THE STRATEGIST

WATERFYRE RISING 5

NADIA HAN

PROSE & CONCEPTS

For those with the "fyre" to persevere.

.

.

.

"The wound is the place where the light enters you."

– Rumi

COPYRIGHT

PROLOGUE
ARROW

MY HEART HAMMERED as I sat on the city bus, waiting for my stop. The short ride seemed so much longer than usual. Why was the bus going so slowly?

I glanced around at the crowd on the bus, spying to see if those dangerous men had followed me. An old lady wearing a straw hat with a daisy sat two seats in front of me. Two teenagers giggled across from her. They had probably skipped school like my friends and I had today. Three men took up the back seats of the bus.

I'm safe.

I released a slow breath, even though nerves ravaged my stomach. I didn't see anyone resembling those gangsters who had killed that man, but that didn't mean they wouldn't come after me later.

Why did the man with the slash on his face let me and my friends go? Was it a trick to follow each of us? I glanced outside the bus, but saw nothing out of the ordinary. People were friendly to you when they wanted something in return. What did he want? Was I being paranoid?

Probably. But I had good reasons.

I trusted very few people. Life was a bitch. The only people worth my time were my four best friends.

The bus finally pulled over for my stop, and I stood from my seat, slipping my backpack onto one shoulder. I got off the bus but didn't go straight home. Home wasn't that safe either. The wound on my shoulder still stung from two nights ago. I didn't tell my friends about my dad's drunken assault this time. It was old news by now, and they would have made a big deal out of it . . .

Life was hard, and I didn't want it to be more difficult. My mom died when I was twelve, and my life turned to hell. At fifteen, I'd gotten used to the ugly side of life. On terrible days, I wondered if foster care would be better for me. Then again, who knew where Social Services would send me?

I did my research, and I'd rather be home with my abusive father than with abusive strangers. The world was a messed-up place. If my dad went to jail, I'd be an orphan and thrown into a messed-up foster care system. What if they took me somewhere far from my friends? What would I do? How would I meet with them to continue our WaterFyre Rising video game venture?

No, these boys were all I had.

There was one place I could go besides home. I yanked the door to Pam's Diner open and entered my safe haven. It gave me a place to go when I had nowhere else.

"Hey, you're *early*." Pam eyed me as she wiped a table with a white cloth. She had curly red hair and freckles. She was in her mid-thirties and the owner of this restaurant, the place where my mom worked before she died of liver failure.

Deep down, I knew my mom had died of heartache. My

dad wasn't a good husband or father. He was before he started drinking.

"Yup." I forced a smile and slid into my usual corner booth, placing my backpack beside me. Seeing Pam made the erratic bat wings flapping in my stomach calm a bit.

"Got homework to do?" Her brown eyes warmed on me.

"Yup," I lied.

Teachers didn't give us homework when it was so close to the end of the school year. But I knew she was trying to get information from me like she always did when I came here to get away from my alcoholic dad. She knew he'd hurt me before, and she'd called the police.

I'd stayed with Pam for a few weeks while everything was sorted out with my dad's arrest. I didn't want to be a burden to Pam or go to a foster family, so I lied and said he'd only hit me once. Dad promised to stop drinking and attended his AA meetings. But he didn't take long to fall into the old routine. Pam didn't know that, and I didn't want her to worry. She'd already done enough for me. I spent time at one of my friends' houses whenever I could.

Avoiding my dad had been my survival method.

"Let's feed that brain of yours." She studied me carefully. "What do you want to eat?"

"The usual."

"No fever?" She placed a hand on my forehead, and I jerked. "You okay? I've never seen you this pale." She slid into the seat across from me. "Wanna tell me what's going on? Did your Dad—"

"No. I'm just tired. My friends and I are working on a video game, and I've been staying up late." That wasn't a lie. Just not the whole truth.

"Oh, that WaterFyre Rising thing, right?"

"Yeah." She was the only other person who knew about my passion.

Pam smiled. "Your mom would've been extremely proud to see you chasing your dreams like this." She rose from the seat. "Food will come right up. And don't you *dare* pay me." She pointed at me with her index finger. "I need some help in the back room when you're done, okay?"

I nodded. "Thanks."

My dad always left some lunch money for me on the kitchen counter. I guess that was when he was sober and remembered he had a son still in school. I'd saved that money to pay Pam, but she never took it. So in exchange for feeding me, I took out the trash and broke down boxes for her. She said my mom was her best employee and didn't mind helping me.

"By the way, your dad is eating with a woman on the other end," Pam said before walking to tend to another customer.

Shit.

If he caught me skipping school, he'd beat the crap out of me and kick me out. I slid further down the booth. He could probably recognize the back of my head. I didn't understand why he kept drinking when he knew it changed him.

Maybe I reminded him of his responsibilities. Or maybe he was stressed and needed someone to hit. I'd fought back a few times. But he was bigger and stronger than me. Though he didn't hit me when he was sober, he ignored me. Neglect was also a form of abuse, wasn't it?

Abuse came in all shapes and sizes.

But what could I do? My friends would help me, but I

didn't want to burden them. Besides, it was embarrassing for people to know how shitty my life was.

I snuck a peek down toward the other end of the diner. His back faced me. A pretty Asian woman smiled across from him. Then the door chimed, and four Asian men dressed in black suits entered. My stomach clenched. Did the gangsters send their men after me?

I slid further down the seat so they couldn't see me. I shouldn't have come here. What if they destroyed Pam's restaurant?

Their footsteps sounded elsewhere. They weren't here for me after all.

"It's time to go home, Angela," said one man.

"I don't want to go," said a woman.

"Your father won't like it."

"Go home with them, Angie," said my dad.

A dispute occurred between my dad and the woman, but she eventually said, "Fine."

I heard them exit the diner. I glanced out the window, which was partially hidden by the flower bushes.

My dad held the woman's hand until one man broke them apart. Who was she?

"Stay away from her," said the man with a snake tattoo on his neck.

Angela wiped the tears from her eyes. She tried to reach for my dad, but the men ushered her away. Was she his new girlfriend? Mom and I had suspected he'd been cheating since he always came home late and never gave a straight answer. That had made her sad and worsened her condition. How could an injured heart heal the body? I'd never forgive him for that.

"I won't hurt her," my dad told Snake Tat.

"Just do your job, and you'll get paid. If you don't, you know the consequences." Snake Tat smirked and escorted Angela into an expensive black car with dark windows.

What was my dad doing for these dangerous people?

CHAPTER ONE

"ANY NEWS ON AIMEE YET?" Dad asked. The worry in his voice practically seeped through the phone.

I hated that he was going through this stress. It wasn't good for his weak heart.

"Not yet, *Ba.* But I've got a lead. Aimee's a smart girl, so don't worry." I stared at the picture of the unique nine-year-old girl splashed on my computer screen. She had big, curious eyes and adorable dimples. But it was her brilliant mind that stood out from everything else. "They won't harm her. If anything, I'd be worried about *them.*"

He let out a laugh, which was what I'd wanted.

"The not knowing is killing Will and Susan," he said. "They've lost so much weight."

Will and Susan had helped my dad and me during a difficult time in our lives and were practically members of our family now . . . Aimee was like a niece to me. Will was the doctor who'd taken extra care of my injuries back then. If it weren't for him, I would've developed other issues beyond the physical wounds.

When Aimee was abducted while on a field trip to the zoo, the shock shook us all up. Dad and I had tried our best to live a quiet and simple life in Northern California after my mom died. But deep in my heart, I had known this day would come. My connection to a dangerous crime family would eventually come back to haunt me.

"I'm doing my best, *Ba*. And I'm doing it discreetly," I said, trying not to give him any reason to worry about me too.

"I kept replaying the video from that day, Viv. They took her in broad daylight."

That meant these people didn't care if they were caught, which made them even more dangerous.

But I said, "A mistake. And we'll catch them for that."

Though the kidnappers wore masks and abducted two other girls, Aimee was the only one who hadn't been found. Or rather, she was the only one they hadn't released. The other classmates were released that evening at a shopping plaza. They'd been forced to wear blindfolds, which prevented them from seeing their kidnappers.

I knew they'd released the girls to distract the public. Aimee was a prodigy. She was a target because of her brilliance. *Just like my mother.* Mom had been a prodigy, and she made a lot of money for The Triad, an organized crime syndicate that dealt with extortion, sex trafficking, illegal gambling, drug trade, and the laundry list went on and on.

My grandfather, Stephen Kwan, who went by the nickname King Viper, was the leader of The Taipan Triad until his death eight months ago. Around the time of Aimee's abduction. I hadn't seen my grandfather in years. Though he was a dangerous man, he loved my mom and me and ensured our lives would be undisturbed by members of his faction.

But he was no longer alive to keep that promise. I knew

little about the honor system within a crime organization. Was there such a thing? How long could one man's word hold power after his death?

Had The Taipans taken Aimee? I wasn't sure, but my intuition told me to look in that direction.

My dad coughed, and I could hear him drinking something.

"We'll find Aimee, *Ba*. I promise. I don't want you stressing out. And I don't want Rose calling me about your condition either."

Rose Tran had been his nurse for the past few years. They'd become friends, and I could tell there was something more between them. But Dad didn't want to admit anything to me.

He hadn't dated since my mom died, and Rose was the first woman who'd caught his interest. She'd taken great care of him and always called me when Dad was being stubborn about his medication and workout routine.

Dad sighed. "I know, I know. I'm trying not to add to your burden—"

"You're not a burden to me. I want you to focus on your health. Don't worry about finding Aimee. That's my job."

"I don't want you putting yourself in danger. Will and Susan wouldn't want that either. Promise?"

"Yes, I promise," I agreed.

It was the best I could do without flat-out lying to him. To find Aimee, I had to step close to the snake pit. Danger was part of the game. A scared little girl was waiting for someone to save her.

Was she still alive?

Stop it. Don't think like that.

They need her. They won't hurt her.

The voices warring in my head drove me crazy. My life had been consumed with finding Aimee. I'd resigned from my pediatric dental position and moved to Providence to start a new practice. It was eight months since she'd been kidnapped. Most people would have assumed she was already dead, but I knew in my gut that Aimee was alive.

"I'm going to buy some fruits and flowers for the altar. I'll make a donation to the temple too. Your mom, our ancestors, and all the gods and goddesses will watch over you and Aimee."

"Thanks, *Ba*." I smiled as I imagined him making the offer. Believing that there was a higher power protecting me brought him peace. Dad's parents had taught him the Vietnamese tradition before they both passed away in a car accident. I never got a chance to meet them.

"Let me know if you need anything from Agent Stone or me."

Aimee's parents had hired a private investigator to help locate her. So far, he had discovered nothing either.

A knock sounded on my door, and Dakota, my dental assistant, poked her head in. The look on her face told me it was an urgent matter.

"Have to go, *Ba*. Talk to you soon."

I hung up the phone and glanced at my watch. Three hours until the wine expo. I had time.

I walked to the dental chair and sighed when I saw Chicken standing with an older woman with gray hair in a twisted bun.

Chicken was a tall, lanky man with a kind face and a full heart. He wore a black T-shirt and jeans. His dark hair was swept to one side, looking like one of those K-pop stars that Kaylee loved so much. I didn't know why people called him

Chicken, and I never asked. He was known in the area as a thoughtful man who cared for his grandmother and her friends. My office treated many of them, and most didn't have dental insurance.

"How can I help you?" I asked the young boy, who was holding a hand to his cheek.

"Max has a bad toothache that's getting worse. His grandma is here with him," Chicken explained. "They don't have—"

"I'll take a look." I patted Chicken's arm, stopping him from stating the obvious out loud. Other patients were around, and I didn't want anyone complaining about my good deeds. People could twist things for their own gain, which could cost me. I couldn't afford any setbacks. My time in Providence was to find Aimee. Then I could return to California and resume my simple life.

"Thanks." Chicken nodded and tucked his hands into his jeans.

I led Max into the exam room. Chicken and his grandmother stood against the wall.

On the stool, I scooted closer to the eight-year-old boy. "What's going on, buddy?"

Wincing, he pointed to his right cheek. "It hurts a lot."

"He didn't sleep well last night," said the grandmother.

I looked at the fearful boy. "Don't be scared. I'll take good care of you. Cavities are afraid of me. Now, open wide."

"Dr. Vo has magical powers." Chicken winked at me.

With a quick review, my heart sank. "You have an infection in your primary molar." I looked up at Chicken and the grandmother. "It needs to be removed. I can do it right now."

"Please," said the grandmother.

Max beamed when everything was done, carrying the plastic baggie filled with a toy, a fancy toothbrush, toothpaste, and floss. "Your adult tooth will fill in that space soon. Make sure you brush and floss twice a day. No candies."

Max nodded.

"Thanks for squeezing us in," Chicken said as the boy walked to the front desk to check out.

"Are you related to Max?"

"No. He lives in the same complex as my grandmother." He reached for his wallet. "Can I give you some cash to cover part of it?"

"Don't worry about it." I waved a hand. "I have a fund for these kinds of situations."

"Thank you," Chicken said.

Max and his grandmother were busy putting on their coats in the waiting area.

I told Allison, my officer manager, to use the Kindness Fund to pay for their visit. Most dentists would call my deed an unprofitable business practice because I wasn't making money, but I didn't care. A kid went home pain-free today. If I were his parent, I'd want that for him too.

When my dad was a dentist, he also had a Kindness Fund. My mom thought it was the most wonderful idea, and they'd started dating because of that.

The only thing the visit cost me was time. I could've filled that slot with someone who had insurance, but I was helping a family who couldn't afford dental care. This was why I wasn't a wealthy dentist. *And don't even get me started on what some dental offices charge these days and what insurance suits claim is "unnecessary."* There were dentists sitting on the Board of Directors for dental insurance companies and the candy industry. Everything came back to money. The entire world was corrupt.

Walking back into my office, I shrugged off my lab coat and hung it on the rack. I washed my hands and prepped myself to look decent for the International Wine Expo event.

Out of habit, I checked my phone for the newsfeed from New England. Sometimes, the smallest details could provide clues to Aimee's whereabouts. The local station had a segment on the wine expo and several of the notable attendees. An old image of Arrow and his ex-girlfriend splashed across the screen. Sylvia Ormon was a gorgeous brunette and looked like a supermodel.

An uncomfortable feeling sprouted in me. Surprised at the strange sensation, I rubbed my stomach.

He'd asked me on a date twice, but I'd declined, so I had no idea why I was experiencing the sudden pang of jealousy.

Wealthy men like him would attend a wine convention. I'd probably see them tonight. Or maybe miss them all together. I just wanted to get there, do what I needed to do, and head home.

Not wanting to think about him anymore, I swiped to another news page. Governor Fenner was being interviewed about his opposition to Whiz Kidz's purchase of an old building owned by the state. Apparently, he wanted more money from the nonprofit organization. I rolled my eyes at the greedy politician with a head of spiky silver hair. Whiz Kidz was an exceptional organization that offered talented children a way to broaden their abilities. I didn't understand why anyone would oppose that, especially if the old building wasn't being used.

Enough of the news. I grabbed my purse and headed to the wine expo.

CHAPTER TWO

ARROW

"KEEP ME POSTED ON THE RENOVATION," I said to my warehouse manager in Texas. I glanced at my watch, ensuring I had enough time for a quick stop before the wine convention started.

"Will do," Joshua said and reiterated the plan before ending the call.

A former employee had stolen a large order of my CheckMate wine, which hadn't been for sale yet. I'd been prepping it for this wine convention this evening. James Chin had burned down part of my warehouse, which now needed extensive renovation. He'd also killed someone and hidden the body under the wooden floor of his office. The dead body wasn't one of my employees, and the authorities were still working on identifying the man. The rebuilding and wine replacement had cost me time and money. I'd been trying to locate the asshole for months.

He can't hide forever.

Pushing the frustration aside, I stopped by Pam's condo to drop off her late birthday present. I had promised to visit her two weeks ago, but my business trips and her vacation plans with her boyfriend, Jarrett Packard, got in the way. Both were retired and living their best lives.

"Thank you. You didn't have to." She beamed and kissed me on the cheek. She still had curly red hair, but it was mixed in with layers of silver. More freckles dotted her face.

I loved and appreciated her as though she were my mother. If she hadn't been around, my life would have been different. I sat beside her on the living room couch and watched as she peeked into the box full of gift cards.

"Goodness, Arrow. I don't need all of this."

"You and Jarrett can eat out every day for the next year." I offered her a big hug.

"He's at the gym right now. I wish I had the same motivation as he does. Need to get over this stupid cough before I can make myself go. I love fall, but I always get sick."

"You want a trip to Florida?" I asked. "I can book a flight for you and Jarrett."

She laughed and patted my cheek. "We just got back from Bermuda. I want to stay put for a while."

"Okay. Just let me know if you want to go anywhere."

She placed the gift box down and studied me. "Where are you going looking all dapper?" She brushed her hand down my black tux.

"A wine convention. There's two bottles for you." I gestured to the bag on the dining table. "Don't get drunk now."

She stared at the bag of wine and sighed. "You've made something ugly beautiful. Your mom would've been so proud."

Most people who had an abusive alcoholic father would steer clear of booze, but not me. I'd used my experience and created a successful business from it. I was no alcoholic, but I learned about alcohol and its effect on human psychology.

"I hope so," I said, checking my phone. "I've got to run. Say hello to Jarrett for me."

"I will." She embraced me. "I'm proud of the man you've become."

"You helped raise this man." I smiled as she teared up.

As I headed to my car, a couple walked by with a little girl who looked to be about six years old. The guy reeked of alcohol.

"I don't want you visiting your fucking mom," snarled the guy with the beard.

"She's not well, Rick. I *have* to see her," she said.

A *thwack* sounded, and I knew what he'd done. The child screamed, and I whirled around to find the woman against the side of the car with a hand to her face. The little girl clung to her mom's leg, crying.

"You do as I say, you hear me?" he seethed, jabbing a finger at the woman's forehead.

"Don't hit my mom!" cried the little girl.

He grunted at the little girl and reached for her.

"No!" The mother held onto her child while he yanked at her arm.

Fury ignited in me like a dormant volcano. It rose and surged out of me. I stalked over, clasped the guy's arm, and threw two punches into his face.

He fell back and shouted, "What the fuck, man?"

I stood in front of the woman and child. "If you lay another hand on her or anyone else, I'll fucking kill you."

"It's none of your business!" the asshole shouted while his busted lip bled.

"It is everybody's business when you harass a woman and child in public. Makes me want to know what you do behind closed doors. The police should look into your history."

"Mind your own business, fucker!" He charged at me.

I let him get a swipe on my shoulder, and I pretended to wince. Then I broke his arm and a couple of fingers and called that self-defense.

I gripped his neck, had a good squeeze, and whispered into his ear, "You stay away from them. If I find out you're anywhere near them, I *will* end you. And no one will know where to find you."

"Who the fuck are you?" he gasped as his face turned pale.

"Your fucking nightmare." I looked into his eyes. "Stop drinking. Get help."

Rage thrummed through my blood. Moments like these made me wonder if I was contributing to the deterioration of society. But was the alcohol to blame, or was it the man who had a choice?

The little girl's cry snapped me out of my rage.

I forced myself to calm and looked at the woman and her daughter. "Both of you okay?"

"No." She crouched and held her daughter tight.

"Leave him," I said. "You need a safe place for your daughter."

"He's going to kill us."

"He's not my daddy," said the frightened girl.

"No, he won't go near you." I crouched to be at eye level with the girl. "What's your name?"

"Bella," she said with curious blue eyes.

"Oh my God!" Pam rushed over to the woman and child

and looked at me. "I heard a commotion and looked out the window. The police are on their way."

Apparently, the asshole lived in the same condo complex as Pam, which I owned. What a small world.

I called a member of my legal team to come and assist the mother and daughter and deal with the drunken fucker who was slumped against the wall of the building. Rick was the woman's boyfriend, and his name wasn't on the lease, which made it easy for me to prevent him from entering the building.

"I've got to go," I said to Pam. "Let the police watch the security footage. If they need my statement, I'll be happy to stop by the precinct in the next few days. Or they can call me."

Pam nodded. "Don't worry. Go do what you need to do. I've got it."

Anger and frustration warred inside me as I drove toward the La Luna Hotel. I thought my dark past had fallen into the abyss, but seeing the violence and fear on the woman's and child's faces proved the past was a ghost that could appear anytime to piss me off.

I tried my best to calm myself before I had to greet the press and all the wine lovers. I wanted to kill that asshole. He was just like my father, whom I should have killed. But he died shortly after getting out of prison. Karma eventually caught up to him.

My mom loved him, and I loved him before he started drinking. I remembered little about those years now because the dark years became more prominent in my memory.

Alcohol was a fucking monster that sucked the life out of people. It transformed people. And here I owned a successful empire of it. Alcohol wasn't the only thing that could cripple the psyche. Society assigned blame to certain things that weren't fully responsible for certain illnesses.

Anything in the extreme wasn't good for anybody. Alcohol could be used as medicine and as a liquid that numbed the mind. A knife in the hand of a chef differed from a knife in the hand of a killer. Alcohol was a thing that couldn't make its own decision. A rock on the ground wasn't responsible for someone using it to break a window.

I *chose* to turn alcohol into a drink and profited from it. I wasn't the only wine company in the world. But I used the profit to aid those suffering from alcoholism and other diseases. Was I doing the right thing? I wasn't sure.

The entrance to Remi's hotel was crowded. I pulled up to the valet, got out of my Maserati, and gave the key to the young man.

Shrugging off the irritation, I steered my mind toward the wine convention. Would CheckMate make it to the next round?

CHAPTER THREE

VIVIAN

"SEE YOU ON TUESDAY," I told my staff and headed out.

I didn't work full-time at the office. Dr. Jillian Jones was the general dentist, and Dr. Nancy Goodwin covered for me a few days a week for pediatric needs. I spent the extra time searching for Aimee and teaching at the Martial Arts Studio. I enjoyed the exercise and teaching other women how to defend themselves. Knowing self-defense would have helped me when I was younger.

I slid into my car and saw the Kuromi—a stuffed toy—in the back seat. It was a bunny wearing a black jester's hat and a devil's tail that belonged to Kaylee, a brilliant thirteen-year-old girl. Two years ago, I became her guardian when her mom passed. Kaylee's mom had been good friends with my mom, so I took her in because she didn't have any other family.

I sent her a text.

Vivian: *Hey. I'll be home late tonight. Eat the leftovers or frozen pizza in the freezer.*

Kaylee: *We're getting McD's.*

Vivian: *Not healthy.*

Kaylee: *Neither is pizza or leftover lo mein.*

What every parent said about teenagers was correct: they were little devils.

Kaylee: *Help me test out my new app, and I'll eat all the salads you want.*

I rolled my eyes.

How dare she give me an ultimatum?

Kaylee was an extremely intelligent girl, and I was happy she found her calling creating apps with her nerdy friends at an afterschool program at Whiz Kidz. But I didn't have time to be her guinea pig. I wasn't much help with her previous app, which was a game like Tetris. I didn't have the patience for that. But she had since moved on to something more fun.

You're her guardian. Support her dreams.

I blew out a breath. She didn't have anyone but me.

Vivian: *Okay, but only because you aced your last math test.*

Kaylee: *Promise not to go back on your word?*

I glanced at the clock.

Vivian: *Yup. Gotta go. Chat later.*

Kaylee: *Thanks! I'll create an alias for you. Just play along. Better not go back on your word. (smile emoji) (heart emoji)*

Was that a threat?

This girl, I swear.

Shaking my head, I shoved the phone into my purse and headed to La Luna Hotel. I parked in the garage, entered the elevator, and headed toward the event. I was probably under-dressed in my tapered dark pants and pale yellow silk shirt. *Whatever.* I wasn't here to impress anyone, negotiate a business deal, or buy a boatload of wine. I was here for information.

I entered the foyer with a giant chandelier and exotic flower displays. A fountain sprayed water from a water lily pond near the front desk. I walked up to the counter and retrieved a flyer for the International Wine Expo.

"Prepare to spend a lot of money, dear," said the woman with the chic French twist in a black top and matching skirt. "I spent way too much."

"Everyone deserves a treat now and then." I smiled.

She placed a hand on her heart. "Wine and desirable men? There's just something about that blend, you know." She shivered to emphasize. "If only I were in my thirties again."

I laughed. "You're beautiful. Enjoy the wine."

Dating wasn't on my mind these days. I had no time or energy. It didn't help that the last guy I dated was such an asshole. I kicked him to the curb after only one month. That was before I moved to Providence. My mind had been on Aimee.

I had no interest in connecting with The Triad, but I made an exception today for Aimee.

The signs for the wine expo took me down a hallway into an extravagant ballroom with a magnificent display of wine from all over the world. I browsed the rows, searching for the Tai Lok wine with the snake logo. The wine belonged to The Taipan Triad. The inland taipan was the most venomous snake known today. That serpent insignia represented how ruthless and deadly The Triad could be.

I was acquainted with the Tai Lok wine representative in attendance today. But I didn't know if Calvin Wong would help me. Despite that, I had to try for Aimee's sake.

A section of the event was roped off from the public crowd. The VIP area displayed more glamorous centerpieces and appetizer tables. Men in tailored suits and women dressed in designer gowns chatted around tall tables. The lifestyle of the rich and powerful differed from mine. I was underdressed compared to them.

As a pediatric dentist, I could demand a lot more money than a general dentist. I wasn't in need of money. I was content with my life.

Stop lying.

Fine. My life was missing something . . . A spark? A dream? I didn't know. I had a thriving career, but that didn't fill the emptiness in me. The violence I'd witnessed and experienced as a child took something from me, and I never got it back.

That part of me died along with my mom, and it was also something I'd never let anyone know. Tears welled in my eyes, but I blinked them away. It would be embarrassing to cry in public for no reason.

My eyes scanned the VIP area and connected with a man I didn't want to see today. Arrow Holt had a face that looked like the God of Fury and the God of High Sexuality combined into one irresistible being. The power he exuded forced me to take a step back.

I inhaled a breath to gather myself from the imbalance he had caused in me. Arrow was like an unexpected storm that came and disturbed my inner peace. Every time I was near him, I got flustered, and being flustered wasn't something I needed *or* wanted.

By now, he probably detested me for rejecting him not once, but twice.

Three women stood beside Arrow. One of them was his

ex, Sylvia. They seemed like more than friends. Were they back together? The other two women, a blonde and another curly-haired brunette, ogled at him as he made eye contact with me. The women followed his gaze in my direction. I looked away and walked off to browse the wine aisle.

Talk about magnetism. I couldn't free myself from his eyes fast enough. His stare was like some invisible power pinning me in place. No wonder those women were stuck to him. This was another reason I didn't want to go to dinner or duel with him. A man surrounded by pretty women was often tempted to stray. Of course, I was assuming based on experiences and what I saw in celebrity gossip.

He'd be a major disturbance in my life, and I wasn't ready for another storm, even if it was the most gorgeous disruption I'd ever seen.

I shook off the unease and focused on finding the Tai Lok wine.

Where was Calvin Wong? On the surface, no one knew the Tai Lok brand was associated with The Triad, but I knew. Nerves churned as I walked further down the aisle. Would Calvin help me? Would he still remember me? It had been so long ago.

Aimee was just another missing child among a long list of missing children. Her case was no longer a priority for the police or the private eye they'd hired, so I had to take matters into my own hands.

I stopped by a magnificent wine display with two fancy pots of live bamboo. One was filled with black bamboo, and the other green. I glanced at the Bambooze Series of the CheckMate Black and CheckMate Red labels. The tagline read: *Make all the right moves.*

"If you drink enough, I'm sure you've got all kinds of moves," I muttered with a laugh.

Intrigued, I picked up a bottle to examine it. I'd heard about bamboo wine but had never tried it.

"Would you like a taste?" His deep voice vibrated on my skin, making me shiver.

I turned and looked up at a set of magnetic gray eyes that belonged to an untamed wolf. Arrow Holt was a gorgeous man with hidden fine prints. If I weren't careful, I could sign my life away without knowing it. I'd been around dangerous men before. Most of them wore masks.

What mask are you wearing, Arrow?

"Is this your brand?" I asked.

He nodded, and the intensity of his eyes sent a series of tingles rushing up and down my body.

What the heck was wrong with me?

It had been a month since he asked me out to dinner. I was surprised he was still friendly instead of keeping his distance. Maybe I was just one of many women he'd wanted to date. So my rejection meant nothing.

I shouldn't wonder what would have happened if I had said yes. It didn't hurt to wonder, right? According to the relationship column in one of the magazines in my office, imagination was a healthy way to overcome difficulty or any sort of inner barrier.

Arrow got brownie points for respecting my wishes. But right now, it was awkward standing next to him, knowing what had transpired between us.

Arrow grabbed the bottles of CheckMate Red and CheckMate Black, placed them into a bag, and handed it to me. "Try them. Let me know what you think. They're new to the market."

"Oh. Let me pay you." I took the bag from him, and our fingers touched.

A zap of energy sparked, and my body heat increased a few notches. I wasn't sure if he noticed it because he grabbed a postcard and wrote his number and email for me. "It's a gift. In return, I'd love your honest opinion. Share it with the girls. I'd like to know what they think too."

It would be a great reason to meet up with Audri, Michelle, Kiera, and Natalie. I'd canceled on them twice this month.

"Thanks. I'll share these with them."

Something told me not to accept the wine, but I blamed it on my overcautious mind. How could I not suspect people? A smart girl stayed away from trouble, right? And Arrow Holt had trouble written all over him. So why wasn't I returning the bag to him?

"What brings you here tonight?" he asked.

It was a simple question, but the words caressed my face and neck. A seductive shiver slithered up my spine, but I willed myself to appear unaffected by his presence. His voice. His eyes. This man was like a King Cobra—a threat to my sanity.

"Saw it advertised and thought I'd swing by to check it out." I smiled.

His gray eyes considered me, probably weighing how much truth was in my statement.

Ten percent truth.

"If I had asked you to join me at this wine convention back then, I would've gotten my yes, correct?"

Oh, God.

CHAPTER FOUR

ARROW

I KNEW VIVIAN WAS LYING, but seeing her flustered turned me on more than it should have. In this public arena, where I should mingle with people to boost my new bamboo wine, I was more enthralled by her sudden appearance than anything else.

Something was obviously wrong with me. Perhaps because I'd been working nonstop for months trying to complete the campaign for CheckMate. My mind and body weren't functioning properly. But if I were to admit, I hadn't been myself since laying eyes on her.

I'd always been drawn to mysteries, and Vivian was exactly that—a uniquely shaped box wrapped with an enticing dark velvet fabric. What treasures was she hiding?

In the Navy, I'd been tasked with dangerous operations that required my investigative skills to complete the missions. With my experience, I should also know when to abandon a mission, especially when it wasn't safe or beneficial to me. And yet here I was, still trying to unravel a truth that could hurt me.

She rejected you, asshole. Move on.

No woman had ever *rejected* me. When I wanted a woman, I always got her. So yeah, I wanted to know why. When I had asked her if she was seeing someone, she said no. If there was no other man, then why didn't she want to go on a date with me?

"It would have been a no as well." She looked at me. "I'm not ready to date, Arrow."

Now that was a truth I could accept. I saw it in her brown eyes. But there was also something else there. Pain? Sorrow? Fear?

"Let me know when you're ready."

"There are a lot of beautiful women over there who are waiting for you." She gestured to the group of women who had surrounded me since I'd arrived. My ex stood with her social media friends.

The first time I met Vivian was at the Krazee Tavern, where she had demonstrated her martial arts skills with precision. I was intrigued and asked for a duel. That was when I got my first no.

"But they can't kick my ass the way you can."

She laughed, and it was a pure and beautiful sound that made me smile.

"And that ability attracts you?" Curiosity bloomed in her eyes.

"Damn right. I'm a man intrigued by a challenge."

She changed the subject and gestured to the wine bottles on the table. "Why bamboo?"

"Why not? It's different and profitable. Unlike grapes, bamboo is versatile. It can be made into furniture, build homes, create materials for clothing, eaten as food, and made into drinks, not to mention used for medicine, which

Forrest is an expert at." I held up a bottle. "When I see something extraordinary, I go all in studying it. *Unravel* it. Make it *mine*."

Her lips opened slightly as though she was releasing a slight gasp. Her eyes connected to mine. The topaz in her iris shifted to a darker shade. What was she thinking?

"Sounds very methodical. Like a business transaction that would garner you profits."

She was partially right. That was a proven business practice that made me successful. But why did her comment rub me the wrong way?

"Vivian?"

A man with short dark hair interrupted us, and I immediately didn't like him. I recognized him as the Tai Lok representative I hadn't met yet.

"Calvin," Vivian said with hope in her voice.

Okay, I HATE him. Why didn't she react to me the same way?

He stepped closer and placed a hand on her shoulders, surveying her like he had every right to. "You look amazing. It's been so long."

I wanted to push his hands off her, but that would make me look stupid, irrational, and out of character. Definitely out of character. I needed to be the Arrow Holt who ran a successful wine empire to ensure my bamboo wine made it to the second round of the competition.

I was here for clues involving The Trogyn, not to fight over a woman. It irked me that, for a moment, I'd forgotten *why* I was at the convention.

What the fuck had gotten into me?

How did they know each other anyway? Was he the reason she didn't want to go on a date with me?

Something uncomfortable stirred in my gut. She wasn't mine *yet*. I had no claim to her to do anything.

"I'm Arrow Holt." I offered my hand. "Tai Lok is an exceptional wine."

He shook my hand with firmness. "Calvin Wong. Yours is fabulous. My boss has been raving about it."

Calvin stood a couple of inches shorter than me, but he was built. He had a good posture that conveyed confidence and sharp eyes that told me he couldn't be trusted.

He looked at me, then at Vivian. "You also know Vivian?"

"We have mutual friends," I said.

Vivian looked at Calvin with a serious expression. "Do you have a minute? I'd like to speak to you privately, please."

Irrational jealousy surged into me. *He* was the reason she was at the convention. Why?

My strategy to give her time and space had shifted. On a battlefield, a methodical plan ensured victory. I wouldn't stand around while an enemy posed a potential threat to what was mine.

"Arrow!" Remi waved me over. The look on his face showed me he had pertinent information regarding our reason for this wine expo.

I turned to Calvin. "Good luck tonight." My gaze slid over to Vivian. "See you soon."

It was a promise.

As I walked toward Remi, I scanned the growing crowd of wealthy men and women from around the world who received VIP tickets to this special event. They'd vote for the wine label that would head to Monaco, where it would be showcased at the Monte Carlo Hotel Resort. This was a hangout place for elite members of The Trogyn, a dangerous crime organization that had become a threat to me and my friends.

"Is that Vivian?" Remi asked.

Remington wore a dark suit that resembled mine. Ever since he'd been with Audri, joy oozed from him. His short dark hair had grown a bit long, but those sharp blue eyes remained the same as when I'd met him all those years ago. He had masterminded the WaterFyre Rising game back when we'd been teens, and I couldn't be more grateful to be part of it. My life could've gone horribly wrong if it hadn't been for my friends. I'd probably be serving several life sentences.

"Yeah, that's Vivian," I said, not wanting to speak any more about her right now. "Hosting this event at La Luna was an excellent idea." I glanced around and lowered my voice. "Cameras working? Anyone look suspicious?"

He smirked. "All set. There are people in attendance I don't recognize."

"Who?"

"People who have more money than us."

Though my friends and I were prominent figures in the business arena, we knew there were others wealthier than us with their own circle of powerful acquaintances.

"Let's go check them out."

CHAPTER FIVE

VIVIAN

CALVIN LED me down a hallway into a small room that looked like an office with warm-colored walls. He closed the door as I took in the rest of the room. A round table with four chairs sat in the center of the space. A long couch and other cozy furniture adorned the lounge area.

He pulled out a seat for me, and I sat down.

"How are you?" Calvin asked, folding himself into the chair across from me. "It's been a while. You grew up. You look . . ." He studied me. "Fabulous."

I blushed at the compliment. "You grew up as well. Looking better than the scrawny boy I remember." Calvin and I were the same age.

He wasn't the twelve-year-old boy who had helped me once. Now, he stood around six feet tall, and he'd been working out based on his muscular form. He'd played an important role in my past, and I had wished he had the chance to get out of The Triad like my family did.

I had so many questions for him, but I feared that the dark past would come flooding back if I asked. Then ugly things would start floating like debris, disturbing me. It was best to leave the past where it belonged.

"What's going on?" His hands moved to a steeple in front of him.

Nerves twisted my stomach. "I know it's odd to just come out of the blue after so many years and ask for your help, but I don't know what else to do."

"Help with what?" His eyebrows furrowed.

"Are you still heavily involved with The Taipans? Or are you just working for their wine label?"

He smiled. "They're my family, Viv. My dad lived and died as a member of The Taipans. And so will I."

The members of The Triad valued brotherhood, respect, and honor. I'd learned that these definitions varied between people and circumstances.

The elders seemed to value honor more so than the younger generation. One time, I witnessed a punishment at my grandfather's massive house when I'd gotten lost and wandered around. I hadn't seen my grandfather's fury until that day when he beat a man to death. But that man had raped and killed a member's wife. What kind of "brother" would do that?

At that moment, the line between right and wrong blurred for me. I never told my parents what I'd witnessed.

"Why didn't you get out?" I asked. "You loved astronomy. You could have . . . made a difference in the world."

He sat back in the chair, surprised by my statement just as much as I was. It wasn't my business, but I couldn't help it.

"Like what you're doing? I hear you're a dentist in California. Why are you in Providence?"

"Before I answer your question, I just wanted to thank

you for helping me back then. I would've died if you hadn't stopped him."

His expression turned serious. "I'm sorry about your mom."

"Where's Ghost's body?" I asked about the monster who tortured me and my mom. "I heard he died. Is it true?" My voice grew, and it surprised me.

I shivered as the memory flooded my vision.

"You little shit. Tell me where your mom is hiding the key." Ghost holds a branding tool. I recognize it from a TV show. "Tell me!" he shouts.

He's wearing a clown mask. Fear grips me. I hate clowns.

He comes closer to me and tilts his head. I race toward the door, but then he stabs me with the tool, and my skin sizzles.

I thought the anger had subsided after all these years, but it had lingered like an awful toothache that came and went as it pleased.

"Grandpa never wanted to talk about Ghost whenever I asked." I swallowed as my throat went dry. Grandpa probably felt guilt for not being able to save my mom or help me.

"He's dead."

The confirmation loosened the knots in me.

"Ghost is in the past." Calvin's firm voice anchored me to the present.

"How did he die? Why didn't Grandpa tell me?"

"It took time to locate Ghost. He went rogue and murdered another member's daughter. His father, Rattlesnake, had begged your grandfather to be lenient. That didn't happen. Eventually, Ghost was caught, tortured, and tossed into the sea." Calvin looked at me. "After your mom's death, no one from The Triad could disturb you and your father."

I thought Grandpa had resented me and my father. He had wanted Mom to marry a Chinese business executive that would benefit The Triad, but Mom loved my dad. Dad was Vietnamese American, and he wasn't part of The Triad. Grandpa had never reached out to me or Dad after Mom died. It was like my mother was the only connection he had to us. When she died, our relationships severed as well. But I supposed he cared about us in his way.

"King Viper wanted to protect you. The less you know, the better."

Grandpa was a ruthless man, which was how he'd become The Triad tycoon for The Taipans until his death from a heart attack eight months ago. Knowing that I was related to a ruthless gang leader wasn't something to be proud of. It was a shameful family history that I never shared with anyone. No one would have wanted to be friends with me. They'd have thought I'd send someone after them if they wronged me.

"He would've wanted you to attend his funeral," Calvin said, not knowing the truth.

I *had* attended the funeral, but from afar. I didn't want anyone to recognize me. My appearance would have stirred up too much uncertainty. *Why is she here? Does she want The Triad's money?* The last thing I wanted was a target on my back.

"It's better that way," I said. "Where's Ghost's father? He must hate me."

"Rattlesnake died two months ago from a gunshot wound. He's made a lot of enemies."

I wanted to know who was left if their members kept dying like this, but I refrained from asking.

"How are your wounds?"

I blinked at the question. "They're still there."

"You could've removed them. Some plastic surgeons can—"

"Some wounds are worth keeping, Calvin. They remind me of the evils humans are capable of."

Calvin didn't say anything. He knew the malice that existed in the world he lived in. Did he ever have a good night's sleep? Did he ever feel guilty for killing people?

"I'm not here to talk about the past," I said. "I'm looking for a nine-year-old girl named Aimee Chen. She was abducted eight months ago."

He leaned on the table. "And you think we have her?"

I couldn't read his face. "Do you?"

His lips curved. "That's a dangerous question, Vivian."

Calvin served The Triad, which meant he had to be careful of what he told me.

"Aimee is like family to me. Like a niece. I can imagine how terrified she is because I was once that little girl."

"Why do you think we have her?" he asked, still not showing any emotion.

"Because she's a prodigy. You people have a tendency to use children with brains. My mom was one of those kids, remember?"

Grandpa had ensured he used his daughter's exceptional memory and mathematical abilities to benefit The Triad.

"Your mom wasn't mistreated," he said. "She's the daughter of King Viper. No one would dare hurt her."

"And she died, remember?" I reminded him. "Abuse comes in many forms, Calvin. Sometimes, the worst scars are invisible."

He opened his mouth to say something, but closed it.

"I haven't heard about any children being used for anything." But something flickered in his eyes.

Had I been wrong to suspect The Triad?

"Can you ask around and let me know?" I looked at him. "Please?"

A smirk slid onto his face. "Is this a business negotiation, Vivian?"

This conversation was transpiring into something I didn't know how to navigate. I didn't want to do business with The Triad.

But this is your only chance.

"It could be. What's your price?"

He crossed his arms. "That depends."

"On what?"

"Your ability to comply."

What the hell?

Caution flared as I tried to figure out what he wanted. Something wasn't right.

You're talking to a triad member, Vivian. It's not supposed to be right.

I stared at him, weighing the pros and cons of this negotiation. Could I trust him? No, but I *needed* him. A little girl needed me. He knew something. He had to, which was why he was being cryptic. I needed any clue he could give me.

Even if The Taipans hadn't taken Aimee, he could find out who had her. Surely they had connections within underground society. Money and power could buy information. Calvin was my key to Aimee.

I crossed my legs, trying my best not to look disturbed about making a negotiation with a Triad member. "Okay, but I have some criteria."

He arched an eyebrow. "Go on."

"I'm not committing any crimes. I'm not hurting anyone, and I'm not going against my morals."

"Morals." A laugh bubbled out of him as though he'd never heard of such a word. "Fine."

"We have a deal." I extended my hand out to him for a shake.

Calvin held my hand for too long. For a moment, I wondered if we could've been good friends if circumstances had been different. He dwelled in a dark world that I was familiar with. How could anyone survive in a world with that much violence, pain, and sorrow?

"I'll be in touch," he said.

Despite my deal with Calvin, I had a backup plan. A man known as The Tip at an underground club could get me information—for a price. The problem was that I didn't belong to the Midnight Chaoss club and needed a creative way to get in.

I couldn't rely on a single source of information, so I'd been training a certain special skill to ensure my acceptance. I had to prepare myself for when the event occurred, and right now, I'd absolutely fail.

CHAPTER SIX

ARROW

"YOUR WINE MADE IT!" Remi punched me in the bicep. "Things are sailing beautifully." He gestured to the screen, which showed my Bambooze series making it to the next round.

Pride overflowed in me to see my wine on the top tier among other fabulous brands. "Let's see how they do in the final round."

My wine would compete with the Piedmont Perilli from Italy and the Tower Estates from Australia. These wealthy families had been in the business long before me. I felt privileged to be among the masters.

Would my mom be proud of me? I wasn't sure. Her husband was an abusive alcoholic, and her son was a billionaire with a degree in enology, running a successful wine empire.

I'm not my father.

"You've now been welcomed into the prestigious wine circle. There's no doubt someone from The Trogyn will be there."

In the past, I'd participated with my other brands in the Decanter World Wine Awards, organized by the British magazine *Decanter*. The Mundus Vini competition in Germany and the AWC Vienna from the European Union were two other prestigious wine awards that had boosted my business.

Though the Medici Medallion Award wasn't a large competition like the others, it was the most prominent. The competition wasn't open to anyone. Candidates had to be nominated. So I was surprised when I got a nomination. I was grateful to whoever had submitted my Bambooze series to the award committee. The winning wine would be in the Monte Carlo Hotel and the restaurants around the resort for three months.

This promotion would push my wine empire forward, no doubt. Aside from that, this was an opportunity to network and mingle with the international wealth, where the elite members of The Trogyn dwelled.

"We're getting close," I said to Remi.

He nodded. "Which means we need to be extra careful. They're probably getting too close to us."

After we'd destroyed several of their moneymaking businesses, they had no choice but to uncover who was behind it all. Remi stopped a sex trafficking ring, while Royce eliminated the human trafficking and drug operations that were linked to the Providence Police Department. Grayson discovered and took over the tunnels that were used to carry out these illegal acts, and Forrest destroyed a large sex-trafficking ring after his girlfriend had fallen victim to it. These operations had been on the news for three days and were never spoken about again.

One clue flared to life: sex trafficking was their biggest moneymaker.

My boys and I had to be careful about our actions. We knew The Trogyn was trying their best to unravel us. We could've made unforeseen mistakes along the way. Despite that, we had to keep moving forward.

"Do you know any of them?" I gestured to the group of judges consisting of sommeliers, enologists, wine experts, gastronomes, wine merchants, and journalists.

"No. But I'm sure networking with them would only benefit us."

We made our way through the crowds toward the judges. I shook hands with them, thanking them for the opportunity. I discovered the next competition would have a new set of judges.

"Remington!" A man in a white suit waved him over to a table with other men. One of them was Prince Allard, the adopted son of Prince Garnier, who was the current ruler of Monaco, the sovereign city-state on the French Riviera.

As I scanned the room, I studied the wealthy and powerful people in attendance. Some gathered at tables, drinking wine and eating fancy appetizers, while others mingled. Were any of these people elite members of the crime organization? What if The Trogyn launched an unexpected attack? Was I prepared for that kind of destruction? My body tensed at the possibility that everything I'd worked hard for could crumble.

A man in a dark suit was also surveying the crowd. He stood in the corner by a tall floral vase. Our eyes connected, and he offered me a slight nod before making his way to the wine display. Two men approached him, and they chatted.

"Congratulations." Calvin approached me, offering a

smile I didn't trust.

It was hard to trust anyone in this competitive arena, especially your competitor in wine *and* women. My caution about him increased with his friendliness toward Vivian. I knew little about him, but that would change.

I didn't like the fact that he appeared close to her. Like he knew her well. Did they have a history? I didn't like that thought and crushed it.

Something about Vivian made me want to unravel her. The more she pushed me away, the more I was intrigued. Arrow Holt didn't give up that easily. Persistence and determination were my strategies to success—to survival.

Vivian was the first woman to fascinate me this much. Most men would have understood and respected her rejection and moved on. But I wasn't most men. Something about her called to me, and I had to find out what that was.

Maybe Calvin had information for me.

"Congratulations to you as well. The Tai Lok wine is fabulous."

"Thank you, but it didn't make the second round this year." He tucked his hands in his pant pockets. "We'll try again next year."

Curiosity thrummed in me, and the words came out before I had time to craft a more diplomatic question. "So, how do you know Vivian?"

Calvin looked at me for a moment. "We have a history that goes way back." A smirk slid onto his face. "How do you know Vivian?"

I didn't like the way he said her name. It was too intimate.

What the hell was wrong with me? Since when had I been jealous of a woman like this? We hadn't been on a date.

She wasn't mine. Hell, I didn't even know if she was attracted to me.

She declined your date.

That didn't matter. Maybe she'd been busy. Something was seriously wrong with me for all the excuses I'd been making.

Calvin's smirk told me he suspected there was something between Vivian and me. Why not let him believe it?

"We have common friends, and we have a history." It wasn't a lie. There was a history of me dreaming about her and asking her on dates. A history of me seeing her at my friends' houses.

History could be defined in many ways, and he hadn't been specific.

Calvin nodded and changed the subject. "Why bamboo wine? You have success with your other brands. Sacred Sins is an exceptional Merlot, and Sensual Enigma is a delicious Chardonnay."

"Success comes with exploration."

"You're right. Success comes when you venture out to discover new things."

A man with a dragon tattoo on his neck approached. "Calvin, you need to resolve something."

Calvin wasn't just a wine representative. Who was he?

He excused himself as Remi came over to me. "Have you heard about the Reimann family?"

"One of the wealthiest families in Europe. They own most of the banks. But I don't know what they look like." I glanced around the crowd to see if I could spot one of them.

"They're quadrillionaires," Remi said. "Rex Reimann is CEO of Reimann Corporation. He just left with some wine."

"What are they doing at a small wine competition?"

"Probably making business deals." Remi jerked his chin toward a table with city officials. "You missed out on Governor Fenner."

"His reelection is coming up, and he's trying to rally his supporters."

There were too many powerful people at tonight's event. It was hard to tell who was there for wine and who had a separate agenda.

But then again, Remi and I were there for wine and a separate agenda.

With my wine moving into the next round, I could relax a bit.

"Your demo for Level Five looks good. When do we get to see the rest of it?" Remi asked.

"Soon. Now that round one is over, I'll have more time to work on it."

My game took the players to various countries, destroying their leaders to gain control of that territory. Though it had all the components of a compelling game full of intrigue and excitement, there was one missing piece I couldn't place. My brain needed a rest before I could jump back in.

"Take your time. Rushing it won't help. It didn't for me." Remi grabbed a glass of wine from the host and sipped. "Right now, we're all focusing on uncovering members of The Trogyn. The game is still a second priority."

He was right. If that crime organization ended us, there wouldn't be any game. My thoughts wandered back to Vivian and Calvin.

My evening wasn't going to end when I got home. I had some investigating to do.

CHAPTER SEVEN

VIVIAN

AFTER DOING some more research on Calvin, I wasn't sure if reaching out to him had been such a great idea.

The stress I'd been dealing with clouded my brain. Calvin Wong was currently vying for the top seat in The Triad against another member. He had climbed the ranks over the years and had become a trusted member. His father died a few years ago. The Triad had respected his father, and that respect had been passed onto Calvin. Creating a fake identity to join specific group chats had gotten me enough information that exhausted me.

I didn't want to think about violence and death anymore. I showered, slipped into my silky pajamas, and slid into bed. Kaylee was already in bed because she was heading to a Sanrio event in Boston with her friend Violet tomorrow. Violet's mom, Grace, was driving them to look at all the stuffed animals and K-pop collectibles.

Kaylee had saved her allowance money to spend at this event. She finished the lo mein and also ate the salad in the fridge. She told me my account for her Heartstrings app was all set up. All I had to do was play along and interact. She needed all the feedback I could give her.

She kept her word, and I'd keep mine.

I couldn't believe Kaylee created a dating app. Should a thirteen-year-old girl be doing this? Should I allow this? What was the right way to raise a teenage girl? She was smarter than most kids her age. Even if I stopped her from doing what interested her, she'd probably go behind my back to do it anyway. So, taking part in her project would help me monitor her. With her brilliant mind, she could make this world a better place.

Arrow's face invaded my mind as I tried to clear my thoughts so I could fall asleep.

Can you let me know when you're ready?

I hadn't met a persistent man like him. Most men would have moved on already. Was this a game to him? Maybe he liked a challenge, and winning a date was the prize he'd aimed for.

You're overthinking again.

My phone buzzed on the nightstand, and I grabbed it to see a notification from Heartstrings.

You have two heart tugs. One yellow heart tug and one red heart tug.

What did they mean?

I had planned on looking at the dating app tomorrow when I wasn't so tired. But the tugs intrigued me. Sitting up in my bed, I clicked on the icon with two adorable smiling hearts connected by one string. An adorable logo that illustrated the app beautifully.

I browsed through the app. Colored hearts rated the connection scale. Yellow meant a wonderful friendship. Pink meant a potential love match. Red signified passion, while black meant not a chance.

Goodness. I wasn't sure how I felt about this coming from Kaylee. She was only thirteen years old! She shouldn't be thinking about these things!

Remember when you were a teenager?

Being a guardian to her was like being a parent, and I had no experience whatsoever. I was more like a big sister to her. But I also lacked experience in that area—I was an only child.

"Who are these people?" I asked no one in particular.

Curiosity had me checking out the red heart tug. What made the match? More importantly, what kind of profile did I have?

What the hell was I thinking, trusting a thirteen-year-old girl to set up a profile for me?

You're just helping her test out a prototype.

Still, I had to know everything.

I smiled at my alias, Tulip, which showed an image of a single yellow tulip. She knew I loved yellow tulips. They reminded me of joy and new beginnings in the spring.

Oh my God.

I gasped at the preferences in my profile.

Preferences: *A man with brains who can buy me whatever I want. Stable job. Funny.*

Age: *Late twenties.*

Hobbies: *Fishing and martial arts. Shopping. Good food.*

Dislikes: *Fakers. Mean people. Bald men.*

Laughing, I shook my head.

Likes: *A lot of things. Ask and find out.*

Tagline: *N/A*

I guessed she left the tagline for me to add. I had no idea what to put there.

Who was going to read all of this? I'd never used a dating app before. One of my former hygienists met some guy through a dating app, and he turned out to be on the FBI's Most Wanted List.

Creeps were all over the place, even on the internet. I had to protect Kaylee from this. Who was she working with at Whiz Kidz? Were they doing enough to ensure the kids were safe from online criminals?

The red heart linked me to someone with the alias DonutDude. He managed a donut shop, loved to eat donuts, and wanted to find someone special to share his love for donuts and other pastries. He was on a mission to lose weight and needed a partner to take walks with. I couldn't help but laugh at the description, but I silently wished DonutDude would find his DonutGirl soon.

How was the calculation done? What happened behind the scenes to match my profile with his? I had to talk to Kaylee about this. This donut guy and I would not work out. If this app was going to be something real, she needed to revise the matching calculation.

If this was a prototype in its testing stage, who were these people? Did she know them? How did she know them? Whom did I have to hurt? Did the people at her afterschool program know about these things?

Gosh, I needed to have a chat with her tomorrow.

I clicked the other profile with the "friendly" tug. It showed he was online.

He sent a wave of a hand.

I waved back.

I read his profile with the name Bullseye and an image to match it.

Preferences: *Here for friendship.*

Age: *Thirties, but sometimes I forget.*

Likes: *Fishing. Playing video games. Sports. Doing nothing.*

Dislikes: *Dentist, alcoholics. Too many to list. Ask me.*

He sent me a text:

Bullseye: *You like fishing?*

Tulip: *Yup.*

Why did he dislike the dentist? I wasn't sure if this friendship could happen.

Tagline: *Weirdo looking for someone weirder.*

That tagline made me laugh. It took me out of my stress bubble. Maybe I could be friends with a weirdo.

Tulip: *Are you a creep in disguise?*

Bullseye: *Are you?*

Tulip: *Maybe.*

Bullseye: *Why so suspicious?*

Tulip: *Why not? The world is full of dangerous creeps. Trust no one.*

Bullseye: *Then why r you on a dating app?*

Tulip: *Weeding out the creeps.*

I didn't know why I said that, but if he were truly a creep, that statement would have made him more cautious. I had to protect my Kaylee.

Tulip: *How did you find out about this app?*

Bullseye: *A friend told me about it. You?*

Tulip: *Same.*

Bullseye: *The app says we could be friends.*

Tulip: *But you could be a sixty-year-old, lonely creep trying to lure young girls.*

I had no idea why that thought kept flashing in my head.

Bullseye: *Could say the same about you too. Are you a serial killer?*

Tulip: *With a dental drill as my weapon. (scared face emoji)*

Bullseye*: Evil. So evil.*

I didn't realize talking to a stranger about random things would relieve the stress I'd been carrying. I'd never chatted with an online stranger this much. But if he were a creep, I had to ensure he wouldn't get near Kaylee.

Two hours later, I yawned and texted.

Tulip: *Gotta go. Past my bedtime.*

Bullseye: *Okay. Good night, Dental Drill.*

I grinned at the ridiculous nickname. The device was actually called a dental handpiece. I logged out of the app, unsure when I'd be back on.

As I closed my eyes, Arrow's face splashed across my mind. What would it be like to date someone that intense? Someone who demanded attention without saying anything. Someone who seemed to follow a strict chart, not missing a single step? I'd probably be bored to death.

Then my mind wandered to Bullseye. What did he look like? For all I knew, he could be a grumpy old man who showered once a week, had an STD, and only came online to defraud people.

I'd never gone to bed with two men occupying my mind. For now, the distraction gave me the reprieve my mind desperately needed.

CHAPTER EIGHT

VIVIAN

MY LAST APPOINTMENT for the day had called to reschedule. My back and neck had been bothering me, and it was because I hadn't been working out. The stress had taken its toll on my body.

I left work early and went to Martial Arts Studio for a good workout. Even though the studio had increased its space, it had maintained the boutique-style atmosphere with cream-colored walls, daylight bulbs, and pretty potted plants everywhere. You could tell it was owned and managed by women. The three T's: Tina, Tammy, and Tabitha. All were close friends. They reminded me of my girls.

When I'd first signed up, there were only a handful of male members. Now, the number of men and women was about equal.

"Hi, Tina." I waved to the adorable front desk receptionist. She looked like a brunette version of Reese Witherspoon.

"Hey there!" She rounded the counter and gave me a welcoming hug. "Haven't seen you in a while. How are you? The students were asking about you the other day."

"I've been busy. Can't keep up. I heard you hired a few other instructors."

"We did. But they miss *you*. No one teaches the tiger and snake formations like you."

"I could do one next week."

"Awesome. You let me know what day is good for you, and I'll set it up."

"Okay. I'll check my work schedule and email you."

There was a beginner's kung fu class in the large studio room and a tai chi class at the end of the hall. The renovated gym would be crowded in a couple of hours when people got off work.

I changed into my workout clothes and stepped onto the mat, stretching my legs and arms. Stress had tightened my muscles. I shouldn't have let my body go so long without exercise.

I'd have loved to teach more self-defense classes. If my mom had known how to defend herself back then, she would be alive today, and my body wouldn't be scarred. Then again, I'd never expected someone close to the family would hurt me and my mom.

Keeping people at a distance was the best method. It was hard for me to trust people, which was probably why my relationships never lasted. The last guy cheated on me after seeing my scars. He wanted a perfect woman and never asked about my scars. I wasn't even jealous when I saw him walking down the street with his new girlfriend.

What did that say about me? I supposed I was never that invested in the relationship.

Arrow's face popped into my vision. Why did I keep thinking about him? Would he react the same way if he saw my scars?

You're here to relieve stress, not add to it.

As I cleared my thoughts, three people came into the room. One of them was the man who had just occupied my thoughts. The two women found a spot at the front. This room had little fitness equipment. It was more of a spacious room, allowing people to stretch, do yoga, practice martial arts on the wooden training dummies, or use the punching bags.

Arrow took up a corner opposite from me. He wore dark knit pants and a short-sleeved top. His back was to me, and I took my time studying him. My body warmed from the way his muscles bunched. I couldn't take my eyes off his attractive form.

Then he turned and met my gaze. "Hey! What are you doing here?"

He approached me, and his magnetic energy surrounded me. Embraced me. I'd never met a man who could make my body feel so much without touching me.

What would happen if he touched me intimately? Curiosity and fear warred with each other inside me.

I left them to battle as I replied, "Hello. I didn't know you go to this gym."

Arrow shrugged. "The gym I normally go to is being renovated, so only a section is open. That means a lot of sweaty people confined to a smaller place. No thanks. This was close by."

One woman punched the wooden training dummy while her friend kicked the sandbag. My conversation with him at the wine convention seemed so long ago. He had looked gorgeous in a suit, but he took my breath away in casual workout clothes.

Though I didn't want a relationship, I could still appreciate an attractive man when I saw one.

Arrow's eyes sparked. "You're here to relieve stress?"

I nodded. "Yup."

"Me too. Let's spar. It's better than fighting those wooden dummies." He bounced on his feet. "I'd love a good opponent."

Arching an eyebrow, I considered his suggestion. This wasn't like his last request. This statement came out casual, with no hint of anything other than a simple workout.

Stop overanalyzing. Maybe the guy just wants a good exercise.

I had nothing to lose. And he was right. Sparring with him would be more challenging than the dummies.

"Okay." I took my position across from him, still unsure if dueling with him was the right decision.

I didn't have time to contemplate as his arm swung out, initiating the duel. I deflected with my forearm, my warm skin kissing his. The contact ignited a circuit of energy that zinged through me, energizing my muscles and tissues. The potency forced a sigh from my lips. I glanced up at him, and my heart skipped at the magnetic gray eyes on me.

With a wink, he shifted his stance, and we sparred with arms, hands, and legs. Did he feel that burst of energy? Or had it just been me?

My heart hammered, and sweat beaded my forehead.

He hooked his arm over mine, pulling me flush to him. Heat increased, making me wonder how my body would react if I were naked with him.

"You enjoying this duel?" he breathed.

"Yeah. You?" My eyes followed the glistening sweat sliding from his forehead to the side of his face and down to the column of his neck. My gaze fixated on the pulse thumping there. I didn't know what got into me, but I pressed a finger to his neck, feeling the pulse thump against my skin.

"The best duel I've had in a long time."

When I realized what I'd done, I immediately retracted my finger. He didn't seem to notice that gesture and continued to spar.

I swung my arm, trying to trick him, and threw a kick at his shin, but he dodged. Then he swung a leg into my shin, throwing me off balance. I dropped to the mat, and he was on top of me. The feel of him over me had me yearning for more.

"Surrender, and I'll let you live." He grinned, looking down at me.

Laughing, I tickled both sides of his ribcage, forcing him to roll over. Then I leaped onto him. "Who needs to surrender now?"

His smile widened as he wrapped his legs around me, gripped my arms with his, and somehow rolled me over to be under him again. What kind of duel was this? This sparring had transformed into something more, but neither of us was going to acknowledge that.

The people in the room were probably watching us, but I didn't care. The anxiety that had dogged me when I came into this studio was now replaced by arousal and the loosening of muscles obtained from an excellent workout.

"Surrender," he demanded.

"No." I shifted, curled my leg, and kneed him.

He rolled over, and I jumped to my feet, taking on the tiger stance. "You need to work hard if you want me to surrender." I beckoned him with my fingers. "Come on."

A crooked smile formed on his lips as he charged at me.

CHAPTER NINE

VIVIAN

I DROPPED Kaylee off at the airport this morning. She was joining her Whiz Kidz team in Texas for a robotics contest for a week. Her team had made it to the national competition, and I was so proud of her. On top of her good grades at school, she was doing fantastic at Whiz Kidz.

Last night's workout with Arrow had been extraordinary. The chemistry between us was something I'd never experienced. The hour flew by, and I wanted to continue sparring, but he had to go. He didn't ask me when I'd return to the studio, and I didn't ask him. A part of me wished he'd asked.

I didn't like this internal confusion. How could I want a man to continue pursuing me when I'd turned him down? What was wrong with me?

I'd slept like a log last night and decided I deserved a latte from Sunshine in a Cup Café across from my apartment. I walked into the shop, got in line, and glanced toward the tray of blueberry muffins to my right. My staff would love a treat.

When I got my order of six muffins and a latte, I headed

out as Arrow was heading in. He wore a gray felt coat over a navy suit, looking deliciously sophisticated and dangerous. God, he was so gorgeous.

He smiled and held the door for me. "Good morning."

Joy thrummed in my body like I'd just gotten a dose of caffeine in my bloodstream. All I had to do was look at him, and my body felt invigorated. He could be my morning latte.

"Good morning!" I replied too excitedly.

He glanced at the box in my hand. "I guess you have an appetite after last night."

"It was a good workout. Thank you."

"It was indeed. Have a great day."

"You too."

He *had* moved on. Sadness and disappointment clung to me as I entered my office and got to work. What did I expect?

I should be the one to move on. I was the one who didn't want any complications or distractions. And here I was, standing in the middle of my mess. No one got me here. I placed myself in this dilemma, and I had to get myself out of it.

The next day, I had my special training class so I could enter Midnight Chaoss. Missing that class wasn't an option. I'd invested too much time into it. Kaylee thought it was weird that I was taking a hip-hop class, but I told her it was just another workout for me.

"But you're a kung fu master," she had said.

"And?"

"Why do you need to find another exercise?"

"Because it gets boring if you do the same thing repeatedly. Speaking of exercise, you need to exercise too. Wanna come?"

"Nope."

I knew she'd decline the offer. Though she was a smart girl, she was like a lot of teenagers—lazy. She had promised to learn self-defense from me later this year.

After work, I changed into my workout clothes and headed straight to class. The evenings had gotten darker during the late fall season. A sense of melancholy filled the air, which was peaceful and beautiful in its own way.

I entered the brick building and raced up two flights of stairs. The hallway had a collection of eclectic art on display from the artists occupying the studios on the first floor.

My instructor Lamar and his son Dion were patients at my dental office. I'd already taken three lessons from Lamar, who knew about the underground club. To enter Midnight Chaoss, I had to pretend to be his cousin, Jayden, who was sick and wouldn't be attending any events there. Jayden was part of a gambling ring that often visited the club, so he had a VIP ticket. He walked with a pronounced bounce and a faux half-limp. Basically, I was learning how to do the pimp roll. Special events occurred there, and I was waiting for the call from Lamar to inform me when I could attend.

Do you know how hard it is to walk like that? Like your pants are falling off while trying to look cool and confident? Gosh, if my pants were falling off, trying to be cool would be the *last* thing on my mind. But I had to play this character well in order to use his identity. I wasn't familiar with hip-hop fashion. On top of that, I'd never been good at acting, so this entire ordeal could be a disaster if I didn't prepare well.

I'd never imagined I'd ever say this, but Vivian Vo had to

master the pimp roll. What if Calvin didn't come through for me? This plan would ensure I had another way to find Aimee. If Dad found out about my plans, he'd beg me to come back to California. Knowing his weak heart, I'd oblige because I didn't want to lose another parent.

I wasn't doing this only for Aimee. Saving Aimee was like saving my mom—saving the girl who never had a normal childhood. In some way, I was also saving myself.

Mom had exceptional mathematical skills. Her mind was like a high-tech computer. She could solve difficult equations as though she were coloring a book. The answers came easily to her. On top of it all, she had an impeccable memory.

Music boomed as I entered the studio.

"Dr. Vo!" Fourteen-year-old Dion walked out of the small studio and fist-pumped me. He had a bright smile and short, dark hair. He wore a sweatshirt with jeans and fancy sneakers.

"Hey! I didn't know you'd be here today."

"My dad said I could teach you today. He has desk duty because his leg is in a cast."

"Oh, no! What happened?"

"He tripped on something on the floor."

"Where is he?"

He gestured to the other end of the studio. "In his office."

As I made my way there, I passed a room where an instructor was teaching a hip-hop dance class.

Lamar, Jayden, and their friend, Willy, had rallied the community to support my practice when it first opened. This was because I'd given Lamar and a few other members of his family necessary treatments that weren't covered by their insurance companies. A friendship started between us, and I told him I was looking for information about a kidnapping.

He'd told me about a man named The Tip who hung out at Midnight Chaoss. Apparently, he could retrieve information for a price—the more difficult to obtain, the higher the price.

When I arrived at the office, I found the door open.

I knocked on the opened door, getting his attention. "Sorry about your leg. How are you doing?"

Lamar glanced up and beamed. Dion had his father's warm smile. Unlike his son's short hair, Lamar wore his in long dreadlocks.

"Torn ligament. I'll be out for a while. If you don't mind, Dion's been dying to teach you. He thinks I'm too boring. But if you're uncomfortable with him, you'll have to wait until I'm healed. That could be over a month. Tamara is being very strict about my injury this time."

"She should be," I said. This wasn't his first time with a leg injury. "I'm fine with Dion teaching me. I'm curious what he offers."

After catching up with Lamar for a few more minutes, I walked into the small studio where Dion sat on the long couch by the wall. His two friends were beside him. The rest of the room was an open space with hardwood floors and a wall of mirrors.

"Okay, I'm ready to learn," I interrupted the boys, who were all engrossed with their phones. "Dion, your dad said you've got some ideas for me? Bring it on!" I smiled at my patient, who recently had a cavity filled.

Dion looked up from his phone and grinned. "I do. I can help you ace it, Dr. Vo!" He turned to his friends. "She's cool. She's my dentist, and she's learning how to walk, yo."

He jumped up from the couch and crossed his arms, striking a pose. His friends laughed.

"You gonna teach her something she already knows? That's weird, yo," said the boy with spiky blond hair.

Dion rolled his eyes. "These are my dumb friends, Tim and Raul."

Raul had olive skin and curly dark hair that went past his ears. Tim had short blond hair and braces. All the boys wore jeans and T-shirts. These kids must not be cold. Here I was, wearing an oversized sweatshirt over a long-sleeve shirt with knit pants.

"Nice to meet you both." I waved at Tim and Raul. "I'm playing a guy in a play. He has a certain walk I need to master," I lied, and Lamar had already agreed to keep the story consistent. Teenagers didn't need to know I was embarking on something illegal. "And Dion is gonna help me do it, right?" I patted his shoulder.

"That's right! C'mon." He gestured for me to follow him to the center of the studio floor and faced the mirror.

"Just watch me and mimic."

Dion loosened himself up while Tim and Raul stood nearby, making a rhythmic beat with their mouths. Dion stepped forward, walked, and added the dip and faux-limp. He looked so natural doing it.

I tried my best to follow his movements and failed miserably. My hips swayed in the wrong direction, and my legs felt too stiff. I was off-beat and couldn't perform the "dip" of one side of my body. I felt like a kitten in the body of a duck. It wasn't working out the way I'd hoped.

Tim snickered, but Raul elbowed him.

Dion made a face, lifting a clenched fist at his friends. Then turned to me. "Try again, Dr. Vo."

How was it I could pull out an infected molar with swiftness, precision, and ease but stumbled on a walk? I couldn't give up with these kids watching me.

Insecurity flushed onto my cheeks as I gathered courage and tried again. I watched myself in the mirror, saw how horrible and silly I was, and burst out laughing.

Dion, Tim, and Raul joined in on the laugh.

"You've gotta loosen up, Dr. Vo," said Tim.

"Pretend we're not here," added Raul.

"I've got it." Dion lifted his hand. "Pick a song with a good beat, Tim."

"We'll help you win the Oscars." Raul walked up and fist-pumped me.

"You mean the Tony Awards. Oscars are for movies. I'm in a small play." I loved that these boys felt sorry for me and wanted to help.

"We can make our own award show. It's called the Providence Oskars with a K," Dion teased.

More laughter erupted in the room, and I realized how much fun these kids were. They truly made tonight's lesson unforgettable.

Tim chose a beat I didn't know.

Dion jerked a chin at Raul. The boys walked around me, and Dion rapped.

Yo, yo, yo, Dr. Vo.
I want no more fillin'
Just put my grill in
That'll complete my style
For when I pimp roll up to the ladies and smile.

Dion emphasized the last word and beamed. All the boys laughed as they each performed the pimp roll in their own way. Their silliness and joy warmed me up and set me free. When they rapped again, I joined them and mimicked their moves. I felt less embarrassed and didn't overthink the moves. I didn't care how foolish I looked. After a while, I was sweating and realized we'd been rapping and pimp-rolling for about thirty minutes. This was one evening I'd never forget.

Wait until I tell Kaylee about the dentist rap.

Before I left, I thanked the boys for their time and made another appointment for next week. When I got home, I practiced again and again. Since my body was accustomed to the movements, I wanted my muscles to remember everything. Just like with kung fu, I could only get better with practice.

That session and a hot shower cleared my head. While I ate three fresh spring rolls and a papaya salad for dinner, I read all of Kaylee's texts and loved all the pictures she took of the robotics projects from kids all over the nation. I replied to her messages and told her I loved and missed her.

While in bed, I logged into Heartstrings, wanting to talk to Bullseye. I shouldn't, but I enjoyed chatting with him. Besides, we were only friends, and there was nothing wrong with talking to your friend, right?

Why don't you text the girls?

I immediately shoved that thought away. I didn't have the urge to chat with them tonight. It was already ten, and if he wasn't online, I'd take that as a sign from the heavens. It meant God wanted me to go to sleep.

When I logged on, the active symbol glowed in his profile.

He was online. Joy burst within me, and I sent him a message.

Tulip: *Hi.*

Bullseye: *Hi back.*

Tulip: *Why are you online?*

That was a stupid question, but it was too late to delete it now.

Bullseye: *Why are you? (smile emoji)*

Tulip: *Bored.*

I didn't want him to know I was looking for him.

Bullseye: *Me too.*

Was he lying too?

Tulip: *I guess this app is perfect for people like us. Lol.*

Bullseye: *We need a life.*

Tulip*: Lol.*

Bullseye: *Did you get a lot of heart tugs today? I got five.*

Jealousy stirred in me. I guess a lot of women wanted to talk to him.

I checked my page. No heart tugs.

Tulip: *No. You're my only friend.*

Bullseye: *You're my only Tulip. (smile emoji)*

Heat flushed my cheeks. He was probably referring to their profile pics, but I didn't care. It had been a long time since I felt this giddiness.

Tulip: *You must be a great catch.*

Bullseye: *Obviously. (wink emoji)*

Tulip: *So arrogant.*

Bullseye: *Nothing wrong with confidence.*

Tulip: *Why don't you have a girlfriend?*

Bullseye: *What makes you think I don't?*

My heart deflated.

Bullseye: *I don't have one.*

My heart immediately felt full again. Oh, God, I was like a teenager unable to control the bliss.

Tulips. *Why?*

Bullseye: *Waiting for the right one.*

Tulips: *Define that.*

Bullseye: *Then you have to tell me your perfect guy too.*

Tulip: *Deal.*

Bullseye: *A woman who I can fish with.*

I paused a moment. He *knew* I enjoyed fishing. Was he teasing me? Was I reading too much into his message?

Tulip: *That's it? I'm sure you can find someone like that.*

Bullseye: *I don't know anyone.*

Was he tossing out bait to see how I would take it? Was it possible to be attracted to someone I didn't even know? I knew Bullseye's personality from the chat, but I didn't know what he looked like. Could this be a good way of knowing if you like someone despite their appearance?

Maybe Bullseye was some antisocial weirdo who never went out and spent all his time online. Was he an online predator? My intuition told me no, but I couldn't trust myself right now.

Tulip: *What other traits are you looking for?*

Bullseye: *Intelligence. A kind heart.*

I noticed how he didn't say beauty or wealth. Maybe he knew the online game and knew exactly what to say. I was trying to make him look bad to discourage this growing attraction.

Bullseye: *Your turn.*

Tulip: *Someone I can share my burden with.*

Bullseye: *You're stressed? Gimme.*

My smile grew. He knew exactly what to say. Bullseye was either a dangerous man or a nice guy.

I had to change the subject.

Tulip: *Why do you like to fish?*

Bullseye: *Clears my head. Practice patience.*

Tulip: *Are you not patient?*

Bullseye: *Sometimes.*

Tulip: *What do you fear most?*

Bullseye: *Dentist.*

Shit.

Tulip: *Why?*

Bullseye: *Had a terrible experience as a kid.*

I could understand that. So many people had extreme anxiety going to the dentist.

Tulip: *When was your last checkup?*

Bullseye: *. . .*

Tulip: *You could have a cavity and not know about it!*

Bullseye: *(shhh emoji) (smile emoji)*

Tulip: *What's one thing that would make your dental visit better?*

Bullseye: *Quieter tools.*

Tulip: *I love the dentist.*

Bullseye: *(shocked emoji) This friendship isn't going to work out.*

Tulip: *On shaky grounds.*

Bullseye: *Tell me about your dream guy. Three words only.*

Tulip: *Exceptional. Smart. Funny.*

Bullseye: *You're describing me! (wink emoji)*

Tulip: *Tell me about your dream girl. Three words.*

Bullseye: *Extraordinary. Exotic. Mysterious.*

Tulip: *You like solving mysteries?*

Bullseye: (bullseye emoji)

Tulip: *Why? Isn't that too much work?*

Bullseye: *Nothing worth having comes easy.*

I let that statement hang in the air for a moment.

Bullseye: *You there?*

Tulip: *Yeah. Had to get a drink.*

I lied because I didn't know what to say.

Bullseye: *You never told me what you fear.*

Tulip: *Clowns and sizzling sounds.*

Bullseye: *I get clowns. But sizzling? Why?*

Tulip: *(shrug emoji) Sometimes fears make little sense.*

I didn't know him well enough to share that part of me yet.

Bullseye: *You're weird.*

Tulip: *At least I'm not boring. (smile emoji)*

Bullseye: *You're lying to me.*

Tulip: *Huh?*

Bullseye: *Sizzling. There's a reason.*

Tulip: *(eye-roll emoji) Nope. What's your longest relationship?*

Bullseye: *Ahhh. Changing the subject now? (smile emoji)*

Why was he so hung up on the sizzling comment?

Our conversation continued, and he stopped asking about the sizzling issue. The more I chatted with him, the more I discovered things about myself. I remembered that carefree version of me that had been lost so long ago.

My chest tightened. I was developing feelings for this stranger. I was stepping into the danger zone and didn't know what to do about it. Arrow's face intruded into my thoughts, and guilt gnawed at me.

Let me know when you're ready to date.

Arrow was waiting for me? Was he just saying that, or was he truly waiting? I couldn't trust someone like him. He was a man who had a lot of options. Would he toss me aside once he got what he was after?

The last two encounters with him had been casual and friendly. He didn't appear like he was still waiting for my answer.

I had suppressed my attraction to him. Arrow seemed to demand complications, whereas Bullseye didn't. Confusion sparked in me, but I stopped it.

I wanted an easy evening with no complications. I returned my focus to the mystery man tugging at unfamiliar places in my heart.

CHAPTER TEN

VIVIAN

I WOKE up at five in the morning, wondering why I couldn't fall back to sleep. It was Sunday, and I could sleep in. I *should* sleep in. But no, my body had other ideas.

I couldn't believe I stayed up past midnight texting with Bullseye. I was lonely, crazy, or bored. Perhaps all of the above. I didn't recognize this strange person in me. Actually, I sort of recognized her. She was a version of myself I hadn't connected to in a long time. This version didn't have worries or fears weighing her down. This version was the girl who went fishing by herself and talked to fish before she released them back into the waters.

One incident changed that, scarring me forever. After my mom died, I was afraid of a lot of things. That fear suppressed my emotions, and I think I forgot how to find that joy again. How could someone forget to be happy? Happiness should come easy, right? I was happy when my little patients smiled at me after a difficult procedure. I was happy knowing Dad was safe and at peace. I was happy that I could take care of Kaylee and not leave her alone in this cruel world.

But your soul is missing something.

I supposed I could never truly be happy if I were always on guard, scanning the horizon for any incoming threat. Being prepared was better than being attacked unexpectedly.

On that fateful day, I experienced two extreme emotions. That day had started out bright, beautiful, and full of hope. I had worn a new yellow shirt with pants to the party with my mom. My dad was out of state at a dental conference. By the end of the day, I was severely injured, and my mother dead.

Mom had exceptional talent, and I wished she got to live a longer life. Grandpa used to take her along on all of his business trips. All she had to do was look at a document, and she'd memorized everything on it, including account numbers. The information was used to blackmail his enemies.

She was both an asset and a threat because she knew a lot of confidential information. Only a few people knew about her ability. They just assumed that Grandpa adored his daughter and wanted her by his side. Over time, the work exhausted my mom mentally and emotionally. She didn't want to memorize numbers to hurt others, even though they were her father's enemies. She didn't have many friends. Her close friend was Kaylee's mom, Angela.

I often wondered how life would be for my mother if she had used her skills for something outside the crime organization. She could've been a rocket scientist. She could have created something innovative to improve the world. Yet she was trapped in a corrupt society that abused her ability.

I didn't want that for Aimee.

Why didn't Mom leave The Triad earlier?

You don't abandon your family.

Duty. Family responsibility. As an only child, her duty as the daughter of a ruthless triad leader was to support her father. If she left him, he would die. She was an asset not only to him but to the entire organization. An inexplicable honor system demanded a brotherhood and sisterhood amongst the members.

My chest hurt, and I placed a hand over it.

Stop making yourself sad.

I didn't know why all these memories came flooding back at this moment. Were they reminding me I'd gotten distracted from my goal?

Releasing a sigh, I returned my thoughts to the two men who had started me down memory lane—Bullseye and Arrow. Two men. Gosh, having two men occupy my mind was surreal.

Bullseye made me remember my inner joy. He had an easygoing personality and a sense of humor, making me want to go fishing again. Arrow's magnetism and intensity tugged at my deepest desires. It was as though he understood my pain, sorrow, and secrecy without me having to tell him anything. To know that someone had that ability to see straight into my soul terrified me. Even I didn't want to look within myself sometimes. In some strange way, it made me feel less lonely, knowing he could see me in a way no one else could.

I was torn between two men. Guilt nibbled at my conscience. What should I do?

Something was wrong with me. I was struggling between two men, one of whom could be a creepy serial killer pretending to be some nice guy. Maybe Bullseye was acting out a character in the same way I was learning how to do the pimp roll. Maybe he was married and cheating online. Or maybe he was trying to scam me out of money like those women I'd heard about on the news.

Ugh.

I needed a chat with the girls. Their insight into this ridiculous dilemma might help me. They'd scold me if I told them I was interested in someone I met online. Hell, I'd scold myself.

I had to meet Bullseye. I had to know what he looked like. Comparing the two would help me choose. Was Bullseye as handsome as Arrow? Did Bullseye have the magnetism of the gray-eyed wolf? Arrow's soul-searching eyes made me think of an alpha wolf who knew his way around a dangerous terrain. I shivered, imagining his eyes on me.

Take a walk and clear your head.

The park near my apartment would be perfect to clear my head. It wasn't big, and no one would be there at this early hour. The fresh air would help me decide on my next step.

I climbed out of bed and looked outside. It was still dark on this early December day. The apartment was in a nice and quiet area just outside of Providence. After washing up, I walked by Kaylee's bedroom. I hoped she was having fun in Texas with her classmates. They'd be back next week. I was so proud of her. She was definitely not awake right now. That girl would sleep all day if she could.

After sending her a good luck text, I dressed in a sweat-shirt, sweatpants, and a puffy coat. I tucked my phone into my coat pocket, stepped into my sneakers, and headed to the nearby park.

It was cold and dark at six in the morning, with the crisp chill nipping at my face. A peak of light glowed on the horizon, ready to wake up the city. The sun had another hour before it could warm up the day.

I tucked my hands into my coat and braced for the cold. The unpredictable New England weather differed from the warmth of California. But I'd spent time in New York with my family when Mom was alive. The Taipans had factions in New York City's Chinatown. So this cold weather wasn't new to me. I didn't mind it. The gloomy atmosphere made me more introspective.

Normally I listened to music during my walk or jog, but not today. I wanted to immerse myself in the city's dawn as it woke and yawned, preparing for the brand-new day. Providence was a busy city, but not as chaotic as New York or San Francisco. It was a quaint size with all the city amenities, but not as crowded. I preferred solitude over groups of people. Preferring my space and privacy didn't mean I was antisocial.

I crossed the street to the park. As expected, no one was there. In about an hour, people would be out walking their dogs, jogging, or sitting on the benches with coffee in hand. So I got to steal this quiet moment for myself.

As a self-defense instructor, I'd cautioned my students to be careful when going out in public alone. I'd tell them to avoid impractical times like late at night or super early in the morning when the world was still asleep. I'd remind them to be smart about their choices. And here I was doing the opposite of my instructions.

I didn't always practice what I preached.

The swoosh of cars passing by became the background music to my ears. Two people exited a café from across the street. My mind was blank, and I was taking in images and sounds like a camera scanning the area. I took a big inhale, filling my lungs with fresh oxygen. As I exhaled, I heard faint footsteps behind me. I'd been trained to sense these minor details. Learning martial arts had taught me to be more aware of my senses.

Maybe the person was just out walking like me. I sped up, and the footsteps increased. What the hell?

Stay calm. Stay alert.

I removed my hands from my coat pocket, preparing for whatever was to come. Nerves mounted as I began a light jog. Then, the person also started jogging. I could hear their movements. Was I freaking myself out for no reason?

I stopped and whirled around, ready to see who was behind me. But I slammed into a brick of a body. The sudden shock and power shoved me backward.

"Are you all right?" Arrow asked, gripping my arm and pulling me to him.

I looked up at his gray eyes. Under the lamppost, they appeared even more animalistic. The gray irises shifted as they stared at me. My heart quivered as though his gaze seared right through my eyes and traveled straight into my heart. The sensation was palpable—something I'd never experienced before. There was this irresistible danger to it. The kind that made me feel alive.

My phone rang, and I stepped away from his grip. Pulling out my phone, I saw Calvin's name flash on my screen. Had he found Aimee?

"Hi, Calvin."

Arrow's face tensed as he watched me.

"Hey, are you free to meet me?"

"Where? When? Do you have news for me?"

"Yup. Meet me at Over the Moon Café."

"The café in downtown Providence?"

"Yes."

"Be there in twenty minutes." I slid my phone back into my coat pocket.

"Where are you going?" Arrow inquired. "I can give you a ride."

"You don't have to."

"I'm just parked over there. Besides, I haven't had breakfast yet."

A car ride would save me time. I considered him for a moment.

"Aren't we friends?" he asked.

"We are."

"Then accept my friendly gesture." His stomach growled.

I smiled. "Okay. Let's get you breakfast."

"Thanks." He rubbed his stomach and ushered me to his Bugatti, a different car from the Maserati I'd seen him in.

I only knew the name because Audri's boyfriend also had one, but his was slightly different. Arrow's car was worth more than I made in four years combined. This was another reason I kept my distance from him. We lived in different worlds.

He opened the door for me, and I slid in. The interior was even more beautiful.

"Is Calvin helping you with something?" he asked as he drove toward downtown.

"He is."

"Were you guys in a relationship?"

Arching an eyebrow, I studied his profile, and his jawline seemed tense. "No. Why?"

The tension on his face relaxed. Or was that my imagination?

"Just wondering."

Was he jealous?

I looked out the window as warmth bloomed in my chest, and a smile crept onto my face.

The sun had risen, casting a warm glow over the entire area. Like the sun, my feelings for Arrow and Bullseye needed to be cleared up so I could move on. I had to get back on track and remind myself why I was in Providence. That temporary fun I had last night with Bullseye had to stop. It seemed surreal and too selfish of me. A little girl was waiting for me to find her, and I was flirting with some stranger.

Bullseye could be a kidnapper for all I knew.

I turned and looked at Arrow. The sunlight cast shadows onto the angles of his face, making him appear almost ominous and dangerous. As though sensing me, he turned and met my gaze.

"Do I have something on my face?"

"Shadows are dancing on your face."

"Oh yeah? What do I look like?"

"You look like a man preparing for war. A strategic general quietly laying out his attack plans to ensure victory."

He smirked. "You're not wrong."

Oh. What was going on? Who was he going to war with?

Why was he following me?

Before I could ask, he parked the car. "We're here."

CHAPTER ELEVEN

ARROW

I DESPERATELY WANTED to know what she was thinking while she studied my face. I'd felt the heat of her gaze and couldn't resist looking at her to find out. She was good at hiding her emotions. But there was one thing I was certain of: she *was* attracted to me. Perhaps not to the same extent as my attraction to her. But it was there, like a whisper surrounding both of us.

After hearing their brief conversation, there was no way I'd let Vivian meet Calvin without my presence. It wasn't just jealousy warring inside me. Curiosity piqued when he asked to meet her right away. What was so important?

After a thorough research, I knew who Calvin Wong was. He dwelled in a violent and dark world. The Triad wasn't a place for someone like Vivian. She could get hurt. I didn't like her hanging out with him. But what could I do? Somehow, they were friends.

I opened the door to Over the Moon Café and accompanied Vivian inside. Two lines of people filled the space. One line had people waiting at the counter for Chinese pastries.

The second line was to order pancakes, sausages, eggs, and other regular breakfast items.

I spotted Calvin sitting at a table in the back corner. "He's over there."

When he saw me approach with Vivian, surprise and disappointment splashed on his face.

That's right, fucker. She's with me.

I pulled out a chair for Vivian and took the seat beside her. "Good morning, Calvin."

"Morning." Calvin glanced between Vivian and me. Questions sparked in his eyes, but he didn't ask them. Instead, a casual question emerged. "Do you guys want anything to eat or drink? They have excellent coffee here." He lifted his cup.

Vivian turned to me. "You should get something."

I was hungry, but I didn't want to wait in line and miss their conversation. "I can wait."

"Your stomach's going to growl again."

I smiled. "Do you want anything?"

"A latte with oat milk, please." She beamed.

I got up, glanced at the line, and sighed. At this rate, Vivian and Calvin would finish their conversation by the time I got the order and returned. I got to the front of the line. "Ladies and gentlemen, I have an emergency, and I'd like to request a favor from you. I'll pay for all your orders and buy you a gift card to come back here if I can place my order *right now*. You cool with that?"

"Fine with me, sweetheart," said the old lady, who was next in line to order. "Come here."

"I'm fine with that!" shouted the group of college kids.

Everyone smiled and agreed. I paid five thousand dollars upfront and told the cashier to ring up everyone's order to include a hundred-dollar gift card. She could keep the rest or put it toward the pay-it-forward fund, which was in a container on the counter.

"Thank you!" cheered everyone in line.

I returned to the table with Vivian's latte, my coffee, and three muffins.

"Here you go." I placed the latte down for Vivian.

"Wow. That was fast. Thank you."

I took my seat, offered Calvin a blueberry muffin, and smiled.

He glanced at the long line and arched an eyebrow. "I'm not a muffin kind of guy, but thank you."

"You really don't have any updates for me?" Vivian asked.

"Sorry, no," Calvin replied.

"But you said you had something for me."

"I asked if we could meet. You just assumed." He leaned back in his chair and smirked. "I just wanted to see you."

Vivian blinked, and I kept my gaze on Calvin.

Was he testing my feelings for Vivian? He was holding back information because of my presence.

"When do you think you'll have something for me? I don't have time for games, Calvin."

"I just wanted to see if you remember our deal."

"What deal?" I interjected.

Vivian's lips twisted as he looked down at the table and back up at Calvin. "You have my word. Get me all the information on Aimee, and I'll fulfill my end of the bargain."

"Are you blackmailing her?" I eyed Calvin as the need to protect her coursed through me.

"She needs my help. There's a price for everything."

Calvin offered me a sly smile. "You should know this, Arrow."

He neither admitted nor declined.

"No, he's not," Vivian said. From under the table, she placed a hand on my thigh to stop my inquiry or to calm my anger.

I placed my hand over hers, keeping it where I liked it.

She tried to yank it away, but my grip was stronger.

Something was going on between Vivian and Calvin, and I had to find out. Anything to do with Calvin wouldn't be good for Vivian. Was Calvin helping her as a friend or member of The Triad? Either way, danger was lurking around her.

I didn't like the way he looked at her. The possessiveness in me surged. "Any man who blackmails a woman deserves severe punishment."

"Is that a threat?" he asked, showing no fear.

A man who was used to violence should be accustomed to placing fear on others. Having served in the Navy and traveling to remote areas of the world, I'd seen my share of monsters. My rough childhood, along with those worldly experiences, had created a monster in me. Sometimes, you have to be the most terrifying monster to deal with the worst of humanity.

"It's a promise." I held his eyes. "And I'm a man who keeps his promises."

Laughing, Calvin leaned on the table. "It's best if you focus on your bamboo wine so another employee doesn't sabotage it."

How the fuck did he know about that? This was confidential information. I made sure no one outside of Holt Enterprises knew that a former employee had stolen an order of my wine prototype and sabotaged the warehouse.

James Chin had been missing for months. But I'd find him and make him pay. The fucker had cost me millions of dollars in damages. What had he done with the three cases of wine? I'd searched the black market for any resale, but nothing had shown up.

Could James have been working for The Triad and stolen my goods for them? The Tai Lok wine from The Taipans triad was a successful brand long before my Bambooze Series came about. It didn't make sense, but there could be another agenda I wasn't aware of.

My jaw tightened. "Do you have anything to do with my stolen wine or damaged warehouse?"

"No."

"But you know who does?"

Something flickered in his eyes. He didn't need to reply. His eyes already told me what I needed to know.

"Where is James Chin?"

"I don't know," he said as his phone rang. "If you find him, let me know." He glanced at his phone, his brows furrowed, and tucked it away.

Had James screwed with him too?

"I'd appreciate the same gesture."

Calvin offered me a nod and turned to Vivian, who had been keenly listening to our conversation. She had stopped trying to free her hand from mine. If she wanted more information about what Calvin and I discussed, she could tell me about her deal with Calvin.

"I've got to go." Calvin rose from his seat just as his phone rang again. "I'll let you know what I find on the girl," he said to Vivian.

After he left, I clasped Vivian's hand more tightly and brought it up to the table. "I like holding your hand." Her small hand was soft but also firm. I loved how it fit into my wide palm like a puzzle piece finally falling into its perfect place.

"Why?" she asked, but didn't take her hand away.

"Because it revitalizes me. Gives me energy like a charging station, a battery, a blazing sun." Her lips curved, and I continued. "Like a rare crystal with magical powers. An antidote for my foul mood."

Her eyes flickered with amusement. "You didn't look angry when you were creeping behind me at the park."

I cleared my throat. "First, I wasn't creeping. You were lost in thought, and I didn't want to frighten you. I gave you time to yourself while I followed behind. Then you started jogging, so I caught up to say hello. But you turned around and slammed into me."

As she searched my face for the truth, her irises turned a dark brown. I wanted her to trust me. She had no reason not to.

"I had the park to myself until you came along."

"You like taking walks in the early winter mornings?"

"Not really. I needed fresh air to clear my head."

"Something bothering you?" I caressed my thumb over her hand.

"Just need to figure out a few things. Why are you up early on Sunday morning?"

"Working."

"Maybe you wouldn't have foul moods if you stopped being a workaholic."

"Just to clarify, I wasn't in a foul mood when I saw you at

the park. But that changed when you went to see Calvin. He likes you."

"No, he doesn't." She made a disbelieving face. "He has information I need."

"He said he wanted to *see* you."

"He's lying."

"Why?"

"Because you're here." She leaned in, her face inches from mine. "Why are you really here? You could've just dropped me off and headed back to work."

I lifted her hand to my lips and caressed it. Branded it with my lips. "Because I wanted him to believe that you were with me."

"But we're not together."

"But we should be." I smiled at her. "What information are you waiting for? What girl is missing? Maybe I can help you."

A woman wearing a long coat burst into the café, looking frantic. "Please call the police! There's a body of a little girl around the corner!"

Vivian gasped as the color drained from her face. She darted out of her seat, rushing over to the lady. Her voice trembled. "Where's the body?"

CHAPTER TWELVE

VIVIAN

I GRIPPED Arrow's hand tightly as we rushed out the door.

Please don't let it be Aimee.

I couldn't believe we were still holding hands, but I didn't care. I needed stability. I didn't know how I'd react if the body belonged to Aimee. I might collapse into a heap of sorrow on the ground.

The woman led us to a corner where a small body was wrapped in a large blanket. I trembled as I approached. Arrow released my hand and wrapped his arm around my shoulder, pulling me close.

As I stepped closer, my stomach churned. The lifeless face of a little girl with blonde hair greeted me. She was carefully wrapped in several blankets as though someone had taken the time to bundle her up and protect her from the chilly weather.

Tears filled my eyes as I imagined what that poor girl had gone through. Who had killed her?

"Don't touch anything!" a woman shouted at a man who took a notecard tucked between the blankets.

"FTM. Maybe it's her initials?" He placed the notecard back and stepped away. "She's so young . . ."

Aimee could already be dead. What if her body was wrapped in a blanket somewhere, and no one had discovered it yet? Emotions flooded me, and I couldn't keep it together. I turned into Arrow's shoulder and cried.

Arrow ushered me away from the growing crowd and wrapped both arms around me, cocooning me from the cold and chaos. At that moment, I felt safe and protected. This wasn't the same protection and safety I felt with my parents. This was different. This was something I'd never felt with a man before.

But I could be too vulnerable right now to decipher my true feelings. Fear and worry collided in me, and I didn't know what to do.

When the police arrived, I watched as the EMT took the girl.

"Check all the nearby cameras." A detective gestured to one of his men.

Arrow took my hand in his again. I looked at our joined hands and wondered how it all happened. I didn't wake up this morning with plans to hold hands with any man. The predicament between the two men had occupied my mind.

But my heart was hurting too much to think about that now. Arrow's gaze fixated on something across the street. I followed his gaze to a group of people watching the crime scene. Who was he looking at?

Nausea rose in me, and I returned my attention to my body.

I yanked at his hand. "Can we go now? I don't feel well."

He looked at me, and concern filled his eyes. "Okay."

CHAPTER THIRTEEN

ARROW

"YOU DON'T HAVE to come up. I can get to my apartment fine." Vivian walked past the front desk and waved at the security guard. "Hi, Marvin!" Then she headed toward the elevator door.

I was right beside her. "You don't look fine. Besides, it's common courtesy to invite your savior up for a cup of coffee."

"My savior?" She stepped into the elevator, and I followed her inside.

"From the cold. I was your charger just now." I slung an arm around her shoulder, pulling her close to me. "Didn't you feel warmer from my touch?"

She rolled her eyes, but didn't push my arm away until we got to her apartment door.

"Shoes off." She entered and placed her shoes on the rack.

I did the same. She didn't know I also took my shoes off at my house. When my mom fell ill, I'd kept the house as clean as possible. Germs weakened her immune system. My dad had complied with the rule when he was sober.

"You want milk and sugar in your coffee?" she asked.

"Black is fine." I walked to the window and looked outside. "It's a friendly neighborhood with great potential."

"I like the quiet here. Make yourself at home."

"Thanks." I walked to the living room, sat down, and noticed a Whiz Kidz folder on the coffee table. "You know about Whiz Kidz?"

"My sister Kaylee loves that place. The program funded her trip to Texas."

A framed picture of Vivian and Kaylee caught my eye. "I didn't know you have a sister." I studied their faces. Kaylee was mixed race, whereas Vivian wasn't.

Vivian handed me the white coffee cup. "I'm her guardian, but we're much more like sisters. I took her in when her mom died."

"Have you been to Whiz Kidz?" I asked, wondering if she'd seen me there.

"A few times when I dropped her off or picked her up. Why?"

What should I say? I had to be careful.

"It's a great place for kids to go after school or on weekends." I studied more pictures of the two of them. "I wish I had something like Whiz Kidz back then."

"Kaylee is thrilled there. It's perfect for her. I'm helping her test out this app that she created."

Holy fuck.

Tulip. Could Vivian be Tulip? Surprise, excitement, joy, and fear burst in me. I couldn't believe this.

If I told Vivian that Whiz Kidz was my nonprofit organization, she'd know that I was Bullseye. Kaylee had also asked me to help her test out the app. I'd been flirting with someone who went by the name Tulip, thinking it was just some random woman.

Had Kaylee arranged all of that?

But she couldn't have known I would connect to her sister, right? The app tugged Vivian based on the data on her profile. Besides, Kaylee didn't know I liked Vivian. She only knew I was interested in a gorgeous dentist. That was all I told her a while back. Could she have remembered my interest and set us up?

Based on what I knew about the clever girl, she was probably behind this. I'd need a chat with the little brat later. If I had dug deeper, I would have known that Kaylee lived in this building—*my property*.

I'd been so concentrated on Vivian that I'd missed a few key details. What else had I missed?

Vivian didn't need to know I'd purchased this apartment building so that I could monitor the cameras within the building and outside of it. It was how I knew she went to get coffee at Sunshine in a Cup and had gone out early to walk alone that morning. I had programmed all the cameras to detect her facial features and alert me when she went out.

Stalker creep.

I wasn't being creepy. I was being *protective* of her after seeing her with Calvin at the wine expo. He was in The Triad, and that spelled trouble with a capital T. Besides, I'd bought this building as an investment when I'd first met her. The camera thing was new.

I'd share everything with Vivian after I talked to her sister.

Vivian sat next to me. Color had returned to her face. I didn't think she'd appreciate any surprises right now. Especially about a stranger who had flirted with her too many times online.

"You okay?" I asked. "Who's Aimee?"

"A little girl who's been missing for nine months now. She's the reason I'm in Providence. I have to find her."

"Do the authorities know?"

She told me the story and why she believed Aimee was with The Triad.

"So you went to the wine expo to ask Calvin for help?"

She nodded, and the knots inside me unknotted. "Do you think he'll help you?"

"I don't know. He seemed sincere, but I have to try. He's my only connection to The Triad." She looked at me. "I don't know why I'm telling you all this. I shouldn't."

"Why not?"

"Because I don't know you well enough."

"We can catch up now." I took her hand in mine again. "Time to charge up."

Vivian stared at me, but I could see a small smile emerging. "Are you always like this?"

"No." The question brought me to a pause too. She brought out a lighter and happier side of me. I didn't enjoy holding hands with any other women. I had to think about this further—this change I didn't even realize was happening to me. "I guess I just like holding your hands."

"Why don't I believe you?"

"You *should* believe me." I shifted so I could look her in the eye. "Most times, I'm not like this."

"I know. You have this intense demeanor, like a powerful magnet that pulls people to you."

She'd been observing me. "But I failed at attracting you."

"You didn't fail," she admitted, and her cheeks flushed. "I'm just . . . careful."

I brushed my fingers across her cheeks. "What are you afraid of? I won't hurt you."

"It's hard for me to trust people, Arrow."

There was so much to her, and I wanted to unravel every secret she was hiding. But I didn't want to bombard her with questions when she was dealing with so much.

"You can trust me." I squeezed her hand.

She considered me with her brown eyes, and I loved that I could see she was slowly welcoming me into her world.

"You have a face that makes it hard for me to trust."

"What does that mean?"

She traced my jawline with her fingers, tantalizing my skin with her seductive movement. My cock hardened in my active pants. She noticed, smirked, but said nothing.

Did she know she had power over me? No woman had made me *want* the way she did.

"It means you're a stunning man." Her eyes gleamed. "In my experience, stunning people get bored and stray." Her face was so close to mine, and her perfume hypnotized me.

Was she testing me?

"Let me show you that your analysis is wrong." I crushed my lips to hers, loving the way her soft lips molded to mine.

She whimpered, and my tongue slid in to meet hers. She tasted as perfect as I'd imagined. A mystery flavor that was uniquely hers.

Heat pulsed between us, and she broke the kiss, bracing a hand on my chest.

She looked at me and licked her swollen lips. God, she was fucking beautiful.

"I don't get bored easily." I traced her bottom lip with my

index finger. "Especially not with something I've wanted for a long time. You just gave me a wicked taste of you." My lips hovered over her ear. "And I want *more.*"

When she shivered, I smiled.

Then my phone rang, and I cursed. She smiled, hopped off the couch, and busied herself in the kitchen.

I took the call from the PI, who had news about my former employee, James Chin. A recording from the Boston Casino showed someone who looked like him.

I had to go check it out before he escaped again.

Vivian returned from the kitchen with some strawberries and pineapple. "You want to take some to go?"

"I would love that, thank you."

Before I left, I reached for her hand. "I meant what I said. I want more."

CHAPTER FOURTEEN

VIVIAN

IT HAD BEEN a few hours since Arrow kissed me, and I could still taste him. I didn't know what had gotten into me earlier when I'd seduced him on my couch. I wanted to know what it felt like to kiss him.

He was a fabulous kisser. But I didn't know if we could start anything. Though he said I could trust him, I still needed to know for myself. That would take time.

I swung my attention back to reality instead of the fantasy that could get me into trouble. I called my dad to update him on my progress. News about the little girl's body would probably reach him soon, so I wanted to soften the shock.

"They're running the girl's DNA now," I said. "Hopefully, they'll locate her parents soon."

"That's good," Dad said. "By the way, a tip came in the other day about a girl matching Aimee's description in Florida. Turns out, it was some drunk man wanting the reward money." He sighed. "I'm scared, Viv."

"We have to cling to hope, *Ba*. She's an asset to them. They won't hurt her."

An awkward moment of silence swayed in the air. We both knew that Mom had been an asset until one of the members went rogue and hurt her and me. Hope pushed us forward to another day. So, no one mentioned that painful past.

"Oh, there's a new Vietnamese restaurant in town," my dad said. "They have the best *phở*. I'll take you and Kaylee there next time you visit. How's she doing?"

I updated him on Kaylee, and I could imagine him smiling on the other end.

"She's lucky to have you. Her life could have been different."

"You mean *us*. She adores you," I reminded him.

"Aimee reminds me of Kaylee. They're both brilliant kids. Did the final adoption papers go through yet?"

"Yes. I want to throw her a party to give her the news. She'll be thrilled."

I'd been Kaylee's guardian for two years now. She didn't know that I had officially adopted her. The process had taken a while, but everything finally went through. She'd be happy to know she could be with me and my dad forever. She had a family now.

Though Kaylee never brought up the adoption topic, I knew she yearned for a permanent family. Every time she spoke about her classmates and their families, I could see the hesitation and sadness in her eyes.

As far as she knew, I was her temporary guardian until the court decided otherwise. According to her, this family wasn't truly hers yet.

I tried my best to give her what she needed, including

love. Despite that, she was a smart girl. She understood what the counselors had told us at the initial meeting. They had to see how I performed as a guardian since I had a busy life and had never had a child, sibling, or even a pet to take care of.

Joy burst in me as I imagined celebrating with her. She'd be my forever sister. I was only thirty and loved the idea of having an interesting and vibrant thirteen-year-old girl around me all the time.

The work day had taken a toll on me, and I yawned. "I'll keep you posted, *Ba*. Say hello to Rose for me. I'm heading to bed."

Instead, I sat on the couch, replaying the day. I went from walking to clear my head to meeting Calvin, holding hands with Arrow, seeing a dead body, and having Arrow kiss me. He'd turned me on, and my body was having trouble forgetting what had occurred.

Despite all of that, the thing I clung to right now was Arrow holding my hand. It gave me more comfort than I realized. It was special and different from the kiss.

I looked at my palm. Warmth bloomed there every time I envisioned us holding hands. At that moment, I knew I had to let go of the illusion of Bullseye. He was an imaginary vision from an app. I hadn't seen his face.

But Arrow was real. He could elicit a range of emotions in me. Today, I saw a glimpse of joy I hadn't seen in him before. There was another side to the dark and intense man I met a while ago. Not only that, but I also witnessed the change in me.

When he held my hand, it was like a key to something I didn't fully understand. All I knew was that something unlocked inside me.

I didn't need a man to make me feel safe. I could defend

myself. But the protection and safety Arrow offered was more like a secure home where I could pour out all my secrets and fears and not be judged.

It was time to end it with Bullseye.

Bullseye: *Hi.*

Tulip: *Hi.*

Bullseye: *How was your day?*

Tulip: *Good. Yours?*

Bullseye: *Not so chatty today?*

Tulip: *I won't be logging in anymore.*

Bullseye: *Why?*

Tulip: *Busy*

Bullseye: *You seem different tonight.*

Tulip: *Had an exhausting day. But I figured out a problem. (smile emoji)*

Bullseye: *What kind of problem?*

Tulip: *A guy problem.*

Bullseye: *Want to tell me about it?*

Tulip: *Nope.*

Bullseye: *(sad face emoji)*

Tulip: *Thanks for being a good friend. I'll miss our chats.*

Bullseye: *Me too. Chatting with you was the highlight of my evenings. (thumbs up emoji)*

Tulip: *Good night.*

Bullseye: *Sweet dreams.*

Feeling better, I hopped into bed, grabbed a pillow, and wished that Bullseye would find his dream girl because I was already taken by the man who'd kissed me today.

CHAPTER FIFTEEN

ARROW

MY VISIT to the Boston Casino in search of James Chin turned out to be some guy who looked like him from the profile, but when I got up close and sat beside him at the poker table, I knew it wasn't him.

Nothing would stop me from searching for him. He'd pay for the stolen goods and damages. I'd add in a hefty interest rate that would be paid with physical pain. The fucker infuriated me, but compared to other issues at play, he was a minor problem.

When I got home, I showered, slipped into my boxers, thought about the kiss, wanted more of the kiss, and browsed Heartstrings to see what details had linked me to Vivian. She had ended the chat, and an air of sadness lingered after the screen dimmed. I could see my reflection on the phone, and it showed a man completely obsessed with a woman.

She'd had an emotional day, and it showed in the conversation. What was her guy dilemma? Was she interested in someone else? I raked a hand through my hair and let out a dry laugh. I'd never allowed a woman to get me worked up like this. It clouded my judgment, and who had time for that?

Apparently, you do.

I'd been doing a lot of things aside from the tasks on my to-do list. Chasing after Vivian had been a fun distraction at the beginning. She was a mystery that had called me, like a mission I had to complete. But now she was something else. There was this pull I couldn't resist. The closer I got to her, the more the mystery grew. She was like a compelling book that sucked me in the more I read it, and I had to find out what happened next.

More than anything, it was the way she made me feel. The other details might not be as prominent as how my heart hammered when I looked at her or how my fingers yearned to touch her.

The damn kiss was the catalyst that cranked up my desire for her. I licked my bottom lip, still tasting that mysterious sweetness that made me feel like an idiot.

I used to make fun of my friends when they talked about their significant others. They had all seemed foolish. But here I was, standing in that same emotional pool, wondering what the hell had happened to me.

I had no explanation for my actions. Like buying the building she lived in so I could have access to all the cameras. Like paying off the customers at the café so I didn't have to wait in line and miss her conversation with Calvin. Like "bumping into" her when she went for coffee at that café across from her apartment or ensuring she was safe when she went walking at the butt crack of dawn. Not only that, but I'd also asked the owner of the Martial Arts Studio to alert me when Vivian went to the gym. I'd told them I wanted to ask her to be my private martial arts instructor.

My focus had been on The Trogyn, but now that concentration was also on Vivian and The Triad, specifically The Taipans. Were they working with The Trogyn? Was Calvin also a member of that organization?

Vivian could get hurt by these dangerous people. Was I being overprotective? Probably. But it was better than being sorry.

This was all my speculation, but I had to see everything from a bird's eye view. I had to imagine the possibilities because that was how my mind worked. A strategy had to be established and implemented to eliminate disasters. A well-thought-out strategy could steer a dangerous situation to have a different outcome.

However, Vivian was someone I couldn't steer my way. She had seemed unaffected by me until recently. The kiss and the handholding changed everything.

Since when had I been obsessed with holding her hand?

I laughed out loud to myself. The sound bounced around the walls of my office. I could imagine all the furniture, paintings on the wall, and even the hardwood floor laughing back at me.

The fool who wouldn't give up.

Did she have feelings for Bullseye? It was still me, but an uncomfortable feeling stirred, knowing she had feelings for another man while holding my hand.

But he's you.

But *she* didn't know it was me.

When I held her hand, it felt so right. She also welcomed it because she didn't extract it from my grip. I hadn't expected the dating app to reveal so much to me.

Vivian had confessed she had trouble trusting. I had to tell her the truth soon. But how could I do it without appearing untrustworthy? I didn't want her to think I was toying with her emotions.

I got up from my desk, walked to my wine cabinet, and poured myself a glass of CheckMate Black. The dark liquid slid down my throat, warming my stomach.

I returned to my desk and thought about the man I'd seen at the crime scene.

What was he doing there looking at the dead body of that little girl? Was he just a regular bystander who walked by? I doubted it. I'd seen him at the wine convention, and he'd offered me a nod.

Who was this man? Did he know me? Had we met, and I'd forgotten?

No. I had an excellent memory, and I would remember if I'd met him. He wasn't some regular guy who went unnoticed. He was well dressed both times I'd seen him. Money and power oozed from him. I had to find out who he was.

Who was that little girl? She appeared to be eight or nine, maybe even younger. Perhaps the authorities had her information in their missing children's cases. The DNA test would confirm that.

Did The Triad have Aimee?

I didn't want Vivian anywhere near The Triad, but she was already immersed in it, which meant I had to keep a closer eye on her.

The PI could help locate Aimee quicker. He had exceptional resources that the police didn't have. Besides, the city had too many cases to work on. He'd been instrumental in helping me and my friends destroy The Trogyn's businesses.

I finished my wine, grabbed my phone, and called him at his current number. He changed phone numbers every two weeks to protect us and himself.

He told us to call him O.R., but we were used to just calling him our private investigator.

"Can you prioritize a missing child's case?"

"Yeah. Send me a pic and any info you have."

I forgot to ask Vivian for a picture. It was too late to bother her now.

"I'll send it to you tomorrow via email."

"Great. Thanks."

Our conversation ended, and I went into my bedroom to get ready for bed. Was Vivian thinking of me as I was thinking of her?

Then my phone rang, and my brow furrowed at the name on the screen.

CHAPTER SIXTEEN

ARROW

"WHY ARE YOU STILL UP, KAYLEE?" I glanced at the clock that had just ticked to midnight.

"You said to call."

"I was expecting a call sometime tomorrow." I'd texted her earlier, before my trip to Boston.

"But I'm busy tomorrow."

I swiped to the robotics agenda in my email, and it wasn't packed. But I left that detail out.

Leaning back against the headboard, I said, "You planned it, didn't you?"

"Huh? What are you talking about?"

I rolled my eyes. "Your dating app. You asked me to test out Heartstrings."

"I asked a bunch of people."

I could almost hear her smile on the other end.

"Are you trying to set me up with your sister?"

"How's the chat going?" She giggled, excitement filling her voice.

I knew it! "I could twist your arm for this."

"That'd be considered child abuse, and I'd have to report you to the authorities. But Vivian would have already gotten to you first." She paused. "Just as a warning, the police will be kinder to you."

Christ.

She sounded so serious. "You know I'm joking, right?"

She laughed. "You know I'm joking too, right?"

I couldn't help but smile. "How old are you again?"

"Thirteen going on thirty. That's what Viv always says."

Kaylee would be a force to be reckoned with when she got older. "You're not spying on our conversation, are you?"

"No!"

I had already blocked that ability. She was creating the app that was being supported by *my* server. So I had access to everything. A team of people was dedicated to teaching and helping young kids amplify their talents. But kids often did unimaginable things, so this program had to be monitored closely. I'd been more involved in Whiz Kidz until the recent months when my concentration had gone to The Trogyn and the fucking asshole who stole my wine.

"Good, because I'd delete the entire app."

"You can't do that!"

"I certainly can. You're doing this through Whiz Kidz, which is *my* business, remember?"

"But *I* created it."

"Yes, you did. Creating a cool app and ensuring it works properly demands responsibility, Kaylee. Didn't you listen to the instructor about personal and social responsibilities?"

"I did, and don't worry," she said. "Besides, I don't care what two adults talk about. Probably boring shit."

"Language."

"Stop! You sound like Viv! She doesn't like it when I

swear. You cuss sometimes when you're talking to your team."

Shaking my head, I said, "I'm an adult, so I can do whatever I want."

"*So* responsible."

I smiled at her annoyed emphasis. "How did you know Tulip and Bullseye would get along?"

"I didn't. But Viv is single, and so are you. You said you like this dentist, so I assumed you have a thing for dentists. My sister is smart and beautiful. So . . . do you like her?"

Kid, I'm obsessed with her.

But I wasn't going to share that. Who knew how she would twist it?

"I do."

"Then ask her out! Duh! She needs a break. All she does is work and look for Aimee. I don't even know if she's still alive." She sighed. "But I don't have the heart to share that with Viv."

I could imagine the pressure and fear around Vivian.

"I didn't know the two of you would connect on Heartstrings. The details on your profile probably connected to something on hers. I created both of your profiles and added things I knew about you. Did you change anything?"

I'd included fishing in my details, and she also enjoyed fishing. Maybe that was what linked us together.

I didn't want to keep her on the phone any longer. It was getting late. "Next time, I want you to tell me what you're planning, okay?"

"Okay. Can you keep this between us?" she asked.

"Why?"

"Viv would be angry with me for manipulating stuff."

"All right. You owe me one."

"Okay," she said. "But I deserve a reward too."

"For what?"

"For connecting you to the woman of your dreams!"

She laughed. "Good night!"

She hung up, leaving me shaking my head at the truth in her statement.

My phone buzzed, and three reminders popped onto my screen: wine campaign, WaterFyre Rising, and Ormon's reopening.

I had to review the international wine campaign for my Bambooze Series. Even if CheckMate Black and CheckMate Red didn't win the final round, I'd be part of the top tier and could use that in my promotions.

I had to sit down and think about what I wanted to do for Level Five of WaterFyre Rising. The feedback from my friends had been glowing, but there was something the game needed that I couldn't understand yet.

I had to attend a banquet at Ormon's Restaurant this Friday. The renovation wrapped up only a few days ago. It was a popular Italian restaurant chain owned by Kenneth Ormon, my ex's father. I'd dated Sylvia for a few months until she hinted at a ring and marriage, which forced me to end things quickly. I wasn't ready to be attached like that. Despite the ending of our relationship, she suggested her father stock my wine in all of his restaurants. Though I'd rather be working on my to-do list, I had to attend the reopening of his restaurant to show my appreciation.

CHAPTER SEVENTEEN

VIVIAN

IT HAD BEEN a super busy week, and by Friday night I was exhausted. The weather was warm for early December. I didn't mind the rain pounding on my windshield because it was better than a snowstorm, which we would have gotten if the temperatures had dipped a few degrees lower.

Christmas was approaching, and I had to prepare gifts for my family and office staff. I'd think about those things later. Right now my brain just wanted food, a shower, and my bed.

I drove toward Ormon's Restaurant, which had fantastic comfort food. They just reopened after expanding. Tonight would be the perfect evening for some takeout and a movie with Kaylee. She'd been watching this Korean drama about a demon falling in love with a human. That would be a great distraction for me to rest my mind and unwind.

When I ended my friendship with Bullseye from Heartstrings, a peculiar sadness lingered around me. I knew I was doing the right thing by not clinging to some infatuation with him. Like I said, he could be someone I detested in real life.

But online, where the lens of reality was blurred and half-truths became distorted, a demon could be beautiful, and that terrified me.

The clown-faced man who had killed my mother and traumatized me as a kid flared in my vision. Bullseye could be wearing a mask too. I couldn't risk my life like that again. I had to be careful. Living like this required me to suspect people. It prevented me from getting close to anyone, but I felt safe.

As I pulled up to the restaurant, a car was leaving, and I snatched the off-street parking spot. The restaurant parking lot looked full. I'd already called in my order of spaghetti and meatballs and chicken alfredo with some garlic breadsticks. I pulled up my hood, got out of the car, and headed into the restaurant.

"Sorry, we're swamped tonight." The hostess with the snowflake pin apologized for the delay. "Your order should be out shortly."

"No worries. I understand." I sat in the chair and waited. More people came in for pickup and crowded the space.

An Asian man with brown hair smiled at me. "I picked the wrong night to come here."

"We all did," said the woman next to me. "But they're worth it."

A pregnant woman glanced around the waiting area, but all the seats were taken.

I rose. "You can take this seat."

"You're so kind. Thank you so much!" She huffed out a breath and sat down.

"You're welcome."

Laughter boomed nearby, and I glanced over to a party in the large room.

My heart palpitated when I saw Arrow standing with his ex. She'd been with him at the wine expo too. If they weren't together, then why was she always with him? Why did he kiss me and kept asking me out when he already had her?

Sylvia wore a black dress that accentuated her curves. Jealousy slithered through me. I didn't have curves like her. She gripped his arm, leading him to a group of men. He shook hands with the men and laughed.

Sylvia patted his cheek while he spoke to a man with silver hair.

Were they still together? The affection she had for him was obvious.

I was confused and hurt. Had I gotten the wrong message from him?

I want more.

His words echoed in my head.

Liar.

My fingers curled, hating myself for loving the way he had held my hand. My mood soured as I realized I'd misinterpreted his gestures. Maybe I was seeing—wishing for something that wasn't there. This was why I kept my distance from men. They couldn't be trusted. Just when I was about to give him a chance, he ruined it.

I got my food, and I didn't know why, but I glanced at them once more. Sylvia had her arms hooked around his neck like she was going to kiss him.

Sylvia was a successful influencer of several brand names. She wore their clothes and used their beauty products, promoting the items to her millions of followers. Some of whom were celebrities. She lived in the limelight, whereas I preferred a private life.

Did Arrow like those kinds of women? Clearly, I wasn't his type.

I looked away and rushed out of the restaurant. As I darted to my car, I noticed a man standing outside the restaurant wearing a clown mask.

Fear spiked in me, and I completely froze in place. He looked at me and tilted his head. Then he strode off, blending in with the crowds of people on the sidewalk.

My body trembled, and I got to my car, slid inside, and dropped the takeout bag in the passenger seat.

My heart raced, and I took a moment to breathe.

Ghost is dead. Stop freaking yourself out.

That was just someone who liked clowns.

I placed a hand on my erratic heart as I turned on my car engine and activated the wipers. Someone carrying about a dozen birthday balloons headed into a family restaurant across the street. Was the clown hired for the party?

Was I overreacting?

CHAPTER EIGHTEEN

ARROW

I THOUGHT I'd seen Vivian Friday night, but it was raining outside, and the restaurant was packed. I'd been thinking about her too much, so every time I saw an attractive woman, I assumed it was her.

Wished it were her.

This longing was becoming an annoying distraction. I should concentrate on other things demanding my attention, but she was like a firefly flickering her light while I wandered along my dark path. How could I not follow? She could lead me straight into hell, and I didn't have the willpower to resist.

Arrow: *Hi. How's your weekend?*

She didn't reply.

I continued working on Level Five, which was a multiverse that allowed the players to hop around various countries to search for villains to destroy. I wanted to create a power that encompassed water and fire elements, but nothing seemed distinctive enough to make my game stand out from my friends' worlds. My creativity had been sluggish, and I needed to fix that.

My mind had been occupied trying to find the asshole who betrayed me, ensuring my Bambooze Series would be well received and locating elite members of The Trogyn. Aside from that, Holt Enterprises was growing exponentially, and it needed my attention to oversee the expansion. One wrong move could put all my work in jeopardy.

I glanced over at the wine cabinet in my office. Wine from all over the world was on display. Most people would think I loved wine and all forms of alcohol. But they'd be wrong. My relationship with it didn't start out with affection.

I hated it. My body jerked as it remembered the reason for my hatred and dark memories poured out of me.

"Where the fuck have you been?" Dad slurs from the couch, glaring at me with glassy eyes.

The stench of alcohol reeks in the room, making me want to gag. There's already an empty bottle of whiskey on the table.

Fear makes me squirm as I slide off my backpack. Every time he drinks, he becomes a monster. He didn't use to drink like this. Something happened to him one day, and he changed. When Mom was still alive, she tried to help, but she was too sick to do much. I think his drinking made it worse for her.

I hate him for that. I may have a father, but I feel just as lonely and abandoned as if I'm an orphan.

"I was studying at Remi's house."

"You're an hour late." He sneers and pushes himself up from the couch.

"I told you what time I'd be home this morning—"

A fist connects to my face, and my head snaps back. The

force sends me against the side table, knocking everything down. I fall to the ground as my vision blurs and pain bursts on my cheek.

"Don't you dare talk back to me!" He kicks me and pulls out his belt. "You live in MY house. You follow my rules. Understand?"

"Stop!" I shout and brace for the attack as he whips the belt, hitting my leg.

At fifteen years old, I'm not strong enough to fight back, but I do it anyway. I kick him and he falls back. I get up, but my leg hurts so bad. My nose bleeds from the punch.

"I'm going to kill you!" He glares at me with eyes I don't recognize.

"Go ahead—KILL ME!" I charge at him, but he whips the belt at me. I grip it and stare at him. "I'd rather be with Mom than you!"

He curses, and his eyes darken with rage. I'm going to die tonight, but I don't care. The fear that should be with me is immobilized by the pain coursing through my body. Every part of me burns.

My body jerks every time the belt slams into my shoulder, my arms, my legs, and my back. I'm face down on the floor, curled into a ball, ready to die. Ready to be with my mom.

A knock sounds at the door, and he stops whipping me.

"Who is it?" he growls.

"We're here to collect."

"Fuck." He drags me into my bedroom and shuts the door.

I don't know who came. All I hear is Dad apologizing. How come he never apologizes for hurting me?

You must survive. Get strong. Live your life.

I hear my mom's voice and glance around. My head is

throbbing. I'm probably imagining all this, but I cling onto her voice because it's my lifeline.

After that beating, I continued to hang out with my friends as much as I could. I stayed out of my dad's way. If there were parental forms that needed his signature, I forged them. I'd come home when he was at work. I learned self-defense from YouTube videos and worked out in the basement of Pam's Diner to build my strength and muscles to fight back. My life had been rife with fear and abuse until I graduated high school and joined the Navy. It was the escape that altered my life for the better.

I shook my head clear of the heavy memory. So strange how the human body could remember the pain as though it lived inside every cell. The misery I'd experienced made my Navy SEAL training seem less difficult. I'd survived a horrible obstacle no child should ever have endured.

Despite what I'd been through, I was curious about alcohol and studied it while I was in the Navy and even after I left it. I had to study the beast that made my father into a monster. And now I owned an empire that sold alcohol.

Alcohol was a weapon that could heal or harm. Alcohol was found in alternative medicine like the concoctions that Forrest had developed. I offered wine as a means to entertain, to help the mind relax. But for those who didn't have a strong will to know their limits, this could be a detriment.

Sometimes I wondered if I was responsible for all the alcoholics out there. Deep down, I knew I wasn't, but the thought lingered. I chose this path because I needed to understand the source of my dad's illness, and I realized, though alcohol contributed, it was not the main reason.

My dad had a choice, and he *chose* to drink. He *chose* to overdo it.

I stared at my phone. Vivian hadn't replied to my message. I pivoted and texted someone who would reply.

Arrow: *How's your weekend, Kaylee?*

Kaylee: *Good. Gonna hang out with Violet soon.*

Violet was also a student at Whiz Kidz.

Arrow: *Is Vivian home?*

Kaylee: *Yes. But she's not in a good mood.*

Arrow: *What happened?*

Kaylee: *Dunno. She came home with takeout last night, looking distraught.*

Arrow: *Was the takeout from Ormon's?*

Kaylee: *How do you know?*

Arrow: *Wild guess.*

Kaylee: *Oh. Anyway, Viv said nothing's wrong when I asked.*

Arrow: *She's not replying to my text.*

Kaylee: *Text her again. I can see her at the kitchen table.*

Arrow: *Ok.*

What happened last night? Did something happen at her office? Had she actually been there and seen me at the party?

Arrow: *Any plans for the weekend?*

No reply. Vivian was avoiding me. But why?

Kaylee: *Her phone just buzzed with your message. She looked at it and went back to her laptop. You're in trouble. (devil emoji.)*

Arrow: *(dunno emoji)*

Kaylee: *Maybe she's PMSing. Gotta go now!*

Arrow: *Have fun.*

What had I done?

CHAPTER NINETEEN

VIVIAN

I DIDN'T USUALLY work on Saturdays, but I made an exception today. I'd squeezed two urgent appointments in for my patients who had trouble getting in during the week.

Having performed one urgent extraction and a lingual frenectomy, a laser procedure that treated tongue-ties, I drove home in my car. I'd offered this laser treatment when I had my California practice too. It had helped so many mothers trying to breastfeed their infants. If the connective tissue under the tongue was too short or too tight, that could prevent babies from latching on to breastfeed. If untreated, some people grew up with a lisp. But every case was different and needed a thorough analysis. It made me happy to make a difference without breaking people's bank accounts. I didn't charge people as much as I should.

On one hand, the lower fees helped people but also made them question my skills and professionalism. But repeat patients knew how good I was. On the other hand, I wouldn't be saving enough for my retirement.

But I wasn't doing this work for money.

People assumed I was happy with a successful career. Sometimes, I was happy. But most times, I was as alone as a hawk, hunting in the sky. Was the hawk ever sad? Did it wish it had a companion to soar with?

Maybe the hunter was alone because it didn't want to rely on someone. Doing things my way was easier and more efficient. I didn't have to explain anything to anyone or wait for any outside approval.

No one could get close enough to hurt me. But that also meant I could never be intimate with anyone either. My dad and Kaylee were the closest to me. But even then, I hardly shared my private thoughts with them.

But damn it. This yearning to let everything go blazed through me. For some stupid reason, I'd wanted to share my burden with Arrow. My heart had cracked open a little for him on the day he'd kissed me. I'd been too vulnerable.

I hated when my mind wandered back to him. Shaking him away, I steered my thoughts back to how I could make a difference in the world. I was a Vietnamese-Chinese-American individual with a blend of culture to share.

If I had all the money in the world, what would I do? I'd create the most exceptional dental tools for my patients to make their visits feel like a spa retreat. I had ideas, but had shoved them away because I didn't have a clue where to begin. Wasting my time on farfetched things wasn't beneficial to me. But that didn't stop me from dreaming about a larger dental fund to help those who couldn't afford care. I'd love to open dental clinics in places that didn't offer dental care. While parts of the world thrived with new technology, other parts were still stuck trying to find basic needs. I'd start with Vietnam and China because they were my roots.

I blinked and realized I was halfway home when I

stopped at the red light. I'd been driving mechanically, not paying attention to the road. That wasn't good at all.

A burst of laughter drew my attention to the sidewalk. Arrow stood with his ex, Sylvia. *Ugh.* In two days, I'd seen enough of them.

I get it, universe. You're telling me to move on.

Couldn't I just let my emotions roll through me at their own pace? I couldn't just take out the disappointment and sadness in me as though they were teeth extractions. If things were that easy to discard, no one would have issues.

Jealousy emerged in me. I shouldn't be jealous. I'd been the one who kept rejecting him. But I didn't like seeing him with her. A car honked from behind me, and I jerked at the sudden disruption.

"Green means go!" a man shouted.

I waved a hand to apologize to the angry guy behind me.

Arrow turned in my direction from all the honking as I sped off.

Enough was enough. It was time to vent. When I got to my apartment, I texted the girls.

Vivian: *Wanna meet up tonight?*

Audri: *Come over to my place. New jewelry just arrived.*

Michelle: *I'm out of state. Send pics.*

Natalie: *Sorry. We're in Paris visiting my mom.*

Kiera: *I'll be there!*

Vivian: *See you soon.*

I had to do something for myself tonight. Something fun that would put me at ease. I didn't want to think of men. If I saw another man, I'd probably stab him with something.

I called Kaylee. "How are you doing?

"We're about to watch another movie," she said with a mouthful of something.

Kaylee was at Violet's house for a sleepover this weekend. Violet lived with her mom one floor below ours.

"I'm heading over to Audri's. Call me if you need anything."

"I won't need anything. Have fun!"

Kaylee was the most responsible teenager I'd ever met. Sometimes she acted as though she were my mom. She spewed wisdom that kids shouldn't have. Kids these days know more about things than adults give them credit for.

I always knew where Kaylee was, and she always knew where I was. That was our deal, and she'd never disappointed me.

Knowing that she was safe allowed me to let loose. Tonight, I needed my friends to cheer me up. I needed their sound advice. Just their presence was good enough as well. Maybe after tonight I'd rekindle my friendship with Bullseye on the app. Or maybe I'd meet someone new.

But no. That would be for all the wrong reasons. Whatever. I'd think about that later.

I arrived and parked on the side near Audri's massive studio. Remington had added the addition to their home not too long ago for her to work at home when she wanted to. She had a gorgeous flagship store downtown inside the same building as Natalie's clothing collection.

I walked to the lounge area of Audri's studio, where Kiera sat on the comfy couches. Her long brown hair was tied into a ponytail.

"Where's Audri?" I asked.

"Getting appetizers for us."

I placed the bottles of CheckMate Black and Check-

Mate Red on the wooden coffee table. I needed to get them out of my apartment once and for all. They reminded me too much of *him*.

"Oh, I haven't had either of these yet. May I?" Kiera reached for a bottle and examined it.

She had the glow of love around her. She and Forrest recently got engaged, and I'd agreed to be one of her bridesmaids. They hadn't set a wedding date yet because Kiera was taking her time.

"Open it," I said. "They're for us tonight."

"Where did you get these?" she asked, pouring herself a glass. "I heard Forrest talking about Arrow's new wine, but it wasn't ready for the market yet."

"I attended a wine expo. Who knew there were so many types of wine around the world?"

"It's big business." Kiera sipped and purred. "So good."

Audri walked in with a platter of appetizers. "I want some." She wore her black hair in a side braid.

"Sorry. My bad." Kiera laughed, pouring Audri and me a glass.

I sipped the wine, letting it seduce my mouth before swallowing. It had an earthy flavor with a mild level of sweetness.

"Did you know that bamboo wine has medicinal properties?" I'd done my research when I first got the bottles.

"Forrest uses bamboo for his alternative medicine," Kiera said.

"The wine can potentially help with digestion and lowering blood pressure," I added.

"In moderation," Audri added. "Anything to the extreme reverses its effect, right?"

"Yup. That goes with anything. Even food." I reached for

a small dumpling and popped it into my mouth. I sat on the soft floor pillow close to the coffee table.

"I love how light it tastes," Audri said.

"Arrow gave me the wine. He'd like your honest feedback."

"How come he didn't give us a bottle?" Kiera looked at me suspiciously above the rim of the wineglass. "What's going on between you two?"

"Nothing!" I said too quickly. "He was at the wine expo and gave me some to bring home. He asked for an honest review. That's all." My heart raced for no reason.

"Uh-uh." Kiera wagged a finger at me.

Audri placed a hand on my shoulder and said in an amused tone, "We don't buy it."

Oh no. I recognized that look in her eyes. Audri sat down beside me.

"Buy what?" I played coy and made everything worse.

The girls laughed.

"Your ability to lie is awful." Kiera beamed.

"We've all been there, babe. Tell us what's on your mind. You started the text earlier, so you *have* something to tell."

"What if I just missed hanging out with my girls?" I finished my wine, and Kiera refilled it.

"You've missed the last few gatherings and now you're suddenly in need of one? You need our advice. C'mon, we're all ears." Audri propped an elbow on the table, resting her chin on her palm, eyeing me.

Kiera did the same.

I grinned at the curious faces looking at me. They could read me. I'd declined the last few invitations because of more pressing matters. Following up on clues regarding Aimee's whereabouts took time. I had to fly back to meet with the judge on Kaylee's adoption case, and my dad had an urgent heart surgery. But I didn't tell them any of this.

They had given me the privacy I needed. That was genuine friendship, wasn't it? The wine relaxed me just as I had hoped. I had to eliminate these feelings for Arrow. Maybe they could tell me he was an ugly jerk, that I'd be better off liking someone else.

Yes. Perfect.

What should I tell them?

"You're having a private conversation with yourself." Kiera smiled at me. "Want to share?"

I couldn't hide anything from them.

"We're friends, aren't we?" Audri asked. "Do you trust us?"

"Of course, I do."

"Then why didn't you come to the last outing with us?" Kiera narrowed her eyes.

"I had to take care of my sister."

"What?!" Kiera scrunched up her pretty face.

"You have a sister?" Audri asked.

"How come we don't know about her? Why haven't we met her? She could have joined our girls' nights."

I opened my mouth and said, "Oh, I thought I already told you." But then I realized I had shared nothing about Kaylee. I didn't want to complicate my life in Providence when I would be returning to California as soon as I found Aimee. I hadn't expected to find an amazing circle of friends.

"I'm her guardian, her big sister. Kaylee is only thirteen years old."

"Girl, we know you're a private person. But when you're friends with me, *I* need to know these things." Kiera fluttered her eyes. "I don't bite, you know."

"You can trust us." Audri squeezed my shoulder. "I'd like to meet Kaylee."

I nodded. "Sure. She'd love to browse your jewelry store."

"I'd love to give her a tour." Audri got up. "Speaking of which, I have a new collection for you to check out."

"Are you hiding anyone else?" Kiera asked.

"No." I laughed. "It's just me and Kaylee here in Providence." I gulped down the wine, and Kiera opened the bottle of CheckMate Red since the black label was empty.

The red label had a lighter sweetness compared to the black label. Both were delicious in their own way.

"You can tell us how you became a big sister *after* you tell us about Arrow." Kiera winked.

Audri glanced out the window. "Speak of the devil. He just arrived with a box of wine. The boys are hanging out in the man cave today."

Oh, God. Nerves spiraled in my stomach as though a thousand butterflies had broken free from their cocoons. But then the image of him smiling with his ex at the restaurant and on the sidewalk earlier popped into my head, and I scowled.

I *wanted* his attention.

"If you wanted me that much, why are you with your ex?" The thoughts came out of my mouth before I could stop them.

"Arrow can't hear you." Grinning, Kiera pushed herself up. "Want me to go get him?"

"You'd better not!" I yanked her back down and wrapped an arm around her neck as if we were dueling.

"Help me, Audri!" Kiera pretended to choke.

We both laughed like idiots.

Releasing Kiera, I sighed. "Yes, I'm attracted to him. But I don't trust him."

Audri and Kiera listened intently.

"He's asked me out several times, but I've always said no." Needing more warmth for courage, I gulped down the wine. "I think he moved on just as I was thinking of giving him a chance."

"What makes you think that?" Audri asked.

"I saw him with his ex twice this week. She was all over him."

"Who's his ex?" Kiera turned to Audri.

"Sylvia Ormon. Social media influencer."

"Oh. I remember her now. They didn't last long. She seemed more into him than he was into her," Kiera said. "He's never brought her to any of our get-togethers."

"Never?" Curiosity sparked in me.

Audri shook her head. "Nope, but I don't know why."

"We have a close-knit group." Kiera stretched out her legs. "Maybe he's being extremely selective about who he shows off?"

"I was seeing someone on a dating app too," I blurted out.

"What?" Audri and Kiera's eyes went wide as I told them the story.

CHAPTER TWENTY

ARROW

WHEN I FOUND out that Vivian was just a few rooms away from where I was, I wanted to rush over and demand why she was ignoring me. If I had done something wrong, I needed to know.

But I had a few things to discuss with Remi and Forrest first. The other guys could catch up later when they returned.

"Did you hear about the deceased body of a little girl from the other day?"

Remi nodded. "It has to be The Trogyn."

"Or their enemies." Forrest raked a hand through his dark brown hair. The energy around him was lighter and more joyful these days. Probably because of his engagement with Kiera.

"My thoughts exactly," I said. "Maybe someone is trying to give us a message? A clue to something?"

"It could also be a trap." Remi sipped his wine.

I was going to tell them that Vivian was also looking for a little girl, but I held back. What if this information wasn't disclosed to everyone yet? It was her story, her business to tell.

"Sex trafficking and human trafficking are huge money makers for The Trogyn." I reached for a shrimp dumpling from the appetizer tray and popped it into my mouth.

"And they're pissed that someone is making them lose money." Forrest downed the wine. "I'm surprised they haven't retaliated yet."

"They will once they find out who we are."

Ice formed in my stomach as I thought of the potential violence they could cause.

Remi turned to me. "Are you all set for your Monaco trip?"

"Yeah. There's nothing else for me to do but show up. Do you remember a tall guy with dark hair wearing an expensive gray suit at the wine expo?"

Remi furrowed his eyebrows. "None stood out to me. Why?"

"I saw him at the scene where the little girl's body was found." I folded my arms across my chest. "He was among the crowd of spectators. Could've been a coincidence."

"Maybe." Forrest danced his fingers on his wineglass. "But we all know there's no such thing as a coincidence. Have the PI look into him."

I had planned to, but I didn't want to add more to his plate. His priority was finding Aimee for me.

"Have you guys heard from Slash?" Forrest asked.

"He's working on something and will reach out to us soon. But he's also trying to spend more time with his wife."

Slash was a former member of The Trogyn and the man who gave us a second chance to live. He'd been working behind the scenes with us to get us info on the crime organization.

A burst of laughter erupted in the hallway.

"The girls are having too much fun," Remi said with a grin.

Was Vivian thinking of me?

CHAPTER TWENTY-ONE

VIVIAN

"OUR VIVIAN HAS BEEN HORNY!" Kiera gaped at me.

"It's not that kind of app!" I defended myself, wondering why I put myself through this.

"Tell us about the app," Audri said.

I told them how Heartstrings was created by a thirteen-year-old girl.

"One, Kaylee is a genius." Audri held up a finger. "Two, that's not dating, honey."

"It's not?" I asked, grabbing another throw pillow and tucking it behind my back against the edge of the couch for extra comfort.

Kiera laughed. "Not even close, babe. You were just chatting with a stranger who gave you an option to compare to Arrow. This dude helped you figure out what your heart wanted."

"Why didn't you ask to see his picture?" Audri asked.

"Because she feared it would be some pervy old dude who would ruin her fantasy." Kiera grinned.

"Looks shouldn't matter," I protested.

"But they *do*." Audri emphasized with her hand gestures. "Especially in the beginning. First impression is *everything*. You see a hot guy, and that sparks an attraction. Then once you get to know him, that emotion grows deeper. I don't care what the books or therapists say. Looks matter to some extent."

"You're telling me you were attracted to Remi's looks first?" I asked.

"I thought he was cute when we were teens. Then he grew into a handsome man I couldn't resist. My impression of him was planted in my mind years ago. It became *more* as time went by."

"Same here." Kiera poked a meatball with a fork and popped it into her mouth. "I always thought Forrest was hot, but he was way out of my league."

"What do you mean?" I'd never had this kind of conversation with anyone. It fascinated me how my friends started their relationships with their men.

"His girlfriends were all doctors or nurses. I wasn't a science girl with several college degrees, so I assumed I wasn't his type." She reached for the tray of earrings and held up a glittering pair. "I want to buy this," she said to Audri.

"Each of you gets to pick a pair from my new collection. It's my gift to you." Audri smiled. "Wear it and promote it for me."

"Thanks! You know I will," Kiera said.

"That's so sweet, Audri. Thank you!" I reviewed her jewelry and chose a simple golden spiral earring.

Audri turned to me. "Life has an intricate plan full of twists and turns, taking you in circles. But you'll eventually end up with the person you're meant to be with."

"Give him one date and see how it does," Kiera said. "What should we call this Super Spy Girl mission?"

Oh, God.

"You thought we forgot about the SSG, didn't you?" Audri winked and reached for the bottle of wine, but it was empty. "I'll be right back."

"I thought about giving him a date, but then I saw him with Sylvia."

"Maybe you misunderstood the situation. Were they hugging? Kissing? Holding hands?"

"No," I said.

Sylvia was waiting for him to kiss her at the restaurant and he didn't push her away. I wouldn't stand around watching it happen.

"Maybe they're still friends. Why don't you ask him?"

"On what grounds?"

"Just be straight with him. Ask *all* the questions." Kiera grabbed a grape from the fruit bowl. "If his answers settle your nerves, then you have nothing to worry about, right?"

"He asked for a duel once," I said.

"Go kick his ass. Loser pays for dinner." Kiera elbowed me in the ribs. "He's a great catch."

"And smart too. Very thoughtful. *Methodical.*" Audri returned with two more bottles of wine. "He used to work for several companies creating their user interface."

"What's that?" Kiera asked the same question I had.

"He tests out strategies to help companies attract clients. Like choosing colors that people would most likely be drawn to, the shape of the buy-link box, where to place data that would have the most clicks. Stuff like that. He gave me some tips for my jewelry website and referred me to a former colleague when I wanted to hire someone to do it full time."

"Forrest said he has a degree in enology too." Kiera popped the cork.

I didn't know too many people who studied the science of wine and winemaking. What prompted him to go that route?

For me, my dad inspired me to be a dentist. I remembered this little girl coming in with tremendous fear on her face. Dad had comforted her, transforming her fear to courage. From that day on, she always came in with a bright smile. Her fear had dissolved. I'd seen too many children and adults with that kind of phobia.

I slid a gaze out the door that led to the other room, wondering what Arrow was up to in the other room. If I had known he'd be here, I wouldn't have come.

Ridiculous. Don't give any one man that much power.

It wasn't fear toward him . . . It was fear of me seeing something I *wanted* but not having the courage to go after it. A relationship would disrupt my responsibilities.

"Anyone want a tarot card reading?" Audri asked, waving a colorful deck.

"You read tarot?" I asked.

"Not really. But there's a little booklet that'll give us the interpretations." Audri took out the deck and began shuffling. "I just got it yesterday. One girl on my design team had a reading with The Silver Rose—some well-known psychic— and bought her deck. I hear it's hard to get a reading from her."

Audri gave me a few cards to look at it. The art was mystical, dreamy. I'd gotten a fortune reading one time during the Lunar New Year at a temple, but that was based on Chinese Astrology where each year carried the energy of a certain animal. I loved how different cultures had unique ways of interpreting life. Life was unpredictable and not set in stone. It was all about our choices and how we lived our lives.

Choices. What should I choose? A chance at happiness or to stay annoyed and unhappy?

I'd never had a tarot card reading before. "Sure, why not? I'm open to see what the universe has to say."

"Me too." Kiera glanced at the cards. "It better not be anything bad."

"Nothing is truly bad. It's how we look at it."

Kiera arched an eyebrow. "What are you, some kind of witch?"

Audri chuckled. "If I'm a witch, you're all witches too."

"And *bootiful* bitches." Kiera snorted, making me laugh.

I could tell the wine was getting to my friends.

"Audri's right though." I shrugged. "What could seem bad at the moment may actually be perfect in the long run."

Kiera poked me in the ribs. "Witchy bitch!"

"You're drunk," I teased.

"I'm not. And even if I am, it's fine. It's been a while since you joined us. Tonight we celebrate Vivian!"

"Celebrate what?" I asked, my brain growing foggy.

"Celebrating your SSG mission," Kiera said. "What should we call it?"

I shook my head. "You seem more excited about it than I am."

"That's how it is." Kiera waved a hand. "When it was my turn, I was so nervous. There wasn't room for any excitement."

"It's normal." Audri bumped shoulders with me. "I felt the same with my License to Kiss." She told me about her sumo wrestling with Remi.

"My mission was called Opals are Forever, and Michelle was From Iceland with Love," Kiera said. "And Natalie had The Man with the Golden Angle."

I couldn't hold in my grin. "A ninety-degree angle is pretty hot."

Audri tilted her head and considered me. "Your mission should be The World is Not Enough or A View to a Kill."

Arrow's kiss resurfaced in my head. "How about A Kiss is Not Enough?"

"Something you need to share?" Amusement gleamed in Kiera's eyes.

"We kissed once," I admitted.

"How was it?" Kiera asked.

"Exceptional." Heat bloomed in me just remembering that moment.

"We want all the sexy deets." Audri wiggled her eyebrows.

I rolled my eyes. "I don't know the details about the 'mission' yet."

The mission needed a purpose. What would it prove?

"That can come later," Audri said.

Kiera refilled her wineglass and topped mine off too. She lifted her glass. "Tonight we're going to let everything go and just be happy, okay?"

"Okay." We clinked our wine glasses.

I couldn't help but see love beaming from Kiera. It was contagious. Love could change a person inside and out.

"It's time for your reading, girls!" Audri shuffled the cards again and spread them out on the rug. "Just a warning —I'm not a psychic. I'm following directions from this booklet and using my intuition to help with the interpretation."

Kiera reached for a cheese cracker while I tried the apple tart. I needed something sweet to contrast the recent bitterness in my life.

"Each of us is going to pick a card and see what message it has for us." Audri nudged me. "You get to go first."

"Why?"

"Because you're the only one who's unattached right now. We've got our men, but the world is limitless for you."

"I don't define my world by a man."

"Neither do we," Audri said. "But they help us see our potential and therefore, expand our world. You'll understand soon."

I didn't know what she meant. I was still irked at Arrow for making me believe something that wasn't true. And that stupid clown from yesterday had terrified me more than I'd like to admit. So my mood was all over the place.

I inhaled a breath.

What do you want me to know, universe?

I skimmed my fingers along the cards while keeping my mind blank. Then I randomly chose a card and flipped it over.

"Woohoo!" Audri beamed at the Lovers card.

My heart drummed for no reason. "I should pick another card. I wasn't thinking about anything."

"No!" Kiera stopped me from taking another card. "They say you receive the most accurate reading when you're not expecting anything."

"How?" I stared at the two lovers inside a golden ring.

"Because that's when your mind is most open to opportunities," Audri said. "Because you're not clinging to a specific outcome."

The Lovers card scared me.

Did it mean I was hoping for love? Needing love? Receiving love? Or was love out of reach?

Maybe the card picked up my thoughts from days ago. Before I saw him and his ex.

"I don't think it's true." I dropped the card on the rug.

"Let's check out the meaning." Audri flipped through the booklet, found the page, and read it. "When this card shows up in your reading, it signifies a relationship is on your mind. Communication is paramount right now. You can safely share your feelings with someone you trust. That's us." Audri gestured to herself and Kiera. "It's time to make an important decision. Consider your choices carefully. Open your heart to opportunities."

"That's a great reading!" Kiera beamed.

A relationship was on my mind. It was time for me to decide. Heat bloomed on my cheeks for no reason. Or was that the wine?

Audri gave herself a reading and got the Six of Wands, which signified recognition. She was receiving an award for her volunteer work and donation to an animal charity. She was creating a pet accessory line soon.

"Where's Ignis?" I asked Audri about her adorable cat. The last time I came here, he ran off somewhere.

"He's upstairs in his little condo. Getting neutered isn't fun, so he doesn't like people right now."

"He's such a little fluff. I love him," Kiera said as she picked a card and flipped it over.

She got the Three of Cups, which foretold a time of celebration. Kiera was engaged, and a wedding was in her future. Seemed pretty accurate.

I swayed and shook my head. "I guess I had a little too much wine."

"Let me get some jasmine tea," Audri said and looked at Kiera. "Stop giving Vivian wine."

Kiera held up her hand. "Wasn't me. She poured it herself."

"Stop her then."

"Kiera can't stop me. I'll attack her with my snake form." My fingers formed and mimicked a snake's head. "Sssssseeee?" Why did I sound strange?

Kiera laughed. "Oh my gosh. She *is* drunk."

"I'm not. Just sleepy." I snuggled into the massive throw pillow, wanting to sleep.

Audri laughed. "She's definitely not driving home."

"I know who should take her," Kiera whispered to Audri.

"What are you guys talking about?" I asked, only half-hearing them.

Another voice joined their conversation. But I wasn't paying attention because the pillow was so soft. I loved how my face fell onto it, making me so comfortable . . .

CHAPTER TWENTY-TWO

ARROW

WEARING HER WINTER COAT, Vivian slept in the passenger seat while I drove her old Toyota RAV4 home. I pulled into the parking garage and turned off the engine. She needed an update to this car. I didn't want her stranded somewhere, especially now that winter was in full swing. With her dentist salary, she could afford a newer car. Why didn't she?

I glanced over at her, all curled up in the seat. She had a smile on her face. I reached over and tucked a strand of hair behind her ear.

She cracked her eyes. "Are we there yet?"

"Yes, we're home. Ready to get out?"

She studied me and reached over to touch my chin. "You have a gorgeous face, you know that?"

"You think so?" I smiled, loving how open she was because of the wine. I could stay here just chatting with her, but it was cold and late and she needed to rest. "C'mon, I'll help you get home."

I'd get an Uber to pick me up later so I could retrieve my car from Remi's place.

Vivian traced my jawline with her finger like she had done before. Her touch ignited all kinds of sensation in me. "I dreamed about you the other day."

My smile widened. "What was the dream about?"

"I was furious with you." She pouted. "You wouldn't give me a piggyback ride." She giggled, and her cheeks bloomed a bright pink, but that could've been the wine's effect.

I'd never given anyone a piggyback ride in my life.

My eyebrows furrowed with fascination. "What's up with the piggyback ride?"

"I don't know." She sat up in the seat and clasped our hands together on her lap. "It's just something casual and friendly, kinda like holding hands." Her eyes fluttered closed again.

It was *not* like holding hands, but I would not debate that with a drunk woman right now.

She opened her eyes, looking sad. "I was very mad at you the other day."

"Is that why you didn't reply to my texts?"

She nodded and shifted in her seat. "I was hurt. And angry. And confused." She placed a hand on her head. "Ugh. I shouldn't have drunk so much. It's your fault." She settled back into the seat.

I didn't like knowing I had hurt her.

"Let's get you home, and you can tell me what I did wrong."

"I'm comfy here." She smiled and snuggled into her coat, looking too adorable.

"No, it's too cold. We're both going to get sick." I couldn't believe what I was about to say. "If you comply, I'll give you a piggyback ride."

What had gotten into me? I'd think about that later.

Her eyes widened with excitement. "Really? This must be a dream, but it's a happy dream and I don't wanna wake up yet."

I got out of the car and went over to her side. She opened the door, swung her legs over and stretched out her arms like a baby wanting to be carried. Her trusting smile did something to my chest.

I knew she was drunk, and that she wasn't acting herself, but having her look at me with warmth and trust made me yearn for her affection even more. Was this a version of Vivian that she hid from people? The lighthearted woman radiating with carefree joy and trust?

Alcohol manipulated the mind, and I couldn't believe the girls had drunk so much of my wine. Some people told the truth when they were under the influence. Others got violent or retreated into a corner, shutting the world out.

Something told me Vivian had a desire to break free from all the restraints holding her back. I desperately wanted to know what they were. I wanted to unchain her so she could be free.

I knew what being trapped felt like.

Gripping her hands, I pulled her out of the seat, shutting the door. She embraced me and snuggled into my chest. "You're like a blanket. So warm. So perfect." Then she sniffed at me. "And you smell *so* good."

Go on. Keep the sweet talk coming, baby.

I'd be a fool if I didn't capitalize on this affection. Only a stupid man would let this opportunity slip by. I wrapped my arms around her, protecting her from the cold.

She peered up at me. "Are you sure you're strong enough to carry me? I don't want to hurt your back."

"I'm strong enough for you, Tulip."

She giggled. "I like that nickname."

I crouched. "Hop on, baby."

She climbed onto my back and wrapped her arms around my neck. Her warm breath tickled my ear and sniffed me again. "I love the way you smell."

Grinning, I secured her legs around me and walked into the building, heading to the elevator. The security guard glanced at me, recognized who I was, and smiled.

I owned this building so I could do whatever I wanted, no matter how silly it seemed. But a piggyback ride was reserved only for her. I got to the elevator and waited. No one was in the hallway. Not that I cared if someone walked by.

She pinched my cheek. "You're so adorable! I love piggy-back rides."

I laughed. "You're so weird." The elevator opened, and we got in.

Her floor arrived, and I made my way there.

"I'm gonna cling to you forever." She tightened her arms around my neck and kissed my cheek. "Thank you for being so nice."

I paused a moment, allowing her words to settle in me.

When I walked again, I slowed my steps.

"This is the nicest dream I've had in years."

She slid off my back, and I missed the connection. She dug into her purse for the key and opened the door. I kicked off my shoes and hung up my coat. She wobbled, so I removed her coat and shoes and helped her to the couch.

"You should go to bed," I said.

"No." She grabbed my hand, dragging me down beside her. "I want to keep dreaming. I enjoy holding your hand."

The admission made me smile. She was confessing so many things tonight. What would happen when she found out tomorrow? Would she even remember anything?

"So what did I do that made you ignore my texts?"

She sneered at me. "Are you back with your ex?"

"No. Why do you think that?"

"I saw you and her at Ormon's. She was all over you. I didn't like it." She extracted her hand from my grip. "You lied to me. I thought you liked me."

"I *do* like you." I snatched her hand back into mine. "Very much. Let this sink in: I'm *not* seeing anyone. I was at the restaurant for business. Just networking."

She scowled. "But I saw you and her on the sidewalk earlier today too. Why are you always with her?"

"You're the one who's always on my mind."

"I am?"

"Yes, Tulip. I can't stop thinking about you."

CHAPTER TWENTY-THREE

VIVIAN

THIS WAS the best dream I'd ever had. Arrow just drove my car home and gave me a piggyback ride. He told me he couldn't stop thinking about me. My heart felt like it wanted to burst out of my chest. I'd never been this happy.

I grinned like a fool, even though I should have been sleeping. My head was pounding, but I didn't care. I shouldn't have drunk too much with the girls, but it had been such a fun evening.

Right now I was tired, relaxed, and happy. I wanted the dream to last forever.

I snuggled closer to him while holding his hand. His musky cologne made me feel so warm and fuzzy, like a perfect fireplace kindling a chilly night.

I'm not seeing anyone.

I remembered Kiera telling me about lucid dreaming when you knew you were dreaming and you could decide in the dream. This had to be a lucid dream because he was telling me things I wanted to hear.

I looked up at his gorgeous face.

"Arrow?"

"Yes, Tulip." He looked at me.

I smiled and gave him a loud kiss on the lips.

CHAPTER TWENTY-FOUR

ARROW

I WAS A LUCKY MAN TONIGHT.

Sitting with her on the couch, I listened to her talk about random things. Some of it made sense. Some of it didn't, but it didn't matter. Just being with her was worth it.

I'd never sat with a drunk woman for this long. I stayed away from women under the influence because they got clingy, and I couldn't deal with it. But with Vivian, I wanted her to cling to me. I loved how she rested her head on my shoulder like she was used to it.

"We should go fishing." She looked up at me.

"We can."

"Do you like to fish?"

"I do."

"You're a fabulous catch." She slurred her words, smiled, and demonstrated reeling in a fishing rod.

I laughed and patted her head. "You're a cute drunk, baby."

She placed a hand on her head. "I didn't mean to drink

so much. It's not me, but I had fun with the girls. I made an exception for tonight."

There was a hint of sadness in her voice.

"There's nothing wrong with having fun with your friends."

"I'm tired. I need to sleep. Can you get me my pajamas?" She rose from the couch and wobbled, but I caught her. "They're folded on the chair in my bedroom."

She leaned against me as we made our way into her bedroom. We walked past Kaylee's bedroom. I could tell it was hers because of all the Kuromi stuffed animals on her bed and the Sanrio characters on the wall.

Vivian sat on the edge of her bed while I grabbed her cotton pajamas from the chair and placed them beside her.

"I should go wash off my makeup and brush my teeth, but I'm exhausted."

"Need help?" I extended my hand.

"Yeah."

I stood behind her with my arm wrapped around her waist, making sure she didn't fall over and hit her head. While she brushed, she paused and smiled at me in the mirror. "I love this dream."

"It's not a dream."

"Yes, it is." She finished brushing, took out her makeup kit, washed her face, and returned to bed.

"Now be a good girl and go to sleep."

"Okay, Nemo." She giggled, pointing at me. "I hooked you and caught you, remember?"

"You did." I smiled and wondered if I should remind her when she was sober.

I'd never been more entertained than tonight.

She took off her gray sweater revealing a gray tank top

underneath. Part of me wanted to leave her bedroom, but the other part desperately wanted to stay. The battle between good and evil warred inside me, but advantage of a drunk woman wasn't my thing.

"I'll give you some privacy."

"No! Don't go. If you go, this dream will end. *Stay*." She pointed to the chair beside the bed.

She wanted me to stay. I had to be a gentleman and comply with the lady's wish.

Vivian stripped out of her jeans and pulled on the cotton pants. When she turned to hop into bed, I saw her back. I stiffened, and my breathing hitched.

I stopped breathing for a moment.

Her back.

"Vivian," I said when I got my breath back. "Don't move."

"You want a bedtime hug? Come here." She opened her arms, welcoming me in.

I wrapped my arms around her, my hands caressing the ridges of scars covering her back. What the fuck happened to her?

"Can I see your back?" I asked.

She broke the embrace and pouted. "Why?"

"Because I want to see it. Please?"

"Okay, but only because you asked nicely."

I sat beside her, and she turned her back to me. I lifted her tank top to see the rest of the back. My chest constricted as emotion erupted in me. My heart cracked from seeing the destruction on this beautiful woman.

Was this why I'd been drawn to her? The pain and the sorrow trapped within these scars had called to me. Who had done this to her? I ran my fingers along the uneven surface. Some sections had a rough texture. Had she been burned?

How had she survived this torture?

I thought my scars were bad. But compared to hers, my wounds were nothing.

"How did you get all these scars?"

"An evil man."

"Who?" Rage spiked in me. "Where is he?" My fingers curled into fists, ready to pound the fucker who had tortured her like this.

She turned around and patted my cheek. "He's not important."

He is very important, dammit.

The urge to kill him coursed through me, changing my entire mood.

She tucked herself in, looking exhausted and sad. "He's dead." She stared at me for a while as tears welled in her eyes. "Thanks for asking. This has been the most perfect dream of my life." She reached for my hand as her eyes fluttered close. "He can't hurt me anymore . . ."

While she drifted off to sleep, I held her hand, trying to process everything.

My plan to call an Uber vanished. I wasn't going anywhere. I wanted to stay by her side. The need to protect her coursed through me like magma churning beneath the surface of the Earth. I had to know the complete story when she was sober.

She shifted, removed her hand from mine, and curled into the blanket, facing me. I lay beside her, studying her lovely face.

She looked so peaceful. But behind the peaceful façade dwelled a dark story. Her scarred back flashed in front of me.

How long had she had these wounds? I noticed a circular wound of raised flesh on her lower back. That appeared to have been caused by something else—like a branding tool.

"What in the world happened to you?" I brushed her hair away from her face.

The scars appeared like they'd healed, but had she truly recovered?

Those kinds of scars lasted forever. I knew this because I couldn't forget the wounds on my body either.

I couldn't sleep as I wondered what her life had been like. Did Kaylee know about Vivian's story?

My phone buzzed with a text from the PI.

PI: *JC spotted in Providence at Midnight Chaoss.*

He sent me a pic of a man amongst the fighting crowd. That club required a special invitation.

Arrow: *Can you get me in?*

PI: *You'll need to wear a mask.*

After I gave him an alias I wanted to use, I ended the call and prepared to find the fucker.

Vivian shifted, murmured something, and fell back to sleep.

"Sweet dreams, Tulip." I squeezed Vivian's hand. I didn't want to leave her, but this was my chance to apprehend a man who had stolen from me.

CHAPTER TWENTY-FIVE

ARROW

I'D CALLED an Uber to retrieve my car from Remi's and rushed into the twenty-four-hour store to buy a blue mask. I got some markers and drew a bullseye on it since my alias was Bullseye.

I'd heard of Midnight Chaoss but hadn't considered going there. I'd been focusing on luxury clubs where elite members of The Trogyn visited. Midnight Chaoss wasn't a classy club by any means. On the surface, it appeared like a nightclub with dancing, food, and music. But it also hosted illegal gambling—a fight club for humans and animals.

This would be the perfect place for James Chin to hide. The fucker had worked at my Texas warehouse for eight years. He had moved up the ladder from a forklift driver to a manager.

I parked a block away from the alley where the club was. Midnight Chaoss was below a twenty-four-hour gym called Chaoss Workouts. I strode by a group of thugs trying to hook up with two girls. Another group of men wearing masks stood huddled, smoking in the corner.

I recognized a strange version of Iron Man, a cat, an alien face, and Elmo. I supposed my half-assed mask wasn't that bad compared to theirs. An icy breeze blew by and I pulled up my hood. The temperature had dipped to zero tonight.

I walked into the gym, which was pretty busy given the midnight hour. I walked up to the receptionist and told him I was Bullseye and here for the special training.

He gave me a red bracelet and pointed to the back room. "Down two flights of stairs, and you'll see a black door. Scan the bracelet on a monitor, and someone should let you in."

As I approached the door, music boomed. I scanned the bracelet, and the door opened.

A guy wearing a polka dot mask let me in. "Welcome. Are you betting tonight?"

"Most likely. But I want to browse first." I hadn't had time to research this place thoroughly, but I got enough info from the PI.

I walked by two men wearing red masks.

"The Rottweiler will destroy the Husky." He held a ticket in his hand and entered a room with a sign that read *Animal Exhibitions*.

I walked around, scanning the area for a man with a raccoon mask. The image the PI had sent showed James Chin had momentarily taken his mask off to eat at the food court. Another image showed a man wearing the same clothes in a raccoon mask. The PI had hacked into their servers using his facial recognition software. He had access to advanced equipment that my boys and I didn't have.

A fight erupted between two men. A security guard wearing a red mask broke them up.

I found the food court filled with people standing at tall tables and sitting on the benches.

A man removed his bear mask to munch on fries.

"Why do people wear masks?" I asked. "I'm sweating."

"To protect our identities, especially people who are putting up big money." He shrugged. "I'm not one of those high-rollers so I don't care."

On the far right, I could see two martial artists fighting with crowds cheering for whoever they had bet on.

"There's a fight next week. Lot of cash on the line. You coming?"

"Maybe." I glanced around. "I came with my friend, but I lost him in the crowd. He's wearing a raccoon mask. Have you seen him?"

"Yeah. He was just over by the bar. They're serving outstanding drinks. Surprisingly, they have excellent wine here."

I stalked to the bar and glanced around for a raccoon face, but didn't see anyone.

Sliding onto the stool, I said to the bartender with the lion mask, "I heard you have excellent wine."

"We do. It's a special kind." The bartender leaned in. "It's bamboo wine."

"Oh." This had to be my stolen wine. "I've heard about bamboo wine but never tried it."

"I have. But this is top-notch." He poured from a black bottle that I immediately knew was mine. A new label— Monster's Gate—covered it.

"Try it." He placed the glass in front of me.

"Do you mind if I take a picture of the bottle? The label is awesome."

"Yo, that's what I said."

He gave me the bottle, and I took several pics of it,

including the tiny serial number embedded into the bottom of the glass. "Thanks."

I sipped the wine. This was definitely my product. A prototype that I was going to send out to my tasting team before it was stolen.

"This *is* incredible. Where do you get this? I'd like to buy some."

"Not sure." The bartender looked up and smiled. "But you can ask him. He delivers the wine." He gestured to the man with the raccoon face by the hallway. "Maybe he'll know where you can buy more."

I studied James Chin as he stood talking to a man with a dog mask.

"Jimmy!" the bartender hollered. "He wants to know where you got the wine."

Jimmy looked my way, stared at me for a moment, and darted away.

Fuck.

I chased after him down the hallway and heard a door slam. I darted out the back door, which opened to the side parking lot. A black car screeched down the alley.

You can't run from me, James Chin.

I called the PI. "I lost him. He took off in a black car. Can you check the surveillance for the plate numbers?"

"Will do."

"Thanks."

Maybe the plate number would offer a useful address.

CHAPTER TWENTY-SIX

VIVIAN

I WOKE with a pounding headache and cursed myself for overdoing it with the girls. My limbs felt like they were made of lead. Turning to the side table, the clock showed seven in the morning. I bolted up in bed, thinking I was late for work. But then I realized it was Sunday. I didn't have to get to the office early to prep for anything.

I blew out a sigh of relief as I flipped through my Sunday routine. First, I needed to get some painkillers to ease the headache. I had grocery shopping to do for the week. Kaylee would be back from Violet's place after lunch, and we could catch up.

I hadn't had a chance to really talk to her about Heartstrings and where she was getting volunteers to help her. As I pushed the blanket away, I noticed my pajama pants but not the matching top. I had on my tank top from yesterday, and my sweater was draped over the chair.

How in hell did I do all that and not remember a damn thing?

How did I get home? This was terrifying.

Did Audri or Kiera drive me? They'd also been pretty drunk.

I raked a hand through my messy hair. Though the evening had been fun, I had placed my life in jeopardy. Who had driven me home? Audri probably asked Remi to drive me home and she probably accompanied him. She was thoughtful like that. Or it could have been Kiera and Forrest.

Had I said something stupid or private while I'd been under the influence? *Oh, God.*

Kaylee could never know I'd gotten sloppy drunk, somehow made it home, and lost all my memory of what I'd done.

What kind of role model was I?

Yesterday seemed like a blur. I remembered seeing Arrow with his ex, which pissed me off, so I went to hang out with the girls.

I remembered receiving the tarot card reading and seeing Arrow at Audri's, but that was it. Why was everything so foggy in my head?

Because you enjoyed way too much alcohol.

Groaning, I walked into the bathroom to wash up. Hopefully, the water would freshen me up and clear my head. I vaguely remembered talking to Arrow. Or was that a dream? I thought I dreamed about someone giving me a piggyback ride.

After washing up, I sent Audri a message.

Vivian: *Hey, how did I get home last night?*

Audri: *Arrow drove you home.*

Vivian: *I don't remember anything.*

Audri: *You were so drunk!*

Vivian: *Lesson learned.*

Audri: *Do you remember your SSG mission?*

I let my brain catch up. *Oh.* I'd admitted my attraction to him.

Vivian: *A Kiss is Not Enough*

Audri: *Keep me posted. Gotta go shopping with my mom. Chat later!*

Vivian: *Okay. Thanks for having me over. (smile emoji)*

Audri: *We'll do it again soon. (heart emoji)*

Anxiety clawed at me. Arrow had driven me home. Had I embarrassed myself? Had I said or done something I'd regret? What if I snored? Vomited?

This was worse than what I'd originally thought. A hot shower would clear my head. As the hot water sprayed on me, clarity slowly returned.

I remembered sniffing his cologne. Gosh, what was wrong with me? What else had I done? Did I dare try to remember everything?

After the shower, I made coffee and took two painkillers. The shower had relaxed the stiffness in my body a little. I'd never been hungover in my life. I got dressed and headed out to the store. When I walked by the security desk, Marvin smiled at me. He had a beard and looked like Santa's brother.

"You feeling better, Ms. Vo?"

Amusement glinted in his blue eyes.

"Please call me Vivian," I reminded him. "I feel a lot better. Did I make a fool of myself last night?"

"No. Your man was very nice. He gave you a piggyback ride."

Oh. My. God.

"What?! Through *here*?" I gestured to the main entrance where anyone could see me.

"Want to see?"

"Please." Curiosity and fear twisted my stomach. "Are

you breaking any rules?"

"No one will know." He winked. "I've been here for twenty years—I can make the executive decision to show my favorite tenant a video of herself." He waved a finger. "And this isn't because you keep giving me and Mary those delicious blueberry muffins." He tapped his round belly.

I always bought an extra box for him and his wife whenever I stopped by the store. He'd helped me move in when I first got to this apartment.

"You're the best." I smiled and walked behind the counter to look at the monitors.

He clicked on the screen. The video played, showing me looking like a monkey on Arrow's back. My face was burrowed into his neck.

I sniffed him! Embarrassment flushed through me. Where was the black hole when you needed it? I wanted the ground to open up and swallow me right now!

Arrow had a goofy grin on his face as he walked toward the elevator.

"Oh my God!" I covered my face with my hands.

"You had a fun night?" Marvin asked.

I looked at him with wide eyes, wondering what he was thinking.

Then realization hit him and he waved a frantic hand. "No! No! I was referring to the fun night that got you drunk. Not what you and your man did in your apartment."

I wanted to laugh and cry at the same time.

"No worries, Marvin. I knew what you meant. I'm just horrified by my actions. Don't mention this to Kaylee ever, okay?"

Nodding, he zipped his lips with his fingers.

My phone buzzed, and I reached into my purse. Maybe it was Kaylee replying to my message about what she wanted for lunch.

But the text wasn't from her.

Arrow: *Morning. Feeling better?*

"It's him." I looked up at Marvin.

He smirked. "Tell the boss I said hi."

"Boss? What do you mean?"

"He owns this building. When he took over and noticed we hadn't gotten a raise in two years, he gave us an enormous increase."

I couldn't believe it. Why didn't Arrow say anything about this to me?

I gaped at Marvin. "When did he buy the complex?"

"About two months ago. The owners were retiring and didn't want the extra stress. It's a prime location."

I made Marvin swear not to show that video to anyone and drove to the store, which was three blocks away. Grabbing a shopping cart, I tried to focus on what I needed to buy instead of Arrow's text, which I hadn't replied to. I needed some time to process what had happened yesterday.

Had I asked him for a piggyback ride? Where had that idea even come from? My face heated as the image blazed through my mind. I laughed and cursed at myself.

How else did I embarrass myself? How could I face him after that?

Why hadn't he run far away from me?

None of the previous men I'd dated would ever have agreed to a piggyback ride. Why did Arrow agree? Had I promised something to him?

I'd held hands with some of my previous partners, but

none of them had the same power. Everything with Arrow was more intense, had more meaning. When he held my hand, it was a gentle act of possession, an obsession—something deep that I didn't understand yet.

I felt a sense of belonging to him. Like I'd finally discovered a secret place all to myself. Perhaps I was overanalyzing and reading too much into it, but that was how I felt.

After my mother died, Dad and I often went camping by the lake. It was the only activity I enjoyed. I'd always find a nook where I could sit and fish that wasn't on the pier. That private spot was my sanctuary. I felt safe sharing my secrets with the water, the trees, the bugs, and the fish. I used to imagine sitting by the lake, immersing myself in nature and the silence. As I did so, my troubles floated out of me and into the lake, feeding the fish, bugs, and plants. Then I would imagine them smiling as they transformed what was ugly into something useful. My troubles became food for them. How silly was that?

In some odd way, holding his hand brought me back to that sanctuary.

For a moment I emptied my mind, and the reality of why I was in Providence surfaced. Where was Aimee? Who had her? Were they feeding her? Was she sleeping in a safe place? Anxiety made me tense. The issue bounced around my head, increasing the pressure in my temple. What could I do to find her quicker? I was doing my best.

As far as I knew, the private investigator Matt Stone, whom Aimee's parents had hired, hadn't found anything worthwhile either.

Sensing the surge of stress, I forced myself to calm.

Breathe. Relax. You can only get things done with a clear head.

A crashing noise yanked me back to reality. Shit, I'd just crashed into another shopping cart.

Earth to Vivian!

"Sorry," I apologized to the woman with a full cart of groceries.

My mind was all over the place today.

Just get your groceries. Everything else can wait.

I checked my phone and Kaylee had replied that she'd like pizza, wings, and fries for lunch. She'd also like more snacks to take along to her afterschool program at Whiz Kidz, and *phở*, the Vietnamese beef or chicken noodle soup she loved so much. I hadn't made it in a while. I usually just ordered at the Vietnamese restaurant. It was easier to go out since it was just the two of us. But I supposed I could stop by the Asian market to get the ingredients to make it for her.

I pushed the shopping cart to the produce section and grabbed a bag of green grapes.

"Hi. Fancy meeting you here." Arrow was also pushing a shopping cart, but his was already full of fruits, vegetables, boxes of oatmeal, a carton of eggs, antacids, overnight protection pads, and a pack of pork loin. Who was he shopping for?

Tingles rushed down my spine from his presence. Yesterday's event flared, and my heart raced.

"Hi." I could feel heat traveling from my toes up to my face.

"How are you feeling?" he asked with concern on his face.

"A lot better, thank you. Sorry I didn't reply to your message. Busy buying food to prepare for the week. Looks like you are too." I gestured to his cart.

He stared at his cart and smiled. "Yup. Busy week

ahead." He picked up a package of overnight pads, arched an eyebrow, and dropped it back into the cart.

With his wealth, he didn't need to go shopping. Didn't he have a personal assistant? A personal chef that did all the cooking for him?

"You cook a lot for Kaylee?"

I turned to him. "You know Kaylee?"

"I run Whiz Kidz. I only recently discovered that you're her guardian." His eyes gleamed.

"So how do you know that I'm her guardian?" Why wouldn't the tingles stop?

I steered my cart to the pasta and sauce aisle, and he followed me.

"I'm a volunteer for her Heartstrings app."

My heart thundered. I stopped the cart and gaped at him. *Oh no.* It couldn't be true. I didn't know if I could receive any more unexpected news today.

"You're . . . Bullseye?"

Nodding, he smiled and offered his hand. "Let's do this the right way. It's very nice to meet you, Tulip."

I felt like I'd just entered a brand-new day where the script and characters had altered, playing different roles.

This was the plot twist I didn't expect.

Somehow Arrow had been at every corner of my life since I arrived in Providence. Wherever I went, he was there. Even this meeting in the grocery store . . . Did he live nearby? I assumed he lived in his billionaire neighborhood, wherever that was.

But then again, I just discovered that he owned my apartment complex. So he could work around the area. Or maybe he had an apartment in the same building and didn't tell me! At this rate, anything was possible.

"There it is!" A woman in her sixties wearing a pink hat stalked up to him. "Young man, you took my cart."

Arrow glanced at the cart, gasped in surprise, and turned to them. "I'm so sorry! I wasn't paying attention. Must have taken yours by accident." He gave it back to them. "Please forgive me."

The pink hat lady exchanged glances with her friend in the fur coat. "It's okay, right, Vera?"

"Of course, Nora," Vera replied. "We understand. You were busy flirting with this pretty young lady."

They both offered me a sweet smile.

"I was indeed." He smiled, not even trying to deny it.

"Did you ask her out?" Nora propped a hand on her hips.

I couldn't believe this. Who were these nosy women?

"I did."

"And?" Nora looked at me and then back at him.

Arrow smiled at me, waiting for me to answer. *I'm gonna kill him for putting me on the spot.*

"I'm not ready for a relationship yet," I said.

Vera placed a hand over her heart. "Did he do something to make you unsure, sweetheart?"

"Unfortunately, I did. And I'm sorry for it."

Vera elbowed Nora, and they both grinned.

Vera looked at me. "Forgive him, dear. Life is too short. Give him a chance. He stole our cart as a prop to woo you. That deserves something."

Were these women his sidekicks or something? Did he hire them for this act? I narrowed my eyes at him. But his attention was on the women, full of amusement.

"You make a lovely couple," Nora said and pushed the cart down the aisle with her chatty friend.

For a moment those women reminded me of the girls. Would we act like them someday? Would we interrupt people's business in public like that?

Amusement sparked in his eyes. "They're not wrong. You should listen to your wise elders." His eyes bored into mine. "Give me a chance."

I didn't know how to act today when so many unexpected things were tossed at me.

"Did you hire those women?" I studied him.

"Absolutely not." He gave a weak laugh. "I wouldn't even know where to find outspoken old ladies."

"How did you know I was here?" I asked. "Are you stalking me?"

"It's not 'stalking.' It's research when I'm monitoring surveillance around my properties. I saw you leave the complex and head this way."

I wanted to ask how he could access the city's traffic cameras too, but decided against it. A man like him could buy anything.

I had a lot of questions for him, but one blazed through my mind.

"Why did you give me a piggyback ride?"

"Because you asked for one."

Embarrassment flushed to my face. My body should be used to this emotion by now, but it wasn't. I covered my face with both hands as my cheeks inflamed.

He gripped my arms, drew them away from my face, and pulled me into an embrace.

"It was the best evening I've ever experienced," he said. "I've never given anyone a piggyback ride before. It's reserved only for you."

I veered back to look at his handsome face. A sigh escaped me when I saw baby blue specks in his irises.

His thumb stroked over my cheek. Energy zigzagged down my spine and back up.

"There's nothing to be embarrassed about. It was the highlight of my evening after the kiss you gave me."

I gasped. "What? I *kissed* you."

Laughter flashed in his eyes as he pointed to his cheek. "It was wet, loud, and sloppy."

"We love wet, loud, and sloppy, don't we?" Vera said as she and Nora strode by and winked at us.

"I'm going to give my Frank a wet, loud, and sloppy kiss when I get home," Nora said.

"My Ed would take that as an opportunity to get a little saucy." Vera held up a bottle of hot sauce to her friend.

"Nothing wrong with adding a little spice!" Arrow told them.

The women burst into laughter, and so did I.

"Give him a chance to show you some spice, sweetheart," Nora purred, and Vera howled.

"Did she just howl?" I asked.

"She did."

We stared at the interesting women as they disappeared around the corner.

"What just happened at this grocery store?" I asked. "It's like a scene out of some strange sitcom."

"The Checkout." He slung an arm around my shoulder.

"What?"

"That's what the sitcom should be called."

We both stood in the sauce aisle laughing like idiots. The laughter was exactly what I needed to release the tension in me.

After a few more seconds, I gathered myself and looked at him. "Why are you here?"

"I came to ask you if you'd like to have dinner with me."

My SSG mission of A Kiss is Not Enough came to mind. I'd always wondered if he'd move on after he got the date he wanted. Would one date be enough for him?

"Duel with me. This won't be like the sparring at the gym," I said. "The loser has to do what the winner asks."

"Okay," he agreed instantly.

"But I didn't give you the rules yet."

"I don't care about the rules." He shrugged, looking too confident. "I'm gonna win, and you're going to be my girlfriend."

It was a firm statement with no room for errors.

"When and where?" he asked.

"I haven't thought of that yet."

"Think fast and tell me."

I hadn't gotten that far. I needed to digest everything that had occurred today before I could plan my mission.

Arrow accompanied me for the rest of the shopping trip as though we were a couple. Somehow, he invited himself to my home for when I made *phở*.

His phone rang, and he picked up the call while I got milk and eggs.

"I've got to go." He leaned in and kissed me on the cheek. "I have to return the friendly gesture you gave me yesterday." Something flashed in his eyes. "You just gave me the courage to do something I feared most."

"What's that?"

"Going to the dentist. See you in a few days."

Then he left me standing there perplexed, aroused, and excited.

CHAPTER TWENTY-SEVEN

ARROW

FLAPPING bat wings wreaked havoc in my stomach as I pulled into the parking lot of Healthy Smiles Dental Care, and my phone rang.

"Hi, Sylvia," I said.

"Hey, babe. What are you doing? Where are you? I got invited to Real Rumor's banquet in New York next week. Want to be my date?"

Why hadn't she moved on? Our relationship had ended a while ago. She hadn't taken the breakup seriously, even when I went on dates with other women. She believed I needed a break from her to realize who was best for me.

A woman who didn't resonate with my heart wasn't best for me even if she was beautiful.

"No, I can't. I'm busy."

"No, you're not." Irritation stirred in her.

"I'm busy, Sylvia. Ask someone else to accompany you."

"But I want *you* to come."

"We're not a couple anymore," I said calmly.

Silence hung in the air, and I could imagine her fuming as she always did when she didn't get her way.

"Are you seeing someone?"

"Yes." It wasn't a lie. In my head, I was already seeing Vivian.

"Who is she?"

"No one you know."

"Is she in our circle of friends?"

I was never in her circle of social media friends. I'd met two of her friends *once*.

"She's a simple girl. Not in the limelight."

Vivian was anything but that. However, I wasn't going to add fuel to an already crazy fire.

She snorted. "That's not your type."

I didn't have time for this. "She's what I need."

"You don't know what you need yet."

Perhaps not then, but I was beginning to understand my needs now. Needs and wants were different things. But Vivian fulfilled both requirements for me.

Like all my previous relationships, Sylvia had served as a temporary satisfaction until she got too clingy and hinted at marriage. I had wanted something that didn't require all my attention, and Sylvia demanded all that.

"Sylvia, we're just friends."

"What about the wine expo in Monaco?" She huffed. "Are you accompanying me there?"

"I already have a date. You should ask Eric or Tyson." They were wealthy bachelors within her circle.

"Tyson has asked me out several times, you know. But I told him I belong to you."

I glanced at the clock on my dashboard. I didn't drive all

the way to the dentist to sit and chat with her in the parking lot.

"You *don't* belong to me, Sylvia. I've got to go to my appointment."

"Fine. I'm going with Tyson." She hung up.

I sighed, shoving the conversation from my mind. How much clearer could I be with her? I didn't have the energy right now. My thoughts swung back to the reason for the sick feeling in my gut.

Don't be a wuss. Only little kids are afraid of the dentist. Not a grown ass man like you.

Holding Vivian's face in my mind to give me courage, I headed to the front door. Nerves wrung my gut as I stood staring at the Healthy Smiles Dental Care sign with a joyful tooth image that didn't make me want to smile at all.

Anxiety tightened the muscles in my shoulders and legs. A chill rushed through me. Sweat warmed on my hands, and I clenched it away. I forced myself to breathe regularly as the shortness of breath was another symptom I detested.

I hated how dentophobia had turned me into a weak person. A negative experience from when I was eight years old had transformed into a monstrous disorder. While lying in the exam chair for a filling, I had choked from the water running to the back of my throat. I couldn't breathe, and it freaked me out. From that horrible experience I'd developed this strange aversion to the equipment. The sounds of the drill and water suction triggered an awful sensation in my body.

My former dentist had suggested hypnotherapy and acupuncture to help me relax. Nothing helped. Whenever I had any work done, I asked to be sedated. Few people knew this about me. Not even my friends. This wasn't something

I'd discussed over a casual dinner, during a video game, or at a sporting event.

The shame and embarrassment were too much.

I was a former Navy SEAL who had conducted high-risk operations in all kinds of dangerous situations where I'd captured and killed high-level targets. Now, I ran a billion-dollar empire that had its own risks and danger, and yet I succumbed to a mere visit to the dentist.

Pathetic.

This was a hurdle I had to overcome. Vivian would be the person to assist me. I was due for a cleaning a year ago and kept canceling it.

I released a heavy sigh and prayed she had an opening for me. I didn't make an appointment because that would've intensified the anxiety.

A little boy about six years old stared up at me. "Hi." He wore a Batman knit hat and matching gloves.

"Hello," I said.

"I have a cleaning today." He beamed. "And then the office is gonna give me a bag of goodies with some toys in it. And then my mom is gonna get me some McDonald's. That's my favorite restaurant."

"That sounds wonderful. You like going to the dentist?"

"Yup! Dr. Vo is my favorite dentist! I get to watch Peppa Pig on the TV!"

I glanced behind me, and his mom was chatting with another woman.

"You're not afraid of the dentist at all?"

"Nope," he said with pride. "Some of my friends cry when they go. Not me. There's nothing to be afraid of." He rolled his eyes, and his whole body followed the motion.

Show off.

"You're a brave boy."

He studied me with curious blue eyes. "Are you getting your teeth pulled today?"

"No."

"Are you afraid of the dentist?" he asked.

I didn't answer the question.

Looking serious, he moved closer and placed a tiny, gloved hand on my thigh because that was where he could reach. "Everything will be okay." He patted my thigh. "My uncle is *super* afraid of the dentist too. One time, I went with him for 'moral support.'" He used his tiny fingers to emphasize the quotation.

I laughed out loud, and the sound rushed down the street. This kid was growing on me.

"Do you have someone to hold your hand?" he asked innocently.

I did, but not for dental moral support.

"Your bravery gives me courage, kid."

He smiled as his mom approached. I opened the door for them to enter first.

After they checked in and sat in the waiting area, I asked the receptionist, whose nametag read Allison, "Does Dr. Vo have any openings for an urgent appointment?"

Allison smiled. "One moment, please. Let me look. Someone called in to cancel earlier." She clicked a few times. "You're in luck. She has an opening in an hour."

"Great. Can you put my name down?"

Allison furrowed her eyebrows. "Umm, Dr. Vo only sees kids."

"Oh." Disappointment stirred in me. I should've known this. "Can I speak to her for a moment? Please? She's a friend."

"Of course. What's your name?"

I gave her my name. Ten minutes later, I sat across from Vivian inside her cozy office.

"I'm a pediatric dentist." She leaned into the table. "Adult patients are treated by the general dentist, Dr. Jillian Jones."

I also leaned into the table. "Which means you have *more* knowledge than a general dentist. I want *you* to work on me." When I heard unintentional sexual innuendo, I smirked. "In more ways than one."

She rolled her eyes, and a crease slowly formed between her eyebrows. "This isn't grocery shopping where you get to pick out your fruits and vegetables. A hygienist could clean your teeth."

I sighed, and disappointment probably showed on my face because she studied me for a moment. "Do you have a dentophobia?"

I twisted my lips and nodded.

Amusement flickered in her eyes, but it soon turned into compassion. She got up from her seat, walked over to me, and gripped my chin as though she was going to tell me to open wide. Instead, she said, "I suppose I could squeeze in a *big* baby for today."

I smiled and yanked her onto my lap.

She shrieked at the sudden gesture, and I couldn't help but kiss her. Her lips were soft and welcoming. She didn't kiss me back, but that was expected. She was the cautious type—except that one time at her apartment and when she was drunk. I wanted her to kiss me again. I wanted her to *want* me.

Breaking the kiss, I stared at her flushed face. "Shh. Or your staff will come rushing in."

She licked her lips, and I couldn't take my eyes off that sexy little tongue.

"You have no idea how much I want to kiss these beautiful lips." I ran my thumb over her bottom lip. "And taste that curious tongue of yours." I bent down and licked her bottom lip. When she gasped, my tongue slid in and greeted hers.

Fuck.

It was better than I remembered.

Another lick. Another taste. I was sucked into a world I could never come back from.

Decadent.

Delicious.

Dangerous.

Heat shot straight to my dick and throbbed. She didn't push me away, and I took that opportunity to explore her mouth. When her tongue played with mine, I moaned. When she sucked on my tongue, I almost came.

Fuck.

I loved the way her lips wrapped around my tongue. It made me want her mouth wrapped around my cock too. My cock throbbed as the vision flashed across my mind. I'd never been aroused at a dentist's office. This would be a new experience that could trump my fear. Vivian was the perfect distraction.

She placed a hand on my chest, eased back, and breathed, "I'm working."

"I know." I grinned. "You're doing a fabulous job, Tulip. Do it again."

Smiling, her eyes darkened. "I mean, I'm working at the office. You're causing too much trouble for me."

"But you love it."

I could hear her heart racing. The bulge in my pants had grown exponentially, achingly pushing against the fly of my jeans. Could she feel it? I shifted her ass into the appropriate position.

"This is what you do to me. Be a caring dentist and help me deal with it sooner rather than later."

"It seems like you have a different agenda for coming here." She tried to get off my lap, but I secured her with both arms, wrapping them tightly around her.

She laughed. "Let me go. What are you doing?"

"Holding onto my lifeline."

"I have a schedule to keep up with." She rose to her feet and straightened out her white coat. "I'll do my best to make your cleaning comfortable." She placed a hand on either side of my shoulders. "Many people suffer from this phobia. Just try to imagine a pretty or safe place. I can even play gentle music for you."

"But I'm an adult, Tulip. I shouldn't have this ridiculous fear."

"We all have fears, Bullseye. Including me."

I liked her calling me that. It was our connection before we knew we were linked to each other. "What do you fear?"

She waved a finger. "There's only room for one phobia today. I'll tell you that if you win the duel." Her face beamed.

"Well, that just means I will *have* to win now. Hurry and set a date and time."

"Come on. Let's get your cleaning done so I can take care of my other patients." I followed her to an exam room.

"Thanks for squeezing me in," I said when she gestured to the exam chair.

"You're welcome." She looked at the tray where someone had already set up the tools.

"There's another place I'd love to squeeze into." I smirked at my bluntness. What was the point of hinting when I could be direct with her?

She narrowed her eyes at me. "If you keep this up, I'll have to *squeeze* your neck." She demonstrated with her hands.

I laughed as she placed a napkin over my chest and reclined the chair.

"Do you want to listen to music?" she asked.

"No thanks." I placed my hand on her arm. "I'm going to keep my gaze on you. It'll ground me and make me think of sexy things, so the loud noise and splashing water won't bother me. Okay?"

"Okay." She smiled warmly and placed a pair of goggles on me. "This will protect your eyes from any sprays. Just concentrate on your breathing. In and out through the nose. You'll be fine." Her caring voice soothed me.

My heart raced when she asked me to open wide, but I stared at her and wondered about her scars. That kept my fear at bay.

CHAPTER TWENTY-EIGHT

VIVIAN

WHAT HAD TRIGGERED HIS PHOBIA? What had happened to him? Phobias could paralyze a person to where they couldn't function properly. The human mind was such an interesting mystery.

It must have taken a lot of courage for him to be vulnerable in front of me. When I got home tonight, I'd replay the kiss and his body's reaction to me. If I thought about it now, I wouldn't be able to do my job well.

No one had wanted me this much. Part of me relished in it. But the cautious side had me staying a few steps back, not fully giving in. What if all this was just some game that men liked to play?

Stop thinking. Focus on your patient.

His slow breathing told me he was trying his best to concentrate on that instead of the noisy equipment. If I had innovative equipment, it would help people recover from this phobia faster. With all the technology available today, why hadn't they invented something beneficial to the dental industry?

I had a few ideas for better equipment, but I had no clue where to get started. Plus, I didn't have the funds to work on something like that. For example, a silencer for my handpiece would be awesome. No more loud noises. Kids would love it.

Sound was very important to a person's mental state. People listened to certain music to relax or get into a certain mood. A loud drill was as far away from relaxation as one could get. On bad days, I found the sound of the handpiece irritating as hell.

If the weapons industry could invent a silencer for a gun, why couldn't they create one for a handpiece? It would be so easy for them.

Not enough money in dentistry.

Well, not general dentistry, but certainly cosmetic dentistry. The beauty business made loads of money, but I had no interest in servicing that community.

He flinched when water sprayed on his cheek. "Sorry." I wiped it with his napkin. "You're doing great, by the way."

He nodded, and I knew he wanted to say something but couldn't.

He had fabulous hygiene and beautiful teeth for someone who hadn't been to the dentist in a year. The fear probably motivated him to take extra care of his teeth.

When we were done with the cleaning, I performed a quick x-ray. After reviewing it, I said, "You're all set. No cavities. Keep up the good work." I gave him a bag with a toothbrush and toothpaste.

"Thank you." He took the bag and peeked inside. "No toy?"

I smiled. "We need to save those for the little kids. And you're welcome."

A serious expression splashed onto his face. "I've never had such a comfortable dental experience. Be my dentist from now on."

I arched an eyebrow at his demand. A man accustomed to shouting orders didn't usually ask for anything. But I wasn't the type to comply with orders either.

"Is that a request or a command?"

He smiled. "It's a plea."

"I'll think about it. I made an exception for today's visit. Consider this as repayment for you taking care of me while I was drunk."

"I'll pay you extra to be my dentist."

"It's not about the money, Arrow. If I become your dentist, then other adults would also ask me. I would have to decline, which would make them angry, and so on. I don't have time to deal with that."

"I could come in after hours," he said, trying to look adorable.

I laughed. "Are you planning on having a lot of cavities or something? Right now, you're good until the next cleaning, which would be in six months."

"See? You can be my dentist twice a year. That's not bad at all."

An idea percolated in my mind. I let it simmer while I considered his request.

"If I agree to be your dentist, can you help me with something? You know more people than I do."

"How can I help?"

I told him about my silencer idea, and he beamed. "That's *brilliant*."

His excitement and praise did something to my heart. I hadn't shared this idea with anyone until today. It felt wonderful to have someone understand where I was coming from.

"You have the specs?" he asked.

"Just a rough sketch, but that's it. I don't know where to go to have it produced or have the funds to—"

"I'll invest in it. One hundred percent. We'll find a company to create the prototype." His eyes held mine. "It's a fantastic idea, Vivian. I want to help you make it happen. Hell, if they had that invention back then, it would've helped me."

I gawked at him. I hadn't meant for him to offer the capital for it. From chatting with the girls, I knew he was a former Navy SEAL. So I had hoped he could tell me what company made weapons or would be interested in my idea. I wouldn't mind selling it to them for a percentage of the profit. But it appeared like he already had a business proposal in his head.

I tapped his forehead. "You already have a strategy in place, don't you?"

"Always. Especially with something I'm passionate about."

Curiosity nudged me. "Did you have a strategy with me?"

Something gleamed in his eyes, but he only gave a little truth. "You have no idea."

I wasn't sure if I should be wary of his plan for me or be excited that he thought that much about me.

My phone buzzed in my pocket, and I reached for it.

Calvin: *Got news on Aimee. Meet me here tomorrow. GO ALONE.*

Then he sent me an address to a restaurant I hadn't been to.

"Who's that?" Arrow asked.

"Calvin."

"What does he want?" The softness in his eyes turned edgy.

"Nothing important."

"He has news for you?"

I nodded but didn't elaborate. I had to go alone. For whatever reason, Calvin didn't want Arrow there.

"That's good." Arrow inhaled a breath. "Let me know what happens after." I needed to follow up with the PI to see if he'd found anything on Aimee.

A knock sounded on the door, and my assistant, Dakota, peeked in. "Your next patient is ready."

"We're all set. Can you please schedule him for his next cleaning with me?"

"Sure thing. Come this way," said Dakota. "You're her first adult patient."

"I'm her biggest baby," he told her, and she laughed.

I smiled and wondered if my relationship with him was developing faster than I had anticipated.

What if the swift speed prevented me from seeing all the obstacles along the side?

CHAPTER TWENTY-NINE

VIVIAN

THE NEXT DAY, Kaylee didn't have school because of staff development. I'd taken the day off to catch up on errands and prepare for my meeting with Calvin later.

"I want to know everything." I sat at the kitchen table, staring at Kaylee as she swallowed a bite of the pepperoni pizza.

"What do you want to know?"

"Did you know I was chatting with Arrow on Heartstrings?"

She shook her head. "No. Not until recently, when he found out you were my guardian."

I narrowed my eyes at her suspiciously. She was giving me a half-truth. I could tell by the way her eyes darted back to the pizza.

"Kaylee, you know how I feel about dishonesty."

She twisted her lips. "I swear I didn't know the app would connect the two of you or that he even knew you. I asked a bunch of people to volunteer for my app." She picked up the pizza. "I like Arrow. He's smart, and he teaches us lots of things even though he doesn't have to. He spends a lot of time at the center, hanging with us."

That was something I didn't know. I assumed he just funded the organization like most wealthy people who used that as a photo op to write off their taxes and so forth.

"And."

"One day, he said he was interested in this dentist. And I thought of you. But I knew you weren't interested in anyone after that jerk Connor cheated on you." Her eyebrows bunched. "You should've kicked his ass. Actually, you punched him."

"Language."

She clamped a hand over her mouth. "Sorry. It's true though." She shrugged and took another bite of her pizza. "I don't know why, but I like the idea of you and Arrow together. He's cute, and you're gorgeous. I know we're here to look for Aimee, but that doesn't mean you can't like a guy. Nothing has changed for me. I'm still going to school, doing my thing, and praying that we find her soon. I miss her."

I loved that Kaylee and Aimee got along. They had bonded over their affection for Sanrio characters. What was Aimee doing right now? Was she eating pizza? Or was she locked up in some room, crying for someone to save her? I understood the terror she was experiencing. I'd been a desperate girl, hoping someone would save me on that day when Ghost tortured me. That trauma was ingrained in me.

"We'll find her." I leaned back in the chair and crossed my arms. "So you didn't set us up?"

"Nope. The app did that. Guess it works! It used your profile data and randomly chose some tugs for you." She finished her pizza and gulped down her lemonade. "Do you like him?"

"Something like that."

"Yes!" She punched her hand into the air. "My Heart-strings app is the best!"

I didn't want to tell Kaylee that Arrow had pursued me before I met him on the app. But I also liked Bullseye. I supposed I got the best of both worlds.

"Are you mad at me?" Kaylee asked.

"No. I'm sorry I haven't stopped by Whiz Kidz as often as I'd like. If I had, I would've known you knew Arrow."

As we cleared the table, my phone buzzed with a reminder that it was time to meet Calvin. I prayed he had good news for me about Aimee.

CHAPTER THIRTY

VIVIAN

CALVIN HAD BEEN specific about me coming alone. What had he found out about Aimee?

I'd dreamed about Aimee last night. I hoped she knew her parents and I were still searching for her. That we'd never give up.

I needed to make time for Christmas shopping for Kaylee as well. My dad called yesterday to let me know he'd be in Vietnam with Rose for the holidays. I was happy he was going away with her. Rose had taken care of him in more ways than one. I knew Dad was hesitant about starting a new relationship. He'd told me once that my mom was his soul-mate, and he didn't want to betray her by loving another woman.

That had been years ago, and I prayed that one day he'd understand that Mom would've wanted him to be happy. My parents' love for each other was the ideal relationship I had dreamed about all my life. Would I ever find someone who loved me that deeply?

Mom left The Triad because she loved my dad. She left

a dangerous family for a more peaceful life.

Arrow's face popped into my mind, and I smiled at our impending duel. He was the first man to make me feel safe and hopeful. I wasn't as tense or stressed about everything when he was around. But I didn't want to depend on someone else. What if things didn't work out between us? Where would that leave me?

Dependence made a person weak, and I'd been relying on myself for too long to change my routine. Yet I couldn't help letting myself go when he held me.

A reminder buzzed on my phone. Kaylee was staying late at Whiz Kidz because she was presenting her dating app to the software team, along with the other kids. I would've attended to support her, but I couldn't miss this important meeting with Calvin. Kaylee promised to send me the recording of her presentation for me to watch later.

I walked into Bella's Bistro, and a youthful and vibrant atmosphere greeted me. It had interesting artwork on the colorful walls and unique lighting running across the ceiling. At four in the evening, the eclectic restaurant was packed with people. Three people stood waiting at the pickup section. A group of students huddled in the corner with their drinks, backpacks, laptops, and phones.

A few college students with their Brown University and RISD sweatshirts occupied a couple of tables by the wall. The lively restaurant was in a shopping strip with an adorable boutique, flower shop, and two other restaurants farther down. I planned to take Kaylee here one day.

I ordered a chai latte, got an empty table by the window, and waited for Calvin.

A minute later, Calvin arrived wearing a beanie hat, a

leather jacket, jeans, and boots, looking more exhausted than the last time I'd seen him.

"Hey." He smiled, pulled out a chair, and folded himself into it.

"You want anything to eat? Or a drink?"

"No thanks." He glanced around the restaurant, probably looking to see if Arrow was around.

"He's not here." I sipped my drink. "You asked me to come alone, so here I am."

He smirked and leaned into the table. His expression turned serious, and I was afraid of what he was about to say.

"I've got some news for you."

My stomach knotted from the somber tone. "Did you find her?"

"Yes and no."

"What does that mean?"

"I saw someone who looked like her in Chinatown and at the front of the Boston Children's Museum. I parked my car and went to look, but couldn't find her. She was with a man both times, but she didn't look terrified."

"Maybe she was scared. Maybe he forced her to act that way."

"Could be. The girl looked like her." A kid from a nearby table dropped a drink on the floor, drawing his attention away for a moment. When he turned back, he said, "I've got some stuff I need to deal with. I won't be able to continue helping you. You should head to Chinatown and the Children's Museum. Ask around. Maybe someone recognized her there." He met my eyes. "Consider our deal nullified, okay?"

"Our deal with the mystery price?" I asked.

"Yeah. That one." He smiled.

"If you had continued to help me, what would've been the price?"

"A date."

My eyes widened. "Why?"

"Because I want to annoy Arrow." He shrugged. "Just to see what he would do. He seems very protective of you."

I rolled my eyes. "You have that much time on your hands?" Shaking my head, I asked, "When did you see the Aimee lookalike?"

"Yesterday. I was in the city for a meeting." He sighed. "I know it's not the best news, but it's something you can work with."

"Thank you. It's useful information. Right now, anything is helpful. It gives me hope," I said. "I'll check it out." He looked tired, making me wonder if there was chaos within The Triad. "Is everything okay with you?"

He flicked me a look. "Dealing with traitors is never okay—"

The fire alarm shrieked out over the crowd, startling everyone. My body jerked from the loud noise.

"Let's go, everyone!" shouted the chef and the hostess.

People rushed out of the restaurant.

"Let's get out of here!" Dion rushed out with his group of friends.

If I had seen him earlier, I would have gone over to say hello. He fist-bumped Tim and Raul, who had come from somewhere. Then the boys rushed off around the corner.

Calvin and I walked across the street, where everyone was standing around. I didn't see any smoke. The fire alarms were blaring all along the strip mall. What had happened?

"Protective and possessive," Calvin muttered and

glanced at his watch. "Gotta go. I'll let you know if I receive more info on Aimee."

"I thought you can't help anymore?"

"I'm not obligated to help you because we no longer have a deal. But that doesn't mean I won't if time becomes available."

I appreciated his gesture. "Thank you for meeting me today."

When he left, I stood on the sidewalk watching the fire engines and police cars arrive. The firefighters went into the stores. They returned a few minutes later and told everyone we could go back. It was a false alarm.

Suspicion percolated in my head. This was no accident, and I knew who was responsible. The idea hadn't dawned on me until now. The perfect distraction to disrupt everything. My lips twisted in annoyance, and I decided it was time to confront him.

CHAPTER THIRTY-ONE

VIVIAN

KAYLEE ASKED if she could spend the weekend at Violet's place because Violet had asked her for a girl's weekend together. I called Grace to make sure it was all right with her. I didn't want my sister to intrude if she already had plans.

"Of course. Kaylee is like my second daughter. And Violet loves hanging out with her. They entertain themselves. I don't have to do anything but feed them."

"Thanks, Grace."

I felt bad Kaylee was always over there. Violet had also spent a few nights here, but Kaylee knew I preferred privacy, especially when I was digging into Aimee's whereabouts. It was better to keep outsiders away from what I had to do.

After giving Kaylee some money to chip in for the food, I headed over to Arrow's place.

My brain had been keeping track of all the places I'd bumped into him. A well-thought-out picture had formed in my head.

I had called Audri, asking for his home address on the pretense that Kaylee wanted to send him a thank-you card for letting her join Whiz Kidz.

I wanted to surprise Arrow, catch him off guard. He was a methodical guy accustomed to planning, and I wanted to unsettle him. I could've asked him, but he'd suspect something. I didn't want him to know I was coming over.

Glancing in the mirror, I ensured my makeup and hair were perfect, pausing to fix the rebellious strand of hair that wouldn't obey.

Shit.

What was I doing? I'd never cared this much about my appearance, especially when I was peeved. I didn't like being manipulated, and he'd manipulated me. Hadn't he? Somehow, I'd fallen into his trap. *Ugh.*

Snow fell slowly, and there was something peaceful about driving on the street while the gentle flakes flew around me. Maybe I shouldn't have come all this way to give him a piece of my mind. But I was halfway there already, so I might as well get it over with.

I would've worn snow boots if I had known about the snowfall. The meteorologist had said something about flurries, not the increasing flakes flying around. Maybe I was at the tail end of a snow squall that would end soon?

The GPS told me to turn in five hundred feet.

As expected, he lived in a posh area with homes I could never afford. *Gosh, look at the gorgeous Christmas lights everywhere.* They were so beautiful. I followed the GPS to a house that was the farthest from everyone else in the neighborhood.

If I were spending that much money, I wouldn't want to

be close to my neighbors either. Unlike the other homes, he didn't have Christmas lights. It looked dark and sad compared to everyone else. Why didn't he put up any lights?

I pulled into his driveway and spotted *five* garages. Who needed this many cars?

CHAPTER THIRTY-TWO

ARROW

THE HOT SHOWER after the workout in my home gym was exactly what I needed to clear my head.

I'd received enough information about Vivian's past to make me want to wrap her in my arms and tuck her away someplace safe. No wonder she had built a barrier around herself, keeping one foot in the dark and one in the light.

I'd been drawn to her because of the misery she'd experienced. But I wanted more details about her life that no one else knew. I wanted an invitation to her secrets—into her heart.

I should focus on my wine competition in Monaco, but my thoughts were on Vivian. I threw on a T-shirt and cotton pants and went into the kitchen to see what I wanted for dinner. A few takeout orders had been delivered earlier today because it had been a work-from-home day for me.

My doorbell chimed, surprising me. The clock on the wall showed it was seven in the evening. Who could this be?

I checked my security camera and smiled at the image of

Vivian standing at my front door. How did she know where I lived?

I yanked the door open. "Hello, Tulip. How did you know I was thinking about you?"

She didn't give me a warm look like I'd hoped. But I thought the scowl on her face looked cute. She was so beautiful, and warmth spread all over me just seeing her at my home. She wore long boots that accentuated her thighs and a short, puffy coat. I had the sudden urge to strip everything off her.

"Welcome." I took her arm, ushering her into my home.

She shook off her long boots, and I grabbed her coat.

"We need to talk," she said, tossing her purse onto the chair.

"Sure, but can I have dinner first? It's been a long day. Have you eaten?"

She shook her head. "Not in the mood."

I gripped her chin and gave her a quick kiss on the lips. She blinked, and the tension on her face diminished about fifty percent.

"I don't enjoy seeing you angry or stressed. Did I do something wrong again?"

"Yes," she said, licking her bottom lips.

God, I fucking loved that gesture. My cock hardened every time her pink tongue swept over her bottom lip.

It must have been something obscene if she drove all the way here to see me.

I folded my arms over my chest and studied her. "Maybe it was my idea to lure you here."

She rolled her eyes. "I thought about that too."

Joking aside, I was curious about what prompted this

visit. She looked tired, angry, and in need of a distraction from it all.

I placed a hand on either side of her shoulders. "Eat first, and we can talk after. Your muscles are tight." I gave her a gentle massage.

"Harder, please." Her shoulders relaxed for me. "Didn't know you were a masseuse."

"Not a masseuse. I'm just *very* good with my hands," I whispered into her ear.

"So this is how you seduce those women." She stepped away.

"You're the only one I want to seduce."

She looked around my home and walked toward the living room.

"The other women had to seduce me." I reached for her arm.

She shifted and blocked my arm. Then she threw a sharp attack, which I dodged.

Vivian sized me up, and I found that fucking hot. "Ready for another duel?"

Oh, she had no idea. "Been ready for you, Tulip."

"Get ready to lose, Bullseye."

CHAPTER THIRTY-THREE

VIVIAN

THE DUEL SEEMED appropriate for the moment. Frustration whirled in me, and it needed an outlet.

Since he was the reason for my frustration, he had to deal with my rage.

The way he looked at me added a layer of feelings I didn't want to acknowledge. But maybe it was what I needed to move beyond all these feelings.

I had planned on finalizing the rules of the duel and what I'd get out of it. But right now, I didn't have the energy to care about rules and regulations.

Arrow had wanted to be with me from the beginning. He had continuously pursued me even after I'd rejected him twice. He was either a fool or a determined man who didn't back down. Regardless, I admired his persistence. And to be honest, it made me feel special that I was his target. So I shouldn't have been too angry with him, but I was.

I was an emotional mess because of him, and that needed a resolution today.

"If I win, you'll do anything I ask?" He eyed me.

Was that the original deal? I vaguely remembered something like that. At that time, I wasn't sure what I wanted him to do. In truth, A Kiss is Not Enough was to determine if he was serious about me or if I was simply a means to an end—little more than winning a game. That after he got what he wanted, he'd push me aside to focus on someone else. This operation posed a threat to my heart though. My attraction to him had grown despite my refusal to let him affect me.

But if I didn't go along with this duel, I'd never know the truth.

"Sure," I said. "But you won't win."

Arrow paced the massive living room with neutral-colored walls and modern furniture in shades of grays, blues, and browns. He surveyed me like a wolf eyeing his prey. His gray eyes gleamed as though he knew the conclusion of the duel before it even began.

Too confident and sexy as hell.

He wore a black T-shirt and knit pants, which allowed him swift and easy movements. That was an advantage I didn't have. I wore jeans and a thick sweater.

Oh well.

I hadn't prepared for a physical battle when I came here this evening. A verbal battle had been on my mind, but the influx of emotions spawned something I had to deal with now.

"What martial arts did you study, Bullseye?" I asked, watching him the way he watched me.

"Krav Maga and Shaolin Kung Fu. You?"

I hadn't studied Krav Maga. It was an Israeli martial art combining fighting techniques from judo, aikido, karate, boxing, and wrestling. That was too many variants for me. My focus had been on the five classic animal stances from the Shaolin Kung Fu: the dragon, tiger, leopard, snake, and crane. The way animals fought to survive in the wild intrigued me because people often had to fight for their survival too. Each style didn't mimic the actual animal, but its essence and temperament.

"Shaolin."

"Which animal is your favorite?" he asked with a smirk.

A smirk that had a dare etched on it.

"This one." I charged forward with my snake head stance, an open-handed technique where the fingers were clenched tightly together. The tips of the finger created a hard surface to attack. I aimed for the soft spot on his neck, but he blocked it with his dragon claw and grinned.

I pivoted and switched to a crane beak, striking him in the arm and chest. He fell a step back and considered me, sweeping a gaze up and down my body. I didn't know why, but my body tingled from his inspection.

He inhaled a deep breath and took on the tiger formation, making him look like a feral beast ready to apprehend his enemy. His fingers formed the tiger claw, which was effective for tearing and grabbing.

Arrow came at me, but I blocked it and dodged his other hand. A battle erupted between us in a series of swinging arms, swift hands, and powerful kicks. His moves were controlled, speedy, and strategic. I wasn't sure if I could win this duel. My mind spun, trying to figure out how I could defeat him.

Somehow, he gripped my sweater, pulled me flush to him, and kissed me on the cheek. "That's a swan peck."

"There's no such thing," I retorted, extracting from him.

"It is now. It's my personal style inspired by you." His

arrogant smile turned to something else. "You're fucking turning me on with this battle."

The statement took me by surprise. At that moment of pause, he gave me a delicate kick to my shin and grabbed my shoulder with his tiger. But I got away, hopped onto his couch, and jumped onto his back like a spider monkey.

Sliding my forearm around his neck, I nipped at his ear. "This is the deadly monkey choke and the spider bite."

He laughed, knowing I'd just made them up. To my surprise, he secured my ass with his hands and ran around his house.

What just happened here?

I laughed because it was silly, absurd, and unexpected. The duel had pivoted to something entirely different, with me on his back for another piggyback ride. It seemed like that was an ongoing theme between us.

"What are you doing?" I asked. "Put me down!"

"Trying to make you dizzy so you can lose." He stopped and pressed my back into a wall with a mirror across from us.

I bit gently on his neck and felt his racing pulse.

He met my gaze in the mirror. "I love the way your sex is pressing into my back, Tulip." He shifted and wiggled, bringing my core even closer to him.

A moan released from me, and he grinned, knowing exactly what he was doing.

I'd never been in this aroused position and didn't know what to say.

"How about we call it a truce?" he asked.

I swallowed, caught my breath, and slid down from his back.

He turned around and braced his arms on either side of me. "You're the ambush I wasn't ready for. You've knocked all the sense out of me. Especially with the monkey choke and spider bite."

My heart drummed, and I wondered if he could hear it.

He breathed near my ear, inhaled my hair, and growled. "We have to deal with this attraction, Vivian. It's unavoidable."

I lifted my face to stare up at his hungry gray eyes. Spears of cool blue burst from his irises, creating a mesmerizing mosaic that drew me in even more.

He ran his knuckles down my cheek, and electricity zipped through me. This man could command my body in unimaginable ways. The sexual energy was spiraling out of control. I didn't want to analyze anything. I just wanted to feel him touch me.

He was right. This explosive attraction needed to be dealt with. The duel shouldn't have increased the attraction, but it did. I loved that he was my match. If we had continued, he would've defeated me. He was a lot bigger and stronger than me.

For tonight, I wanted to be taken care of.

A Kiss is Not Enough could be confirmed after tonight. Would Arrow move on once this attraction was dealt with?

Would I?

Could I?

I placed my palms on his chest, feeling his warmth and heartbeat. "Arrow?"

"Yes, Tulip?"

"Kiss me."

CHAPTER THIRTY-FOUR

VIVIAN

ARROW'S LIPS crashed into mine with a masculine growl. I moaned at the onslaught of hungry lips, curious tongues, and greedy teeth. It was like an explosion of need that had been dormant for too long.

For me, it was an eruption from years of keeping my desires and emotions on a straight path. But right now, I wanted the detour. I wanted to take a different route without a planned destination.

His tongue dueled with mine, and the taste of him added fuel to my wildfire. He had sparked something in me when he'd asked me out the first time. But fear and responsibility forced me to keep my distance. The distance had kept me safe, but it also prevented me from exploring what I truly wanted—what I desperately needed.

Arrow lured that explorative part of me out and indirectly guided me to his home tonight.

The kiss intensified, and we were like two heated creatures clawing at each other. He offered, and I took. When I offered, he growled like a beast. I loved how he devoured me. Possessively. Hungrily. I surrendered to his ravenous mouth and his skillful tongue. His curious hands explored my breasts, ribs, and stomach, igniting another fire that had me trembling for him. The heat escalated, and I gasped for air. His open mouth dragged over my face and down the column of my neck.

I wanted more of him. The muscles in my inner thighs tightened. Heat burst in my center, blooming to every crevice of my body. My legs trembled, and I slid my arms around his neck, clinging to stability. My fingers threaded into his hair, pulling him closer.

I'd never felt this overwhelming need to be close to someone. I didn't understand it.

He lifted me with powerful arms, and I wrapped my legs around his waist.

"I'm going to fuck you all night." He sucked my bottom lip as his hands cupped my ass, carrying me away from the wall.

"Okay," was the only word that escaped me.

Arousal flooded my mind and blurred my ability to communicate properly.

Arrow dropped kisses to my jawline and pressed his hot lips to the pulse on my neck. I panted from trying to keep up with the furious energy between us. He tossed me onto the couch, smirking like a wolf ready to feast. When he shoved my jeans off, a whisper of cold air skimmed down my body. The searing heat from his gaze chased the chill away. He stared at my yellow underwear with hearts all over. Embarrassment flushed through me. I should have worn a solid pair or lacy underwear.

"Adorable," he said, dropping to his knees. He pressed

his face to me, inhaled, and kissed me through the underwear.

The visual of it almost undid me. I'd never watched a man adore me the way he did. With my past relationships, the intercourse started right after our clothes were off. But Arrow was taking his time to discover me, which did something to my heart.

He nudged my thighs apart and palmed my core, massaging my bud tenderly while his gray eyes darkened like a storm. I loved that I was the reason for the transformation on his face. He was an intense man with so many facets—dark, tender, thoughtful. But I also sensed a ruthless side that called to me. I was a lucky woman to experience this sexy enigma of a man.

When his fingers played with my bud through my underwear, I moaned, writhed, and turned into a gooey mess.

"You like me touching you, Tulip?" His voice was decadent sin, dripping down my body. Each sizzling drop was like an otherworldly kiss that seeped into my skin, traveling all the way to my heart.

"Yes," I whimpered, gripping the couch cushion for stability.

My underwear flew off, landing on the floor. His face was so close to my sex, and I could feel his breath caressing me. I should be insecure about what he saw, felt, and smelled. But I was too aroused to even care.

"Beautiful. Sexy. All mine," he crooned.

I made a sound full of plea and something else.

He smiled. "A wine lover can taste all the secrets in wine. I want to taste all your secrets."

His thick tongue swiped over me once, twice, watching

me respond. I cried, bucked, and desperately wanted more. His hands held my thighs in place as his tongue worked its magic.

"*Fuuuck*, Vivian. You taste so good."

Heat, need, and lust flooded me. My body levitated. Or was I hallucinating? My fingers dug into his thick hair, and my eyes rolled back, absorbing the wonderful sensation coursing through me.

"More."

I didn't know the request came from me until he lifted his face and smiled. "Don't worry, Tulip. I'm giving you everything tonight."

He buried his face between my thighs and feasted like a starving animal. Need spiraled in me, pushing me closer to the edge. Higher and higher until nothing held me back.

"Arrow!" I cried as a powerful surge of bliss whipped me over the edge.

"That's right, baby." His tongue intensified.

Unfamiliar sounds of ecstasy poured out of me. Was it a groan, a moan, a growl? *Jeez*. I didn't recognize my own voice.

My body quaked as I slowly descended back to reality. But he kept eating me as liquid fire leaked out of me.

"You're a sex god, Bullseye," I said, thinking I could live my life like this forever.

He pressed kisses to my thighs.

"Did I hit the mark, Tulip?"

I smirked. "Right on the spot."

A goofy grin appeared on his face as he rose. "Be right back." He rushed off somewhere.

I stretched out on his wide couch. The room seemed cold

and empty without him. I missed his warmth, his touch, and his lips.

That tongue. *My God.*

I glanced out the window and noticed the snow had fallen exponentially. The forecast had been light snow for today and tomorrow. But it didn't look like it at all. I'd just gotten a new snow brush, so that shouldn't be a problem when it was time to go home.

When he returned, I realized he was still fully clothed, and I was half-dressed with my sweater still on. The obvious bulge tented his cotton pants. He stared at me, and I wanted to know what he was thinking. My heart twirled at the stunning man looking at me.

I sat up on the couch and crooked a finger. "Come here."

Arrow padded over, wearing a sexy smirk. "Yes, Tulip." He bent down to kiss me with those lips that had just devoured my most private part.

I gripped his shirt. "I want to see you. All of you. Take it off."

His shirt flew off, landing on the floor. I released a sigh as I examined this gorgeous man standing before me. Well-defined muscles. Smooth skin. Firm abdomen. I spread my palm over them as though introducing myself. I lingered around his amazing abdomen. It felt like a slab of indestructible granite.

Then I noticed some scars on his ribs.

He probably saw the curiosity in me and gripped my wrist. "Questions later. Something else is begging for your attention." He guided my hand to his bulge. "I need you right here, Warrior Goddess."

"What does that make you?" I dragged down his pants and boxers and gasped at the glorious cock.

Oh. My. God.

"Warrior God, what else?" he said. "I think we should duel every day so we can end up like this."

His statement floated around me like a cloud. I was only half-listening to him. My concentration was on the thick, throbbing cock begging for my touch. Maybe it was the other way around—I desperately needed it.

I clasped my fingers around his powerful stalk, and he moaned. As I stroked him, I studied his face. It was full of restraint and desire like a taut rope slowly shredding at the edges. How long would it take for him to snap?

I wanted to make him erupt.

"I need that sexy pink tongue on me." His voice hitched. "*Right now.*"

CHAPTER THIRTY-FIVE

ARROW

SHE OBEYED and licked the length of my cock while her brown eyes connected to mine.

Fuuuccck.

It was the most beautiful thing I'd ever seen. Heat sparked from where her tongue loved me. I'd been dreaming of having her do exactly this for the longest time. But nothing prepared me for this powerful sensation searing through me. It was like a storm racing through my blood vessels, so fucking hot.

I let out a loud growl and fisted a hand in her hair. She knew her power and continued to stroke and lick me as though she was fulfilling her appetite. When her tongue swirled around the crown, I thought I was going to erupt. But I gathered everything I had to hold back. I wanted to savor every drop of pleasure she offered me.

This beautiful woman was loving my dick. I wanted this moment forever etched into my mind.

When her mouth took me, I crooned, "Vivian."

Her mouth was warm and soft. Her mischievous tongue teased and tormented. I slid in further, touching the back of her throat. She gagged, paused, breathed, and let me drive in deeper.

So fucking sexy.

So fucking beautiful.

So fucking mine.

My heart pounded in my ears as the pressure increased. No woman had looked so perfect and glorious sucking my cock. She changed up the pace from slow to fast to slow again. She drove me crazy. I was clinging to the precipice, trying my best to hold it together. I didn't want to come in her mouth this first time.

She released me with a pop and licked her lips. "Is that what you needed?"

I released a guttural roar. "Fuck yes. But I need more of you." I gripped her sweater, yanking it off, followed by the yellow bra that matched her underwear.

Adorable and sexy all rolled into one.

My hands possessed her breasts, squeezed them gently, and teased her pointy brown nipples. I claimed a delicious nipple, suckling it while my hand massaged the other breast. She tasted like something I couldn't define, but I knew it was mine. Her flavor. Her scent. Her softness. They all belonged to me. Somehow, I knew it.

Like I knew I had to go after her the moment we met. It was a mere feeling. A powerful intuition that pushed me forward.

Her moans became a song to my heart. I could listen to it all day and night.

She melted into my touch, surrendering to my mouth. I

wanted to touch her everywhere. When my hands roamed to her back, she tensed.

I drew back and looked at her face. "What's wrong?"

"Nothing," she said, looking away.

I clasped her face with two hands, making her look at me. "I don't believe you. Did I hurt you somewhere?"

"No." Embarrassment flushed on her cheeks, and I knew.

I pulled her into an embrace, and my fingers caressed her back. "If it's your scars, I'm not bothered by them. I have scars too."

She released a repressed sigh and relaxed in my arms.

She drew back, and worried eyes stared at me. "You're not turned off by the imperfections?"

"No. Why would I be?"

She didn't reply.

"Did someone tell you that?"

I didn't know anything about her history, and I wanted to kill the bastard who had hurt her.

She chewed on her bottom lip, and I wanted to erase any insecurity she had about being with me.

I tapped her forehead. "Listen to me. I'm not bothered by your scars. Your wounds don't make you imperfect. They define you as my wounds define me. It took me a long time to understand that." I kissed her forehead. "Think of your scars as trophies you've earned to survive this cruel world. You're a survivor, and that makes you perfect for me."

Tears brimmed in her eyes, but she held them back.

"May I see them?"

I'd already seen them when she was drunk. But this was different. I wanted her to share her wounds with me willingly and openly.

She considered me for a moment and nodded. She'd given me permission to see her wounds, and that was sacred to me.

I turned her back to face me and examined her scars more carefully this time. I'd been too shocked the first time to study them.

Vivian flinched when I ran my fingers along the scars desecrating her back. Parts of her skin appeared like they'd melted. She'd been burned. Was it a fire? Two raised flesh sections in her lower back caught my eyes. They had a circular shape with an abstract design in it. My stomach knotted, recognizing what kind of tool had caused it. Someone had branded her. Who was the fucker?

Rage pulsed in me, but I didn't want it to ruin this moment. I'd ask her more details later. Right now, I wanted to soothe her.

"The scars have turned into something beautiful." I dropped kisses all over her back.

"Arrow . . ." she whispered, turning to face me.

Emotions filled her eyes as she touched my face. The delicate gesture signified something more. It was more intimate than I could explain. It was as if her touch whispered something to me. Like an appreciation that words couldn't express.

"I want to see your scars," she said.

"Whatever you want." I shifted so my back faced her.

The cushion dipped when she rose to her knees. I heard a soft gasp, but she didn't touch me. Her scrutiny warmed my back.

I'd seen my scars before. They looked like intersecting lines all over my back. I'd gained several other wounds during my days with the Navy, but the original scars from my childhood carried more weight. Pain caused by a loved one was difficult to heal.

CHAPTER THIRTY-SIX

VIVIAN

WORDS CLUNG to my throat as I tried to figure out what to say to him.

His scars were just as bad as mine. My heart ached. The last thing I expected coming to his home tonight was this—that we were similar. We both swam in misery in our life.

I placed my palm on the crisscrossing lines. I pressed my palm into it, wanting to absorb his pain.

"Who did this to you?" I asked, placing a kiss on his back the way he had mine.

It sounded strange, but something had lifted from me when he'd pressed his lips to my scars. I didn't expect that tenderness from the powerful, and magnetic man he presented to the world—the man I had initially feared would break my heart.

When he didn't reply, I wrapped my arms around him, my body pressing into his back. This gesture was more intimate than any sexual encounter I'd ever experienced. He had touched a part of my soul tonight. But I wasn't going to share that.

I kissed the side of his face. "Whose butt do I need to kick for you?"

Laughing, he shifted and somehow dragged me onto his lap easily. I was cradled in his arm while completely naked.

But I wasn't even insecure about it. Something shifted between us tonight. Maybe it was because we both saw each other's darkest wounds. Nothing else could measure up to that.

He looked down at me. Emotion swirled in those irresistible gray eyes that seemed to tell me an entire story of his life.

"Would you do that for me?" he asked, brushing strands of hair from my face.

"Yup." I ran my fingers along the light stubble on his chin. "I need a name and an address. Then I'll start my attack plan."

His smile widened. "Using what?"

"Haven't you read the *Art of War*?"

His eyes gleamed with amusement. "You've read it?"

"Let me tell you a secret, pal." I lowered my voice. "The comic book version is fabulous."

His laugh roared through the living room. His body shook with me still cradled in his arms.

"Didn't know there was one. I read the English translation of the book when I was in the Navy."

"The comic book version is out of print. But the strategies and philosophies are still the same. You just have to apply it to modern contexts. People don't ride horses into battle anymore."

"No. We use cars, planes, and other advanced technologies."

I poked him in his abdomen. "So . . . who gave you those scars?"

It should feel strange that we were having this serious conversation in the nude. Minutes ago, sexual energy thrummed in this room. But right now, a rare intimacy—even friendship—stirred between us.

I cherished it more than he could ever know.

I wasn't into wars or war strategy, but I was interested in how people survived during turbulent times. My kung fu master had given me the comic book version a long time ago when I first started learning self-defense. It was probably inside some box in storage.

"I'll crush your enemy with my snake attack. I'll even add in a few crane pecks into his eyes. Then another two pecks on his heart meridian that governs all his organs. He *will* know extreme pain and—"

His mouth met mine, and I was flat on the couch with his weight over me, his cock growing hard, hot, and throbbing against my skin. I loved how he kissed me tenderly this time. Our mouths sought each other as though we were trying to travel deeper to find out more about one another.

This wasn't the ferocity he'd shown me earlier. This was delicate, meaningful, and penetrating.

His tongue caressed mine, and I returned the favor. It was as though we were telling each other love stories with our senses.

He drew back and looked down at me, his eyes full of emotion. "Time to fuck you all night, Tulip. Any objections to that?"

"No objections here." I smiled, opening my thighs wider for him.

He shifted, reached for the condom pack on the floor,

ripped it open, and put it on. I didn't remember him getting the pack. But my focus had been on more important things, like the sexy man who looked like he wanted to possess me.

Heat pooled at my core again, and he glanced at it. A wolfish grin stretched his face.

Growling, he sat on the couch, bent toward my sex, and licked me again. "You're so fucking ready for me."

He shifted so his knees were on the couch and dragged me closer as he positioned his thick cock at my core. My heart jolted from the flood of warmth in his eyes.

When he slid into me, he looked at me, and I knew this union was different.

This was special.

I wished I could wrap the sacred look and raw emotion into a precious box where I could cherish them forever. Where I could take it out to remember this moment.

My breath hitched as he drove deeper into me.

"Fuuuck. You're so tight," he crooned.

He felt so good inside me, so full. So perfect. He pulled out and slammed into me again and again. I moaned with each powerful thrust.

I pulled his face to me and kissed him all over—his lips, his jawline, and his forehead. I couldn't get enough of him.

He pumped harder and harder, and my body thrummed for release. His body tensed, and I knew he was on the edge too.

"Look at me." He panted. "Come with me."

"Arrow!" I cried as the powerful orgasm ripped through me, blinding me, but not before I saw the grin on his face.

"You're mine. Remember that." He groaned, and I felt the shockwave of pleasure inundate his body. He fell onto me, bracing one hand so he didn't crush me.

I bit into his shoulder, loving the scent and taste of a satisfied man. Seconds later, he removed himself from me, went to wash up, brought a towel to clean me up, and resumed his position next to me on the wide couch.

We stayed like that for a while and wallowed in bliss and relaxation. I couldn't remember what we talked about because I dozed off.

CHAPTER THIRTY-SEVEN

ARROW

SHE LOOKED SATISFIED, adorable, comfortable, and perfect in my arms. I pulled over the soft throw from the couch and covered her naked body.

My body hadn't been this relaxed in a while, but I was too wired to sleep. I replayed the evening in my head. She'd gotten me aroused from dueling with her to fucking her. I loved how she responded to me. Turning my face, I inhaled her hair. Her floral scent got me all excited again.

The most profound moment that stood out to me wasn't the sexual encounter. It was the discovery and sharing of our wounds. We got to touch each other's scars. When she put her hands on mine, her healing intention penetrated the surface of my skin to where the darkness lived.

I couldn't put it into words, and even now, I couldn't express it. But I knew what she wanted to do when her hands touched my scars. She wanted to erase the pain etched into the scars the way I wanted to remove hers.

Whatever happened between us today ignited a new

warmth inside me. Like a fire had erupted to kindle my dark soul.

I shifted her, removed my numb arm, and retrieved a larger blanket, throwing it over the smaller throw. I got dressed, grabbed the laptop from my office, and settled in the lounge chair across from her, watching her sleep for a moment. My chest constricted, and I wasn't sure why. I'd been attracted to her physically, but this evening intensified my feelings for her to another level I wasn't ready to face yet. It wasn't just the sex. It was the connection, the way she made me feel at the deepest level.

What had I gotten myself into? My mind had been cluttered with finding the asshole who had stolen from me and destroying The Trogyn. Caring about someone posed a threat to my mission. This hadn't been my initial strategy at all.

You got distracted, moron.

I had to pivot and reevaluate my strategy to ensure the thief was punished and The Trogyn destroyed.

What if my new plan pushed her away? I didn't like that. I'd take a few days to let things settle in my mind before making any further decisions.

I looked outside the sliding door, which gave me a view of the spacious backyard. The meteorologist was wrong again. About eight inches of snow were already on the ground. Light flurries, my ass.

I searched for the news, checking for the latest weather forecast. A fucking blizzard? Apparently, the precipitation had shifted, and now we had a Nor'easter named Betsy hammering part of New England for the next forty-eight hours.

Vivian shifted, made a soft sound, and curled into the

blanket. She looked so cute. And she was now stuck with me for another two days.

Smiling to myself, I got up from the lounge chair, walked over to the sliding door, and looked up at the dark sky. "Thank you."

This was another gift I didn't expect to receive today, but I was happy it had occurred. I returned to my seat and emailed my assistant to shift my schedule around. I had an international call tomorrow and Sunday. Those could wait.

I had a special guest to attend to. Vivian had come here tonight all wired up, ready to confront me. I had a feeling what she wanted to know. Somehow, she connected all the dots of what I'd done. I knew she'd find out eventually, but this was too soon.

I opened the file the PI had given me on Vivian's family history. Her grandfather, Stephen Kwan, or King Viper, had been The Triad tycoon for The Taipans. He passed away and there was no current leader at the moment. The Taipans ruled New York's Chinatown with business in several cities around the world, including Providence. Like other crime organizations, The Triad dealt with illegal activities. Now I understood her connection to Calvin.

Were The Taipans working with The Trogyn? I couldn't help the thought.

The file wasn't complete, and I had more questions for Vivian when she was ready to share. How involved were her parents? Was that how she'd gotten her wounds? Did someone from The Triad do that to her? Who would dare injure the granddaughter of a leader?

His enemy.

Was she close to her grandfather? Why was she really in

Providence? It seemed like the woman sleeping on my couch carried a lot of dark secrets. I wanted to keep her safe.

I checked my email for anything pressing since I'd abandoned everything the moment she appeared on my doorstep. The email from the Medici Medallion Award committee reminded me to send in the name of the guest who would attend the event. I looked over at Vivian.

My phone buzzed with a text from Sylvia. She probably got the same email.

Sylvia: *We're going to the Medici together, right?*

Wasn't I clear the last time we spoke?

Arrow: *No.*

Sylvia: *Who are you going with?*

Arrow: *Not sure.*

I knew who I wanted to go with me, but I hadn't submitted a name yet.

Sylvia: *Why are you doing this?*

Arrow: *Doing what?*

Sylvia: *We're good together. My father loves you.*

Arrow: *We're not in a relationship.*

Sylvia: *I can wait.*

Arrow: *I'm seeing someone.*

Like I told you last time.

Sylvia: *Does she suck your cock the way I do?*

She got this way when she was drunk.

Arrow: *Are you drunk?*

Sylvia: *No. Two bottles of your wine don't do shit to me. Christ.*

Sylvia: *I'm touching myself while I think of you, handsome. (tongue emoji)*

Arrow: *Stop drinking. Gotta go.*

Sylvia: *I want your cock in me right now!*

A series of explicit demands followed, and I blocked her.

"What's wrong?" Vivian asked. "Why are you staring at your phone?"

I raked a hand through my hair, trying to shrug off the ridiculous conversation with Sylvia. I had no idea why I'd dated her.

"Nothing important. There's a blizzard slamming into Providence for the next forty-eight hours. Snow total is expected to be somewhere near two feet."

"What?" She shot up on the couch, the blanket and throw falling off her, revealing her naked body to me.

She glanced down, gasped, grabbed her clothes, and shoved them on quickly. "I need to leave *now*. Kaylee needs me."

I wasn't going to let her leave. If she had to, I'd do it with her. "Is she at home?" I asked.

"She's sleeping over at her friend's, who lives one floor below us."

"With Violet?"

Vivian nodded.

"Then you can call or text her. Let her know you're stuck at my place. Tell her to stay at Violet's."

"I can't do that—put Kaylee's life in someone else's hands."

I grinned at her protectiveness. "Aren't Violet and Kaylee good friends?"

"How do you know?"

"Because I run Whiz Kidz, remember? They're both in the program. Call Violet's mom. I'm sure she'd understand." I came over to sit next to her. "Besides, the city is shut down. Only essential workers may travel."

"I can't believe this. The meteorologist was wrong."

"That's one occupation where you can be wrong many times and still keep your job."

A small smile emerged on her lips, and she sighed. "I need to see." She walked over to the sliding door. "Wow. If I had known there would be a blizzard, I wouldn't be here."

"But God had other plans for us." I draped an arm around her shoulders. "He wanted you to come to my house tonight." I looked at her. "And I'm so glad you came."

Thunder boomed, and Vivian jumped at the sound.

I embraced her. "Thunder snow is something special."

Lightning flashed through the dark sky while snow whirled around from the howling wind. She relaxed in my embrace, but said nothing.

I pulled back and looked at her. "You came here tonight because you needed answers. I'll give them to you if you agree to one thing."

She arched an eyebrow. "Why is there an ultimatum for *my* questions?"

I smirked and shrugged. "Because I need a yes from you."

She narrowed her eyes. "Then I won't ask."

"Then you'll never know the reason. And you're dying to know."

"Do you want to duel about it?" she inquired.

"No. Because if we duel, I'll end up devouring you again."

She pouted. "Agree to what?"

"Date me."

Amusement gleamed in her eyes.

"You said you'd give me an answer when you're ready to date. We just did something that only couples do." I pressed my lips to hers. "Say yes and make me a fortunate man."

"That doesn't sound like a question."

I smiled. "Will you be my girlfriend, Tulip?"

She rose onto her toes. "I'm not sure where this relationship will go, but I'm willing to give it a chance. So yes."

I gave her a wet, loud, and sloppy kiss, and her stomach growled.

"Let's eat, and then I'll answer all your questions."

CHAPTER THIRTY-EIGHT

VIVIAN

I SAT at his kitchen table, which was smaller than the dining table. The turn of events baffled and excited me. I didn't come here this evening to end up being his girlfriend.

I glanced out the window where fat snowflakes covered the sky. "Can I help you with anything?"

"Nope. Just sit and watch me heat up food."

I smiled at his quick movements. He was warming up meat lasagna and Thai chicken basil fried rice.

I picked up my phone, texted Grace about being stuck at a friend's house because of the storm, apologized for the inconvenience, and asked if Kaylee could stay over until I got back. Grace responded immediately, telling me not to worry and that Violet was thrilled to spend more time with Kaylee.

Next, I texted Kaylee, who was probably asleep.

Vivian: *Hey, how you doing? I'm stuck at a friend's house, thanks to this blizzard. I'll see you on Monday when the roads are cleared and it's safe to drive. You can stay with Violet and Grace until I come back.*

Kaylee: *Okay. Where are you?*

Vivian: At Arrow's house.
Kaylee: Tell him I said hi!
Vivian: What are you doing up?
Kaylee: Watching a show with Violet. Going to bed soon though.
Vivian: Don't stay up too late.
Kaylee: Ok. Are you and Arrow dating?
Vivian: Yes.
Kaylee: Yay! Can I tell Violet?
Vivian: Okay. Good night.
Kaylee: Night. Love you!
Vivian: Love you too.

My heart warmed at her response.

"What are you smiling about?" Arrow placed down the steaming containers of food on the table. Then he got plates, utensils, and some napkins.

"Kaylee is thrilled we're dating. She's sharing the news with Violet."

He bent down and stole a kiss from me. "She knows I've had my eyes on you for a while. I always get what I want."

I rolled my eyes, and he laughed. "What do you want to drink? I have wine, tea, juice, and water."

"Water is fine, thanks."

He got me a glass of water and one for himself, then sat across from me.

"Thanks for the food." I scooped some lasagna and the fried rice onto his plate and some for me.

"You're welcome." He dug in, looking smug as he ate.

It felt oddly strange how comfortable it was being in his kitchen eating with him. My A Kiss is Not Enough mission popped into my head. I couldn't wait to share this news with the girls soon. For me, the mission wasn't complete yet.

It needed time to settle. Would his attraction to me fizzle out eventually? Or was he truly serious about this relationship?

I didn't know him well enough to determine anything yet. But I knew he made me feel alive, loved, and protected. Those were emotions I hadn't felt with any man in a while. I wasn't referring to parental love because my dad provided a safe haven for me growing up after that awful incident that killed my mom. This powerful affection Arrow showed me was different.

My dad would be elated to know I was dating again. Now, he could stop asking about it. He didn't like my previous boyfriend, Connor, whom I punched in the face when he put his hands on me in a drunken fit.

"I can see your mind going a million miles an hour. What are you thinking?" he asked as he spooned up some fried rice.

"Wondering if my dad will like you."

"What's there not to like?" He grinned. "When can I meet him? Isn't he retired now?"

"How do you know?" I arched an eyebrow.

"I know a lot of things about you. But I still have some questions."

"You looked into me?"

Why wasn't I surprised?

Because you also looked into him.

But my information was just stuff splashed on the internet. The information he retrieved was confidential.

I had a feeling it was going to be a long night of talking. But that would be okay because I wasn't going anywhere. I could sleep in tomorrow.

Crap. I only had the clothes on my back.

I looked up at him with embarrassment. "Do you have anything I can change into?"

"My T-shirt, sweatpants, and sweatshirt are on the chair in my bedroom for you."

I gaped at him. "How did you know I'd ask?"

He tapped his forehead. "Because it's logical. You're staying here for the next two days. You didn't bring clothes, so you need them. You also need a toothbrush, which I have."

I supposed a billionaire who ran a successful empire had to think ahead and anticipate his next step.

"You had a strategy with me, didn't you?"

He smirked. "Of course. Things worth having require strategy, patience, and the ability to pivot when necessary."

When we finished eating, I changed into his clothes, which were loose on me. I rolled up the sweatpants, and the T-shirt fell below my knees, as did the sweatshirt.

"You look cute. Come here." He opened his arms to me.

I sat down on his lap. "I have three questions for you."

"Hit me."

CHAPTER THIRTY-NINE

VIVIAN

"HOW DID you know I went for a walk that morning? I know you have access to the apartment building, but I wasn't anywhere close to it."

He told me what I'd already assumed. He had hacked into the city cameras.

"You broke the law."

"It's research, and no one got hurt." He pulled me closer. "Don't tell me you haven't broken the law either."

"Is there a person who hasn't broken some kind of law?"

Amusement gleamed in his eyes. "Wanna tell me what law you broke?"

"No. We're focused on you right now. So you created a scenario to walk with me in the early chilly morning?"

"Yes. Since you didn't want to date me, I *had* to create 'fated' moments for us to meet."

No man had gone through this much to be with me.

"Did you buy the building before we met?"

He smirked, and I knew the answer.

"Arrow, do you go around buying properties for no reason? Isn't that wasting money?"

"It wasn't for no reason. I was *investing* in the prime retail location and in you."

"But you didn't know I would date you."

"You're dating me now, aren't you? Everything in life is a gamble. If you want something, you need to take action and follow your gut."

I didn't know what to say.

"I checked out the area, and this location was perfect. I offered the retiring couple twice what it was worth at the time. The value has tripled since I purchased it because a new office and retail center is being built near your apartment." He touched the tip of my chin. "I always do things with purpose."

Emotions overwhelmed me, and I wasn't sure how to react.

"When I purchased the property, I gave it to my lawyer and team to manage it. I didn't start checking the camera until recently, Tulip. I don't have time to sit there and watch recordings of people coming in and out of a building."

"Is your brain tired?" I tapped his head.

"No." He smiled. "Remember how I opened the door for you at Sunshine in a Cup or how I cut the line to get you coffee and muffins at that first meeting with Calvin?"

I pinched the bridge of my nose, trying to follow all the things he'd done because of me. *So much.*

"Did you orchestrate the fire drill at Bella's Bistro?" I looked up at him.

"I didn't like Calvin having dinner with you. He's a dangerous man."

"But he had information about Aimee for me."

"Which was why I told the kids to give you guys half an hour before pulling the fire alarm."

"But it wasn't just that restaurant. It was the *entire* retail strip." I shook my head.

"I had to ensure he didn't take you to a different restaurant down the street."

The care he put into his plan amazed me. Scared me. With this kind of attention to detail, his enemies had no chance of defeating him.

I patted his cheek and pinched it lightly. "You're unbelievable. You could've gotten Dion, Raul, and Tim in trouble."

"Nah. They're smart kids from my program. How do you know them?"

"They're my patients." Well, Dion was, but I didn't elaborate on how I was introduced to Tim. I'd share that information later. "How did you persuade them to do that?"

"They didn't want to see me sad." His hands cupped my ass and squeezed. "I told them about this guy trying to steal my girlfriend from me."

"Seriously? Oh my God."

"Kaylee also knew my plan. She wanted me to be with my dream girl and didn't object."

"You sound like a crooked adult trying to sabotage innocent children."

"I never said I was a good guy. Besides, I'm teaching them about the real world." He grinned. "They're learning how to bend the rules without hurting anyone."

I covered my ears with my hands. "Stop corrupting kids."

"Oh, baby. I'm training them to survive in the real world. Academia can only go so far. Street smarts are just as important."

He was a brilliant and complex man who had somehow forced his way into my life with methodical steps.

"I never had a chance at avoiding you, did I?"

His eyes bored into mine, and my heart melted.

"I gave you the space you needed, but I made sure I was around enough so you wouldn't forget me. Your mind had to be filled with visions of *me*, especially when and if another man asks you out."

"I don't think there's anyone alive as persistent as you. Why did you start Whiz Kidz?"

"Because I wish I had a place like that to hang out when I was a kid."

"Kaylee said there are beds for kids to stay over."

"There are three floors with beds, a kitchen, and bathrooms. Like mini apartments." Sadness swam in his eyes. "Some kids just need a safe place to stay."

"Can you tell me about it?"

CHAPTER FORTY

ARROW

"HOW ABOUT WE TRADE STORIES?" I brushed a hand down her hair. "You tell me how you got your scars, and I'll tell you mine."

She nodded. "You go first."

She hopped off my lap and dropped onto the couch, snuggling against me like a kitten. I slung my arm around her, loving the intimacy. I could have stayed like this forever.

God, please let this storm last another week.

I was probably the only person in New England grateful for Nor'easter Betsy. Vivian yawned and pressed her face into my chest.

"It's past midnight. Do you want to go to bed first? We can talk tomorrow."

She bolted up. "No! I need to know *now*."

I smiled at her eagerness.

My heart raced. I'd never shared this with a girlfriend before.

"My mom died when I was young. She was sick, and my dad wasn't the best husband or father. He drank, and it affected his personality. When she died, it got worse. He became a monster, and I was his prey." I swallowed, reliving the first time he whipped me.

I told her about the leather belts, and she flinched.

"His work schedule differed each day, so I tried my best to avoid the times he was home. I stayed at Grayson's house or Royce's place whenever I could."

I told her about the time I fought back and blacked out.

Vivian's voice hitched, and she reached for my hand. She interlaced her fingers with mine, and that gesture comforted me more than she could ever know.

"Did you call the authorities?" she asked.

I shook my head. "No. I was too scared that they'd put me in foster care, which might have been even worse. My mom's friend, Pam, called the police, but he got out and was forced to attend AA meetings."

She sniffed, and I looked down to see her crying. "Baby, I'm okay." I reached for the box of tissues from the side table and offered her a tissue.

"You were all alone."

"It strengthened me." I took another tissue and dabbed her eyes, where tears kept flowing. No woman had cried for me except my mom and Pam.

My chest tightened at the raw emotion coming from Vivian. She must've understood the pain I'd endured. I could almost feel the misery releasing within me with the flow of her tears.

How was that possible?

"No more tears, okay?" I cupped her face, kissed her forehead, and placed the box of tissues in her lap, just in case.

"I can't help it." She sniffed.

"The day I blacked out was the last time he whipped me. I worked out, built some muscles, and got stronger to protect myself. But I avoided him as much as I could."

"And you joined the Navy right out of high school."

I nodded. "He'd gotten into trouble and then locked up. He reached out to me once to apologize." My throat tightened. "But words from my father seemed distant after so many years of neglect and pain. I didn't know what to think or say to him. In a deep part of me, I felt his sincerity. Or maybe it was just my secret wish."

"He probably sobered up in prison, and he realized what an ass he'd been."

"Maybe." He shrugged. "But then a few weeks later, someone found his body in a parking lot. He'd been robbed and shot multiple times. I had decided to leave the Navy because I needed a change. His death hastened my return. While I served in the Navy, I studied wine and statistics, two different subjects. When I got out, I analyzed data for companies while continuing my wine studies."

She stared at our joined hands. "Because of your father?"

"Partially. I was curious about alcohol and how it could affect a person. But I also wanted to know how it was created. What process did it have to undergo? What uses did it have? Wine is a science and art. I discovered it wasn't the alcohol's fault that turned people into monsters. We all have choices. The wine didn't ask us to overdrink. Anything to the extreme is bad."

"Like if you had sunny days every day, all the plant life would die. And then animals and humans would follow suit. We need the sun *and* the rain, right? Balance. Harmony."

I smiled at how her mind searched for straightforward answers.

"Alcohol could also be medicine."

"Yes." She squeezed my hand. "Three times a week, my dad drinks a small dose of wine his friend ferments to improve his health. It has all kinds of herbal stuff in it. It's an ancient practice. You know there's a kung fu style called the drunken fist where you mimic a drunken person's movement?" She demonstrated by moving her body in slow motion.

I laughed. "Not my preferred style."

"And did you know that back in the day, the kung fu masters used hand-to-hand touch to transfer good energy into another person's body for healing purposes?"

Nodding, I lifted our joined hands. "Holding your hand is like having the sun kiss my soul through your palm." He squeezed. "It's like a phone line from my heart to yours. We don't need to say anything. A simple squeeze of your hand tells me what I need to know."

"And what's that?"

"That we belong together."

Her face softened when she looked at our joined hands. "I knew a special man was lurking underneath the expensive suit on that day at the wine convention, but I didn't know he was also a poet until now." She caressed my face. "Thank you for sharing your story with me. It means a lot to me."

I kissed her head. "Thank you for wanting to hear it. Now it's your turn."

CHAPTER FORTY-ONE

VIVIAN

I GLANCED outside at the beautiful snowstorm keeping me here with him. This forced proximity was something I read in romance novels but never expected to experience. It wasn't just the storm—it was all the events leading up to this moment.

Did the heavens plan this evening? I couldn't help but think my mom had something to do with it. Perhaps she was watching over me and guided me to Arrow.

I looked at him, swallowed, and shared my past with him.

Wearing my new yellow shirt and pants, I sit at a table in the Lotus Flower Restaurant, waiting for my mom. She's in a meeting with Grandpa and the uncles. They're not my real uncles, but members of The Triad. Mom asked me to address them that way to show respect to the elders. They're all nice to me because Grandpa is their boss.

I see Calvin sitting at the opposite table, talking with two boys older than him. I only recognize Calvin because his dad works closely with Mom and Grandpa. I don't know him that well.

A man with a ponytail brings over a plate of dumplings for me. "You can snack on these. Food won't be served until later."

"Thank you." I grab a shrimp dumpling with the chopsticks and pop it into my mouth. The ponytail man also gives Calvin a plate.

None of my school friends know about my family's ties with The Triad. It's better that way. My mom is the daughter of a Triad lord, but she's been out of the crime organization since she married Dad. Mom is now happy working as Dad's office manager at his dental office.

I don't like coming to New York, where Grandpa does his business, but today was his restaurant's grand opening. Mom wants to visit her father and show her support. My dad is at a dental conference, so he can't make it.

The restaurant workers speak Cantonese as they rush around, ensuring the red tablecloths are perfect with all the plates, cups, chopsticks, and utensils. I can understand Cantonese and Vietnamese because my dad made me go to Vietnamese school. Mom can't speak it.

I text Dad on my new phone, which I got for my twelfth birthday last week.

Vivian: Miss you, *Ba!*

Daddy: Ditto.

Daddy: Gotta go, pumpkin. Giving a speech in 10 mins. Be good.

Vivian: Okay. Love you.

Daddy: Love you too.

I can't wait to return to California. Daddy is taking me

fishing at the lake. We found a cool nook, and I caught a bunch of trout and bass last time.

Smiling, I tuck my phone in the back pocket of my pants and look at the restaurant menu. My stomach growls when I see that the ginger lobster is gonna be served.

"Hi, Vivian!"

I glance up and smile. "Hi, Uncle Ghost."

That's his nickname, and I don't know why they call him that. Maybe it's because of his pale skin.

"You busy?" he asks.

"No."

"Wanna see my new puppy?"

I gasp with excitement. "Where? What's the puppy's name?"

I've always wanted a puppy or a kitten, but Dad is allergic to them.

"It's just next door to the restaurant." He grips the chair beside me.

I see a tattoo of a clown's face on his middle finger.

He wiggles his fingers. "Clowns are cool."

"No, they're not. They're ugly and scary." I don't know anyone who likes clowns except this weird kid in my class who's been diagnosed with some mental disorder.

"Clowns just wear makeup. Like a silly mask." He looks at his watch. "Dinner will start soon. Let's go."

I rise from my seat. "What kind of dog did you get?"

"Chow Chow mix. Can you help me name it?"

"Yes, please!" I glance toward the room where Mom is. "Should I go tell her where we're going?"

"No. You don't want to interrupt them. They're having a very important meeting about money." He takes out his phone. "I'll send Fat Dumpling a message and ask him to inform your mom. He's in there too."

"Okay, thanks." My mom is super smart and has an excellent memory. She's probably helping Grandpa with accounting stuff right now.

I follow him out of the restaurant and into the building next door. Ghost opens the back door and lets me go in first.

He goes down a hallway and opens another door. "The puppy's in here."

I enter, and Ghost flicks on the lights before entering a smaller room, probably to get the puppy. I glance around the space. It's full of weapons—guns, knives, and other scary tools I don't want to look at. I don't think my mom would want me here.

Something feels wrong. Why can't I hear the puppy?

"Does Grandpa own this building too?" I ask.

"Not for long." The bitter tone makes goosebumps rise on my arms.

I'm about to turn around when something burns my back. I scream in pain and stumble to the floor.

"You little shit. Tell me where your mom is hiding the key." He's holding a branding iron. I recognize it from a show I saw on woodworking with my parents. "Tell me!" he shouts.

"I don't know what you're talking about!"

Wearing a horrific clown mask, he comes closer. "Liar. Your mom has the key to millions of dollars that belong to everyone in The Triad. The bitch is keeping it to herself. Tell me, and I won't hurt you."

He's lying. My back hurts so much. He's going to kill me. I shouldn't have come here. I kick him, push myself up, and race toward the door.

"Help me! Mommy!" I scream for my life.

As I reach the door, another searing pain stabs my back. My skin sizzles, making this awful sound and smell. He cackles from behind me. I hate him. I want to use a weapon on him too.

He presses the iron tool harder, and I see stars. I think I'm going to die.

Mommy, Daddy.

My body trembles as I collapse onto the floor.

"Little bitch! You think you can run from me? Nobody runs from Ghost!" He walks over to a counter, drops the iron tool with a clank, and grabs a whip.

I can't move. I'm so weak. My skin burns. What if I don't get to see my mom or dad again? Tears blur my vision. Why is Ghost doing this? I don't understand.

Ghost whips the floor twice, and I flinch. The sound terrifies me. He comes closer, and I gather my strength to crawl away.

I scream as the whip lands on my back, hitting the sore spots.

"This is how we punish our enemies," he seethes.

I want to tell him I'm not his enemy, but I'm in too much pain. He whips me a few more times, then he stops. I hear noises and glance over to see him grabbing a container.

The door bursts open, and Mom runs to me. "Vivian!"

Tears rush down my face. "Mom . . ." I'm in too much pain to say more.

She gathers me into her arms. "What the fuck is wrong with you?" She glares at Ghost.

"Tell me where the key is."

"What key?"

"The key to all the gold and cash! You think I'm stupid?"

He comes closer, bringing the plastic container. "I heard you talking to King Viper! Don't lie to me."

"My father is going to kill you."

Ghost approaches. "If he catches me."

Up close, I see the word acid on the container. I don't know where I get the strength, but I tug at my mom's arm.

"Mom! Go!" I don't want her to get hurt.

"No! Stop!" she shouts. She struggles with him, throwing her body over mine.

My mom's painful screams seep into me. My body shakes as though her scream is inside me.

"Fuck!" Ghost wails, holding his bleeding head with one hand. He got acid on his face and neck.

Calvin stands nearby, looking scared but holding the branding iron with a shaky hand. Voices erupt, and he drops the iron to the ground.

Ghost runs off.

"They're in here!" Calvin shouts.

My mom lies beside me, trembling. The acid is all over her face and body. Blood streams down her face because her flesh is melting. I've never seen skin melt like that. I cry because it's all my fault.

Scooting closer, I want to hold her, but I'm scared I might hurt her. Her eyes meet mine, and I know she's dying.

I choke out. "Sorry, Mommy."

Her eyes flutter closed. I'm so scared. I try to push myself into a sitting position, but fall back. Calvin comes to help me, and I pass out in his arms.

I didn't realize I'd used up an entire box of tissues until Arrow placed two more beside me. My voice hitched as I calmed myself. Embarrassment surfaced, and I looked away from him.

"Don't turn away from me." He gripped my chin gently, lifting it to meet his eyes. "I want to see this beautiful face."

"I'm a mess, Arrow." I tried to wriggle free.

He embraced me with his powerful arms, pressing his forehead against mine. "The most beautiful mess I've ever seen." He kissed my forehead. "Let everything out. Let it go. You'll feel better."

"I just did."

"No one will ever hurt you like that again. *Ever*," he whispered as if he were talking to himself.

I didn't realize how much pain and tension I'd been holding in until now. Seeing my mom's face as she died was the most horrific thing I'd ever experienced. From that day onward, I had retreated into myself, never fully allowing myself to experience joy again.

"It's not your fault that your mom died."

I choked at how he could read me so well. More tears flowed down my face, probably making a mess of my makeup, but I didn't care.

"Everything would've been fine if I had just stayed at the restaurant."

He looked me in the eyes. "He would've found another way to hurt you."

"Probably," I said, completely drained of energy.

"How long were you in the hospital?"

"Two weeks." I paused, remembering the overwhelming pain and grief after the adrenaline had died down. "When I returned to California, my dad's friend—Aimee's father—took extra care of me. He's a doctor at the hospital. Let's just say I had too many visits."

I pressed my face into his chest, inhaling his musky scent that reminded me of a massive sequoia: big, tall, sturdy, and strong. When I was younger, I loved spending time in the forest. Being surrounded by all the giant trees made me feel safe and at peace. Arrow had given me back that forgotten feeling.

Silence filled the room, and there was no awkwardness. I didn't feel the need to say anything. Arrow was giving me the space I needed to recuperate.

After a moment, I asked, "What are you thinking?"

"That I should be nicer to Calvin now."

Warmth blossomed inside me. "He saved me."

"What happened to Ghost?"

"He's dead. But it took a while to catch him."

"How's your dad's relationship with your grandfather?"

"They disliked each other because of my mom. Grandpa blamed my dad for taking his daughter away from him—away from The Triad—which caused a rift between some of the members. Dad blamed Grandpa for putting his wife in danger by leading a crime organization. Despite that, they remained cordial because of me."

More conversations flowed between the two of us for another hour. He had so many questions. With each answer I gave, I felt lighter and eventually drifted off to sleep.

CHAPTER FORTY-TWO

ARROW

I CARRIED her to my bed and tucked her in. She looked peaceful, and I knew part of that was the release of her horrendous story to me.

A hurricane of emotion stirred in me as I tried to figure out if Ghost was who I thought he was. I remembered seeing a clown tattoo on a man's middle finger once. How did Vivian know he was truly dead? What did Calvin know about Ghost? I needed to talk to Calvin.

My attitude toward Calvin had changed since the story. He'd been there on that awful day and had saved her for me. But that didn't mean I wasn't cautious of his intentions with my woman. He'd been a boy then, but now he was a man. And any man who looked at her would want her.

Externally, Vivian didn't appear weak or vulnerable. She could fight like a warrior. But tonight, I saw a part of her that still needed to be nurtured and protected.

She was still hurting about her mom's death and blaming herself for it.

After washing up, I slid into bed beside her, took her hand in mine, and fell asleep.

CHAPTER FORTY-THREE

VIVIAN

I WOKE to a delicious aroma filling the room, making me hungry. Sprawled across his massive bed, I ran my hands over the smooth sheets. The sheets on his side looked crumpled. I smiled at the thought of him sleeping beside me.

I took a moment to let yesterday's events sink in. I'd come to his house, dueled with him, fucked him, shared my past with him, cried like a fool to him, and slept in his bed. That was a lot of major changes in one day.

Feeling refreshed and energized, I walked into the bathroom, washed up with the new electronic toothbrush he'd left out for me, and took a quick hot shower. The hot steam relaxed me even more. After that, I used the unopened facial cleanser he had on the counter to remove my makeup as best I could. I got dressed in the same pants he'd given me, but no underwear.

I walked into the kitchen to find him standing at the stove wearing an apron that looked brand new.

"Good morning." I stood beside him as he used the tongs to transfer pieces of burned bacon onto the white plate.

"Morning, beautiful. How did you sleep?"

"Great, thanks. You?"

"Best sleep I've ever had." He smiled.

"What are you doing?" I gestured to his apron, the tongs, and the skillet.

"Making you breakfast." He looked so serious, it was cute.

I crossed my arms, staring at him. "I thought you didn't cook."

"I don't. But I'm making an exception for you." He bent down and stole a kiss. "*Watch* this carefully."

I studied how he used the tongs to take a breakfast sausage from the pack and place it on the skillet. He continued the process until all the sausages were in the pan. They sizzled, and he turned to me with a goofy grin.

"Okay." I laughed, not understanding his silly request. "You wanted me to watch how you put sausages in a skillet?"

"Yes. Pay attention to the *sound* the sausage makes when it touches the skillet. I want you to remember this wonderful sizzling sound. Listen to it."

He turned the sausage carefully, as though they were precious, and looked at me to ensure I was watching him. His expression was unforgettable. This was a billionaire who ran a successful wine empire, and here he was, all serious about the sizzling sound of a breakfast sausage. I couldn't help it anymore and burst out laughing.

"What are you trying to do?" I placed a hand on his back.

He sighed. "I want you to replace the awful sizzling sound embedded in your mind with this new association—*me* making breakfast for *you*. I've never done this for anyone, so consider it a miracle."

Time stopped for a moment. My heart quivered and

swelled at the realization of what he was doing. I stared at him while he fidgeted with the sausages, almost dropping them on the floor. The horror on his face amused and touched me.

No man had been this thoughtful or taken this much effort to ensure I was healing properly.

I wrapped my arms around him. "Thank you." I squeezed him tighter. "Thank you for thinking of me. And for listening and remembering our conversation last night."

Everything had poured out of me until I was left drained and fell into a deep sleep. I told him about my discomfort with the sizzling sound because it reminded me of the iron burning my skin.

"I think about you all the time."

I smiled into his back and took his hand in mine. "You're my charger too." I swung our joined hands back and forth.

Something serious emerged in his eyes. "Have you ever wanted to remove those scars on your back? There's advanced technology that can repair damaged skin."

I didn't know why, but insecurity bloomed within me, reminding me of my ex. "Does it bother you?"

"No, Tulip." He sighed. "That's not what I meant. You're *perfect* for me. But I just wonder if you've considered repairing them for *yourself*. Not anyone else."

There he was again. The man who could see beyond the norm. The man who was always prepared. I should be used to him by now.

I hadn't attended many social events because I didn't want to wear any dresses that would reveal my back. There weren't a lot of pretty dresses with a well-covered back.

"I didn't see the need to back then. But maybe someday

I'd like to wear a low-cut dress at the back or a bikini for you."

His eyes warmed. "Whenever you're ready, let me know. I know of someone who's excellent at skin reconstruction."

I nodded, appreciating his thoughtfulness. "I've never wanted to remove them because they remind me of the pain. Sometimes, I look at people and wonder what kind of pain they've endured and where it's hidden. Everyone has pain somewhere."

"Pain is pain. We can't measure it. Pain eats at our soul. But *you* gave me a piece of my soul back by sharing your story with me."

I didn't know what to say to that. He always seemed to say all the right things.

"You're the first person to understand me so well."

"Let's keep it that way. I want you all to myself."

After breakfast, I helped him clean the dishes. It was too early to check up on Kaylee, who was probably still sleeping. Snow had covered the backyard like a large, soft blanket. There was something beautiful and peaceful about watching the snow fall. I imagined some goddess in the sky, sprinkling snowflakes everywhere as she flew around.

What if each snowflake was a blessing in disguise? Life was too hectic for people to consider that concept. Everyone was so busy trying to get things done that they missed the beauty around them.

If I hadn't been stuck here with Arrow, I wouldn't have been staring at the snow and wondering about this. I would have been checking my dental calendar, continuing my research about Aimee, trying to get dinner ready for Kaylee, and so forth.

"I want to show you something." Arrow led me into his

office, slid into his leather office chair, and pulled me onto his lap. "Let me know if you recognize this person."

He opened a file and clicked on an image of an Asian man. The man appeared to be in his early fifties. I didn't recognize him, though his eyes seemed familiar, but I wasn't sure.

"Who is he?"

"His name is James Chin. He worked at my warehouse in Texas and stole a large supply of my Bambooze. He also destroyed a portion of the warehouse. A third-shift worker had gone to the bathroom, stayed past his shift, and noticed. The entire warehouse would have been destroyed if he hadn't been there."

"Did anyone get hurt?"

"No. But we discovered a dead body hidden underneath the floor of his office."

"Do you know who it is?"

"Forensics showed it was a male, and he had died about three years ago. They're trying to get a DNA match, but I haven't heard any updates yet."

"You think James is part of The Triad?"

Arrow's eye twitched. "I think he's Ghost."

My entire body tensed. "What? That's impossible." I inhaled a deep breath. "He's dead."

"How do you know for sure? James Chin also had a clown tattoo on his middle finger before he covered it with a new skull tattoo."

"Calvin said the body was tossed into the sea." I glanced at James's face again. "He doesn't look like Ghost."

"Advancement in plastic surgery can do wonders to a person's features."

The acid had gotten onto his face the day he'd attacked me and my mom.

Fear twisted in my stomach at the possibility that he was still alive. Had Calvin seen Ghost's dead body? Or had someone also lied to him?

"We have to ask Calvin."

"There's a lot to do when this storm settles." He took my hand in his.

I could tell he wanted to comfort me because of this sudden news. It had rocked me like an earthquake. All the emotions I'd tucked away on my emotional shelf collapsed. If Ghost were still alive, there was no doubt he'd be after me.

"I debated telling you this later, but I think it's better for you to know now."

"Thank you. I appreciate it."

"You mentioned that Ghost believed your mom had a key to something? Did you ever find out what that was?"

"No. Grandpa thinks his enemy gave Ghost false information, trying to stir up trouble within The Taipans. Mom left The Triad when she married, so she wasn't involved with their business."

"Does your father know anything?"

"I asked him once. He said Mom never mentioned anything to him." I blew out a breath. "I searched through her things, but came up with nothing. Maybe it wouldn't hurt to search once more."

"It's a good idea."

"Do you want to come with me? A pair of fresh eyes might help me see something I missed. I have my mom's stuff at my place in California."

"I'd love to join you."

A memory surfaced, and I gasped. "I saw a man with a

clown mask on the day of the grand reopening of Ormon's Restaurant. You were there with Sylvia."

"The fucker has been watching you." A muscle twitched in his jaw, and his eyes flashed with a deadly calm. His grim expression made me wonder what he would do to Ghost once he found him. "I want you and Kaylee to move in with me."

"Why?"

"Because it's safer here." A crease formed between his brows. "I have three security systems. One of them isn't sold to the public. I got it from a friend in the military."

"Is that why your house is so isolated compared to the others?" I rubbed the crease gently with my fingers.

The tension in his face softened. "Yes."

I swallowed, unsure of what to do. My relationship with him had just started, and I didn't want to become a burden. It was too soon to move in, even though this was a rare situation.

"It is not an inconvenience for me."

"How do you know what I'm thinking?"

"I've wanted you for a long time, Tulip. I *know* your expressions." He tugged at my hair. "Besides, it's a logical thought process of cause and effect—a natural response to my request."

"Sounds more like a demand to me."

"I just want you and Kaylee safe. She could also be a target because of you."

Shit. Why didn't I think of that?

Because your mind has been crammed with too many things lately.

Was there something else I wasn't seeing?

"You're making it hard for me to decline," I said.

"If you decline, you'll break my heart." He pressed a hand to his chest, trying to look like he was in pain. "Please don't break my heart."

His serious expression transformed into one of amusement and warmth. I loved that I got to see so many sides of him. How many more were there?

"Will you make me and Kaylee breakfast every day?" I teased.

"Okay."

"Really? Don't make promises you can't keep."

"I can order a bunch of breakfast food and put it on nice plates for you and Kaylee. That can be defined as 'making' breakfast." He smirked.

I rolled my eyes.

"Humor aside, you should also be careful at your office. We don't know what he's up to."

My phone buzzed from inside the sweatshirt pocket.

"It's Kaylee," I told him.

"Tell her I said hello."

I got off his lap and dropped into the big chair in the seating area.

Kaylee: *Can we invite Arrow to join us for Christmas?*

Vivian: *Why the sudden invitation?*

Kaylee: *Violet is going away with her mom and her mom's boyfriend for the holidays. Arrow spent it alone last year.*

My heart sank. I'd spent Christmas with Dad and Kaylee.

Vivian: *Sure.*

Kaylee: *Cool! Thanks. (smile emoji)*

We texted for a few more minutes, catching up. She planned to watch TV, play board games, and work on arts and crafts. Grace was making spaghetti for lunch and pizza for dinner. Kaylee sounded like she was having a good time. Most likely school would be canceled on Monday. I'd keep an eye out for a call or a text from the school board on Sunday.

I emailed my team, informing them that the office would be closed on Monday because of inclement weather. Allison would call all the patients to reschedule. No one was going to trek out for a dentist appointment in this kind of weather. The city needed time to clear the streets and sidewalks. I didn't mind the extra time to absorb everything I'd discovered.

I sat in the chair and watched Arrow work on his computer. His fingers flew across the keyboard. He paused a moment, and his lips formed a slight pout as he pondered something. My heart swelled as I remembered his attempt at breakfast. The burned bacon and sausages were the best breakfast I'd ever had.

When I'd seen him standing at the stove, my curiosity had been piqued. I hadn't even registered the sizzling sound. The smell of bacon and the sight of him with the apron over-whelmed everything else. My body usually shivered when-ever I heard a sizzling noise or a brief hiss. But it hadn't today.

Fear usually made everything worse, and my active imag-ination didn't help. For so many years, the sounds of sizzling bacon and sausages were like the quick jab of a branding iron. But that horrible association had been replaced by something sacred and beautiful today. He'd given me a price-less gift.

My chest tightened as I considered this powerful emotion stirring inside me.

I got up from the chair and walked over to him. He extended an arm, welcoming me back onto his lap.

"Would you like to spend Christmas with us?" I asked.

His face beamed. "I think the question should be: would you and Kaylee like to plan the Christmas party at my house?"

"Christmas is in two weeks. You want us to move in before that?"

"Your safety is paramount. We can't postpone that." He played with a strand of my hair. "As soon as the storm's over, we're packing. I'll have a team of movers to assist you."

I held up a hand. "Hold on a minute. This is temporary, Arrow. Kaylee and I only need our clothes and some essentials. We don't need movers—we're not moving furniture."

What was he thinking?

He considered my comment for a moment. "Fine."

"Let me remind you that you own my apartment building. So it should be safe."

"It needs a security update. The current system can easily be hacked by those who know how."

CHAPTER FORTY-FOUR

VIVIAN

A WEEK AFTER THE STORM, I drove to Providence Place for holiday shopping. Kaylee was invited to join Violet and her mom for shopping at Copley Place in Boston. Sixty percent of the snow had already melted, leaving the city streets flooded. But no one cared because the rare warm weather left everyone in a good mood. Anything but another blizzard.

My mood wasn't as cheerful though. It was a mixture of fear, worry, and the warning blooming in my heart. Everywhere I went, I was extra cautious. What if Ghost was watching me?

I had tried to make a timeline of his life after he'd murdered my mom. He probably went into hiding and then got a job working at Arrow's warehouse. But now he was in Providence. How long had he been here? Had he been watching me when I was in California? If he'd wanted to kill me, he could've easily done so when I thought he was dead.

Or had he moved on and was now working for someone else? Maybe he was a psycho working for himself.

Stop overanalyzing.

I should stop scaring myself by imagining scenarios that weren't beneficial to my mental state. I needed to clear my head to attend to Kaylee, my patients, and my boyfriend. He was my safety raft when I was too tired to keep swimming. Not only was he helping me find Aimee, but he was also trying to protect me from Ghost, who was his former employee. Arrow's stress level must have increased exponentially.

Calvin wasn't able to meet us until he returned from Hong Kong. Neither of us wanted to have the important conversation over the phone. Arrow and I had made a trip to Boston two days ago. We'd visited several shops in Chinatown, asking people if they'd seen Aimee. I'd showed them a couple of pictures of her, but no one had seen her. We also stopped by the Boston Children's Museum. Arrow knew someone on the Board of Directors who could assist us with the security recordings, but he wasn't around that day.

Today, Arrow stopped at the museum before his flight to Texas to check on his bamboo winery, which I planned to visit soon. He'd made an appointment to meet his friend, who had allowed him into the security office to review the surveillance footage. I hadn't heard from him yet.

This man was doing so much for me, and I didn't know what to get him for Christmas. What did you give someone who already had everything?

I parked my car in the garage and headed to the shops. The other day, Arrow asked me to accompany him to the wine competition in Monaco. From all the images he'd shown me from past events, this would be the most extravagant banquet I'd ever been to. I needed a dress to match it. But that could come after the Christmas gifts.

People were out and about carrying multiple shopping bags. All the stores had some kind of sale going on. I spotted a booth selling Sanrio characters, including Hello Kitty, Keroppi, Pompompurin, Cinnamoroll, and a bunch of others. I had no idea why Kuromi—the bunny wearing a black jester's hat and the devil's tail—was her favorite.

I was never into these characters and lost interest in many things after my severe injuries.

The only things that interested me were the outdoors, fishing, and practicing martial arts. I wanted to defend myself and my dad if anyone ever attacked us. The only girly thing I did was read romance novels or watch romantic movies.

Seeing all the stuffed animals made me think of Aimee. She would love these Sanrio toys and all the cute stationery. She should be home with her parents preparing for Christmas. How was she coping? Had she gotten thinner? Was she warm enough? My stomach twisted just thinking of all the crazy scenarios running through my mind.

I walked up to the girl wearing a Hello Kitty shirt. "Excuse me. Do you have more Kuromi plushies?"

She held up a finger. "Yup! Let me open up a box for you. My coworker called in sick today, so I'm managing two booths." She gestured to another booth that sold anime products.

"Great, thanks."

I purchased a Kuromi plushie Kaylee didn't have, two T-shirts, a stationery set, and matching pens.

Getting thirsty, I entered the Bubble Tea shop and got a sugar cane drink and a little pastry. The indoor seating was taken up, so I went out to look for a seat along the outside. A woman sat at a table working on her tablet. I took the empty table that gave me a view of the Sanrio booth.

Two minutes later, a strange energy entered my space. Having studied kung fu for so long, I could sense energy well. My body stiffened as this erratic energy intruded my space.

"Mind if I sit down?" A woman with a mean face pulled a chair from a nearby table and sat across from me. She had a nose ring, and she was built like a tank.

"Actually, I do mind."

"Too bad." Another woman with colorful hair sat down next to me. She surveyed me with glazed eyes. "You pissed off some people, sweetheart."

"You have the wrong person." I didn't know what she was talking about.

"This you?" She showed me a picture of me and Kaylee standing on the sidewalk a week ago.

Fear and anger collided in me.

"Who are you? What do you want?"

"Stay away from Arrow."

Confusion tugged at me. "Why?"

"You're making him lose a lot of money," said Mean Face.

"He's not himself because of you," said Rainbow Hair.

Irritation flared. "I'm not his financial advisor or his shrink."

Who sent these women? Was Arrow losing money because of me?

"Leave him." Rainbow Hair's voice grew louder, and the passersby glanced our way.

"We're not chained together at the hip." This was ridiculous.

I glared at them and got up to leave.

Mean Face shot out of her seat and yanked at my hair. I dropped the shopping bags and my purse to defend myself. I clasped her arm with one hand, punched her in the face, and kicked her in the leg.

Anger and adrenaline soared in me. Who were these bitches?

Mean Face fell back a few steps, wiped her mouth, and spat out blood on the floor. "The fuck!? She knocked out my tooth!"

Rainbow Hair stepped on Kaylee's gift bag, igniting a new fury in me.

Until now, I'd never had to use my martial arts skills in a public place. I'd never been attacked like this. But I didn't have time to contemplate. Both women charged at me, and a battle erupted in the mall.

They were likely high on something, but that wasn't an excuse for me to be lenient with them. I gave them what they deserved—fists to their faces, punches to their shoulders, and kicks to their legs.

They screamed in pain, but continued to attack me. A crowd surrounded us.

Rainbow Hair threw a fist at me, and I gripped her arm, twisting it. Mean Face limped to the side. The pain on her face made me extremely happy.

My neck stung. Rainbow Hair must've scratched me with her long, ugly nails.

"Tie her up!" An old man tossed me a new tie with the tag still on it.

"Everyone, back away!" Two security guards arrived.

I released Rainbow Hair to them. "They're together." I

pointed to Mean Face. "They attacked me out of the blue, and I want to press charges."

I didn't have to say anything. Witnesses began offering their versions of the event. The EMT confirmed they'd been drinking and were on drugs.

After speaking with the police, I replaced some of Kaylee's gifts and headed home.

What a shitty day. I was so pissed. Who had sent them after me?

"Excuse me," said the woman who sat next to me. She had a pretty face with wavy brown hair and sharp eyes. "Are you okay?" She gestured to my neck. "You have a scratch."

I didn't need to see the EMT for a minor scratch. "I'm more angry than hurt. Thanks for asking."

"It's a good thing you know self-defense. I would've been bruised all over. My name is Elena Sanchez, and I'm a journalist for the local news station."

"Vivian Vo. It's nice to meet you."

She smiled. "I also run an online newspaper called the Musepaper that empowers women and shares inspiring news. I would love to interview you for a write-up on women defending themselves. Not right now, of course." She gave me her card. "Whenever you're ready. People need to hear good news. People need to be inspired these days. There's too much bad stuff out there."

I took her card and placed it in my purse. "Thanks. I'll think about it."

"Brace yourself for your fifteen minutes of fame," she said.

"What do you mean?"

"People were recording the incident on their phones.

You know how social media can twist things around. It could also go viral."

Shit. I didn't want this to affect my dental practice.

"Thanks for the warning."

As I got into my car, my phone rang with Kaylee's name flashing across the screen. Several text messages came from my friends' group chat.

I picked up the call. "Hi, Kaylee."

"Was that you fighting those women?"

"Did it look like me?"

"I recognized you even though your face wasn't clear. It was your snake and crane stances. Who the hell were those women?"

"Language."

"Sorry. But I'm so mad!"

Warmth bloomed in my chest.

"I'm not hurt."

"Yeah, but you could've been." She huffed. "If I'd been there, I would've kicked their asses . . . I mean butts."

"You don't know self-defense yet."

"But I will. Ugh! I'm soooo mad."

I could imagine her face turning red. It felt nice to have a little sister wanting to defend me.

My anger subsided. "They were on drugs, and the police got them. So it's all good." I frowned. "Where's Violet?"

"Violet went to the bathroom. Her mom got roped into talking to some lady trying to sell lotion. I'm sitting in the massage chair browsing the internet. The fight has over a million views already on Real Rumors!"

Kids these days spent too much time on social media. "Don't believe everything you see or read online."

"I know, but this time it's real. And you were attacked." Her voice softened.

"I'm fine. Those women will be in a lot of pain."

I heard Violet say something in the background.

"Gotta go," said Kaylee. "Chat later. Love you!"

I stared at my friends' messages. I needed to get home, shower, and gather myself before I could reply to them.

CHAPTER FORTY-FIVE

ARROW

AFTER A MEETING with my team at the winery and reviewing the shipment that would be sent to Monaco for the wine competition, I hopped onto a flight to Hong Kong to meet with Calvin.

I had requested to meet him, and he'd agreed. I didn't have time to wait for him to return to Providence. A major storm was brewing, and I needed information regarding Ghost.

Yesterday, I had briefed my boys about Ghost. I wasn't sure if The Triad was behind Ghost's wine thievery. The Taipans had their own wine label, but that didn't mean they would try to sabotage my business. The business world could be ruthless, forcing one business to commit crimes against its competitor. And crimes were something The Triad was used to.

I walked into a small restaurant near my hotel. Through the crowd, Calvin spotted me and waved me over. All the tables were taken, making the restaurant lively. The restaurant was probably owned by The Triad, with an illegal gambling den in the basement or somewhere close by.

"I ordered some food for you." Calvin gestured to the seat across from him. He wore a sleek black suit, looking like a businessman ready to close a multimillion-dollar deal.

I pulled out a chair, folding myself into it. The ten dishes of food on the table looked fantastic. "Wow. Thanks. Everything smells fantastic."

"That's because it is. Authentic Chinese food is different from the kind you eat in Providence. Want a drink?"

A cup of jasmine tea and a glass of water were already set for me. "I'm good with these. Thanks for meeting me."

"I didn't do it for you."

"Thanks for meeting me because of Vivian—*my girlfriend.*" I smiled.

He smirked. "Help yourself."

After we ate, I placed my chopsticks down and said, "I don't think Ghost is dead."

His jaw tightened. "I know."

"But you told Vivian otherwise."

"That's what I was told." He pressed his lips into a tight line. "I thought he was dead too. I never saw the body though."

"Who told you?"

"His dad, Rattlesnake." He refilled his teacup and mine. "But he died two months ago."

That couldn't be a coincidence. Vivian's grandfather had died months ago, and now another prominent official. I could only imagine the chaos within The Triad right now.

"How did Vivian's grandfather die?" I asked, trying to connect all the dots.

Calvin looked at me. "It's safer for you to stay out of our

business. You stay on your turf, and I'll stay on mine. This is the only way our relationship will work."

"I'm trying to protect my girlfriend. Right now, she thinks her grandfather died of natural causes. She doesn't need any more stress. If you discover something, give me the courtesy to let her know gently."

Calvin studied me for a moment and nodded. "Someone had been skimming money from our businesses. One of our guys recognized the clown tattoo on his middle finger. But his face had changed."

I showed him a picture of Ghost from my phone. "That's what he looked like when he was working at my warehouse. He stole my wine shipment and sold it to the black market."

Calvin scratched his chin as he stared at the image. "He wasn't working on The Triad's orders, if that's what you're thinking. We're proud of our wine. We don't need to steal from anyone."

Next, I gave him the name of the man whose dead body was discovered inside Ghost's office at my warehouse. "Do you recognize Kevin Seeto?"

Calvin cursed, and the people at the nearby tables glanced over. "He was sent to Texas for business, but never came back. We thought he took our money and ran. We've been looking for him. Ghost also killed him and probably took the money. I'm going to rip this fucker apart!"

I shared my suspicions that Ghost's father had betrayed Vivian's grandfather by letting his son go instead of killing him.

Calvin smiled. "Let's just say that I'm dealing with the issue. The Taipans are my family—my home. It was also my father's home before he passed away from cancer. Ghost killed several members of our family. I *will* get answers."

Even if I didn't get to Ghost, The Triad would.

"Please tell Vivian I'm sorry I wasn't able to get Aimee back to her."

"What do you mean? I thought you spotted Aimee in Boston recently."

"I did." He pursed his lips. "But I just found out that a rogue member kidnapped Aimee because he wanted to replicate what Vivian's mom used to do for The Triad." He tapped his head. "Brilliant with math and an excellent memory. She could memorize confidential info and use it for blackmail."

My jaw tensed. "You into hurting children?"

"No. When I found out, I rushed to his apartment, but someone had broken into it. Evidence showed there were two girls living there. I was too late. He'd been dead for a while when I found him."

"*Fuck.*"

Who had taken them? Another triad member? The Triad's enemy? There were many sick people in this world, and I prayed that Aimee and the other girl were safe.

"The apartment was in Boston, so I scoured the area, but there was no sign of her. She could be anywhere now."

"I checked the recordings from the Boston Children's Museum, but didn't see anyone resembling Aimee. Why would this new kidnapper take her around in public if he had just taken her from someone else?" I thought out loud and looked at Calvin. "The body of a little girl was found in Providence recently. Is that your member's work?"

"He's not that thoughtful. Whoever left that girl's body did it with care. She had a blanket around her. She was dropped off at a busy location where someone would find her quickly. It's someone else's work."

Could this be the work of The Trogyn? A headache bloomed, and I wanted Vivian and my bed.

"Have you heard of The Trogyn?" I asked.

"I have."

"Are you associated with them?"

"My only family is The Taipans, okay?"

That was all I needed to know.

"Let me get this." I reached for my wallet when the waiter came to refill our water.

"No. You're my guest. It's on the house." The corners of his lips lifted. "I'd appreciate it if you stopped pulling the fire alarms whenever I'm at a restaurant. It's annoying."

I laughed. "Only if you're not having it with the woman I love."

Love.

Shit.

The sacred word flew out so casually. So naturally.

Calvin arched an eyebrow, and amusement flickered in his eyes. "Understood."

That subject was dropped, and we moved on to another discussion. After thirty minutes, I thanked Calvin for dinner. We mutually agreed that we would keep out of each other's business. But if I discovered his crime organization was involved with hurting children, I would do everything in my power to destroy him and The Triad.

His response was a smile and a "Good night."

I couldn't tell if there were any underlying messages. What mattered was that my statement was clear as day.

I strode back to my hotel, shook off my suit jacket, and dropped into the chair, letting my conversation with Calvin sink in. But I couldn't concentrate on anything except what I'd admitted to an acquaintance over dinner.

What had been an infatuation had turned into a thorough analysis of my heart. The hinges on my closed heart had creaked when I first met her. Not only had Vivian opened the door and entered my heart space, but she had filled it with her smile, her scent, her pain, her strength, and her ability to heal me.

For the first time in my life, I didn't feel alone.

"I love Vivian," I said the words out loud in the hotel room, letting the sound penetrate the walls and windows and into the sky.

She was the most beautiful target to land at the center of my heart.

This was a profound revelation that I needed to contemplate. Did she feel the same way about me? It was probably too soon for her. It had taken her a while to agree to date me. Her trip to Providence was temporary until she could find Aimee. Would she want to stay there with me?

I could come up with another strategy to ensure she remained in my house. But I didn't want to do that. I wanted to let things flow naturally. I wanted to know—*needed* to know—that she loved me without me having to interfere. Love wasn't a mission or a business transaction for me to complete.

After a moment, I swung my attention back to practical things I could control. My Christmas gift list was short, but I had to get it done before I forgot.

What should I get Vivian, Kaylee, Pam, and Jarrett?

CHAPTER FORTY-SIX

VIVIAN

KAYLEE and I moved into Arrow's house three days ago. His shower was better than the one in our apartment. I stood under the showerhead, letting the hot water run down my body. Then I adjusted the side sprays, letting the force massage my back.

Though the shower helped, I was mentally checked out. It would be an early night for me after I replied to my friends. The chat didn't last long because my brain wanted to rest, and my body wanted to sleep. It was only six in the evening, and I was beat. I'd probably be sound asleep when Kaylee returned from her shopping trip.

After convincing my friends I was fine, I crawled into his giant bed. The fight from today and the ongoing anxiety about Ghost took a toll on me today.

I missed Arrow and grabbed his pillow to inhale his scent. I wished he were here so I could cuddle beside him. The odd incident from earlier unsettled me. It came out of nowhere, and I couldn't help but compare the shock to the news about Ghost being alive.

On top of that, another fear—an uncertainty—ran through me. I was falling in love with Arrow, and I didn't know what to do about it. The more time I spent with him, the more my heart opened. This powerful emotion scared me because if things didn't work out, I didn't know if I would recover.

I hadn't loved a man before. I had prevented myself from letting anyone into my heart until Arrow. Somehow, he'd found his way in and woken up my heart. I was more alive now because of him. He made me feel things, see things, and hope for things I hadn't before.

Love brightened everything for me. I feared that if things didn't work out between us, my life would turn dark.

It had taken a long time to bounce back from my mom's death. A death to my heart a second time would be too detrimental to me.

Go to sleep. Stop thinking.

What was Arrow doing right now? I wanted to hear his voice. But I didn't want to interrupt his meetings if he was in the middle of one.

When he returned, I'd ask him about these two women at the mall. Did he know them?

Missing him and needing to be close to him, I sent him a text.

Vivian: *I miss you. Tired today. Going to bed early.*

Before he could reply, I dozed off.

CHAPTER FORTY-SEVEN

ARROW

I FINISHED my conference call with the marketing team and checked my watch. My flight back to Providence was in four hours, so I worked on my video game. Last night, I'd figured out how to finish my Level Five for WaterFyre Rising. Vivian had inspired a special character that became the fundamental change for the game.

I created a character called The Dentist, an angler who tried to catch an evil amphibian named Tark, a hybrid toad and shark. It possessed unique teeth that could be ground up and used as medicine. The dentist carried a powerful hand-piece and a magical fishing rod with a golden fishing line.

A thrill rushed through me as I added the plot and other details. I was lost in the fantastical world and fell in love with my creation. My phone buzzed, yanking me back to reality.

Vivian: *I miss you. Tired today. Going to bed early.*

I smiled and replied to her.

Arrow: *Miss you more. Good night.*

She had no idea how much I'd missed her during this trip. I placed my phone down and returned to the game. A few seconds later, it buzzed. Thinking it was Vivian, I snatched it up.

But it was Kaylee.

Kaylee: *You busy?*

Arrow: *I've got time. What's up?*

Kaylee: *I need a favor.*

Arrow: *What is it?*

Kaylee: *You have connections, right?*

Arrow: *What connections?*

I didn't like the sound of the question.

Kaylee was too smart for her own good. It scared me how much she knew at this young age. If she didn't have the right guidance, she could take the wrong path and use her intelligence for something bad. She was like me. If I hadn't had my boys and Pam growing up, I'd probably be in prison or dead right now.

Kaylee: *I need you to punish two women.*

What?

Arrow: *You want me to commit a crime?*

Kaylee: *Punishing someone for a crime they committed isn't a crime, right?*

She had a point there, but I wasn't going to answer that question.

Kaylee: *Please don't tell Vivian I told you.*

Something twisted in my gut.

Arrow: *What happened?*

Kaylee: *My sister got jumped today.*

Arrow: *What? I'm calling you.*

"Tell me everything," I said.

Kaylee gave me a brief description of what happened and sent me the link to Real Rumors, a popular social media outlet.

What the fuck? Two women attacked her in the mall, a public place. She defended herself well, but still.

"I'll take care of this. I want you to focus on finalizing the Heartstrings App. Don't worry about this."

"Will you punish them?" she asked.

"In my way."

"Do you need help?"

Christ. "No."

"Thank you."

"Where's Vivian?"

"Sleeping."

"Thanks. Now go to sleep and stop trying to solve crimes."

She laughed and said good night.

After watching the video several times, I sent it to the PI. "Find out who these women are. Thanks."

I wanted to call her but didn't want to wake her. Why hadn't she called me?

Maybe she knew you were working and didn't want to interrupt you, dumbass.

I reread her text message. She sounded tired.

I wanted her to know she could interrupt me anytime. Knowing she'd been hurt and I hadn't been aware of it bothered me. She was a strong woman and didn't need my help. But I wanted to be the first person she thought of when she got hurt.

Who the fuck were these women? What did they want with Vivian? This was no random attack.

CHAPTER FORTY-EIGHT

ARROW

AS SOON AS the flight landed, I checked my phone for information from the PI. He'd sent me an image of the two women who had attacked Vivian standing next to a luxury car I recognized.

Though I was tired from the long flight, I drove to a beauty salon near Ormon's Restaurant, where Sylvia hung out. This shit had to stop. I entered and spotted her in the lounge with two of her friends.

She saw me, beamed, and rushed over. "Hey, babe. Miss me?"

I inhaled a breath. "We need to talk. Privately."

"Sure." She looked over at the receptionist. "Can we use your office, Rachel?"

Rachel nodded, and I stalked inside with Sylvia.

"What is it?" She placed her hand on my arm.

I gripped her wrist, removing her hand from me. "I know what you did."

"What are you talking about?"

I showed her the image. "This is a crime."

She twisted her lips. "That's not me."

"Your license plate is visible when you zoom in. It won't take the police long to link you to the two women who attacked Vivian. Stay away from her." I warned.

Sylvia pouted. "You blocked me!"

"We're not dating, and you were being inappropriate."

"But I love you."

I snorted. "You love the image of me with you. That's not love."

"You're taking her to Monaco!" Her voice rose. "I called the committee and asked them."

"She's my girlfriend, Sylvia. Leave her alone, or you'll regret it."

"My father sponsored your wine. All I have to do is tell him you pissed me off. He'll cancel the business contract."

"Go ahead. I agreed to the contract because it would benefit your father's restaurant. But things have changed. You crossed the line." I stared at her. "Listen carefully: my wine doesn't need your father's endorsement. I don't give a shit whether his restaurant carries my wine. But if you harass Vivian again, I'll ruin his business. And we both know you need your father's wealth to support your lavish lifestyle."

She glared at me as I walked out of the room and slammed the door behind me.

CHAPTER FORTY-NINE

VIVIAN

"YOU LOOK PISSED AND EXHAUSTED," I told him as he shook off his coat, tossed it over the couch, and sunk into the cushion.

His brown hair was disheveled, but he still looked so handsome. I'd missed him terribly.

Kaylee had gone to school, and I'd taken the week off because of the video of me fighting off two women at Providence Place. The video had gone viral with the hashtag #badassdentist.

My office informed me they'd been getting a high number of phone calls for an appointment with me. All my appointments had been rescheduled or gone to Dr. Goodwin, who was the part-time pediatric dentist at my office.

"I *am* and exhausted." Arrow yanked me into his lap. "Why didn't you tell me about the attack?"

"Because I wanted to wait until you got back. It's not that important—"

"You were *attacked*." His voice rose, and his jaw was tense. "That's highly important to me."

I could feel his irritation filling up the room.

I shifted and straddled him, sensing the growing bulge in his jeans. How could he be so angry and aroused at the same time?

"I can tell you now if you'd like." I leaned in and gently nipped at his ear. "What do you want to know?"

His voice hitched. "How much did you miss me?"

I smiled and dropped kisses along the roughness of his jaw. He hadn't shaved in a few days. "Lots and lots. But that has nothing to do with the attack."

"I already know everything about the fight. You should've reached out to me the minute it happened. Bad girl." He gripped my hips, one hand gently slapping and squeezing my ass. "But you did well." His hand slid under my sweatshirt and tank top, claiming a breast.

I'd been yearning for his touch. He rejuvenated me in every way.

Removing my sweatshirt and tank top, he said, "You don't need to worry about them anymore."

"What do you mean?" I moaned as he rolled my nipples between his fingers.

"Now stop thinking about them." He feasted on my breasts, and all thoughts vanished from me.

Heat soared through me from the hungry wolf of a man suckling one breast, then the other. I arched back, grinding my hips against his cock. I gripped at his hair, loving the way he tugged at my nipples and dropped kisses all over my breasts.

"More," I begged.

He growled and crashed his lips to mine, taking what he'd missed. To be kissed and wanted by him made me feel liberated. Like I could conquer the world as long as he was with me. I responded with the same passion, kissing him deeply.

I'd yearned for him the past few days. I'd even come two nights ago imagining all the things he'd do to me. It had been fun thinking of him as the hot and kinky patient coming to my office and having his way with me.

"Oh really?" he asked.

"Huh?" I didn't know what he was talking about. I'd delved into another world just now.

"It's fucking hot knowing you'd pleasure yourself thinking of me," he muttered against my lips. "I'll make your fantasy come true right now."

I'd somehow spoken it out loud. Embarrassment flushed through me.

"Take off your pants, Dr. Vo," he demanded. "I've got a treatment plan for you."

Excitement zipped through me as I got off his lap and dropped my sweatpants and underwear.

He licked his bottom lip while his gaze raked down my body, and I swore my inner muscles rejoiced. I could almost sense his wet tongue on me.

A sly smile appeared on his lips as though he knew what I was thinking.

"Get on all fours. It's time for your checkup."

I got on all fours on the couch and glanced over my shoulder at him. "I thought you didn't like the dentist, Patient Bullseye."

His eyes darkened. "You changed everything for me. Now I want to fuck this dentist every chance I get." He moved behind my ass and massaged my butt cheeks, giving each a slap.

Anticipation warred inside me as I lowered my head to

the cushion. My fingers gripped the edge of the couch as a thrill skipped along my spine. He dragged an open mouth around my ass. Delicious nerves twisted inside me.

"Gorgeous." He kissed my sex, spreading my legs wider. "Mine." He kissed it again.

I released a long and loud moan as he licked and sucked on me.

"Is that what you missed, baby?" he asked and quickened his pace. His tongue thrashed against me, and the sucking intensified.

"Yes!"

"You wanted my tongue inside you?" He entered my channel, and I pushed my ass harder against him, loving his rough jaw against my sensitive spot.

I panted. "Yes!"

"You're so fucking hot, Tulip. I can't get enough of you." He shoved two fingers into me while his tongue fluttered against my bud.

Heat and need increased with every pump and lick until I reached the crescendo.

Pleasure burst through me, and I cried, "Arrow!"

My body trembled as his fingers continued to pump and his lips continued to suck. Ecstasy blinded me. This had to be the most sensational assault on my body I'd ever experienced.

He removed his fingers, and I glanced back to see him stepping out of his jeans and boxers. "Shit. I don't have a condom."

"I'm on the pill," I muttered.

"Thank God." He positioned his cock at my entrance, teasing it. "I love your ass. This is the kind of drill I prefer, Tulip."

He drove into me, slid out, and drove into me again.

I crooned as my body tensed, preparing for another orgasm. He gripped my hips as he pummeled me like a mighty warrior. I loved the feel of his skin slapping into mine.

Arrow lowered his sweaty body to me, and his lips licked the edges of my ear. "I'm never using a condom again."

I turned my face and met his hungry lips. We kissed while his cock sank deeper into me. His body quaked, and he straightened up, pounding me hard.

A roar escaped him at the same time as my orgasm ripped through me.

"Vivian!" He growled while his body trembled.

I loved the animalistic sound that came from him—so wild and free.

He lowered his body over mine without crushing me. "Feeling better?" he whispered.

"Yup. You?"

"Much better."

We stayed on the couch for a while, letting our heart rates subside. Then he walked into the bathroom to clean up and brought a towel for me. I got dressed and asked my man what he meant when he told me not to worry about my attackers. Apparently, he had his people send the women a message. If they came near me again, something "awful" would happen to them.

"Those women were just after money. They don't want to die." He looked at me. "If something like this ever happens again, I need you to tell me immediately. Okay?"

"Okay." I touched his chin, appreciating all the things he'd done for me. I wasn't used to men caring about me like this or me having to share details about my life. It was different, and I was getting used to it.

It infuriated me that his ex was behind all of this. I supposed love pushed people to do unimaginable things. Right now, the warmth bursting inside me made me want to finish his Christmas gift tonight.

CHAPTER FIFTY

ARROW

VIVIAN AND KAYLEE had asked me to add some lights to the exterior of the house to welcome our visitors for lunch on Christmas Day. I'd never decorated my home because there had been no reason to, especially for a single guy living alone. The maple trees glowed, illuminating the wide path to the front door, which held a glowing wreathe that Kaylee had picked out. Vivian suggested I cover the bushes with lights as well. Overall, the ambiance was warm and homey—something I hadn't felt in a long time.

Pam and Jarrett were coming over for lunch today. Last year, they'd traveled to Florida to be with his family. This year, they stayed because he'd just recovered from heart surgery and didn't want to deal with the stress of traveling.

"Wow." Pam glanced at the foyer as she entered the kitchen area. "It's like a whimsical winter wonderland."

Jarrett looked up at the dangling lights that hung from the dining room ceiling and sniffed the air. "I love the magical atmosphere, and it smells so good in here."

"That's because Vivian is making something delicious

for us." I placed a hand to her lower back and kissed her head.

Jarrett placed the bags of goodies they'd brought over by the tree and went to join Kaylee in a videogame in the living room.

"How can I help you?" Pam asked Vivian.

"Oh, you don't have to. Most of the hard stuff is already done. You can just hang out with Kaylee and Jarrett."

"Sweetheart, I want to learn what you're making so I can make it for Jarrett one of these days." Pam pointed to the wall with aprons.

I passed the red apron to her and didn't know what else to do. This was the most people I'd ever had in my home. Kaylee and Jarrett laughed at something while Vivian chatted with Pam. I'd brought Vivian and Kaylee over to meet Pam and Jarrett once, so this was their second meeting.

Warmth bloomed in my chest as I stood at the kitchen counter, organizing what Pam and Jarrett brought. I placed their apple pie and tins of various cookies next to the ham, mashed potatoes, and appetizers I'd ordered from a nearby restaurant. They just needed to be heated.

Glancing around, magic and joy filled me up. The emotion reminded me of the last step in winemaking—the bottling and aging of wine. As joy and love entered me, I let them sit and transform into something profound that couldn't be described. All those past experiences had led me to this incredible moment where I got to savor the meaning of family.

"Okay, I think I got it." Pam gestured to the strainer on the counter. "The Mung beansprouts, Thai basil, and sawtooth herbs are all washed and separated."

Vivian glanced over. "Excellent. Can you get out the

small dishes for the dipping sauce? Squirt the Sriracha and hoisin sauce into them. Thank you!" She returned her attention to the pot of *phở*, a delicious beef broth and one of my favorite Vietnamese dishes.

"Sure thing. I've always wanted to know how to make this."

Though danger loomed around us like a dark cloud, I pushed everything aside to be with those I cared about. These moments were rare, and I wanted to make sure I remembered them.

Vivian had gotten me and Kaylee matching Christmas pajamas with tiny snowflakes. I'd never dressed up like this for the holidays. But I'd do it for her.

"Cute outfit," Pam said. She was like a mother to me, and to see her approve of the woman I loved meant so much to me.

I watched Vivian move around my kitchen with ease, owning it. I could see her cooking for me every day if she wanted to. But if she didn't, we could always order out.

The sense of completion flooded me. She was the missing piece I'd been searching for. She was like the perfect ingredient that made great wine *extraordinary*.

My life had been driven by success, to make my mark in this cruel world. But now Vivian was the center of my world. With her, I'd found my sanctuary.

Vivian also made fried egg rolls for the celebration.

"You have enough food to feed an army." Jarrett came over to get a drink and rubbed his stomach.

"Please take some home later," I said.

I looked at the beautiful display of food on the marble counter. Food ranged from Asian to Western delicacies. I loved the mixture of it. It represented Vivian and me.

Vivian prepped a bowl of soup for each of us. We sat around the dining table with an ivory tablecloth and neutral-colored modern tableware around a strip of decorative garland at the center. A bowl of glowing ornaments sat on each side of the garland, making it the most beautiful dining table I'd ever seen.

With his chopsticks, Jarrett dove into his bowl of noodle soup. "So delicious. Thank you, Vivian."

Laughter and chatter filled my home, chasing away any darkness that had worried me.

After the extremely satisfying lunch, we exchanged gifts. Pam and Jarrett excused themselves so they could make a trip to visit a friend's house for Christmas dinner. I walked them out to their car.

"I like Vivian. She's good for you." Pam's eyes gleamed, and I could tell she was fighting back tears. "Don't mess it up." She kissed me on the cheek. "Kaylee is such a sweet girl. She's blessed to have Vivian and you to guide her."

"You have a beautiful family," Jarrett said.

My family.

My heart swelled. "Thank you."

"Wait!" Vivian rushed out with a bag of food. "You forgot these. I packed a little of everything for you. Be careful with the soup. I don't want it to spill."

Pam embraced Vivian. "Thank you, sweetie."

"I'll need to hit the gym after the holidays." Jarrett smiled. "Thanks for the food. See you soon."

This had been one of the best Christmases I'd ever had.

I pulled Vivian to me. "You should've worn your coat. It's freezing out."

She looked up at me and wrapped her arm around my

waist. "You didn't wear a coat either. Let's get inside!" She dragged me through the door.

Once inside, I led Vivian to the living room. The TV was on some news station talking about the weather forecast.

"Kaylee, come here." I waved her over to the coffee table.

She was curled up on the big chair with a throw pillow and a blanket over her. The big Kuromi stuffed toy was in her arms. That was one of the Christmas gifts from Vivian.

"I'm so full . . . I can't move."

"I have another gift for you."

She bolted straight up and darted beside me in seconds. "Really? What is it?"

I gave them each a black box that matched the one on my lap.

"You already got me a gift." Vivian stared at the black box. "I'm visiting the spa next week."

I had another gift for her, but I'd give it to her later.

"A new phone?" Kaylee showed off her white phone.

Vivian picked up her gray phone. "I don't need a new phone."

"Yes, you do. These aren't regular phones you can buy at the store." I looked at Vivian, and she knew and sighed.

"These are just for us. They're special."

"Why?" Kaylee asked suspiciously.

"It's encrypted, so no one can hack into it. Besides, it holds more data for you to add things to your dating app. The data automatically syncs to my server."

"So I can make changes on the phone instead of the computer?"

I nodded. "The charge lasts longer and can be recharged if it's sunny out."

"Cool! Thanks!" She turned it on.

I turned to Vivian. "These are all under my account."

She had questions, but she didn't ask them because Kaylee was present. I'd spent a lot of money on these high-tech phones to know where Vivian and Kaylee were. It didn't use regular internet. Instead, it connected to a satellite with a team of experts monitoring it.

What if Ghost was planning an attack on them? I had to protect them.

I gave an envelope to Vivian. "Open it."

"You got boring papers for Christmas." Kaylee laughed and ran back to her chair.

Vivian furrowed her eyebrows, opened the packet, and pulled out the documents.

She stared at them, flipped through the pages, looked at me, beamed, and then threw her arms around me. "You were serious about helping me!" She cupped my face and plopped a loud kiss on my lips.

"Ew," Kaylee said and continued to play with her new phone.

Vivian looked at the documents again.

"You just have to finalize your idea and submit the information to him so he can start on the prototype."

"You work fast."

"My legal team will help you get it patented when you're ready."

"Really?" She held a pack of paper to her chest. "This was just an idea . . ."

"A brilliant idea," I reminded her. "And one that could help me too."

Vivian would soon have a silent handpiece that would make dental visits more comfortable for her patients.

"Oh my God!" Kaylee shouted, jumping up from the couch and pointing to the TV screen. "Viv! Look!"

Vivian and I glanced over at the TV.

Joy splashed on Kaylee's face as she squealed. "See?"

A news reporter stood in front of a group of people raising money to help a local restaurant replace their equipment after some vandalism. Nothing stood out to me but one homeless guy wearing a red Patriots knit hat and a ragged brown coat. He stood beside the crowd, holding up a sign with words that didn't make any sense to me.

"What's there to see?" Vivian asked. "It's people rallying support for a restaurant."

"No!" Kaylee walked up to the TV screen and pointed to the sign in the man's hand. "Kuraimee!"

"What's that?" Vivian asked.

"It's a version of Kuromi." Kaylee looked at Vivian and me with hope in her eyes. "It's a message from Aimee."

Vivian gripped Kaylee's arm. "How can you be sure?"

"Because it's something we made up. I told her if I could create a version of Kuromi for her, it would be a cute Kuraimee. She liked that idea because I used her name in it."

Vivian's hand trembled. "She's *alive*."

I wrapped an arm around her. "She is. We'll find her." I hadn't told her what I'd learned from Calvin regarding the death of her grandfather yet.

The news reporter had moved on to something else, but we rewound it, pausing at the man holding the sign.

"'Kuraimee is happi.'" What does that message mean?" I asked. "Happy is spelled wrong."

"Aimee is too smart to spell happy incorrectly." Vivian looked at me.

"She was at McDonald's," Kaylee said. "She loves their

nuggets and fries. They make her happy. It's something I would know. We always talked about silly stuff."

"Maybe the man misspelled it," I thought out loud.

Questions crowded my brain. How had Aimee gotten the man to ask for help? Did she write the message herself? Or had she asked him? Did her kidnapper take her to McDonald's? What kind of kidnapper was this? Were there other kids with her?

"Maybe." Vivian met my eyes. "Or maybe it was intentional. Let's go ask him!"

CHAPTER FIFTY-ONE

VIVIAN

THIRTY MINUTES LATER, Arrow, Kaylee, and I walked around the strip with a McDonald's. Nothing was open on Christmas except the drugstore, gas stations, and two Chinese takeout restaurants. I didn't know if we'd find this stranger with the Patriots' hat, but I didn't want to miss the chance.

What if he'd spoken to Aimee? Maybe she'd given him another message. Maybe he saw the kidnapper.

For all I knew, he could be the kidnapper too. But intuition told me otherwise.

The weather was cold, and the sun had a few hours before dipping below the horizon. Arrow clasped my gloved hand in his as we walked up and down the street, looking for a stranger. People were out and about. Some had joy on their faces, while others looked tired and worried.

What did I look like? Probably a combination of all three.

Today had been a wonderful day spent with people I cared about. I got to cook for the man I loved—the man transforming me from the inside out. A man who knew the chances of us finding a stranger were minimal, yet he didn't object to driving here to search with me.

Magic was in the air for me. But fear and danger also lurked, diminishing the joy I would've felt if I hadn't been worried about finding Aimee.

This was the first hopeful clue because it proved she was cognizant enough to reach out to us. I had feared she was drugged and locked up somewhere. I shouldn't think about those things, but I wanted to be practical.

Glancing around, I said, "Look for the guy with the Patriots hat."

We searched for about ten minutes with no luck and returned to the area around the McDonald's.

Disheartened, I dropped down on the iron bench and released a sigh. "I don't think we'll find him today. We can check back tomorrow." I looked toward the McDonald's entrance. "Maybe an employee saw her."

"I'll have a look at the recordings." Arrow offered me a nod.

He could hack into the cameras inside the McDonald's, including the traffic cameras in the vicinity.

"Thanks." I smiled at him.

Kaylee stood on the sidewalk with her bunny knit hat, looking for the man. She and Aimee had gotten to know each other when Kaylee had moved in to live with me. They'd connected instantly. Kaylee had cried for days when Aimee first went missing.

I could only imagine what she was feeling now. Hope and fear—the same mix of emotions whirling inside me.

"There he is!" she shouted, waving us over. "Hurry!"

We crossed the street, speed walking up to a man who looked at us with fear on his face.

"Excuse us, sir. We need your help."

The man with brown hair and a beard looked at us with suspicion. "Not sure I can help you with anything. I'm trying to find dinner."

"We can help with that," Arrow suggested.

The man's face beamed with hope. "Been tough lately. Shelters are full. Those guys in there are ruthless. It's better to be out here, you know?"

"I've got some food for you. I'll be right back," Arrow said. "If you can help these ladies, that would be great."

Arrow crossed the street, heading to his car.

"What's your name?" I asked. "I'm Vivian, and this is Kaylee."

"Fred Rugg." He smiled, and I noticed a chipped tooth. He probably hadn't gotten a cleaning in a while. "It's nice to meet you."

"We saw you on the news holding a sign," I said.

His eyes sparked. "It worked? A little girl was looking for a friend. She asked if I could make a sign and join the crowd. They were with a news station nearby."

"Is this the girl?" I swiped to a picture of Aimee.

Fred nodded. "Yeah. Sweet girl."

Kaylee looked up at him. "Did she say anything else? Who was with her?"

"Are you the friend she's looking for?"

"I am." Kaylee beamed.

"She was with a well-dressed man. He bought her a lot of food and stepped away when he got a phone call. I sat near her with my single hamburger. She offered me her fries and some nuggets and asked me to write those words on the sign."

"She said if someone came looking for her, to tell them she was going to visit the Mount Centauri Museum soon. Then the man returned, and they packed up the food to go."

"What did the man look like?" I asked.

Fred shrugged. "Tall. Dark hair. Intense look in the eye. You could tell he was rich and educated."

That could also be Arrow's description.

"Did Aimee look terrified?"

"No. Maybe a little nervous. She didn't talk to him much."

Arrow approached and gave Fred some food he'd purchased from the drugstore.

"Thanks, man." Fred beamed and dug into the pack of muffins.

"Fred was very helpful," I said to Arrow.

"Good." Arrow studied Fred and gestured to the word Army splashed across his sweatshirt under his unzipped coat. "You were in the Army?"

"Eight years. Got injured and came home to work for a warehouse. They closed down, then the apartment building I lived in burned down a month ago." He shook his head. "Hard to bounce back."

"Thank you for your service," Arrow said without mentioning his military background. "What did you do in the warehouse?"

"Forklift driver."

"Want a job?"

Fred stopped chewing. "Yeah! Where?"

Thirty minutes later, we dropped Fred off at a hotel in Providence, where he had access to the bus route. Arrow had a warehouse that needed help. He paid for Fred's one-month stay at the hotel until Fred could get back on his feet. Arrow also scheduled an interview for Fred with the hiring manager the following week. On top of that, he gave the man some money to get decent clothes for the big day.

The things that went on in Arrow's mind amazed me.

On the ride home, I said, "You just changed Fred's life."

"You're Santa Claus today!" Kaylee said. "You gave Fred the best gift ever."

I was falling more in love with him every time I witnessed his kind gestures. He gave more to others than what he got credit for.

"Fred needed help, and he gave you the best clue to finding Aimee."

"It was nice of him to help Aimee." Kaylee popped her head between the driver and the passenger seat. "He could've taken her fries and nuggets without doing anything."

"That's why he deserves the help."

"When are we heading to the museum?" Kaylee asked.

"Not today. It's closed. Let's go home and enjoy the rest of Christmas, and we'll figure out when we can go find her."

CHAPTER FIFTY-TWO

ARROW

I SPENT the next couple of days completing the wine campaign for my trip to Monaco. Aside from the competition, other promotional campaigns for my Bambooze Series needed to be approved for TV commercials and social media outlets.

I caught up with my team regarding my other wine labels. Satisfied with their reports and the status of the ongoing projects, I deferred them to my management team for the next few months. That didn't mean I wouldn't check in now and then or that they couldn't contact me if something urgent came up.

I wanted to focus on helping Vivian find Aimee and locate Ghost. My mind worked best when it zeroed in on a target. Too many targets scattered my energy. I had to concentrate. Ghost was a violent and unpredictable psycho. He'd lived a life in the shadows of a fucking clown mask. The plastic surgery to change his looks also revealed how mentally unstable he was.

An unstable man posed a more dangerous threat than a

"normal" criminal. I had to protect the woman I loved at all costs.

In addition, I'd uncovered something that boggled my mind. The recording from the McDonald's was missing for the day Aimee had been there. Someone had gotten to it before the PI.

So today, I took a trip back to the area to investigate. I entered a hole-in-the-wall restaurant attached to an apartment building. It was so tiny that they only offered takeout. I wouldn't have noticed it if I hadn't seen a customer exiting with food containers. They had an older security system, which told me they weren't saving the recordings on any internet services that could be hacked into.

After telling the owner I was a detective looking for a clue about a robbery—which I'd heard on the news days ago—they let me review the recordings. I used my phone and recorded what I saw on their computer. If I had to rewatch it, I'd have a copy. A man walked by with Aimee in front of the restaurant. Though the walk was brief, I saw enough. He was the man I'd seen at the wine convention and at the scene of the dead girl.

Who was he? What did he want with Aimee?

This man had shown up at critical moments. Was he part of The Trogyn?

I had sent his image to Slash, the man who had given my friends and me a second chance at life back when we'd witnessed the crime organization kill someone. Slash was working on a project, so he might not answer me promptly, but I had to try.

Maybe Slash recognized the man since he'd been part of the organization for a while before they sent someone to kill him.

Arriving home, I sat at my desk and allowed my thoughts to stir. Vivian was still at work, and Kaylee was at school. I loved having them in my home. It felt strange to have the house to myself.

My gaze landed on the special bottle of wine Vivian had given me for Christmas called Bullseye. It wasn't a bottle to drink, per se. I could hear something clanking against the glass from inside it. She had made a beautiful label with a tagline that made me smile. *Aiming to fill you up with loving memories.*

She told me to open it when I felt tired, lost, or unstable. Right now, I was bombarded with so many things that I didn't even know what to feel.

I opened the bottle and saw several strips of bamboo card stock. Words were written on each strip. I pulled one out that read: *When you asked me to inform you when I was ready for a date. That moment deserves to be bottled.*

There were so many memory strips within the wine bottle, and I loved that she made the gift especially for me. I'd never received anything so thoughtful.

My phone buzzed on my desk, and I glanced at it.

Slash: *Name is Orion Reimann. Extremely wealthy and powerful.*

Arrow: *Thank you. What business is he in?*

Slash: *Banking. Don't know much about him.*

Arrow: *Is he part of The Trogyn?*

Slash: *Not sure.*

Arrow: *Thanks. I'll take it from here.*

Slash: *(thumbs up emoji)*

I sat back in my chair, letting my thoughts swirl. Who was this elusive man? Orion could be an elite member of The Trogyn. When Slash had been part of the organization, he didn't meet all the elites. The secrecy made them powerful.

Orion seemed to know me. Had he been watching me?

He'd been at the wine expo at La Luna. I searched through the recordings from that day. Orion had somehow avoided all the camera angles. Something or someone was always blocking him.

I searched for his name on the internet but didn't see any images of him. However, there were images of the Reimann family, one of the wealthiest in Europe. The great Howard Reimann was a finance mogul who created the Reimann Sienna Bank after World War I. Howard had a son named Hewitt, who then had two sons of his own, Rex and Ray. Their investments spread globally to the automobile industry, real estate development, beauty products, and even Hollywood.

Rex Reimann—Orion's father—headed the Reimann Corporation. Why didn't more people know about the Reimann family?

Most wealthy families wanted their names to be seen, heard, respected, admired, and feared. Money equaled power, and that kind of power got things done. I knew this because I lived it and took advantage of it. Though it annoyed me that my name was often attached to the fake news with celebrities, I ignored them because they boosted my business.

But the Reimann name wasn't all over the news. Why? Was Orion Reimann working on a secret family agenda? What did that have to do with Aimee? Did he kill The Triad member to kidnap Aimee from her original kidnapper?

This entire scenario grew like a crazy web, making it difficult to decipher. The more I thought about it, the more

Orion Reimann seemed like an elite member of The Trogyn. All the check marks were there: money, power, secrecy.

A peculiar thought nudged me, and I sat with it, looking at the possibilities of Orion's connection to me and my friends. A moment later, a plan formed in my mind, and I sent my boys a synopsis of my suspicion.

My phone rang from a number I wasn't expecting. Why was the Providence Police Department calling me?

"Hello?"

"Is Mr. Holt available?" asked a woman's voice.

"How can I help you?"

"My name is Officer Juanita Lopez. We have a girl named Kaylee Leung at the precinct. She put your name down as her guardian. Can you please come down?"

What the hell?

"Yes. Is she okay? What kind of trouble is she in?" I slipped on my coat and headed out to my garage.

"She's fine. It's complicated to explain. You need to come now."

Nerves gutted me. Was there an accident?

CHAPTER FIFTY-THREE

VIVIAN

"THERE'S an event tonight at Midnight Chaoss," Lamar said.

Shit. I hadn't been practicing my pimp roll. With all that had been going on, it slipped my mind.

"Thanks," I said, trying to replay the walk in my head.

"Just walk like Jayden. His friend Willy knows you're going as him."

"They're okay with me going as Jayden?" I shouldn't be nervous, but I was.

"Of course. You've helped them and the community. This is nothing," he said. "They know you're looking for someone and want to help. Jayden had a ticket, so why not put it to use, right?"

"Thanks so much, Lamar. How's Jayden doing? How's your leg?"

He sighed. "I'm doing well. Taking it slow. Jayden's also improving slowly. We forget the importance of maintaining good health until it's too late."

"I'm glad to hear that. Gotta take care of yourself."

I asked Lamar for Jayden's address so I could send him a care package with healthy goodies.

"That'll make him smile. Thank you," Lamar said. "Be careful tonight. Blend in. Don't stay too long. I don't know if The Tip will be there."

"Got it."

The Tip could retrieve any information for the right price. Maybe he knew the man who had taken Aimee.

Hold on, kiddo. I'm coming for you.

Things were happening too fast, and I was terrified that I'd make a mistake somewhere along the way. I also sensed Ghost around me. The wounds on my back twitched as the memory surfaced, bringing up fear and hatred two things I didn't need right now. They distorted my thinking, and I needed a logical mind to ensure no mistakes were made. Ghost needed to be found and locked up forever.

I took a moment to breathe and ground myself. I checked my phone and saw Kaylee's text message, notifying me she was staying late at Whiz Kidz to finish up a project and wouldn't be coming home with Violet. She also asked if she could sleep over at Violet's since it was Friday. The timing was perfect.

After I sent my approval to Kaylee and informed her I'd be working late, I headed home. Arrow wasn't around, so I texted about running an errand. I'd explain everything to him later. I rushed into the bedroom and stared at my clothes options for Midnight Chaoss. Nerves racked me. I'd never done anything like this.

After seeing my mom die, I'd stayed away from anything unpredictable and dark. But unforeseen circumstances had placed me back at the center of it. What would I see at Midnight Chaoss? I understood it was a gambling center for many things besides playing cards. It was also a fight club. I'd learned martial arts for self-protection, and I didn't like seeing violence portrayed as entertainment.

But I had to find Aimee. Who knew what the man had planned for her? Would he sell her to some asshole across the ocean? How extensive was his network? Had I been wrong about them wanting to use her intelligence?

The research I'd done on missing kids and the sex trafficking trade sickened me. After hearing about Kiera's first-hand experience, I'd vowed to do whatever I could to stop these people.

I wore an oversized sweatshirt—the one Arrow told me to keep after I'd worn it on that snowy day—over a long-sleeved knit shirt and baggy jeans and tied back my hair so I could tuck it under the knit hat. Hiding my gender was paramount in a place full of wild men, dirty money, and flowing booze. Glancing in the mirror, I practiced my pimp roll. No matter how many times I did it, a laugh bubbled out of me. It was ridiculously amusing and so far out of my regular spectrum that it somehow worked. My ability to master it proved that I could achieve anything.

This skill resulted from having fantastic teachers. Dion, Tim, and Raul would be proud of their dentist. Their rap song rang in my ears and made me laugh, which calmed my nerves.

I blew out a breath, slipped on my boots, and drove toward Midnight Chaoss. Not wanting to be close to the club, I found parking in the street one block away. Eight at night on a Friday evening was early for a club, but this wasn't a typical club. The street was crowded with people going to bars and restaurants. The winter weather didn't deter people from going out.

I got out of my car, and walked toward Chaoss Workouts, ensuring I was in character. I walked with a dip, trying to maintain the pimp roll swagger. A group of men strode by without giving me a second glance.

Perfect.

The cold winter air nipped at my face, so I pulled the hood over my head, which was already covered with a beanie. The sign for Midnight Chaoss gleamed in the gym's building. Parked cars had taken up most of the spots along the street. Groups of men filled the sidewalk.

Nerves and adrenaline rose as I walked by them, wondering what awaited me.

CHAPTER FIFTY-FOUR

ARROW

KAYLEE SAT across from me at Becky's Kitchen, formerly known as Pam's Diner. When Pam retired, she sold the business to Becky, who had been one of her employees.

"You're lucky you got off easy. What were you thinking?" I asked, still trying to understand what had brought on Kaylee's rebellious behavior.

I had called my lawyer to meet me at the precinct and made the process smooth.

"Sylvia deserved it." Kaylee broke a fry in half.

"Why do you say that?"

"She hired those women to attack Vivian!" Kaylee's eyes widened. "And *you* did nothing about it."

I sighed. "How did you know about Sylvia?"

She shrugged. "Kids know a lot of things."

"I dealt with it in my way." I leaned into the table. "In a way that wouldn't get me arrested. You're thirteen. I don't want this on your record."

"My dad had one. It's where I'm headed anyway," Kaylee muttered, looking sad and defiant.

"Sylvia claimed you dumped hot coffee on her dress, pulled her hair, and called her a bad word. Then she found her Mercedes scratched with the same bad word painted on her car."

Kaylee stared at me and said calmly, "She *is* a bitch."

I wanted to strangle her, but I also understood her anger and her protectiveness toward Vivian.

At this moment, I applauded all parents and guardians for having the patience to deal with teenage angst. I was probably just as bad at my age.

"Language, little girl." I inhaled a breath. "You're lucky she didn't press any charges. There were videos of you damaging her car."

"No, there weren't." She smiled.

"What do you mean?" I arched an eyebrow.

"Because *you* deleted them."

The fuck? "How do you know?"

Two cameras were nearby, and I'd asked the PI to delete them immediately.

She shrugged. "I know you can do certain things. I've watched you do them at Whiz Kidz. You've talked on the phone, asking people to do stuff for you. You're good with computers, and you have connections."

Christ. I had to be extra careful around this girl.

"Why did you call *me*?"

"Because it would break Vivian's heart." Kaylee sighed. "Please don't tell her. She's taken me in and made me her family. She's my guardian, the best big sister I could ever ask for." Tears filled her eyes. "And it pissed me off Sylvia hired those women to attack her. That's just mean!"

I got out of my seat, walked over, slid into her booth, and slung an arm around her shoulders.

More tears came. "So when I saw Sylvia parking her car, I couldn't help it. She's dressed all pretty, but she's an *ugly, mean* person! I can't believe she's your ex." She glared at me. "What's wrong with you?"

I didn't answer.

I let her cry and spill all her frustration. When she was done, she turned to look at me with embarrassment. "Sorry I got you into this mess. Sorry that you have to buy *her* a new car, which she doesn't deserve. Unless you mean a toy car." A smirk appeared on her lips.

I chuckled. "No, it's an actual car."

She sighed, resting a cheek on her hand. "I'll help you pay for it. You can have all my savings in the bank. Vivian started setting it aside for me."

I appreciated her thought because it showed she acknowledged her mistakes and was dealing with the consequences.

"Don't worry about it," I said. "Consider this a favor. I might ask you for it back someday."

"That sounds *worse*. What kind of favor would a rich guy like you want?" She gave me a suspicious look. "I'll stick to the savings account. I know it's not enough, but I'll pay you more each week when I get a job. Hopefully, I'll get a good job that pays well."

That piqued my curiosity. "What do you want to do?"

"Be a cool influencer who takes down *mean* influencers . . . *legally*." She smirked and sipped her lemonade.

What was I going to do with her? How did Vivian handle her?

Needing to do something, I scratched an itch that wasn't on my head. I didn't know what to say. In front of me sat a brilliant girl with a bright future. I knew little about Kaylee.

All I knew was that she was an orphan when Vivian took her in.

Today, Kaylee had acted out of anger—understandably so—but she also had the clarity to accept her punishment. She knew her crime, and she also knew to call *me* instead of her sister. Right now she was trying to help pay for the cost of the car.

If I could stop Sylvia from creating more trouble, the car was nothing to me.

How could I not help a special girl who was more aware of herself than some adults I'd encountered? To own up to one's mistakes or accept an ugly truth was something a lot of adults couldn't do. Sylvia had refused to accept that she and I were no longer a couple. That refusal had distorted her emotions, which caused her to hire people to attack the woman I love.

Kaylee needed guidance. Her brilliance could benefit this world one day. I saw myself in her. Things could take an ugly turn if she didn't have guidance or a place to feel safe at this vulnerable stage in her life.

She didn't know the extent of her successful Heartstrings dating app. She only knew what my team and I had told her. But the software team had analyzed data that showed success and the potential for immense growth. We could launch it after I discussed it with her and Vivian. This was Kaylee's creation, and my company would give her the support she needed to take it further. But there were more important issues to deal with right now.

"A brand-new Mercedes would take you a long time to pay back."

Kaylee made a face. "Why did she have to be so mean?"

"And being mean back solves nothing," I retorted.

She looked at me. "What did you see in Sylvia anyway? She's not a nice person! Did you see how she wanted to hurt me when I told her I was Vivian's sister?"

It had taken some persuasion to calm Sylvia down. She hated bad publicity, as did most influencers. So replacing her car had forced her to drop the charges, especially when the police couldn't find any proof.

After Kaylee finished her dinner, she got into the passenger seat, and I drove her home.

"Please don't tell Vivian, okay?" She clasped her hands over her lap, looking worried.

"I promise."

"Pinky promise?" She wriggled her pinky.

I rolled my eyes but curled my pinky over her tiny finger. This was the first time I'd offered a pinky promise to anyone. When Vivian entered my life, she brought a lot of unfamiliar things with her. A lot of firsts for me. I'd never chased after a woman the way I did with her. I'd never fallen for anyone so fast and so hard. I'd never given anyone a piggyback ride, and now I was giving her sister a pinky promise.

I didn't have siblings growing up, so I didn't know what it was like to care for someone younger than me. I admired Vivian for taking on the tough responsibility.

Was it difficult for her to juggle her life to ensure it didn't conflict with Kaylee's needs?

"I'm glad Vivian's with you," Kaylee said, looking out the window.

"You didn't like her other boyfriends?"

"No. I only met Connor. They didn't last long though. He was a dentist too, but such a jerk."

Fascination grew. "How so?"

"One time, I went out to dinner with them. He drank too

much and called her names. He also made fun of her scars. I was so mad. They fought, and he got violent. She broke up with him, but he wouldn't leave her alone. His family was 'influential.'" Rolling her eyes, she released a disgusted groan. "I'm starting to hate the word 'influence' and all its variations."

I chuckled at her honesty. But my fingers itched to destroy her ex. "What do you mean they 'fought?' Physically or verbally?"

"Both. But she defended herself and punched him in the face, which pissed him off even more. I guess he's not used to a woman disobeying him. He used to stalk her, but she got a restraining order. That did nothing in the end. He only moved on because he found another girl."

I wanted to meet this asshole. I could imagine the fear he'd bestowed on her and Kaylee.

"Oh my God!" Kaylee shifted her body to look out the window. "*Oh my God!*" she repeated. "It's Vivian! She's doing the pimp roll!" A burst of laughter erupted from Kaylee.

"What?" I slowed the car and glanced toward the sidewalk to see someone in a thick coat with a hoodie doing the Pimp Roll toward Midnight Chaoss. "Are you sure that's her?"

"Yes! She's in disguise, but I'd know her face anywhere. Besides, Dion and his dad have been teaching her the move."

"What? Dion from Whiz Kidz?" I pulled over to the curb. "Why?"

"Yeah. He's her patient. What is she doing here?"

Fuck. Was something happening at the club tonight? That wasn't a safe place for her.

"I'm taking you home. Then I'm coming back here to make sure she's okay."

"Okay," she said. "I'll be at Violet's because that's what I texted her earlier when you arrived at the police station."

Had Vivian received a tip regarding Aimee? Why hadn't she told me? What if something happened to her at the club? Frustration and something else whirled in me.

I needed her to *trust* me. How could she be my woman when she was on some dangerous mission without telling me? That simple gesture crushed my heart.

I saw her text about running an errand. She should've told me about her plan.

We needed to talk.

CHAPTER FIFTY-FIVE

"YOU NEED TO WEAR A MASK." Willy offered me a chipmunk mask. He had a bulky build and long dreadlocks with colorful beads at the ends. His warm smile put me at ease in this loud and crowded place.

"Thanks, but why do we need to wear masks?" I put on the mask and glanced around. "Not everyone is wearing one."

"Jayden always wears a mask when he makes big bets. You're here as him, so it's safer to wear it."

Understanding, I nodded. "Do you know where I can find The Tip?"

"Not sure. He's wearing a mask too. I can ask around. Look for a tall guy with a skull tattoo on his finger." Willy shrugged. "But he might not be here tonight."

Disappointment nipped at me. *Please be here.*

I hoped The Tip could help me get information on the unknown man who had Aimee. Arrow and I could stop by the Mount Centauri Museum next when it reopened after the renovation.

"I'm gonna go check out the fights." Willy gestured to the many rooms down the hall. "Wanna come?"

He was here to gamble, not babysit. Plus, I didn't want him lingering around me as I searched for The Tip.

"No thanks. Don't worry about me. By the way, do you know what kind of mask The Tip usually wears?" There were so many people here in masks. It would be hard for me to pick him out of the crowd.

"I've seen him in a bunch of different ones, but he likes those damn clown masks."

Fear slithered up my spine. Could The Tip be another alias for Ghost? How many did he have? Or was this another coincidence of some sicko who preferred clowns? My stomach clenched as though it knew it were Ghost.

"Thanks. I'll keep an eye out for a clown mask."

Willy nodded and headed over to a group of people wearing matching blue masks.

I strode by a group of men who exited a door. They all grinned and held white slips in their hands. They must have come from the betting area, which I had no intention of visiting.

A sign promoting animal blood sports stopped me. Seriously? I'd heard about these but had never witnessed it. What kinds of animals did they have here? I walked down a short hallway to an area with people surrounding a small cage. People cheered as two roosters fought. I blinked at the horrific sight.

It sickened me to see the injured animal. I swiftly strode out of that room and returned to the main area.

Why would people want to watch animals kill each other? I supposed it was no different from watching MMA fighting or anything of that sort. The violence was too much for me. Was there a veterinarian on call in case these animals could survive?

My gut told me no. If they had cared about the animals, they wouldn't be doing this. I made a mental note to report this place after I got the info I needed.

I didn't like the uncomfortable vibes lingering near me. It had to be Ghost's energy. My body still feared him, as though he had some invisible connection to me. Trauma could do so much to a human psyche, and I'd been trying my best to detach from him. Even when I'd thought he was dead, that unease had remained.

But knowing he was alive had intensified it. I had to face him head-on. I didn't fear Ghost now like I had years ago. Learning martial arts had strengthened my body and mind. But the body remembered things that the mind couldn't control. The muscle tightness, the erratic nerves, and the escalated heart rate would take time to overcome. I willed my body to eliminate the trauma that had embedded itself into my muscles—my cellular memory.

As I searched for Ghost, the wounds on my back tightened, and the nerves bubbled again and again.

Stop it, I scolded my body. *He doesn't own you. I do.*

Even if I located Ghost, would he sell me information? I was in disguise and wore a mask, so I would be a regular customer coming to him for business. Despite this, I had to be extra careful if I wanted to save Aimee.

"You got your boys ready for the shipment?"

A chill skipped down my body at the sound of the familiar voice. I turned to see two men talking in the corner by a tall appetizer table. One man wore a bird mask, while the other had the clown mask I'd seen at Ormon's restaurant.

Ghost.

I calmed my breathing as tingles bombarded me. *I'm stronger and braver now. He has no power over me.*

With each exhale, the goosebumps faded. I stepped over to an empty table and pulled out my phone, pretending to look busy. One thing became paramount as I stood near my enemy. My body had *listened* to me. It didn't panic the way I had expected it to. The fear didn't have the same suffocating grip as it once did. Fear was still there, but I could shove it aside to focus on more important matters. Nothing was more important than getting Aimee back and figuring out how to make Ghost pay for his crimes.

I listened in on their conversation.

"The shipment's arriving next week," said the man in the bird mask. "Time to retire, man. What are they gonna do with those kids?"

Kids?

Ghost shrugged. "Don't know, don't care. Not my business. I'm just making money. You got the wine too?" Ghost asked. "Show me."

"Yeah." He showed Ghost an image on his phone. "What if The Taipans find out you stole their wine?"

Was this why Calvin had looked stressed when I saw him at Bella's Bistro?

"You gonna tell them?"

"Do I look like I want to die?"

"Then don't worry. Keep your mouth shut. Once the money's in your account, I suggest you go on a long vacation, preferably somewhere no one can find you."

Birdman laughed. "You too, man."

"Yo, Tip!" shouted a familiar voice.

I turned to see Chicken, a patient at my practice. He always brought his grandmother and other patients who couldn't afford dental care into the office. He wasn't wearing a mask.

Chicken slipped money into Ghost's hand. Ghost counted it and grunted. "There's a lot missing."

"I'll pay the rest back soon. It's been tough, man."

Ghost grabbed Chicken's shirt with both hands. "You have *three hours* to get me the rest. Add another thousand. If you don't deliver, you're dead."

"I already paid you two thousand for the original five hundred I borrowed." Terror splashed on Chicken's face. "I can't get any more."

"I don't give a shit. Get out of my face!" He shoved at Chicken.

"Yeah, get lost, asshole!" Birdman also shoved Chicken.

Chicken clenched his fist, wanting to fight back, but he didn't, and I knew why. His grandmother needed him. If he fought Ghost now, he'd probably have ended up dead or in prison. I didn't know Chicken well, but I knew he cared for his grandmother and other elders in the community.

I could easily kill Ghost with a metal bar gleaming against the wall. I could avenge my mother. But his death wouldn't bring back my mother or remove my wounds. I wouldn't feel any better having blood on my hands. How could I take care of Kaylee if I were locked up? My dad would probably have a heart attack. How could I love Arrow if I were separated from him?

In my mind, I'd killed Ghost a thousand times. Right now, I envisioned the pipe smashing into his head and cracking his skull with blood dripping down his face as he looked into my eyes and knew it was me—the girl who got away.

Ghost was more useful alive than dead.

Courage and adrenaline filled me as I strode over and interrupted their conversation.

"Yo! My man, Chicken! Haven't seen you in a while. What's up?" I deepened my voice to sound manly and slapped at his back.

Chicken stared at me.

I didn't give him time to ask a question. "I got you." Turning to Ghost, I said, "My pal owes you money? How much?"

"You gonna pay for him?" Ghost asked.

"That's right." I paused and stared at the fiend in the clown mask. The evil eyes hadn't changed one bit. "How much?"

Ghost stared at me for a while. Then he pushed me against the wall. "Who do you think you are, butting into my business? You wanna die?"

I pushed back and punched him in the gut. "Keep your hands to yourself if you want them intact."

He charged at me and threw a punch. I blocked and dodged another fist.

Chicken and Birdman stepped away as Ghost shrugged off his coat, whipped it aside, and cracked his knuckles. "I'll break all your bones, fucker!"

I also removed my coat because it was too hot, and I needed to move easily to fight him. Ghost was a lot bigger than most men. But in a battle, sometimes that didn't matter. A crowd had formed around us. So much for discretion. Where were the security guards? Were there any here?

Ghost's fist came flying at me, but someone's hand gripped his mid-punch.

"What kind of man hits a woman?" Arrow pushed

Ghost's hand away. He wore a Bullseye mask and glanced at me. I could see the fury and concern in his eyes.

"A woman?" Birdman asked.

"Yeah!" I shouted. "Chicken's my friend, and I'll fight to erase his debt." I turned to Ghost. "You in, or are you afraid, asshole?"

Ghost snorted and laughed. "How about I fuck you first, and then I'll break all your bones?"

"And I'll cut off your balls and shove them down your throat before I sever your limbs," Arrow seethed.

A moment of silence thrummed in the room. I could almost sense the darkness slithering up from the concrete floor like evil shadows instigating more violence.

Ghost stared at Arrow, then at me.

"Fight! Fight! Fight!" shouted the stupid crowd. "I vouch for the woman!"

Willy headed toward me, but I shook my head, signaling him to stay out of it. I didn't need to make this messier than it already was.

I yanked Arrow aside and whispered, "What are you doing?"

"What are *you* doing?" he tossed back.

I didn't reply. It would take too long to explain. I could tell he was mad at me for not telling him about tonight. I had my reasons. Still, I understood his anger.

"We'll discuss it later," I said. "Right now, I need to fight him."

"I'm not standing here while a man *attacks* you." He inhaled a deep breath and whispered, "I know who he is."

"Chicken owes him money. The clown is a scumbag loan shark," I said loudly.

The crowd booed him.

"Yo, Tip! I didn't know you loaned money," said someone.

"If I see him hit you, I'll have to *kill* him." Arrow placed a hand on my shoulder. "I don't want you visiting me in prison, Tulip. Let me be the man I want to be for you." His gray eyes gleamed with intensity.

My relentless protector.

It *would* kill him to watch me fight Ghost.

"Fine." I pulled him closer and whispered into his ear, "Knock out a few of his teeth."

Arrow snorted and whirled to face the crowd. "How much does Chicken owe you? Let's resolve this right now."

"I borrowed five hundred," Chicken said. "But the interest came to be two thousand, of which I already paid one fifty. He just added another thousand a few minutes ago!"

The crowd roared. "Rip off!"

"Fraud!" another man shouted.

"The Tip gave himself a huge tip!" someone said and made the crowd laugh.

I could imagine how furious Ghost must be right now. Birdman went somewhere as people surrounded Arrow and Ghost. Did Ghost know who was behind the Bullseye mask?

"If you win, consider his debt erased," Ghost said.

"*When* I win," Arrow corrected and shrugged off his coat, passing it to me.

CHAPTER FIFTY-SIX

ARROW

I KNEW something awful would take place at Midnight Chaoss, but seeing my woman being attacked by Ghost wasn't on the list. He had attacked her once when she was a child. He would never place his hands on her again. The fury that rose in me was something I'd never experienced. It was volcanic, and it coursed through my veins, wanting to erupt with violence. I had to gather all my self-control not to kill him on the spot. That malice had nothing to do with the fact that he'd stolen from me and destroyed my property.

Vivian was the only woman who could drive me to the edge. I loved her, but I also wanted to strangle her right now. She shouldn't be here tonight. She shouldn't place herself in danger like this. Didn't she know how important she was to me?

But she was trying to help her patient. That calmed me a little. *Just a little.*

My fingers curled as I stood across from Ghost, bouncing on my feet and preparing to battle. He probably didn't know who I was, and it was best that way. I had a feeling my love had a plan that required our discretion. Vivian and I needed a long conversation after tonight.

"Who's betting on the Clown Loan Shark?" asked a man in a Batman mask.

Someone laughed.

A person wearing a mouse mask looked at me. "If he's a shark, what are you?"

"A killer whale," Vivian said. "And not from Sea World."

The crowd laughed.

"Killer whales kill sharks. They're the true beast." Vivian punched a fist into the air. "I vouch for Bullseye Killer Whale!"

"It's called a killer whale for a reason! My bet too!" shouted a man with a green mask.

My woman could flip the switch on me like no one else. The anger in me subsided, replaced by amusement. She had gotten the crowd to root for me even though I didn't need them to.

Ghost threw a punch, and I blocked with the tiger claw. As we battled, I discovered he'd also learned some martial arts. It pissed him off when he got no hits on me. His techniques were all over the place, which also meant his mind was unstable.

I pulled back an arm, pretending to punch him. He shifted, moving to where I wanted him. Then I kicked his calf, forcing him to fall back a few steps. I charged forward, punching his chest. One, two, three. Then I pounded his face and cracked his mask.

I could kill him right now. But there was a crowd, and my woman had a plan for our common enemy. I drew back, heaving. The heat was making the mask uncomfortable on my face. I wanted this battle over with now.

His mask dropped to the floor, and two teeth followed it. The face that looked back at me wasn't that of James Chin, my former employee. He'd gotten more plastic surgery.

The crowd cheered. "Killer Whale!"

"Consider that my victory." I stared at Ghost. "Chicken is no longer in your debt. You understand me?"

Ghost spat out blood. "Who are you?"

A smile formed on my lips. Before I could reply, something exploded, and all the lights went out.

CHAPTER FIFTY-SEVEN

VIVIAN

I WOKE to the smell of bacon and chatter. The clock on the wall showed it was ten in the morning. I bolted out of bed and went to wash up. After Arrow had gotten me out of the club safely last night, we headed back home to escape the police crew and the news reporters. Someone had placed a bomb in the club and called in the news stations.

It was probably all over the news right now. Arrow and I didn't talk much during our ride home. We were both exhausted. And the conversation that needed to happen would require a lot of energy. But it would happen today.

Nerves simmered in my stomach. What could I tell him? I'd planned on telling him all about the event. This scheme had begun before we started dating, and everything occurred so fast that I didn't have time to explain. I supposed I could've called him, but I'd been in a rush.

Somehow, that didn't feel like a good reason not to tell him. Would he believe me if I said it didn't occur to me to let him know until it was too late? That it slipped my mind?

That would make him feel . . . insignificant.

Ugh. I didn't know what to do.

As I strode to the kitchen, I heard Kaylee whisper, "Did you say anything about the Mercedes?"

"No, I didn't."

"Good."

"What Mercedes?" I asked, sliding onto the stool beside Kaylee.

"Good morning. How did you sleep?" She smiled and straightened in her seat.

"Fine," I said.

Kaylee slid a look at Arrow, who winked at her. What were they up to? They had bonded over the last few days. Had I missed something?

"Oh, I'm just buying a new car."

"Why? You have plenty of cars." I jerked a chin out toward his garage.

Arrow shrugged. "I like cars. Speaking of which, you're getting a new car too. Something better for snow."

"Mine is fine. Don't need one."

"I already bought it," he said.

I didn't sense any anger in him. Had he forgiven me already? Did that mean I didn't need to have that conversation with him?

Kaylee's eyes widened. "What color?"

"Silver. Just like the one she has now."

"Cool!"

"Hungry?" He gestured to the plethora of breakfast food on the counter.

"You went out this morning?" I asked.

"We both did." He smiled at Kaylee.

I arched an eyebrow, pondering this bond between them. Besides my dad, Arrow was the other male adult in her life.

Warmth bloomed in my chest, seeing how their relationship had transformed just as my relationship with him had shifted tremendously.

Perhaps the main reason I didn't inform him about the club was because I needed the space to do things my way—the way things had been before he appeared in my life. Before I fell in love with him. I was trying my best to navigate being in love with someone. And I made my first mistake by not telling him I'd be putting myself in danger.

"You okay?" he asked, placing a plate full of food in front of me.

"Yeah, thanks." I picked at a pancake.

His phone buzzed on the counter, and he grabbed it quickly. His brows furrowed as he typed something back.

He dropped a kiss on my cheek. "Got a meeting. We'll talk when I get back." His eyes bore into mine. "Okay?"

"Okay." So much for not having the conversation.

He looked at Kaylee. "Don't cause too much trouble while I'm gone. Also, the museum reopens on Thursday."

Kaylee looked at me. "Aimee."

I clasped her hand. "I have a feeling we'll find her on Thursday. We'll need a plan."

Arrow squeezed her shoulder. "Let me know what you come up with."

CHAPTER FIFTY-EIGHT

ARROW

I ARRIVED AT A SECLUDED WAREHOUSE. Four men dressed in black stood outside the door.

"I'm here to see Calvin."

"You're Arrow?" asked one man.

"That's me."

They opened the door for me. I walked down a hallway, making my way toward voices coming from a room. Walking in, I spotted Calvin on the phone by a desk with a computer. He flicked a look at me filled with fury, but then the edgy expression softened.

Calvin probably extracted some pertinent information that left him agitated.

Three men stood at the opposite end of the room, watching another man working on the computer.

"Birdman's ready for me?" I asked Calvin.

"Might be slow at responding, but he's cognizant." Calvin's swollen knuckles showed Ghost's friend had talked.

"You got what you needed?"

His only reply was a grunt and a gesture toward the

metal door on the side.

I'd called Calvin last night as I headed toward Midnight Chaoss, wondering if he'd heard of any event there.

Apparently, he'd received news that a triad member had taken over ownership of Midnight Chaoss and was with Ghost, trying to overthrow Calvin as the next potential tycoon to take over The Taipans. Most of the elders had wanted Calvin to lead, but some members disagreed and had been causing trouble. He had called in the press so they would see the chaos firsthand. The destruction would be an example for those working with Ghost. Calvin made his message clear.

Somehow, Ghost had escaped. I entered the room and shut the door. Birdman, also known as Patrick Choi, slouched in a metal chair with his hands tied around the back. His face was bruised, lips swollen, and one eyelid was so puffy I couldn't even see his eye.

I pulled over a chair from the wall, and the legs screeched across the floor.

Sitting down, I glared at him. "I won't ask you where Ghost is because Calvin already did."

One eye looked at me, and fear gleamed behind it. I had no doubt Calvin had his own way of extracting information. The blood leaking from Birdman's thighs and arms showed his ruthlessness. The pools of blood on the concrete floor looked like a rug around the chair. I was surprised Birdman was still conscious.

"Is Ghost working for an organization called The Trogyn?"

Vivian had mentioned what she'd overheard at the club last night. The fear on Birdman's face confirmed my suspicion.

"Where's the shipment? I want exact dates and times. Who's your contact?"

I knew Birdman had already given Calvin this information.

But I wasn't sure if Calvin would share it with me. He was a triad member trying to keep his business intact, and I was a businessman who understood that. We both had our agendas. A common enemy had brought us together. That didn't mean we were friends.

Vivian was the link between us, and for that, I considered him an acquaintance. He had saved my love back then, and that gave him points in my book.

Birdman didn't answer my question, and I wanted to add more bruises to his injuries. When I rose from the chair and walked over to the rack of knives, pipes, and other tools used in torture, he straightened up. I grabbed a knife with a design on the blade.

From my experience, the anticipation of horrific pain was fear in itself. Just holding the knife in my hand gave him the impression of what I was about to inflict on his already injured body. I didn't need to get blood on my clean clothes. But if I had to, I would.

"I won't ask again." Moving to stand in front of him, I examined the blade of the knife. "I'm not a triad member, but I'm very familiar with getting a man to talk." I met his eyes. "And killing a man where his body will never be found."

In ten minutes, I got all the information I needed and more.

As I had suspected, Ghost had killed his father and Vivian's grandfather. He'd killed two members of her family and recruited several members of The Triad to assist in his crimes. No wonder Calvin looked like he had death in his eyes. He was dealing with several traitors within his organization.

Calvin had his own shit to deal with, and I had The Trogyn.

A smirk slid onto Birdman's face. "You know a Vivian Vo?"

"Why?"

Had he known it was me and Vivian at the club? Probably not.

"I have something to tell you. It can make you rich." He tried to smile with his bloody lips. "But you need to get me out of here. Out of the country."

I arched an eyebrow. "Why should I trust you?"

"There's something I didn't tell Calvin."

Perhaps desperation had forced Birdman to ask an enemy for help. I was curious what went on inside the mind of a man at the edge of his death.

"You need to give me something I can grab onto. Right now, I don't trust you."

"That woman's mother had a key to a safe worth millions of dollars."

"How do you know?"

"I overheard The Triad leader talking to his daughter. I worked in their restaurant for a while. It's not a regular key. Something with a flower design." His eyes sparked. "You get me out of here. We track her down and force her to give us the key. Fifty-fifty." He smiled. "I hear she's a beauty. You can have her first. Then she's all mine."

The knife slid into his stomach, and he gasped as the single eye widened.

"You don't touch or threaten my woman." I shoved the

knife deeper, twisting it and watching his life drain from his eyes.

I'd killed many during my years in the Navy. To see life drain from people was something I'd never forget. Taking someone's life wasn't something I dismissed or took lightly. I had to prevent him from hurting more people.

Birdman was going to die today, whether by my hand or Calvin's. So he should thank me for saving him from more torture.

"You're welcome," I said.

I extracted the knife, wiped it clean, and returned it to the rack. Blood poured out of Birdman as his head lolled to the side.

I exited the room, closed the door, and looked over at Calvin, who sat in a chair talking to one of his men.

"He's all yours," I said.

Calvin got up and walked up to me. "Is he dead?"

My jaw tightened. "He threatened Vivian and left me no choice."

"Stupid fucker." He raked a hand through his hair. "My wine warehouse just exploded."

"Ghost."

Calvin nodded. "And his followers."

"Are you bringing them and Birdman to the farm?"

He smirked. "How do you know about my farm?"

"I dwell in the dark too, Calvin. Part of understanding and navigating the dark terrain is knowing what happens in it."

"Nothing wrong with having a farm of exotic animals that feast on things you want to get rid of. The beasts get fed, and evidence disappears."

"A win-win situation."

CHAPTER FIFTY-NINE

VIVIAN

KAYLEE and I sat inside Arrow's Maserati, heading to the Mount Centauri Museum for their reopening. The event called for casual attire. The late January weather was oddly warm, so we all wore jeans, knit shirts, and lightweight coats.

I stared out the window, looking at the sun, trying its best to peek through the thick clouds. It was like hope trying to break free from all the dark clouds blocking it. But I sensed its strength—its resilience. No matter how many obstacles lay before me, I'd forge ahead. Surrendering wasn't an option.

So many things floated in my mind. Aimee, Kaylee, my dad's health, Ghost, my relationship with Arrow, and the approaching Lunar New Year of the Wood Dragon, or Tết, the Vietnamese version of the Chinese New Year. The past few years, we celebrated in California with my dad, but this year Kaylee and I would do something small in Rhode Island with Arrow. I loved that he was so open to various cultures. Perhaps the Navy had allowed him to see and experience the world differently than most.

I glanced over at Arrow. My heart twirled at how stunning he was. Was he truly mine? Did he love me? Neither of us had said those sacred words yet.

Today, the hard angles of his face were more pronounced than usual. Something was on his mind. He'd been busy the past few days, and so was I. We hardly talked. We didn't get to have our "discussion." Our focus had been securing an error-proof plan to ensure we would successfully locate and rescue Aimee.

What was she doing now? Could she sense us coming for her?

I leaned back in the seat and released a quiet sigh. I didn't want him to know I was stressed. Nerves spiraled in my stomach like it was trying to tell me something. After that event at Midnight Chaoss, I wondered if Ghost had been injured from the blast. When would he come for me? I had something special waiting for him.

What if Aimee wasn't at the museum today? What if all the clues we'd uncovered were just part of my twisted hope, making me see something that wasn't there?

Stop the negative thinking.

It was hard not to see both sides when a child's life was at stake.

"I'm nervous," Kaylee said from the back seat.

Shifting, I reached for her hand. "Me too. But Aimee needs us. Let's stay positive and alert, okay?"

She nodded.

"Try to blend in with the crowd as best you can," Arrow said. "We don't want to seem suspicious with the museum security."

"Are you friends with the owner?" I asked.

"Attikus Mount is a new investor in our WaterFyre Rising video game. I wouldn't call him a friend. Grayson designed the addition to his museum. So they're closer. He's more of an acquaintance to me." Arrow turned to smile at me. "But I could be friends with him if he doesn't cause trouble for us today."

Always so protective.

"Thanks for doing this," I said. "I know it's been stressful."

"It's an enormous task, and I don't want you to handle it yourself. Besides, my friends and I don't like people who hurt children. So we want to get this guy and whoever he's working with."

"I get to meet all your friends today?" Kaylee popped her head between the two car seats.

"Yes," Arrow said.

"I like talking to your friends." Kaylee looked at me. "They're so cool."

"They think you're cool too." I smiled.

She beamed and sat back in her seat.

"I don't think I've attended anything with everyone together," I said. "Usually someone's away for work or something."

"The more eyes looking for Aimee, the better our chances. There's something else I want to check on at the museum."

I reached for his hand. "What is it?"

"I'll explain later. Let's keep our attention on Aimee."

I touched his cheek. "You came to bed late last night. Feeling okay?"

"Just trying to finalize a few things. A kiss would make me feel better though."

"*Ew.*" A gagging sound burst from the back seat. "Gross."

Arrow laughed. "You won't think it's gross when you like a boy."

"They're so annoying."

I glanced back. "I have something special to share with you in a few days."

Her eyes widened. "We're going to Disney?"

"Not telling. You'll have to wait. Practice some patience."

"I'm thirteen. I don't have any. Teenage angst, remember?"

"That's why you need to practice."

She grunted. "That's torture!"

Arrow pulled into the crowded parking lot. "Let's go get Aimee."

"Wow." Kaylee stared at the Mount Centauri Museum. "I like how the three pyramids connect to each other, from smallest to biggest. Cool design."

"Tell that to Grayson," I said.

I'd debated having Kaylee address my friends as Auntie and Uncle to be respectful. But we considered ourselves sisters, so addressing them that way would sound weird.

We met our friends in the grand entrance hall, which was spacious and inviting. It had a high dome ceiling with intricate designs. Paintings and sculptures were displayed in various areas. Some were roped off for protection. The security team walked around the area, ensuring everyone obeyed the Do Not Touch signs.

I saw two wide staircases that led to the upper levels. A wheelchair-accessible ramp was also available beside the two sets of elevators.

Staff members were in abundance, answering questions and guiding people to where they needed to go.

The museum had a special showing of Picasso, Gustav Klimt, and an artist named Nelumbo. I hadn't heard of her, but her floral abstraction was gorgeous. Ethereal and peaceful—something I desperately needed. I'd swing by her paintings later to check them out. Today's mission was to search for Aimee. No other distractions were allowed.

"Hey!" Audri spotted us and rushed over with the rest of the crew.

We exchanged hugs, and they embraced Kaylee. It was their first time meeting her in person.

"You're so pretty," Audri told her.

Kaylee blushed, looking bewildered at all the attention from all the beautiful women.

"I just got a new jacket from my designer friend in Paris. It's too small for me," Natalie said as she untangled a strand of blonde hair from her earring. "I think it'll fit you. It's cool and edgy. Want it?"

Beaming, Kaylee looked at me for permission.

"Sure, why not?" I patted her back.

"Great," Natalie said. "Stop by my office anytime."

"Nice to finally meet you." Grayson smiled at her, revealing a dimple. He had short dark hair, and I could see the sibling resemblance to Audri. "Arrow tells us you're a genius."

All the boys gave her fist bumps. She blushed even more and looked up at Arrow, who stood beside her.

He slung an arm around her and smiled. "It's the truth."

"The dating app is outstanding," Remi said.

Questions erupted, and I told them she wasn't in a relationship. She was *just* learning about app development and created something fun.

"She's focusing on school first. Boys will come later, right?" I looked at her.

"Boys are annoying." Kaylee rolled her eyes. The exact reaction I needed to see.

"You'll need someone smart like you. Otherwise, it'll be boring," Kiera said.

"Who wants boring?" Michelle asked as she fixed the side clip on her long, curly brown hair.

More people entered the museum hall, and we moved to the side, returning to the mission at hand.

Arrow gave everyone a map of the museum's layout. Arrow had shared his strategy with me last night. My job was to look for Aimee with the girls on the first floor. He and the boys would monitor the second and third floors.

"Everyone has a picture of Aimee and Orion Reimann. See anything? Alert the group chat. Be discreet." Arrow jerked a chin at two armed security guards wandering around. "We don't want security booting us out."

Everyone nodded as one.

At first, I wouldn't let Kaylee join us today. This wasn't something I wanted to involve a thirteen-year-old girl in. But she was the one who noticed the clue that Aimee had left for us about "Kuraimee." No one else would have known what that meant.

What if Aimee left another clue today? Kaylee would be the only one who could decode it. Plus, Kaylee was with the girls and me so we could monitor her.

We had discussed notifying the authorities. But Arrow didn't trust them. The man who had Aimee was another wealthy and influential man. What if he had connections to the government officials? We had to play it safe.

Arrow kissed the side of my head. "You good?"

Nodding, I smiled. "All good."

"How about you?" He looked at Kaylee.

She offered two thumbs up.

Satisfied, he gestured for the boys to follow him. "Let's go find her."

My stomach tightened at the thought that there could be a team of kidnappers here. What if that man was working with others? I couldn't imagine a kidnapper taking his captive to an art show. If I were a kidnapper, I'd ensure she was hidden.

Something didn't make sense, but I couldn't let that thought distract me.

I reviewed the map again with Audri, Michelle, Kiera, Natalie, and Kaylee.

I looked at my girls. "Someone needs to stay here in the entrance hall with Kaylee to keep an eye out for Aimee and that man."

"I'll stay with her." Michelle volunteered, draping an arm around Kaylee. "No one will escape our eagle eyes."

Arrow had little info on Orion Reimann and neither did his PI. Who was this man? What did he want with Aimee?

"I'll take the West Chamber." Audri gestured toward the hallway. "Natalie has the East."

"I'll cover the North, and Vivian has the South." Kiera tucked the map into her purse. Her opal engagement ring gleamed in the museum lighting.

Shrill laughter echoed in the lobby, and I looked up and spotted Sylvia with two other women. They wore leather pants with high-heeled, knee-length boots and expensive-looking coats.

"I need to touch up my makeup," Sylvia told her friends. As she headed toward the bathroom, she spotted me and rolled her eyes. Then she glared at Kaylee and muttered, "Bitch," before disappearing into the bathroom.

Kaylee and my friends gasped.

Fury ignited in me. I would have let things slide between us, but no, she had to insult my sister. She wanted a bitch? I'd give her one. The immaturity needed to be dealt with once and for all. I stalked toward the bathroom.

"Oh no," Kaylee muttered.

"Who's that?" Michelle asked.

"Arrow's ex. She's a mean witch."

CHAPTER SIXTY

VIVIAN

I DIDN'T HEAR the rest of the conversation between Kaylee and my friends. Anger, exhaustion, and annoyance spurred me as I pushed the door open. A glance showed me no one else was inside. I locked the door and glanced at Sylvia. She had scattered her makeup supplies all over the counter. I didn't need this immature shit right now.

Remembering my lessons from my self-defense classes, I acknowledged the turbulent emotions whirling inside me and tried to separate myself from the storm. It was the only way for me to resolve this matter efficiently. Anger only clouded my judgment. I gathered everything I had to stay calm. Inhaling a deep breath, I stepped up to her and grabbed an eyeliner from the scattered supplies.

Sylvia shot me a sharp look as I twirled the eyeliner in my hand. Then I gripped it like a weapon, stabbing the air as though it were a dagger.

"Did you know this tiny little thing can puncture easily?" I jabbed it into the air, this way and that. "One powerful stab in the right place can injure someone's heart. Or someone's eye."

She glared at me. I could tell she wanted to bark at me but hesitated when I demonstrated a jab near her throat.

"What do you want?" she asked, keeping her gaze on the eyeliner.

"I want you to grow up." I jabbed it forward as though an opponent was in front of me. Relaxing my stance, I twirled the pencil between my fingers again. "The sharp point can easily penetrate vulnerable human skin. Be careful with this thing. It can make someone beautiful or ugly." I placed the eyeliner back with the other supplies. "As an adult, you need to be careful of what you say and do. There are repercussions to your actions."

Sylvia pouted. "She keyed my car!"

"Was there proof?" I asked, even though I already knew the evidence had disappeared. Kaylee had confessed everything to me. "I apologize for what my little sister did. She shouldn't have done it, and you could've called Arrow. He would've told me, and I would've dealt with it." The fatigue from the past few months surged through the surface, forcing me to release a heavy sigh. "She's only thirteen. Her actions stemmed from the fact that *you* hired two people to attack me in public. Kaylee just wanted justice for me."

Sylvia looked away from my gaze and said nothing.

"If I had wanted justice for myself, I would've sued you. It wouldn't be hard to ask those women to talk. And your perfect persona wouldn't be so perfect anymore."

She looked at me, and fear swam in her eyes.

"But I have more important things to deal with than this immature behavior. We need to talk. Like *adults*."

"I have nothing to say to you," she said.

"Then listen up. One, you stay away from me and my sister." A headache bloomed and pounded my temple. I glanced down at her knee-high boots. "If you don't, I'll shove that heel up your ass until it reaches your throat. The internet would love seeing their beloved influencer like that, wouldn't they?"

She flared her nostrils.

"Just because a man doesn't want you anymore doesn't mean you attack your competition and her little sister." I rubbed my temple, trying to ease the pressure. "Find yourself a man who loves you. Stop wasting your time on someone who doesn't. You're a gorgeous woman, so you shouldn't have any problem finding someone."

Hurt flickered in her eyes, but disappeared quickly. "Does he love you?"

Arrow had never said those words to me. But this conversation wasn't about his love for me. It was about a bully who couldn't accept rejection and was trying to bully me and a younger girl.

"That's none of your business," I said.

"If he hasn't said those words to you, he doesn't. He'll leave you soon."

"Even if he does, I wouldn't hire people to hurt the next girl. That's insane—and illegal."

"She scratched up my car!" Sylvia threw out her arms in defiance.

She glared at me, probably wondering how she could hurt me. If she attacked me, I'd have no choice but to defend myself by breaking her arm.

"I think you've acquired a lot of enemies over the years, Sylvia. You should watch your back from now on. You don't know who could retaliate. People turn ugly when you give them no way out."

I could tell she was thinking about my statement. I was sick and tired of this childishness.

"Arrow said he's replacing your car—which he didn't have to." I gathered her scattered makeup products on the counter and placed them back into the bag. The gesture was like me putting pieces of her back. I didn't know why I did it. Maybe because I also felt like I was scattered.

Sylvia's brow furrowed, gauging what I was doing to her makeup bag. She probably thought I wanted to whip it at her or something.

"He's *my* boyfriend now. So I suggest you move on. I'm very possessive and . . . can turn *crazy*."

Sometimes, bullies needed to know the pain they inflicted on others. I considered myself a decent person, but that changed when those I loved were threatened.

"Are we clear about where things stand?" I zipped up her Versace pouch.

Glaring at me, she seethed, "You stay away from me, and I'll stay away from you."

"Excellent." I watched her shove her beauty pouch into her giant purse.

She shot me a hateful look before stalking to the door without apologizing for the attack. But that was okay—I didn't need one. I simply wanted her to realize I knew she was behind the attack.

Relationships were so strange. They could make people commit horrible crimes. I hoped this eyeliner event would be etched in Sylvia's mind whenever she wanted to hurt someone again.

CHAPTER SIXTY-ONE

ARROW

MY FRIENDS and I split up. Royce, Forrest, and Grayson took the second floor because it was larger, while Remi and I scoured the third floor. People were everywhere, and it was hard trying to locate a young girl and Orion Reimann.

This event served two purposes for me: finding Aimee and confirming Orion's identity. I had been working a lot the past couple of weeks trying to find information on a man who had done everything he could to remain hidden.

But people made mistakes when they were taken by surprise, even extremely skilled individuals. Having worked in the field, I was trained to look for details that others could miss, and I'd spotted something interesting that changed my entire outlook.

My friends and I were in a vulnerable state right now.

As I wandered into the various galleries, I kept my eyes open for a young girl and a man. I passed a group of people listening to a museum guide discuss an abstract sculpture that looked like a god bursting forth from the head of the beast. I wasn't sure what kind of myth that artwork depicted.

A humming sound caught my ear, and I turned. A girl was holding a flyer, walking down a hallway.

I couldn't see her face, but her height and form told me she could be Aimee. I glanced around, and no adults were near her.

As I followed her, I called out, "Aimee?"

She turned, and my heart leaped.

Then she rushed into a room.

CHAPTER SIXTY-TWO

VIVIAN

WHEN I WALKED OUT, my girls and Kaylee stood in front of the bathroom, looking like soldiers protecting their territory. I wouldn't be surprised if they had prevented people from entering the bathroom while I dealt with Sylvia.

Warmth bloomed in my chest. These girls had my back.

They glared at Sylvia's friends, who also glared back.

"C'mon, girls. We have more important things to do today." Sylvia ushered her friends out. "Let's go shopping. Not in the mood for art anymore."

Click, click, click.

I turned to the sounds of a clicking camera.

Elena Sanchez walked up to me and the girls and smiled. "I hope you ladies don't mind me taking your picture just now." She was the journalist who had approached me about a story for her online Musepaper that empowered women.

"You already took it," I said.

"But I won't use it without your permission." She glanced over her shoulder. "I was invited to do a segment on the reopening of the museum. I saw you all standing here with a mission to protect something. You looked like warriors —role models for young girls. I couldn't help but snap a few pictures. May I take one with all of you in it?" She looked at me.

I looked at my girls. "You okay with that?"

"I get to be in the newspaper? Yes, please!" Kaylee exclaimed.

When all my friends agreed, we scooted away from the bathroom sign and posed for a picture with a gorgeous lotus painting behind us.

"Perfect. Thank you so much. I'll send you a link to the article when it's published."

"Thank you." We exchanged contact information, even though I already had hers somewhere at home.

After Elena left, we resumed our mission to look for Aimee. There had been too many distractions. She could have come and gone already.

"Did you guys see anyone resembling Aimee or Orion while I was dealing with the bathroom?"

"No." Audri smiled. "Nothing. We were keeping watch." She leaned in and whispered, "We need another girls' night out so you can fill us in on the bathroom event."

I smirked. "Let's concentrate on why we're here."

My phone buzzed.

Remi: *Anyone hear from Arrow?*

Royce: *No.*

We all replied no too. My stomach clutched.

Forrest: *He's probably in an area with no reception.*

Grayson: *Maybe he's taking a shit.*

Kaylee laughed, and Natalie called her man on the phone to remind him and his friends to watch their language because a thirteen-year-old was in the group.

He apologized, and the group chat went quiet.

What happened to Arrow?

At that moment, I saw a girl with long dark hair walking with a man. They were with a group of people.

"Look," I whispered to the girls. "Near the mosaic artwork."

After texting the guys that we spotted someone resembling Aimee, we made our way over.

CHAPTER SIXTY-THREE

ARROW

AS I RUSHED DOWN the hallway toward the room, I debated stopping to alert the group. But one split second could mean the difference between following Aimee and losing her again. Where did the room lead? I'd inform them once I got inside.

I reached the door at the end of the hallway with a metal plate that read Employees Only. Something was off here. The girl was definitely Aimee, but why did she run into this room?

Because she doesn't know you. She probably thinks you're another creepy kidnapper.

That was a possibility. She didn't look terrified like I had expected. Had she escaped Orion? If so, why hadn't she run to an adult to ask them to call the police or her parents?

Despite the details not connecting properly, I had no choice but to follow Aimee. Vivian had been stressed looking for this little girl, and she was within my grasp.

I stepped into a dimly lit room with comfortable chairs in a lounge area with a big screen TV on a table. This wasn't the conference room appearance I'd expected. I pulled out my phone to alert my friends, but there was no reception.

"Fuck," I muttered.

Though the connection jam confirmed my suspicion, it still annoyed me. This was a high-tech phone that used advanced internet from the government. "How the fuck did he manipulate it? Is he working for the military?"

"Language, Arrow," said a voice from the dark corner. "There's a minor in this room."

Since when did a kidnapper care about profanity around a child?

I'd already sensed his presence when I'd entered. But I wanted to see his next move.

The familiar voice irked me. A part of me felt betrayed, but the other part scolded me for not being more careful—for not seeing the obvious.

Orion Reimann flicked on the lights. He had dark hair and wore a tailored gray suit, looking wealthy and sharp like the man I'd seen at the wine convention. Aimee sat at a table, coloring something. She looked at me and smiled. Guilt splashed on her face, and I knew Orion had made her lure me here.

But why?

Orion gestured to the phone in my hand. "You can alert your boys to come to Conference A now. Ask the ladies to take Aimee downstairs." He looked at the girl. "You can go home now. Thank you for your help."

She nodded and offered him a hug. "Thank you."

Why was she *thanking* him? She should run out the door right now.

When the girls arrived to get Aimee, Vivian had questions in her eyes, but she didn't ask them. She only glared at Orion through the open door.

"We'll talk later." I brushed a hand down her cheek. It had been a chaotic few weeks, and fatigue showed in her eyes.

She offered me a warm smile. "Thank you for getting her back."

I kissed her forehead. "Anything for you, Tulip. Also, don't tell the authorities about finding Aimee yet."

"I have to let her parents know."

"That's fine, but ask them to hold off on alerting the authorities too. I want to make sure we don't jeopardize her safety by alerting the wrong people."

She touched my face and smiled. "Always thinking ahead."

I closed the door and joined my friends standing at the center of the room. We glared at the man who knew too much about us.

Irritated, I stepped forward. "Has it been fun being our PI?"

CHAPTER SIXTY-FOUR

VIVIAN

I EMBRACED Aimee for a long time before releasing her to Kaylee, who gave her a massive hug. Joy and relief burst in me. The anxiety that had weighed me down began to slide off my shoulders. As tears filled my eyes, I imagined my mom smiling from above.

I examined Aimee. She didn't appear terrified or distraught, as I had expected. We all gathered around two tables at the museum café. I had so many questions for her but didn't want to inundate her with them.

Once she got settled, I'd call her parents and my dad. Aimee needed to be surrounded by people who cared about her. She needed to feel safe.

She wore clean clothes, good shoes, and an Armani felt coat. Did Orion buy them for her? This didn't seem like an ordinary kidnapping.

Aimee smiled at my friends, who sat in silence, giving her the space she needed.

After she finished her strawberry shake, I asked, "Are you hurt? Did that man hurt you in any way?"

Aimee shook her head. "Orion didn't hurt me. He saved me."

"What do you mean he saved you?" I exchanged glances with my friends.

Kaylee took Aimee's hands to comfort her.

Though she was only nine, her eyes revealed she knew so much more than other kids her age. The way she reacted to this horrible situation amazed me. Maybe she was hiding the fear underneath the calm exterior? Her parents would need to take her to a therapist to ensure she wasn't repressing the trauma. That could have a terrifying effect on her later on. I understood this because I was still trying to overcome my trauma.

"He saved me from that other man." She looked at me. "They were going to ship me overseas." She rattled off a number. "That's the dock and container number. I heard him talk to a man with a clown mask."

Ghost. Where was he now?

"Wow," Audri said.

"She's better than a computer," Kiera added.

Kaylee wrapped an arm around Aimee. "She's my little Einstein. Thanks for leaving a clue for us."

Aimee hugged Kaylee back. "When Orion stepped away to talk on his phone, I asked the man to help me." She shrugged. "I didn't know if you'd see it . . . But I hoped you would."

"I'm going to make Kuraimee into a real plushie for you!" Kaylee said.

"Really?"

"Yup!"

"Thank you!" Aimee embraced Kaylee once more.

"Did the original kidnappers hurt you?" I asked, fearing

what she'd say. But I had to know.

Fear shone in her eyes. "He was so mean. He hit me a few times."

Anger surged through me.

"Did the clown man also hit you?"

She nodded. "He's crazy. He kept calling me Christine, saying how I'm gonna make him lots of money." Her hands trembled. "He gave me papers with people's information and told me to memorize them. Then he'd test me. If I got it wrong, he didn't feed me."

I wanted to hurt Ghost so badly. He probably held back on hurting Aimee physically. If she looked abused while he took her around, people would question him.

"Christine is my mother's name." I brushed a hand down Aimee's hair. "She was a genius like you. Did they make you do anything? Take you anywhere?"

After another twenty minutes of chatting, my perception of Orion had changed. Apparently, he and Aimee had talked quite a bit. She said his mom was an astronomer and an astrologer, and Orion was her favorite constellation based on the hunter in Greek mythology.

My friends and I smiled as she displayed her intelligence and excellent memory. I wondered if Orion knew who he was spilling info to.

What was his agenda? Why was he helping us?

I pulled out my phone. "I'm going to call your parents now."

Aimee moved to a big, cushioned chair, and Kaylee squeezed in beside her. The two held hands as Aimee spoke to her parents. Tears streamed down her face, and Kaylee helped dab them away.

I wasn't sure what Arrow planned to tell the authorities, but I had to get Aimee back to her worried parents.

"How are you doing?" Michelle rubbed circles on my back.

"An immense relief," I confessed, blowing out a breath. I'd been so wound up that my body didn't know how to react to this sudden lightness. Anxiety over Ghost still lingered, but the catastrophe that brought me to Providence had been resolved.

"The outcome turned out better than I hoped for." Audri glanced over at the girls.

"Someone was watching over her for sure," Kiera said.

I'd like to think my mom had something to do with it. "I'll need to book a flight to take her home."

"You can use Grayson's plane," Natalie said. "He won't mind."

I shouldn't be baffled by the things these billionaires bought, but I was. "Why does he have a plane?"

She smiled. "Long story for the next girls' night out."

"Love makes you do unpredictable things," Kiera said.

Michelle looked at me. "How are you and Arrow doing? He say those words yet?"

My chest tightened as Sylvia's words bounced around my head.

If he hasn't said those words to you, he doesn't. He'll leave you soon.

I didn't know why I was even listening to her.

"Not yet. But I haven't said them either. We've been swamped."

"Who's this Orion guy?" Audri asked.

"Could be a foe or an ally," I said, hoping for the latter.

What were they discussing up there?

CHAPTER SIXTY-FIVE

ARROW

"HOW DID YOU FIGURE IT OUT?" Orion asked, folding himself into the chair. He gestured for all of us to take a seat in the lounge area. "Would you like anything to drink?"

I spotted several bottles of my Sacred Sins and Sensual Enigma in his wine selection.

"Sure." I needed to calm the storm within me.

My boys and I exchanged glances. I had my suspicion when I'd asked him to look up information on Aimee and Orion. He'd taken his time in delivering information about her. But it was my request on Orion Reimann that told me something was up. He'd asked me too many questions.

Not that he didn't ask me questions during prior requests, but his tone and swift reply made me wonder what triggered my PI. Besides, I'd been pondering on the people around me and my friends. Who knew the most information about us? Who knew of all the illegal—yet necessary—acts we'd committed to protect those we loved?

There was only one person—someone we hadn't met in

person. The initials O.R. connected the final dots. He'd told us to address him that way, but I'd been used to calling him my PI. So, a plan brewed in my head.

"No one but you knew about the special phones used at the museum today. My boys did, but I trusted them."

Remi pulled out his phone and smirked. "We also discovered a photo of you at a café in Boston where an 'informant' was supposed to provide info on Orion Reimann."

I'd fabricated a fake story about someone offering information on Orion Reimann in Boston. Orion had showed up and fallen into our trap.

Smiling, he placed the wineglass on the coffee table. "The PI work started as an accident."

"What do you mean?" Remi asked, his jaw twitching.

Though Orion hadn't done anything to harm us—not that we knew of—we felt betrayed by this ordeal. He also kidnapped a young girl. What else was he up to?

"Like you, I have my agenda. When I was contacted to do work for you." He looked at Remi and the others before meeting my eyes. "I discovered something interesting about all of you."

"What?" Grayson asked.

"That you're like me—VATV."

"What the fuck is that?" Royce asked, looking like an angry Thor.

Orion smirked. "Vigilantes against the villains. Everyone in this room has committed deeds that would put us in prison." He looked at Forrest. "Even you, doctor. But we're committing 'crimes' to fight the filth on this planet. Do you agree?"

My friends and I exchanged glances. Orion wasn't

wrong. We'd all done things that would be immoral or even evil in the eyes of society.

"And you helped us because of that?" I asked.

Orion nodded. "The more I helped you, the more I realized that you were men I wanted on my side—respectable men with a mission."

"Why should we trust you now?" Forrest asked.

"I could've used your information against you from the beginning," Orion replied. "But I chose not to." He looked at each of us. "I've done nothing to harm you or your loved ones. In fact, I've saved your women twice."

An uproar sounded in the room.

"What are you talking about?" Remi rose from his chair, followed by Grayson, Forrest, and Royce.

The last thing I needed was a fight. That wouldn't get us answers.

Rising to join my friends, I asked, "How?"

"Your women went shopping three months ago. I intercepted an order to have them eliminated by two eight-wheeled trucks."

I looked at my friends. Fear and relief were splashed on their faces.

Vivian had gone on a shopping trip with the girls a while back. I didn't even want to think about what would have happened if Orion hadn't stopped those men.

"The Trogyn?" Grayson asked.

"How do you know this?" Forrest inquired.

He smirked. "I have a company that's more advanced than NASA. You know little about it, and I prefer to keep it that way. Let's just say that NASA often hires my team to do their work." He rose from his seat, stepping close to us.

"How did you think I got all that secret information for you so quickly? So discreetly?"

I couldn't believe this. It all made sense now. He'd done tasks for us quickly and efficiently. We'd paid him well, but he'd never needed the money.

"I got intel The Trogyn was after you." Orion went to the wine counter and poured himself two fingers of whiskey. "They suspect you're responsible for the last few disruptions to their businesses. And they want payback."

"I knew they'd figure it out eventually." Royce stepped up to the counter and poured himself a glass of whiskey, gesturing to the boys and me if we wanted any. Remi and Grayson nodded, but Forrest and I declined.

"So what did you do?" Grayson asked.

"I deflected information from you as best I could. My men ensured the two drivers never made it." Orion finished his whiskey and put the glass down. "So now the organization thinks you know about their attempts. They've backed up a bit, but not for long." He leaned against the counter, tucking a hand into his pants pocket. "Which is why I needed to meet you. The game has gotten bigger. The stakes higher."

Orion was an asset to keep. If we didn't welcome him, he'd work independently. We were all stronger together.

"When were you planning to tell us who you are?"

"Now. Things are also escalating for me. I stopped the human cargo shipment that Ghost wanted to deliver to the Europeans."

"You saved Aimee from her kidnapper. Why?" I asked.

"Because, like you, I don't like harming children. I'd been searching for human traffickers within the New England area. So, when you gave me her info, I knew where to look."

"Why didn't you tell us you found her?"

"Because they wanted Aimee for her gift. Her recovery would only intensify their search for her. They had to believe they were still getting their 'product.'" Orion smiled. "Plus, her incredible memory helped me locate a few things on my list."

"What do you mean?"

Orion gestured to the room full of paintings and artifacts. He pressed a button on his phone, and the wall with the paintings slid away, revealing a new wall with three interesting paintings. Two abstract paintings and one floral.

Royce walked up to a flower painting about forty-eight by forty inches. "This is a Georgia O'Keeffe."

"It's the *Jimson Weed/White Flower No. 1*. Sold for forty-four-point-four million in 2014. It's the highest-paid painting by a female artist."

"I thought it was in the Crystal Bridges Museum of American Art in Arkansas," Grayson said. He and Natalie often visited art shows worldwide.

"The one in the museum isn't real." Orion turned to look at us. "An elite member hired someone to replicate and replace it."

"How did you get it?" Remi asked.

"That's not important." Orion pressed the button on his phone again. The walls with the previous paintings slid back, covering the *Jimson Weed/White Flower No. 1*. "What's important is that the owner is very angry right now."

"Who is he?" I asked.

"That's what I'm trying to find out."

It made no sense to me, but Orion was an enigma. He probably purchased the painting from someone else for twice the amount.

"What about these other paintings and sculptures? Do they belong to someone too?" Forrest gestured to some abstract seascapes and landscapes and figures on display throughout the room. They were probably worth millions but not as precious as the ones behind the wall.

Orion tucked his hands into his pants pockets. "They belong to me."

"You know what I'm asking," Forrest retorted.

"And that's my answer," Orion replied.

"What are you? A fucking thief?" Remi asked.

Why would a quadrillionaire steal?

Orion laughed. "I'm a collector of fine things. Let's just say some of the paintings in here belong to the members of The Trogyn."

"So they're after you too?" Grayson studied him.

"Which is why we need to take them down." Orion's expression hardened.

"What are you going to do with the art?" Forrest asked.

"Don't know yet." He shrugged. "I'm sure they'll be useful someday. I might gift them to Attikus since he let me use this room for storage." He offered me a smile. "When I learned how important Aimee was to your girlfriend, I wanted to use this opportunity to return her and introduce myself."

"Did you know Aimee asked a homeless man to help her?" I asked.

"Not at first." His eyes gleamed with amusement. "I took her around Boston, bought her things, and tried to let her be a kid. She confessed when she trusted me. That was only after I showed her photos of the children I'd rescued and kept from the news."

Orion admitted he'd rescued the girl locked up with

Aimee in Boston. He'd already returned the girl to her parents. She had been drugged and didn't remember much, but her recovery looked promising.

The image of the little girl wrapped in a blanket popped into my mind. "You saved that little girl with an FTM card in her coat?"

His lips thinned. "She was already dead when I got to her. I wanted to send her back to her family and use that opportunity to show the public a glimpse of their dark world." He looked at us. "FTM—follow the money. People need to open their eyes. Human trafficking is a massive business. Money is truly the root of all evil."

The little girl had been identified recently. Her family had a formal funeral for her in North Carolina. Orion had given her family closure. There were so many families still waiting to hear news about their missing loved ones.

"Why are you revealing your identity now?" Remi asked.

"Because I'm not your PI anymore." His lips thinned. "My enemy has joined the elite club within The Trogyn. We can work together to destroy them."

"We have a common enemy." I looked at my friends.

"And I'd like to invest in WaterFyre Rising."

"Why?" Remi studied Orion.

"It's a brilliant game. You did send me copies of the demos to upload onto a second secure site, you know."

Thirty minutes later we'd learned what he'd been doing, a synopsis of his demo that followed the WaterFyre Rising theme. It seemed like he'd wanted to join us for a while now. We also learned how he'd saved our women the second time. He was a beneficial ally for us.

"Please accept my apology for not informing you sooner

about my identity." Orion looked at us. "We all have agendas. We all have reasons for our actions."

My friends and I looked at each other. Their expression showed they also wanted Orion on our side. He had connections and assets beyond our reach. The man was a fucking quadrillionaire. Money could buy a lot of things, and Orion could be the man we'd been waiting for. He'd been right in front of us all this time.

"You don't need our help," I said.

"No." He smirked.

Asshole.

"But I'd like your help. The more people we have fighting The Trogyn, the better. They're just one of many organizations out there with an agenda." His eyes intensified. "I need intelligent and cunning men like you to help me win this war. Discuss amongst yourself."

Orion wandered the room, reviewing something on his phone while my friends and I chatted. There wasn't much to discuss, but we didn't want to imply that we *needed* him in our circle. That would be a sign of weakness.

"He saved our women," Forrest said.

"Twice," Royce added.

The second time was when Audri, Michelle, Natalie, Kiera, and Vivian had met up at a restaurant in town. The assholes had planned on setting a bomb off in the restaurant. I'd heard about the two dead bodies at the back of the restaurant on the news, but didn't know the reason. Now I knew why, and Orion had my sincere gratitude.

"The fucking Trogyn," Grayson seethed.

"We could use another friend," Remi said.

"What say you?" I asked my friends.

Everyone nodded.

I turned to face Orion. "Does Attikus Mount know you're using his museum for this little business meeting?"

Orion smiled. "He's a close friend of mine." His eyes gleamed. "And he would also be an asset to our VATV club."

Vigilantes against the villains. The phrase made me think of the antiheroes in books, but more complex. This was our unique definition. In the eyes of the villains, we were their enemies.

"Attikus is already an investor in our video game," Remi said.

"Like me, he knows your worth."

I looked at Remi. Questions multiplied in my head, but this wasn't the moment to discuss another man.

The boys and I walked up to Orion.

Remi extended his hand. "Welcome to the WaterFyre Rising Club."

I studied our new member. "When do we get to test out a demo of Level Six?"

CHAPTER SIXTY-SIX

VIVIAN

I WALKED out to the back deck of my cabin that faced the gleaming lake. Arrow wasn't sitting in the chair like he had been minutes ago when he was talking to someone on the phone.

I glanced toward the pier, and my heart skipped seeing him sitting on the edge fishing.

Smiling, I gripped the two glasses of freshly squeezed lemonade and headed down to join him. It had been a chaotic few days after finding Aimee and escorting her back to her parents. I let Kaylee take a few days off from school to hang out with Aimee. Having Kaylee around Aimee would help her adjust better.

Arrow had one of his CIA friends speak to the local authorities about keeping Aimee's discovery private and only telling her family and necessary officials. The CIA had told them an undercover agent had rescued Aimee. If the media got wind of it, it would jeopardize the undercover agent's work at apprehending the human trafficking group.

Aimee would be homeschooled by her mom, which was

better for her adjustment. My dad and Rose were in Vietnam, and he was thrilled to hear about Aimee's return.

Arrow and I needed a break and headed to my lake house. There was still unfinished business to attend to, but we needed a quick respite. I needed to breathe and remind myself that it was okay to pause now and then. I hadn't realized how stressed I was until I was losing so much hair in the shower.

Stress did several things to the body. I'd also taken this week off work to give my body the recuperation it needed. There was so much to process, and I needed the space to do so.

I wanted to cuddle. To be held. Was that selfish of me?

Besides the danger hovering around us, the emotion I felt for Arrow had intensified exponentially, making it difficult to focus on anything else. These feelings also needed to be addressed and resolved.

I tried to imagine my life without Arrow. I couldn't. He was everywhere. In the beginning, he'd inserted himself into my life in memorable ways. Now, he was a permanent essential I couldn't live without. Like the oxygen in the air. Like the water I drank. I needed him in every way.

When I came to Providence, I didn't want a relationship. Too much distraction and the fear of another failed relationship prevented me from wanting more. But I was wrong. Giving myself a chance with Arrow had saved me. I would've continued the sad loop of living without love or joy if it weren't for him.

Arrow wasn't only my lover; he was a man who had reached all the way into my soul and patched it up. The wounds on my back no longer carried weight.

My hands shook as I held the glasses of lemonade while

studying him. He stared at the gleaming lake, which sparkled like a blanket of diamonds had settled on its surface. I studied his contemplative look. He was so handsome. . . My heart ached just looking at him. His brown hair glistened like copper in the sun. He wore ripped jeans and a gray T-shirt, and I wore khaki capris and an old yellow T-shirt. It was a perfect day in Northern California with unusually warm weather this week, but I'd take it. It was a pleasant break from the New England winter.

When he turned to look at me, those gray eyes sparkled, reflecting the glittering lake. He considered me for a moment, and my heart raced. The intense expression showed something was on his mind. Probably the much-needed conversation we never had. I loved his usual air of danger. But my wolf also had a tender side that I got to see. Right now, he didn't appear tender.

Was he all mine? This was something I had to find out.

"There's lemonade if you're thirsty." I placed the lemonade down on the wooden planks.

With one hand, he lifted the drink to his lips. "Haven't had fresh squeezed lemonade in a while." He placed it down and patted the seat next to him. "Sit."

"Any bites?" I asked, reaching for the bag of sliced bread I left out earlier.

"Not yet." He watched me rip off a small portion of the sliced bread, roll it into a tiny ball, and add it to the hook. "You don't use worms or other live bait?" He gestured to the tackle box.

"No. I'm a simple girl." I threw out the fishing line. "In my experience, the trout, bass, and sunfish love the bread. Have you tried using it before?"

"Nope. Maybe they just love you."

What about you? Do you love me?

I smiled. "Let's see who catches the first fish."

I sat beside him with our arms touching. Silence thrummed between us, and it was such a lovely moment.

"Why do you enjoy fishing?" I asked.

He lifted a shoulder. "I fish because I'm not just catching fish." His eyes were on the gleaming lake. "It teaches me patience. I'm discovering myself while being with myself, you know?"

I bumped my shoulder into him. "You're so poetic, you know that?"

He let out a soft laugh. "I guess life can be poetic if you learn how to look at it that way. Why do *you* like fishing?"

No one had ever asked me that question. But then again, I hadn't gone fishing with many people. I ripped off a small piece of bread and tossed it into the lake, offering free food to the fish.

"Part of it is what you just described. Spending time alone with myself is precious. It's like having the fish nibble my trouble away. But I often look at my reflection in the water. There are moments when I miss my mom or am sad about life, and I wonder if the water could remove the sadness and change my reflection. You know, like the water could somehow put a smile on my reflection?" A fish nibbled on the bread I'd thrown into the water and disappeared. "But I realized if I wanted to see the smile, I had to change *me*—the inner me. It had nothing to do with the exterior world. I had to smile to see that reflected in the water. When our perception changes, everything else changes."

He nodded slowly while staring at the water. "That's a wise fishing analogy—and you call *me* a poet?" He bumped shoulders with me as something flickered in his eyes. "Sylvia emailed me saying she didn't want the car anymore."

"Really?" A small smile curved my lips.

"She also wished me luck with my new girlfriend." Amusement gleamed in his eyes. "Know anything about that?

"Maybe she was inspired to be nice after we had a little chat about eyeliner."

"Do I want to know?"

"It's best you don't." I stared out at the trees across the lake.

"So when are you going to do the pimp roll for me?" He elbowed me.

Here comes the long overdue conversation.

"I'm sure you can do it better than me." I sighed. "It was so out of my comfort zone, but I did it for a specific reason."

"A reason you failed to inform me about." The serious expression matched the tone. "I was so worried about you, but I was also angry and sad."

The sadness and disappointment in his voice prickled my skin. A bug landed on the lake's surface, creating a circular ripple as it hopped along.

"I didn't want to bother you. You were working and—"

"I *want* you to bother me about everything and anything. I *want* to be the first to know." He swallowed. "Do you know how heartbroken I was to know the woman I love had put herself in danger without telling me? What if something happened to you? I was terrified I could lose you."

My heart hammered as love erupted like a million butterflies flapping within me.

He secured the fishing rod in the pole holder and

gripped my face. "I love you, Tulip, and it makes me feel insignificant when you leave me out."

Securing my fishing rod to the holder, I placed my hands over his and said, "I love you too, Bullseye."

My lips crushed to his, and he responded with passion. He angled the kiss, deepening it and thrusting his tongue into my mouth. I'd missed this intimacy the past few weeks. Though we lived together, chaos and stress had reigned supreme in our house. But right now, love was the only thing within us, around us.

So much joy radiated from me, and I wanted to hear him say those words again.

I broke the kiss and beamed. "Say it again."

"I love you, Vivian." The words came out slow and meaningful.

I loved how he said the words with my nickname and my real name. "I've been waiting to hear you say that."

"Now you can hear it every day because you're not leaving my side. Just so you know, I've never said it to any woman." He nudged me onto my back, looking down at me.

Could my heart expand anymore?

"What are you thinking?"

He cupped the side of my face with his hand. "That you're the most beautiful woman I've ever met, and you're all mine."

"Come here, my love." I yanked him down for a kiss.

His hand slipped under my T-shirt and cupped my breast over my bra. "I want you," he whispered.

"Bed," I gasped. "Now."

He smiled, got up, and offered me a hand, pulling me flush against him. "You need to tell me everything from now on."

I wrapped my arms around his waist. "I'm used to doing things my way—by myself. I never had to tell anyone anything, and it slipped my mind that day."

"But things have changed now." He touched my face with tenderness. "That's how relationships work, Vivian."

I nodded, understanding that relationships required compromise and communication. "Goes both ways, okay? I also want to know what's going on with you."

"That's a given, Tulip."

"Sounds like this is going to be a long-term relationship."

Confusion flickered in his eyes. "Was there any doubt?"

I told him about my hesitation and suspicion based on his past relationships, which I read about online.

"Don't believe the media. They twist things and make you believe the president is a three-headed alien in disguise."

I laughed. "I know. But the gossip made me wonder, you know? I didn't want to get hurt."

"I'm never going to hurt you, not intentionally. If I have unintentionally, I want to know. Okay?"

I smiled, loving the warmth blossoming in my heart. "I guess I can tell the girls that A Kiss is Not Enough mission is complete."

"What's that about?"

"A James Bond-inspired mission the girls and I created to see if our significant other passes the test." I kissed his forehead. "This is my version of The World is Not Enough." I kissed his nose. "But mine is more meaningful to us. You've wanted me from the beginning. After one kiss, one duel, and one date, I thought you'd be satisfied and move on." I dropped a kiss on his cheek, then the other. "But you didn't go anywhere. And one kiss isn't enough for me either." I plopped a sloppy kiss on his lips, making him grin like an adorable idiot.

"I love that mission. The mission for today is Tulipussy, my version of Octopussy."

A laugh burst out of me. I was surprised there were no ripples on the water because I imagined the fish probably blinked at the sexy statement.

He lifted me, tossing me over his shoulder.

I squealed. "Hey!" I'd never been carried like this. But then again, I'd been experiencing a lot of unforgettable firsts with him. This took second place after the piggyback ride.

Gripping his muscular back, I looked at my fishing line and noticed something yanking at the float. "I got a bite! I caught something! Put me down!" Then I saw the line go still. "No . . ."

"You caught the biggest fish there is—*me*." He slapped my ass. "We'll resume our fishing later."

Arrow rushed me into the house and straight to the bedroom at lightning speed. The hungry look in his eyes sent my stomach churning. He stripped off his clothes while watching me remove mine. Then his mouth covered mine in a deep kiss. All thoughts escaped me but the taste of him, the feel of him.

I fell back onto the bed, loving his weight on me. His hand skimmed down my rib cage, igniting a trail of heat I'd missed. This connection with him was something I'd cherish forever. He dropped kisses all over my face, my neck, and my breasts. I let out a series of moans, surrendering to his hands, mouth, and tongue.

His fingers traveled to the junction between my legs and found me wet and ready for him. As he slid two fingers into me, he looked at me. The love in those eyes belonged to a warrior finding his reason for existence. I didn't know how I knew it, but I did.

My heart quivered, and I released a moan as his fingers glided in and out.

"So perfect." His fingers pumped into me with an irresistible rhythm that made me yearn for more.

I lifted my hips to a different angle while he sucked my breast. My body was on fire from his fingers and his mouth.

"You're mine." He looked up at me.

"And you're mine," I gasped.

"Forever and ever."

A prayer. A promise. The words traveled all the way into my soul.

"Forever and ever," I repeated.

The statement was a promise of ourselves to each other. I didn't know I'd teared up until he brushed a stream from my cheek.

"Tears of immense joy," I said, not wanting him to think it was something else.

"I know." He kissed me again before moving down my body. "You're being worshipped today."

"I want it every day," I said, absorbing the thrill zipping up and down my body. My legs parted for him almost automatically.

He laughed. "Anything you want, love."

Arrow looked at my wet center, and he licked his bottom lip. I blushed even though he'd seen me many times. Growling, he lowered his mouth and licked. He took his time with me. And I loved watching him love me. He wasn't simply pleasuring me; he was genuinely enjoying himself.

Sensations bloomed in me as I writhed under his lips and

tongue. He shifted me to the side and lifted my leg to give him access from a different angle.

"You're fucking perfect," he crooned as he feasted.

The unexpected change in tempo shoved me closer to the edge. I sensed the impending orgasm building and finally exploding in me.

"Arrow!" I gasped and trembled.

He lifted his head, smirked, and plunged into me. He drove in and out, creating this delicious friction that shattered me even further. My body convulsed. My muscles tightened around his cock.

"You feel so good, baby. You love me fucking you hard?"

"Yes!"

He slammed in harder, deeper. He grunted as his hand caressed the spot where we connected. "I love you so much."

I wanted to say I loved him too, but another orgasm flooded my brain. I couldn't muster up a thought, much less a word. The noises coming from me were practically animalistic.

He cried out my name, and I'd never heard anything so beautiful. So possessive. So satisfied.

Liquid heat filled me as he kissed my forehead. "Fucking you is so addicting."

"Better than wine?" I asked, loving the feel of him still throbbing in me.

"If wine has the power to eliminate a man's sorrow, then you, my Tulip, have the power to create unimaginable joy."

I grinned and ruffled his sweat-slick hair. "Where did you learn to talk like that?"

"From having sex with you." He dropped beside me on the bed. "If you want poetry, then you need to have sex with me three times a day, every day."

Laughing, I slapped his chest playfully. "We both need to work."

"I can visit you during your lunch hour. But I think you should visit me in my office. It's bigger." He got up and rushed to the bathroom.

I sprawled on the bed, looking up at the ceiling. This lake house had been my home for the last five years. I loved it. But if Arrow and I were going to make the relationship work, I'd want to see him every day.

Should I sell this place? But the private location was perfect. Maybe I could rent it out.

My thoughts vanished when the gorgeous warrior returned with his cock still hard.

"Stay there." I pointed to him as I got off the bed and dropped to my knees. "Part of A Kiss is Not Enough covers this too." I licked his length and kissed his crown. It wasn't enough, so I gripped his cock. The heat transferred into my palm. I loved how he throbbed in my grip like he was begging me to do all kinds of things to him. I stroked him, and he moaned.

He placed a hand on my cheek. "What mission are you on now, Tulip?"

"A Suck is Not Enough."

He crooned, "Prove it."

CHAPTER SIXTY-SEVEN

ARROW

WE WERE HEADING BACK to Providence tomorrow. Today, we were hosting Vivian's dad, Minh, and his girl-friend, Rose. Kaylee hitched a ride with them.

After lunch, the girls sat on the back deck chatting while I took a stroll with Minh. He had salt and pepper hair, a kind face, and sharp eyes, standing about five inches shorter than me. He wore a baby blue polo T-shirt with jeans.

"Is she really doing okay?" He glanced over his shoulder at the deck. "I know she hides a lot from me because she doesn't want me to worry."

"Vivian is doing fine. I promise."

He looked up at me. "You love her?"

"I do."

Nodding, he looked out at the lake. "That girl has gone through so much. I wish I could have taken her pain away."

"She's the most exceptional woman I know. Her past has strengthened her."

"So you know everything?" I nodded, trying to be careful of what I said to him.

He didn't know that Ghost was still alive. Vivian had kept it from him because of his weak heart. I changed the subject to something more lighthearted as I bonded with my girlfriend's father.

After a couple more hours of quality time, Minh and Rose said their goodbyes. They were returning to Vietnam in two weeks and planned to stay there for a few months. They'd also invited us to visit anytime.

While Kaylee was on her phone checking out all the new members who had joined Heartstrings, I helped Vivian sort through the box of her mother's belongings. Her father had found it in the back of his storage.

Vivian created a stack of books she would donate to the used bookstores. I dusted her photo albums. One album with a floral design caught my eye. I opened it and saw adorable pictures of Vivian as a baby.

"Look at your cute little butt." I smiled, pointing at two pictures of her in diapers.

"What? Let me see!" She grabbed the album from my hand, looked, and gasped. "Oh my God. I'd forgotten about this album." Her cheeks flushed the prettiest pink.

"I want to see all the pictures."

"No." Laughing, she shifted so her back faced me as she continued flipping through her life.

"Gimme!" I clasped her shoulders. "I'll fight you for it."

Vivian gave me an amused look. "Every time we fight, we end up . . ." She trailed off as she glanced over at Kaylee, who wore a contemplative expression, probably missing Aimee.

After a silent moment, we sat reviewing all her baby pictures, Vivian providing context whenever she was able. I got to see the woman I love from the very beginning.

"When will I get to see yours?"

"I don't have this many pictures of me, but you're welcome to look through my one album."

When she closed the album, I held it in my hand, focusing on the design that had gotten my attention.

"Do you know what this is?" I ran a finger over the floral metal design.

She lifted a shoulder. "No. It's just a medallion design."

I shared what Ghost's accomplice had told me during the interrogation.

"So it's not a regular key?" She yanked on the medallion, and it popped up. At the back of the metal emblem was an address and a set of numbers.

"It's . . . a code."

Nodding, her hands shook. "What was my mom protecting?"

I wrapped an arm around her. "Let's see where it leads." I punched the address into my phone, and it showed a storage place in Woonsocket, Rhode Island, which wasn't far from Providence. "We can make a trip there."

Vivian sighed. "What did my mom die for?"

CHAPTER SIXTY-EIGHT

VIVIAN

"YOU OKAY?" I asked Kaylee, who just finished her bowl of cereal. She seemed different after returning from California. Quieter. Something was on her mind, and she didn't want to talk about it. But I wouldn't give up. Teenagers needed their space and time.

I finished my coffee and washed my cup. I'd head to the office after dropping Kaylee off at school. Arrow had already left for work. His task tonight was to pick up a chocolate mousse cake and some Chinese food. I'd already bought her a T-shirt that read "My sister is AWESOME!" earlier this week.

It was Kaylee's special day, but she didn't know it yet.

"I'm okay." She shrugged and grabbed her backpack.

"You miss Aimee?" The two girls had gotten even closer after the incident.

Kaylee nodded. "She had nightmares for a couple of nights. She slept in her parents' room for one night. Then she asked if she could sleep with me the other night."

"It's going to take her time to heal and adjust to being

home and feeling safe again. Life's gonna feel odd until she can find her rhythm. She has people she loves around her, so she'll be okay." I pulled Kaylee into a hug. "Aimee can visit us anytime. You can visit her too. How about this summer?"

"Really?" Joy splashed on her face. "I know she'll be okay. She has loving parents."

"Of course." Wanting to cheer her up, I said, "What do you say about Chinese with your favorite chocolate mousse cake for dessert?"

"Yes!" She punched a fist into the air. "What are we cele-brating?"

"*You*. We're celebrating you, my little genius. My little sister."

She narrowed her eyes at me like I'd just grown a third eye. "Are YOU okay?"

"Yup. Just trying to promote more positive energy. I'm leading by example. So make sure you have a fabulous day, okay?"

"Okay," she said warily as she slid on her jacket.

I wanted to let her know she was now my official sister forever and ever. The adoption had been completed a while ago, but I'd been meaning to do something special for her. I'd been so focused on finding Aimee that I'd let this celebration slip through my mind. This was an overdue celebration.

In my eyes, she had always been mine—part of my family. But I think it mattered to her that it became official. I sensed a longing in her voice just now when she spoke about Aimee and her parents. Kaylee didn't grow up with two parents. Her mother died when she was young, so I could imagine how scared and lonely she'd been.

That would change. I'd make sure of it.

She deserved a party. Arrow and I did too. It had been a

complete whirlwind, one storm after the other. If it were any other man, he probably would have ended the relationship a while ago. I had too much going on, and no man would want to deal with that much stress and danger. Arrow not only dealt with it, but he also took control of it. Like how he'd visited the storage unit with me.

My mom had a lot of gold bars, cash, and a flash drive containing evidence of the corrupt officials The Triad had dealt with. They even had incriminating evidence of other Triad leaders around the world. My grandfather had probably asked her to keep it safe for him.

I didn't want this dirty money. It came with a kind of karma I preferred to stay away from. The Triad lifestyle wasn't for me. I'd give the money to Calvin and hope he would put it to good use. But the giving part wasn't as easy as I'd hoped. Arrow was organizing all of that for me.

"I'm ready," Kaylee said, bringing me back to the moment.

"Let's go."

After dropping Kaylee off, I drove to work. My associate had taken care of my patients while I'd been away. Luckily, there hadn't been any urgent visits. After lunch, I sent Arrow a text message reminding him about the Chinese food and the cake order I'd already placed under his name.

My office manager, Allison, stopped in my doorway. "We have a guy with an emergency. Dr. Jones doesn't have any openings. Do you want to look?"

"Let me go out and talk to him. Maybe I can see what he needs and refer him to another office." I didn't want to take on adult patients. Arrow was the exception.

When I walked out to the front desk, my body tensed. The guy with the toothache was none other than Ghost.

Even after the multiple plastic surgeries, I knew it was him. No matter how much someone changed their face, there were still aspects of them that remained.

His eyes were still filled with malice. My body's instant reaction told me it was him. Intuition didn't lie.

Ghost didn't know I recognized him. He could be here because he wanted me dead. I was the one who got away. But what game was he playing? Was he testing me?

I'd been waiting for him after Arrow threw a punch to his mouth, making him lose two teeth.

Forcing my body to calm, I played along. "How can I help you, sir?"

He placed a hand on the right side of his mouth and winced. "Bad toothache. Can you look? I don't have insurance, but I can pay in cash."

If he were any other patient, I'd help him by using the Kindness Fund I'd set aside for people who couldn't afford dental care. But I didn't want to waste it on him. He had murdered my mother and tried to kill me.

"I'll take care of him." I nodded to Allison and walked toward my workstation, preparing for the exam of a lifetime. I would take care of him indeed.

I sensed the fiery blood of The Triad tycoon coursing through me. My grandfather would be proud to know that his granddaughter understood the power of vengeance. That I'd do anything to protect my family. In the beginning, I'd wanted Ghost to rot in prison.

But what if he escaped? I couldn't be sure he'd leave Dad, Kaylee, Arrow, or me alone. He had to be stopped. I didn't know if Mom would approve of what I was about to do. I hoped she would understand if she were watching me from up there. She didn't want my dad or me involved in

The Triad or anything involving crime. And here I was, preparing for the ultimate crime.

Please forgive me.

I was only callous and vengeful toward evil murderers. Arrow had told me Orion had already gotten to the containers holding the women and children that Ghost was supposed to deliver. Ghost had failed his buyers, which meant disgruntled people were probably after him. Or maybe he'd already replaced the women and children. The thought sickened me. When would this all stop?

"Please fill out this patient form, and we'll get you settled."

Dakota was performing a cleaning for another patient. She'd be over to help me with Ghost as soon as she was done.

My hands shook as I prepared the dental tools. So much for committing crimes. *Such an amateur.* I got out the new device I'd created with an expert at the company Arrow had connected me with, which made dental devices and other high-tech equipment. I'd have to tell Arrow about Ghost. But that could wait until after the exam.

Nausea rose in me, but I focused on my breathing.

Stay calm. Pretend he's just another patient.

I'd reached out to Chicken a week ago to ensure Ghost hadn't approached him regarding the debt that had been squared away at the club. Though Ghost had lost to Arrow, I couldn't take a criminal at his word. Thankfully, Chicken stated he hadn't seen or heard from Ghost.

When Ghost entered the exam room, I gestured for him to lie in the chair. "We need to do some x-rays."

He nodded, allowing Dakota to take the images while I reviewed his patient form. All lies. A fake name, a fake address, and probably a fake phone number. He stated his occupation as unemployed. That was probably true. Committing crimes wasn't an official occupation.

After reviewing the x-rays, I shook my head at the seven cavities and one fractured tooth, none of which resulted from Arrow's punch. I smiled at the empty spots of the loose teeth.

"When did you last visit the dentist?" I asked.

"Can't remember."

"You have seven cavities. I can fix the big cavity today with a crown." I pointed to the computer screen showing the multiple cavities. "You'll have to come back a few times for me to fix the others."

"Shit." His eyes widened.

He wasn't lying about the toothache. The huge cavity was the culprit. "You're going to need regular checkups to maintain healthy teeth." I gave him the standard dental spiel as I began working on his teeth.

Ghost didn't flinch as Dakota and I worked on his tooth. I took the silver crown out of the drawer and sent Dakota to assist Dr. Jones, who was running late with a patient. The process would be easier and quicker with Dakota's help, but I didn't want to involve her in what I was about to do.

It would be so easy to kill him right now. Reliving the nightmare of what he'd done to me and how he'd killed my mother made my blood boil. Though I'd never killed anyone in my life, I could end his life right now with my handpiece accidentally slipping to the back of his throat, causing massive blood loss. *Oopsie.* It would be too easy.

But I didn't want to spend the rest of my life in prison, and I needed information.

Ghost was working with The Trogyn, who were after Arrow and his friends. Apparently, they had also tried to hurt me and my friends. *Assholes.* Who was behind this crime organization? Ghost could lead me to them. Someone was supporting him all these years. Who were his business partners? I wanted all of them in prison.

Arrow had mentioned that members of this dangerous organization ranged from government officials to royalty from all over the world. No wonder the world was a messed-up place. It was ruled by corrupted assholes.

"You doing okay?" I asked, without even thinking about who I was talking to. The dentist in me naturally cared for my patients.

He gave a thumbs up because I had the suction tool in his mouth. My heart pounded in my chest as I positioned the special crown. The expert who created it told me it was the first prototype he'd ever made. I couldn't wait to share this with Arrow. There was a tracker with advanced voice recording and—

Ghost jerked and held up a hand.

"We're almost done." I had accidentally touched a sensitive area on the tooth.

When he was all set, he paid the office one thousand dollars in cash, and that was with the cash discount. I told Allison to set it aside. It was probably dirty money, and I wanted to donate to a shelter.

After finishing my paperwork, it was time to head home. Everyone had already left for the day. I had to document what I'd done with my new crown. I typed up the installation date and the code activation, sent the link to my phone, and texted Arrow.

Vivian: *Ghost came to the office today. Got a surprise for him. Will tell you at home. (smile emoji)*

I glanced at the time on my phone. He was probably on

his way to pick up the food and the cake. This was another thing to celebrate tonight.

Satisfied, I gathered my things and headed out. It was only six in the evening, and there was more daylight now than a few weeks ago. Spring was in the air, bringing with it a sense of a new beginning. I loved this feeling.

Being so close to my enemy today was a new beginning in itself. I was *tending* to my enemy. I gave him the most innovative and expensive crown he'd ever get. Though it had an activation code to erupt in his mouth at my command, I wouldn't do that unless I had to. I preferred he rot poison and take all his accomplices with him.

I got into my car and drove home, but then I remembered I wanted to get some balloons for Kaylee. So I headed to the party store and pulled into the parking lot.

As I got out of my car, someone called my name. "Dr. Vo."

I whirled around to see Ghost close to me. Had he followed me? With the party on my mind, I hadn't paid attention. The smirk on his face told me he didn't follow me to ask about dental care.

Fear twisted in me as I glanced around at the parking lot. There was no one nearby.

"You're not getting away this time, bitch." A fist came at me, and I blocked it, kicking him in the shin.

I wanted to reach for my phone to activate the damn explosion, but he kept attacking me. There was no time to rummage through my purse to turn on the phone. Dropping my purse, I used both hands to defend myself. I clawed at his eyes and his face, wanting to destroy all the expensive work he had done. I dug my nails in as much as possible, scratching his eyes.

He screamed but continued to attack me as if physical pain didn't affect him.

I shouted. "Please help me!"

Laughing like a lunatic, he sprayed something in my eyes. For a moment, they burned, and I couldn't see anything.

Something sharp pierced my stomach. Pain erupted as another stab penetrated me. I blinked, and everything lost focus. Even with the blurry image, I could gauge where he was. Though I was bleeding a lot, I charged at him, but my body didn't have the strength. I dropped to the ground as pain crippled me.

"Hey! What's going on?" someone shouted.

"She's bleeding a lot, honey!"

A commotion followed, but I was in another world. Images of Mom, Dad, Kaylee, and Arrow floated in front of me like a movie.

Tears welled because I knew I was dying . . .

CHAPTER SIXTY-NINE

ARROW

AFTER PICKING up the food Vivian had ordered, I headed to the bakery. I checked my phone while waiting for the host to retrieve the cake from the back room.

My eyebrows furrowed as I read Vivian's text. Fear overcame me. What was Ghost doing at her practice? A thought occurred to me, and I didn't like it. Vivian had wanted me to punch him in the mouth, luring him to her dental practice. But why? What kind of surprise did she have for him? What had taken place at her office today?

A part of me wished she had told me earlier, but there was probably no time if he turned up suddenly.

I called Vivian, but her phone went to voicemail. Something awful stirred in me. I got the cake and rushed to my car.

I called Kaylee, but she didn't answer either. Had something happened to her? I logged into the security tracker app on both the phones I'd given them. It showed Vivian was in Providence at a party store. Relief settled in me. Maybe she was shopping and didn't hear my call. I'd call her back.

Kaylee's location surprised me. What was she doing at the cemetery? Wasn't the cemetery closed at this hour? Was she in trouble?

Fear gripped me as I sped to the cemetery. It was closed. I found off-street parking and hopped over the fence. Using my phone to track Kaylee, I made my way through the cemetery. It had been a long time since I'd visited this place. My mom and dad weren't buried together. Mom had wanted her ashes sprinkled out in the sea. As for my father, I didn't visit him as much as I should have. We had nothing to talk about, and if I visited him, all the painful memories would surface.

I spotted Kaylee in the distance, near a lamppost. She was wearing her backpack. Had she come here after Whiz Kidz? My chest tightened as an odd sensation rushed through me. Why was she standing right in front of *my* father's headstone? Confusion and surprise had me pausing in my steps.

Kaylee stared at the stone. She wiped her eyes with the back of her hand. Why was she crying?

A squirrel rushed by me, and she glanced in my direction. Shock splashed onto her face. Her mouth dropped open but then closed. I approached and looked at her. Sadness swam in her eyes.

"Are you okay?" I placed a hand on her shoulder. "What's going on?"

She turned to look at me with light brown eyes. "I just wanted to see him."

Something quivered in my gut. "Who is he to you?"

Kaylee nodded. "He's my father."

Shock stiffened my spine. "Roger Holt is your father? Are you sure?"

She nodded. "Mom told me about him when I was

younger. He didn't know about me. She said she ended things before I was born. I started looking into him." She cried and threw her arms around me.

Unsure of what to do. I held her as she released the pressure. I had so many questions. Was Kaylee my half-sister? I didn't remember Dad bringing a girlfriend home. But I was hardly home.

A memory sparked in me. I had seen my father with an Asian woman when I was at Pam's Diner. Men who looked like Triad members retrieved her. Was she Kaylee's mom? Had she also been part of The Triad?

After a moment, Kaylee sniffled and drew back, and embarrassment flushed her face. "Sorry."

"It's okay. How did you get here?"

"The bus."

"Did you go to Whiz Kidz today?"

She shook her head. This wasn't like the Kaylee I knew.

"Why do you look so sad, Kaylee? Tell me." I brushed a hand down her hair.

"I don't know," she pouted, looking at her shoes.

"Yes, you do. You can tell me. Don't you trust me?" I wiggled my pinky, reminding her of our pinky promise, which I hadn't broken.

She sighed. "I didn't realize how sad my life was until I spent time with Aimee and her family. She has parents who love her, who always loved her." Tears brimmed in her eyes. "I don't have a family."

"Yes, you *do*. Vivian loves you."

"But she's just my guardian. How long will that last?"

Vivian should've had the surprise party sooner.

"Maybe I'll be living with a new guardian next year," she said, looking like the saddest kid I'd ever met.

"You're not going anywhere. You're staying with us. Understand me?" I choked, unsure of how to tell her she was my half-sister. I never imagined having a sibling. But it made sense now. There was a special bond early on between us.

I looked at my dad's headstone, wondering how he'd feel if he knew he had a daughter.

"I heard you call, but I didn't pick up. Sorry."

"Want to talk about what's bothering you? It'll help."

She nodded.

"Let's talk in the car. It's getting dark out here. Kinda spooky. If a bony hand creeps through the soil, you're on your own, kid." I clasped her hand.

Smiling, she followed me to the car.

Inside the car, Kaylee explained she felt sad because she didn't get to know her parents as much as she'd have liked. Seeing Aimee's joyful family questioned her sense of belonging—her identity. Kaylee didn't even know her father.

I learned that her mom's name was Angela Leung. Angela never informed my dad about the pregnancy. Her family was also involved in The Triad, but she had moved away from her family to start a new life, just like Vivian's mom. They had been good friends, which was why Vivian didn't hesitate to take Kaylee in.

"How long have you been researching about your father?"

"For a while now. But something broke me this week." She shrugged. "I'm just moody, I guess."

"What did you want to know about him?" I studied her.

I could see his high cheekbones on her now.

There was so much I could tell her. But I didn't want to be the jerk to smear the image she had of him. Maybe when she grew up, I'd share my past with her. Perhaps then she'd understand things more.

What she needed right now was love, acceptance, and a place to belong. She belonged with me, just as Vivian belonged with me. One was my sister; the other was the woman I love. Warmth spread all over me. I had gone from a man living alone to having a family member and a woman I couldn't live without.

"I don't know," she said. "I saw a few pictures of him online, but I'm not sure if it was him. Was he a good man? What was his favorite color? Did he have other kids?" She shrugged. "Things like that."

I stared at her for a while, trying to figure out the best way to share the news with her. Maybe I was overthinking this.

"Wanna know something?"

"What?"

"Did you ever notice that my last name is also Holt?"

"I did, but a lot of people have the same last name. Besides, you're a rich guy. I don't think my dad was rich."

I smiled at the brilliant girl, whose logic was clouded by unstable emotions.

She looked at me for a moment. "So . . . do you know him?"

Ah, the brilliant mind returns.

"He's my father too."

CHAPTER SEVENTY

ARROW

WE SAT in silence for a moment as Kaylee stared at me. Questions sparked in her eyes, but she probably didn't know how or what to ask first.

"Are you sure?" she asked, trying her best to hold back tears.

I laughed. "I grew up with him."

"Will you get a DNA test to prove it?" she eyed me. "I . . . just want to be certain."

"If it's important to you, sure."

"Do you . . . do you want me as a sister?" Her lips twisted, showing how nervous she was. If only she knew how nervous *I* was.

"If I could pick anyone to be a little sister, it would be you."

She cried and gave me a big hug. Tears filled my eyes too.

"Okay, kiddo, we'll celebrate this later. Let's go home and share this news with Vivian. She's got a party planned for you."

Wiping her eyes, she glanced at the back seat. "The food

smells delicious. She said we're celebrating me, but I didn't know what she was talking about."

With what we'd learned today, I could share the reason for the party now.

"She wanted to let you know she has officially adopted you."

Kaylee smiled. "Really?"

"All the legal documents were taken care of a while ago. She wanted to give you a celebration, but things got crazy about finding Aimee. She already considers you part of her family, so the party slipped her mind. Don't be mad at her, okay?"

"I'm not." Kaylee nodded. "I love her."

"Me too."

When we arrived home, we didn't see Vivian's car. Unease settled in me again.

"She's not here," Kaylee said.

Fuck. I checked my phone. No messages from her. I called her again, and it went straight to voicemail.

"Kaylee, help me bring the food and cake into the house. Then we'll go find her."

Once we set the food and cake on the counter, I checked the tracker, and my heart dropped.

Fuck.

My chest constricted as though my heart detached and dropped from my chest. I couldn't breathe. Terror sucked the life out of me. I'd been through all kinds of horror when I was in the Navy, but the fear that overwhelmed me right now was much worse.

What if I lost her?

Don't think like that!

I'd never loved anyone the way I loved her. We were planning a future together. She was the only woman who made me want to commit. She spoke to my heart, my soul, my dreams, all the things no one could do. Without her, my life had no purpose.

What was wine without its fermentation or distillation? *Nothing.*

"Are you okay?" Kaylee asked me.

Remembering that I was the adult with a teenage girl beside me, I inhaled and said, "Yeah. I'm just worried about Vivian."

"Where is she?" Kaylee asked.

"At the hospital."

We hopped into the car and rushed over. Now I understood what Forrest had gone through when Kiera was in danger. The mind and body seemed detached. My body felt like it was floating. My mind settled elsewhere, trying desperately to connect.

I wanted to kill Ghost for hurting her. Wanted to rip his body apart, limb by limb. But concern for her stirred me up too much. Kaylee's presence forced me to concentrate. I honed in on the survival skills I'd learned from the military. Remaining cool and calm during chaos ensured my survival.

Though Kaylee stayed quiet, I knew she was terrified. She clasped her hands on her lap and stared straight ahead. I could hear her heavy breathing.

"Don't worry. She'll be okay." I tried my best to sound calm.

Kaylee looked at me, and a mutual understanding passed between us. "She'll be okay," Kaylee repeated.

My little sister was wiser than most kids her age. I was proud to be her brother.

We arrived at the emergency entrance, and I rushed up to the receptionist, asking for anyone with the name Vivian Vo.

She showed us down the hallway where Vivian was sleeping.

What the fuck had happened to her?

An officer was talking to a nurse near the waiting area. He spotted Kaylee and me.

"Officer, is Vivian okay?" I gestured to the room. "What happened?"

"Who are you?" asked the officer with the short blond hair.

"She's my girlfriend."

"She's my sister," Kaylee said.

"I'm glad you're here. I'm Officer O'Dell. Vivian was attacked in the parking lot of Party Supply. Two customers spotted the man who attacked her. We're still looking for him."

I knew it was Ghost.

"Will she be okay?' Kaylee asked, tears brimming in her eyes.

The nurse with the curly hair patted Kaylee's shoulder. "I'm Molly. Your sister lost a lot of blood from the stab wounds. She needed stitches, but she'll be okay."

The tension in my stomach relaxed a bit. *I'm going to fucking kill Ghost!*

"Do you want her belongings?" Nurse Molly asked me. "I was trying to search her purse for an emergency contact but couldn't find anything. I couldn't access her phone either."

"Yes, please." Kaylee followed the nurse.

I requested a larger room for Vivian and didn't give a damn how much it cost. Kaylee had a sleeping cot, and I had mine. I wouldn't leave Vivian unattended. Ghost could return to finish the job if he knew she was still alive, and I didn't trust anyone.

Knowing that Vivian would recover lifted a tremendous burden from me. Still, it would take her time to recover.

Where the fuck was Ghost?

While Kaylee slept in the visitor cot, I was still awake. I sat in the chair beside Vivian's bed, looking at her. Losing blood had exhausted my baby. She looked so pale. The doctor had come in to check on her an hour ago and said all her vitals looked good. She should wake up tomorrow.

I sent Orion a message.

Arrow: *Need your help locating Ghost.*

Orion: *Everything okay?*

Arrow: *He stabbed Vivian.*

Orion: *She okay?*

Arrow: *She'll recover.*

Orion: *I'm on it. He's probably heading to Europe.*

Ghost had been working with people overseas. That could be his next hideout.

Arrow: *Thanks.*

Orion: *You ready for Monaco?*

Fucking hell. I scrubbed a hand down my face. The wine competition was in two weeks. CheckMate Red and Check-Mate Black from my Bambooze Series were all set to go. But I'd recently started a new wine that needed one final touch. It wasn't for the convention. It was for something more important, and I couldn't wait for the world to see it.

I looked at Vivian, wondering if she would be well

enough to attend the event with me.

Arrow: *Yup. All set.*

Orion: *Three elite members confirmed their attendance.*

Arrow: *Who?*

Orion: *Governor Fenner, Judge Oliver Patterson, and Prince Allard.*

What the fuck? I had wondered about their presence at the wine convention in Providence.

It turned out that Orion had been the anonymous person who had nominated my Bambooze wine for the competition.

Arrow: *You wanted me in Monaco.*

Orion: *It's the place for elites. They love wine.*

Once the chat ended, I researched the three members. Governor Fenner described himself as a family man with three grown children. Supreme Court Judge Patterson was in his late seventies with grandchildren. As for Prince Allard, he was the adopted son of Prince Garnier, who was the current ruler of Monaco. Prince Allard didn't get along with his brother, Prince Garnier II, who was the biological son of the present leader. Perhaps this conflict had sent him down the wrong path. Prince Allard had recently married a Hollywood actress and begun calling himself a family man.

Lies. All lies. These fuckers were hiding behind the façade of a loving family man while committing evil crimes behind it. I wanted the world to know their shit.

My mind swirled at how to bring their dirty laundry out to the public.

Vivian made a noise, and I turned to see her looking at me.

"Hey . . . You feeling okay, beautiful?"

She nodded slowly. "Yeah. Where's my phone?"

"You should rest, Tulip. It's past midnight."

"No, it's important. I've got a tracker on Ghost."

I got her phone from her purse and gave it to her. By the time my love finished telling me the story of how she had implanted an entirely new type of crown in his mouth, I couldn't be prouder of her. She could've killed her enemy, but she kept Ghost alive because he was more useful that way. I loved her so much.

"The Department of Defense should think about hiring my dangerous dentist as a contractor," I teased, then kissed her forehead. "You've got fabulous ideas that could benefit them."

She just smiled and looked over at Kaylee. "She doing okay?"

"Yeah. She's a strong girl." I shared the news about Kaylee being my half-sister.

Vivian squeezed my hand as she teared up with joy. Wanting to make her even happier, I told her about her role in my video game.

"I'm The Dentist in your game?"

"The coolest player with a spectacular fishing rod."

She laughed. "I love that Tark's teeth have healing abilities. I want to play it whenever it's ready."

"Get well soon, and you can play the demo."

She clasped my hand tight. "Thank you for including me."

"If I don't include the woman I love, then who should I include?" I kissed her hand.

I let her talk for a few more minutes until fatigue dragged her back to sleep.

Though exhausted, I was energized by the information Vivian had given me. A plan solidified in my head as I prepared for my visit to Monaco.

CHAPTER SEVENTY-ONE

ARROW

I STOOD on the balcony of the Monte Carlo Hotel, staring out at the gorgeous blue sea. Vivian and I arrived yesterday on Grayson's plane. Grayson and Natalie joined us on this trip while my other friends remained in Providence.

Vivian had asked the girls to "babysit" Kaylee while we were gone. We didn't want Kaylee missing any more time at school. She had already missed a few days when we'd brought Aimee back to California.

Kaylee didn't seem to mind all the attention from my friends, who knew she was my half-sister. The DNA test results had come in and confirmed what I already knew. The proof and sense of belonging seemed to make her even happier. Vivian and I would make sure Kaylee had a bright future.

At first, I didn't want Vivian to accompany me to Monaco. It was too dangerous for her, and she was still recovering from her wounds. My stubborn woman told me she would go with or without me. She refused to provide the code to her new crown unless she went with me.

"It's important to me," she had said. "I want to be there with you. We'll capture Ghost together."

I'd only agreed to it under one condition and gave her my demand. After she agreed to go under a different identity, we made it to Monaco.

Vivian was coming as Athena Chapelle, Natalie's fake French cousin. I didn't want Ghost targeting Vivian if he saw her name on the hotel guest list. According to the world, Vivian was still in Providence, recovering from her wounds. Grayson was here to help me locate the elite members and Ghost, while my other boys would monitor events in Providence in case something unexpected happened there.

The stakes were high, and tension had run my body ragged for the past few weeks. I wanted this shit over—I wanted Ghost dead. A massive storm was brewing, and I was doing my best to brace for it.

Two days ago, Orion had sent me a message apologizing that he couldn't attend the event like he had anticipated. He had to deal with a family emergency. I understood and told him I'd keep him posted. He'd been helping me enough already. Besides, family came first.

Though this trip was for the wine event, my focus was on apprehending Ghost and the elite members of The Trogyn.

"I'm ready." Vivian's voice drew me around. "What do you think?"

The mesmerizing image of her froze me in place. All thoughts vanished from me. I read somewhere that beauty was a powerful force in itself. That people rarely understood the meaning and power of it.

I didn't know what that statement meant until this moment when it hit me in the gut, taking my breath away. What followed was a sense of wonder and peace that opened me up. It was as though I was standing in front of the most breathtaking landscape, allowing its magnificence to overwhelm me in the most subtle way. My body and soul released a sigh of awareness that filled me up in the most inexplicable sense.

This was that moment of revelation. I felt like I had dropped into another plane of existence. The world around me seemed to disappear, leaving me with a mostly blank canvas with only one woman on it.

I swore I felt my heart *breathe*, inhaling and exhaling in a slow, rhythmic pattern. An analytical person like me didn't—*shouldn't*—understand it, but I did. It was easy, like my heart had been waiting for this moment when it could break free from the chains of its past.

Bat wings flapped wildly in my stomach as I looked at the stunning woman staring back at me. She wore a red satin gown with thin straps. The tailored bodice hugged her waist, then flared to a full skirt, making her look like a queen. No, like a goddess with more power than a queen.

Vivian had entered my life and opened my closed heart. An open heart could feel, see, hear, and sense things it hadn't been able to before. I was more alive now because of her.

She twirled for me, and my heart skipped. Natalie had designed the perfect dress for my love. The back was especially elegant, hiding the scars. Vivian wore dangling gold earrings and a matching bracelet from Audri's jewelry collection, and Natalie hooked her up with a pair of gold Jimmy Choo shoes.

"You're . . . *beautiful*."

Love was like wine; it intoxicated you. If I were to die right now, I'd be a satisfied man to have experienced this kind of love. Love inflated me like oxygen filling up my lungs, energizing me. There were no words to explain how much I loved her.

Her love was the fermentation and distillation of my soul. Like a beautiful chemical reaction, she had transformed and purified me.

Blushing, she walked up to me, slipped her arms around my neck, and kissed me. "Thank you, handsome."

The kiss was slow and stimulating. I didn't want to leave this room without having her first.

"You're stunning, and I love you."

"I love you more." She stepped back and raked her gaze down my body. The heat in her eyes increased the pressure in my cock to an uncomfortable level.

My breath hitched as she brushed a hand over my black tuxedo with a cream-colored shirt. She adjusted the black bow tie. "You look yummy."

I yanked her flush to me so she could feel what she did to me. "Feel that? That's all for you. You look delicious, Tulip. How about we ravage each other right now?" I bent to nuzzle her neck, and her perfume aroused me.

"No time, Bullseye." She palmed me, squeezed, and gave me a look filled with promised pleasure. "Later, love."

Ten minutes later, we made our way to one of the many luxury lounges. People were out and about. Groups of tourists crowded the various halls as other events were happening at the Monte Carlo Hotel besides the wine competition.

Vivian checked the tracker on her phone for Ghost's location. The last time we checked, he was in Monaco. For some reason, the tracker wasn't working. I glanced around and noticed cameras.

They probably had jammers in place, forcing people to

log into their server for internet services. I didn't want Vivian to log in because their security team could inadvertently access it.

We needed Ghost to lead us to the elite members. After that, his life would end in various scenarios I had envisioned.

The last location put Ghost in a different hotel not too far from the Monte Carlo.

"There are probably high-tech jammers interfering with the connection," I said.

Vivian looked disappointed.

"Don't worry, we'll get him."

My phone was linked to hers and had the same connection issue.

We stood in front of the extravagant wine display. CheckMate Red and CheckMate Black glowed under the spotlight like celebrities.

Next to them were two other wine competitors. It didn't matter who won today. Just to see people buying samples from the adjacent desk made me happy. The exposure would increase profits for sure.

The competition judges were in another room. They'd announce the winner today.

"Look at all the people buying your wine." Vivian beamed.

I'd already met the judges last night at the dinner for all the nominees. There wasn't anything I needed to do today except show up and mingle. Media from all over the world were present as well. I'd met a couple of them last night and told them about a new wine debuting next month. They offered to do a segment, and I returned the favor with free samples being sent to them soon.

The crowd increased as the wine event began. People dressed in tuxedos and beautiful gowns filled the ballroom.

Grayson and Natalie spotted us and headed over.

"You look absolutely stunning." Natalie embraced Vivian.

"You too! I love the purple satin on you. Gorgeous." Vivian twirled Natalie around.

"All good?" Grayson looked at me.

I nodded and glanced around. "Let's hope we spot them soon."

Each of us was responsible for locating members of the elite. Grayson and Natalie would keep their eyes open for the governor and the judge. Vivian and I would search for the prince and Ghost. Since we both had dealt with Ghost, it would be easier for us to spot them.

Grayson and Natalie made their way into the ballroom first. They'd monitor one end of the room while Vivian and I oversaw the other.

I clasped Vivian's hand and met her gaze. "My charger for all things." She smiled as I lifted her hand for a kiss.

The ballroom was decorated like a royal event with extravagant lighting, impressive centerpieces, hanging crystals with flowers draping down from the high ceiling, and silky curtains that enhanced the tables and chairs. This was why the Monte Carlo stood out from other hotels.

A hostess walked by with a tray of various drinks. I looked over to ask Vivian if she would like anything to drink, but she had her phone flush to her ear.

Vivian looked at me and mouthed, "I hear them."

"No, thank you," I told the hostess.

I ushered Vivian away from the crowd to the wall and

listened in. Ghost was talking to the prince, the governor, and the judge.

Keep talking.

Everything they said would be recorded. Human trafficking. Drugs. Racketeering. Money laundering. Then the recording picked up static, disrupting the feed. I couldn't hear everything. Hopefully, the recording would be fine.

No voices came on for the next minute or two. Then an explosion erupted somewhere, and the fire alarm sounded, forcing the sprinklers in the room to activate.

Panic filled the ballroom, and people scattered everywhere. They crowded my space and separated Vivian from me.

"Arrow!" she shouted as frightened people swarmed between us.

I pushed my way toward her. A weapon pressed into my back, and terror slithered up my spine.

"Come with me, or I'll shoot you."

Ghost.

I met Vivian's eyes for a moment before people blocked my view. I didn't want her anywhere close to me right now.

Ghost led me down a hall. "Make a sound, make a move, and I'll blast your guts out just like your father's."

Ghost killed my father?

We entered a conference room, and he closed and locked the door. He wore a blond wig and a black tuxedo, blending in with the crowd.

"You killed my father? How did you know him?"

"He owed The Triad a lot of money. Guess he had a lot of hospital bills." Ghost grinned. "But he owed The Trogyn more. Alcohol and gambling got him into a lot of trouble."

He stood a few feet from me while pointing the gun in

my direction. I could reach into my pants pocket, turn on my phone, and activate the button to end him right now. But that required too many steps, giving him too many opportunities to shoot me. Like Grayson, I'd worn the special Kevlar-infused suit for extra protection, but my face, neck, and hands were exposed.

Ghost had information about my father that I needed to know. "He borrowed money from The Triad for hospital bills?"

Ghost smiled. "From my father, who also collaborated with The Trogyn. They offered us money we couldn't refuse."

Ghost and his father were traitors to The Taipans.

How had I not known about the medical bills? I'd been young, and seeing my mom sick had narrowed my world.

"You didn't know about your family's debt?" He smirked, and I wanted to crater his face.

I said nothing.

He continued, "Money issues turned into a drinking issue. He did extra work for us, which got him into prison. Prison cleaned him up and when he got out, he refused to help us. Blaming us for ruining his family. Saying his son hates him." He laughed. *"Do you hate him?"*

My fingers itched to kill Ghost right now.

"You knew I was his son when you were my employee?"

His eyes darkened. "Fuck no. If I had, I would have burned more warehouses, killed more employees just for fun." He stepped closer. "You've caused too much trouble for me recently, so I did some research on you."

"Why did you kill my father?"

"He chose to die rather than work for me. Wanna know what his last word was?"

Ghost thought he was torturing me by telling me about this. What he didn't know was that this story gave me the much-needed closure to my relationship with my father. Now I understood why he had changed when my mom had gotten sick. The sudden change of character, the abuse, the dark cloud that hung over my family after my mom passed—all of it made sense. My father did illegal jobs to pay for my mom's medical bills when we thought he'd been cheating on her.

I didn't reply to Ghost, so he said, "Arrow."

My father's last word was my name.

I pretended not to let the information bother me and shrugged. "We never had a good relationship. I'm more interested in your relationship with The Trogyn." I shifted my feet, noticing a door on the other end of the room. The door cracked slightly. It had to be Grayson.

Luring Ghost's attention to me, I said, "You're a traitor to The Taipans. You killed King Viper, your own father, and countless members of The Triad."

Ghost flared his nostrils, not noticing I'd made my way toward the rolling office chair.

"They didn't respect me. Never took my suggestions seriously. I should have been the tycoon! My father was useless, wanting to sever ties with The Trogyn, who had provided us with more money, respect, and opportunities than The Triad ever did."

"The Triad is looking for you."

He let out a dismissive laugh. "They've got their hands full right now. I've created a huge financial burden for them. They're too busy trying to fix it. Plus, where I'm going, they won't find me."

"Is that what the governor, the judge, and the prince told you?"

"How do you know about them?"

"Let's just say I'm involved."

Involved in a plan to eliminate them.

"You're with them?"

"Life could bring a lot of surprises." I smiled. "I'm a new member, making my way up to the elites. Do you know other elites?"

Take the bait.

He considered me for a moment and smiled. "Let's meet the prince, and he can tell you himself."

With mighty force, I kicked the office chair into his legs. He fell back a step back, taking him off guard. He shot at me but missed. I charged at him, threw a punch, another kick, and the gun fell to the ground.

Picking up the gun, I aimed it at him. I should kill him, but he needed to suffer first. I blasted his knee. He screamed, cursed, and dropped to the floor. Blood poured onto the rug.

Infuriated, he tried to reach for a chair to throw it at me. "I'm going to kill you just like I did your father!"

I should have ended him for murdering my father and countless other people. But I knew the person he had hurt most was my love. She needed the closure.

A creepy tune that made me think of clowns echoed in the room. Where was it coming from?

The song also distracted Ghost. Then the door swung open, and Vivian stepped inside, looking pissed rather than scared. She held out her phone, pressed a button, and the song grew louder.

The song came from Ghost. Shock splashed onto his face.

His crown could play music? I loved this woman more and more.

"We've recorded everything. You shouldn't have come to me for dental work," she told Ghost. Then she flicked me a look I understood. *Take cover.*

"You bitch!"

He charged at her furiously, and she tapped her phone. "Who has the last laugh now, asshole?"

"Duck, baby!" I shouted to Vivian even though she already knew.

I ran and crouched beside a long table. Ghost's mouth detonated. Parts of his head scattered to the floor. His body swayed and finally dropped to the ground.

I rushed to Vivian, gathering her in my arms. "You okay?"

Though her body trembled, her eyes gleamed with tears as she smiled at me. "It's over."

CHAPTER SEVENTY-TWO

A WEEK after the event in Monaco, I let the debris settle before doing anything else. My life before that trip had been filled with fear, anxiety, and uncertainty. But now, all those emotions had drained out of me and were replaced with love, hope, and joy. With these emotions, I felt liberated.

The emotions stirred in me, making me aware of where I was compared to where I'd been. I witnessed my personal transformation, and that was a gift I'd cherish forever.

Governor Fenner and Judge Patterson were apprehended based on anonymous recordings sent to the FBI and the news stations. Prince Allard was dealing with the problems in his country. Two families had filed lawsuits against the prince for assaulting their young daughters. This was only the beginning of his downfall. The Trogyn were probably livid right now. Their elite members were slowly apprehended, which meant their organization was crumbling.

Ghost had died from the crown explosion, which the authorities believed resulted from a crime organization taking out an enemy. They also said Ghost had pulled the fire alarm to create a distraction for attacking Arrow. Arrow had removed certain audio portions that could incriminate us prior to sending it to the authorities.

My love got the closure he deserved. Though Arrow never talked about his father, knowing what had turned him into a monster made forgiveness possible. Sometimes, forgiveness was the first step to truly healing the past.

Today, Arrow and I were meeting up with Calvin in Newport, Rhode Island. Arrow walked along the seashore, talking to someone on the phone. He gave me privacy to talk. I loved Arrow, and he knew it. There was nothing between Calvin and me.

Calvin sat on the bench beside me, looking at the few boats on the water. Early April was cold, but that didn't stop people from enjoying the sunshine. He wore a brown leather jacket with jeans, looking more relaxed than I'd ever seen him.

"Thanks for the gold and the cash," Calvin said. "Arrow organized everything into one legal business transaction."

"You're welcome."

"Why didn't you keep it?" he asked, referring to the money I'd discovered in the storage.

"It's not my money." I looked at him. His black hair had grown longer. "It belongs to The Triad."

He nodded and smiled. "We used it to rebuild two restaurants and a warehouse that Ghost destroyed. I'm glad the fucker died the way he did."

"I kind of wish he'd suffered a bit more, like going to prison. But then I'd worry about him escaping prison and coming back to find me. So his death was the closure I needed. I saw it with my own eyes."

"You feeling okay?" He met my eyes. "Seeing someone die like that changes you."

"I'm okay." And that was the truth. "I was already immune to the horror after seeing what he'd done to my mom and me."

"You sure you don't want to join The Triad? You'd make a classy criminal." Amusement flickered in his eyes. "You've got the guts for it."

"No thanks." I laughed. "I'll leave that to the experts. Can I ask you for a favor?"

"Anything."

"You're now The Triad tycoon for The Taipans. Will you . . . will you continue to run it as before?"

"You mean the illegal activities?"

"Everything."

He looked out at the sea. "To survive in my kind of world, I *have* to be ruthless, Vivian. I have to show my men and women that they can depend on me. That I can protect them. I have to lead by example. Power and respect. That's how an organization portrays and maintains its success and status." He inhaled a breath. "It's tradition. But I won't harm women and children. That's a business The Taipans won't be involved in."

I was relieved that he was changing the legacy of The Taipans.

"The world is a cruel place. Sometimes cruelty is required to deal with cruelty." I looked him in the eye. "Because it's the only thing it would understand, right?" A seagull flew by and landed in front of us. "After that, you can inject 'softer' methods."

I'd learned the hard way that people could be evil. There was no one method to deal with evil.

He elbowed me. "You're a true daughter of a crime tycoon."

I smirked. "You can't cut down a giant tree with a butter knife. You need a chainsaw."

He laughed. "I heard about your fancy new crown. Mind if I hire you to create a few things for me when the situation calls for it?"

"Not gonna answer that and incriminate myself." I smiled. "But I'll help a friend in need. Just ask."

Arrow approached us with a smile. I got up from the bench and kissed him on the cheek. "Now it's my turn to take a walk down by the shore. You men can have your conversation."

CHAPTER SEVENTY-THREE

ARROW

"DID you have an informative conversation with Vivian?" I watched her walk toward the shore. Her black hair swayed in the cool breeze, making me remember how soft it was and how it fanned out around her face when she was under me.

As though she sensed my gaze, she turned and winked. God, I loved her so much. If wine improved with time, I was a better man every second I was with her.

"You're a lucky man," Calvin said. "I appreciate her generosity."

Vivian didn't want the bad karma associated with The Triad money. Her mother probably saved it for her grandfather. The reason didn't matter anymore. She had returned it.

"What's your plan?" I asked, knowing he had eliminated everyone who was linked to Ghost. "You've been keeping the farm animals busy, huh?"

He arched an eyebrow. "If you ever need someone or something to disappear, you're welcome to use the farm."

I was sitting on a bench chatting with the current triad tycoon for The Taipans as though we were friends.

As though he had the same thoughts, he extended his hand. "Despite our different circles, if you ever need help—you know, like getting rid of someone—you can depend on me, your new friend."

Smirking, I shook his hand. "I might take you up on that offer."

He dwelled in the crime world, and I lived in my world where the lines between right and wrong were so blurred that they created their own color, their own patterns—their own definition.

Villains against the villains.

I supposed that was our fluctuating, morally gray color.

I didn't have a problem stepping over that line to protect those I loved or when something didn't sit well with me.

The man sitting next to me may be a crime lord, but he had tried to help Aimee. He was against hurting children, whereas people with eminent authority like a Supreme Court judge, a governor, and a prince—who were supposed to protect the vulnerable—were abusing them.

The world was a major paradox.

Calvin got a call and rose from the bench. "See you around."

"Likewise. Don't hesitate if you ever need my assistance too." He nodded with appreciation and left, offering Vivian a goodbye wave.

After he left, I strode down to Vivian. She walked into my arms, giving me a big hug.

She drew back, looking up at me. "In the mood for some *phở*? We can grab some ingredients at the store or pick up an order at a restaurant?"

"That can be on tomorrow's agenda. I have something for you in the car."

"What are you up to now?" She touched my face. "Creating some secret strategy to get me to do something?"

I grinned at how much she knew me. "Something like that." My fingers intertwined with hers. "Get in the car and find out."

When she settled in the car, I pulled a black bag from the back seat and gave it to her.

She arched an eyebrow. "What are you trying to do?"

"Just trying to make you smile. That's my mission from now on."

Her face softened as she opened the bag and pulled out the new bottle of wine called *Vivian* with the tagline: *The love of a lifetime.*

She sucked in a breath, stared at the bottle for a moment as though it had a face on it. Then she looked at me with tears in her eyes. "I don't know what to say."

When I first met Vivian, she was like a rare wine that hadn't been created yet. A dream that hadn't been experienced yet. A song that hadn't been sung yet and a magical creation that hadn't come to fruition yet.

But now, all those things were real to me. She was the dream sitting beside me, holding the magical creation that only existed because of her. And joy was the song singing to my heart and soul.

"Just say what comes to your mind right now," I told her. "I don't want a well-crafted statement. I want the raw and real."

"I'm happy. I'm surprised. I'm elated." She placed the bottle on her lap, cupped my face with both hands and kissed me. "And I *love* you. I love you for your ironclad persistence. For how you make me feel worthy. For how you helped me remember joy. Thank you for making me feel so special."

"That's the plan. And you are special." I smiled. "*Vivian* debuts next week worldwide. The world will know how important you are to me. It's one way for me to show you how I feel."

Joy radiated from her as she traced her fingers over the yellow tulip design on the label.

"What are you smiling about?" I asked.

"I'm envisioning our wounds transforming into unique beings. Like they're holding hands and walking off into the sunset with their own happily ever after."

I laughed. "Like two molars wearing crowns with arms and legs?"

Smiling, she patted my cheek. "Look at you. You went from a guy avoiding the dentist to now making jokes."

"All because of you." I kissed her forehead. "One more thing." I reached into my pocket and placed a silver key in her hand.

"What's this for?"

Ten minutes later, we arrived at the building beside Whiz Kidz. With Governor Fenner in custody, no one else opposed the sale of the property.

"I just bought this building. It's still being renovated." I gestured to the brick façade with the ugly blue awning that had to go. "This could be your expanded dental office. You have the space to do whatever you want. I know you like helping the low-income community, and Whiz Kidz also does that. We can do it together."

She placed a hand over her heart, closed her eyes, and smiled. Opening her eyes, she threw her arms around me. "Thank you! Just what I've been thinking."

"Since when?" I narrowed my eyes at her. "Why haven't you told me?"

"Things have been crazy, remember?"

"Tell me. NOW." I trapped her in my arms, preventing her from escaping.

She tilted her chin and beamed. "How about you show me the inside of this new building that would soon be my new office, and I'll tell you what I plan to do for each room?"

"It's not in its best condition right now. There's stuff everywhere."

"I don't care. That's just life, right? Things are scattered everywhere. When we first met, things weren't perfect either. But we saw something in each other." She went on her tippy toes and kissed me. "I like this working phase because I get to see the before and after." She took my hand in hers. "My charger for all things."

Grinning, I swung our joined hands and stepped up to the entrance.

She squeezed my hand. "I have a surprise for you."

"Really? You're hiding a lot from me today, Tulip."

"I'll tell you if you give me a piggyback ride around the building."

A laugh burst out of me as I opened the door and stepped inside. "Get on!"

As I showed her around the property, she kissed my cheek. "I love you." Another kiss. "The secret project has to do with Bullseye."

"Now I'll have to seduce you into telling me everything."

She laughed. "That'll work."

And that was exactly what I did.

I seduced and loved her that day and all the days to come.

EPILOGUE
THREE MONTHS LATER

Arrow

"WHERE ARE YOU TAKING ME?" I asked as Vivian covered my eyes with a blindfold.

Bat wings stirred in my gut, no matter how much I tried to stop them. So I focused on the woman I love, wondering what she had planned for me.

"You'll see."

"Want me to seduce it out of you?"

She laughed, and the lovely sound of her voice energized me. "Okay."

"But it didn't work the last time. You never told me anything about the Bullseye project."

"I was too distracted. I couldn't think straight." She tugged my hand, leading me somewhere down the hallway. "You were in the moment too."

"My fingers, mouth, and tongue were busy."

"You were fabulous, my love." She nudged me down to a seat.

My hands felt around the chair. "Don't tell me you're giving me a cleaning."

Laughing, she yanked off the blindfold. "Ta-da! Bullseye is getting the best cleaning ever to exist."

I laughed at the ridiculous surprise.

Then she gestured to her right. "Let me introduce to you the innovative new dental equipment series called Bullseye. Check out this dental handpiece." She pressed the button, and all I heard was barely a whisper.

"Wow. You did it." A thrill rushed through me, followed by pride.

"I made this for you." She kissed me lightly on the lips. "But these inventions will also help others."

She created a novel tool to counter my fear. If that wasn't love, what was? Emotions overflowed as I studied her showing off the devices.

"Check out the high vac suction and the bendable saliva ejector. You can hardly hear anything. These are just proto-types right now. I'm trying to remove the sound altogether. As I use them, I'll give feedback for improvements." She placed everything back in its proper place and looked at me. "What do you think?"

"I think you're *extraordinary*." I rose from the chair and embraced her. "Thank you for thinking of me, about my fears, and wanting to help me conquer them. Just so you know, my phobia has diminished tremendously because of you." The last cleaning I had with her was a breeze. "I love you so much."

"Ditto."

My heart raced as my nerves intensified. But there was a good reason. I was about to change our lives forever. Despite the joy on her face, she might say no. A memory surfaced of her first rejection of a date with me, but I shoved it away.

I inhaled a breath and dropped to my knees.

Her mouth dropped open. "What are you doing?"

I reached into my pants pocket and pulled out a black box with a brilliant cut diamond ring. "Will you marry me?"

Vivian

My heart galloped, leaped, twirled, and did all kinds of strange things in my chest as I stared at him. My gorgeous lover, protector, and strategist. This man was mine, and I was so grateful he never walked away from my initial rejection. Because of him, I could enjoy life and live it without fear or pain from the past.

We were each other's medicine. Tears filled my eyes. "Yes!"

He slipped the ring onto my finger, stood up, and watched me shift my hand around under the light. "It's stunning. You did an excellent job."

"Kaylee helped me pick it out."

"I love it even more." I couldn't stop staring at the ring on my finger. It made my hand look different.

"I already asked your father."

"When?" I blinked.

"The California visit when we brought Aimee back."

That had been months ago. "You planned this back then?"

I yanked her to me. "I guess you can say you've been my target from the very beginning. And I had a detailed plan to make you mine."

"You're a dangerous man." I looped my arms around his neck. "I can't wait to be your wife."

"And you're a dangerous woman now that you're working part-time making equipment for government spies."

I'd taken the offer from the government to work with their special ops team regarding crowns, dentures, braces, and other dental options that could be converted into weapons when necessary. I figured this job would benefit my fiancé and his friends in their fight against The Trogyn. More importantly, I had the support from the government to create dental tools for my patients at a fraction of the cost to me. So we both won in this collaboration.

On top of that, Arrow and I were opening clinics in remote areas in Vietnam and China to offer free dental care. We'd also hire local dentists to join our organization. My partner in crime had made my dream come true.

"That just means you can't hide anything from me. I will find out one way or another."

"I'm an open book to you, Tulip. How about we share the good news with Kaylee? She'd be thrilled." He glanced at the clock on the wall. "Aimee is due to arrive in three hours with her parents."

"Excellent idea."

Kaylee had handed Heartstrings over to Arrow's team for development. Her interest had switched to unique stuffed toys now. I loved that Kaylee was exploring various aspects of her brilliance. Kaylee and Aimee started their own plushie collection called Stuffed Cuteness, and Kuraimee was their first toy. It was an adorable bunny with four ears, two long tails, and a cool vest. Very soft, squishy, and adorable. I had one in my bedroom.

Of course, my love had worked with his lawyer behind

the scenes to help his sister finalize the legal process so that she and her friend could focus on the creative aspect. He'd also gotten her a team of assistants to help the girls in their business endeavors.

Kaylee didn't know this, but her brother had bought thousands of Kuraimees and donated them to a few children's hospitals and charities around New England. His friends also bought some and sent them to several children's centers around the country. I couldn't wait to see Kaylee and Aimee's reaction to their success. They would be elated when they found out how many Kuraimees had been sold. The plushies also caught the eyes of some K-pop stars who had purchased some Kuraimees.

Along with Aimee's parents, Arrow and I kept a close eye on the girls' success. We didn't want this to overshadow their education. They were still young and they should enjoy their childhood. Success came with stress and outside pressures. Sometimes, those things could destroy a person, especially with the power of social media.

The girls also invited Orion to Kuraimee's debut at Adorable Toys inside Providence Place today. He said he'd be flying in to support them.

In addition, I'd invited Elena Sanchez. I'd gotten to know her after she did a wonderful segment on Empowering Women and Girls using the photo from the museum. Though she didn't know the context of why my girls had been there, she'd used the image to show camaraderie and what it could represent. I knew she would love writing a story about two young female entrepreneurs. Kaylee and Aimee would inspire kids who had a passion for something like them.

As we headed out, Arrow held my hand. I loved that he never stopped.

"I'm craving *phở* tonight." He rubbed his stomach with his other hand. I'd been making the beef noodle soup for him every single week. "Maybe some fresh spring rolls with your special chicken teriyaki too?"

Smiling, I said, "I'll make anything for my *fiancé*."

"I *love* the sound of it."

"Wanna invite everyone over after the toy celebration so we can share the news?" I lifted my engagement ring into the light. "I can make an enormous pot of noodle soup for everyone. But we're going to have to hold off on the spring rolls for another day." They took a while to make, and I wanted to spend more time with him today rather than in the kitchen.

"That sounds perfect, Tulip. Let's go celebrate."

THANK YOU so much for reading Vivian and Arrow's story!

For Elena and Orion's romance, order **The Protege** (Book 6) now!

https://nadiahan.com/books/

BONUS SCENE
THE STARS ARE GONNA BLUSH

Read Vivian and Arrow's **bonus scene here** or scan the code below.

KEEP IN TOUCH

For exclusive content, new releases, and giveaways, sign up to my newsletter.

https://nadiahan.com/newsletter/

Join my **Facebook reader group** for bonus features and exclusive giveaways!

https://www.facebook.com/groups/nadiahanselitebookworms/

ALSO BY NADIA HAN

WaterFyre Rising Series

The Mastermind (Book 1)

The Daredevil (Book 2)

The Innovator (Book 3)

The Inquisitor (Book 4)

Journals

Finding Your HeART

ACKNOWLEDGMENTS

There are so many people to thank. Each year my list grows longer and my heart grows fuller.

Anna, thank you for understanding my voice and seeing into the heart of my story.

Lindsay, thank you for the thorough copy edits and feedback that make my story sparkle.

Violet, I can't release a book without your eagle eye.

Dr. Nguyet Tau, thank you for your dental knowledge and precious friendship.

Sharon, I appreciate you more than you can ever know.

To my wonderful PA, Sara. Thank you for helping me with everything so I can stay focused on my writing.

To my VIPP and ARC teams. What would I do without you? Thank you from the depths of my heart.

To Christina Marshall, thank you for helping me promote The Strategist!

To my readers, thank you reading my stories. Your support means so much to me. Because of you, I'm motivated to write new books!

I'm saving the best for last. Thank you to my husband for being my hero. My ultimate support system. My number one fan. Without you, I wouldn't be able to write and publish these books. To my wonderful children, thank you for your feedback on my book cover colors and sticker ideas and for understanding when Mommy has urgent deadlines.

ABOUT THE AUTHOR

Nadia Han is a dreamer, a visionary, an artist, and a believer in karma and kindness. She lives in New England with her family and spends most of her time crafting stories. When she's not writing, she practices yoga, reads, creates art, explores nature, and eats all kinds of foods.

facebook.com/authornadiahan

instagram.com/authornadiahan

bookbub.com/authors/nadia-han

amazon.com/author/nadiahan

www.ingramcontent.com/pod-product-compliance
Lightning Source LLC
Chambersburg PA
CBHW070233200726
48293CB00005B/1593